Annis

Book One of

The Goddess of Sorrows

By

Mat McCall

In memory of
Elizabeth McCall
1929-2009

Whose life was a struggle from beginning to end, and though
fortune seldom smiled, she never gave up on the ones she loved.
She left behind her a wealth of riches, none tangible,
but priceless and immutable, nonetheless.
And the world was a much better place while she was in it.

And

Nikki and Nick

And

everyone that ever helped or encouraged me in my writing

"I began to imagine, as always at my left side just out of sight, a brazen winged beast that I associated with laughing, ecstatic destruction."

W.B. Yeats.
Introduction to Resurrection.
1934.

"Hear me, you who can hear,
and learn my words. You who know me.
I am the voice that is heard by all,
I am the sound that cannot be grasped."

"I am the silence beyond comprehension,
and the idea never forgot."

The Thunder, Perfect Mind
Gnostic Tractate
Nag Hammadi Library
Loose translation by Mat McCall
Based on G. W. MacRae

Chapter 1

"And syððan is eac þearf þæt gehwa understande hwanan he
sylf com,
7 hwæt he is, 7 to hwan he geweorðan sceal."

"And then there is also a need that each should understand
whence he came, and what he is,
and what will become of him."

Archbishop Wulfstan
Sermo ad Populum

The eagle lifted herself to ride the last vestiges of the warm misty air arising from the coast. At higher altitude, she caught the stronger ice-cold breeze blowing in from the sea and turned into it. Allowing the salt-laden air to fill her wings and take her soaring into the pale of the morning sky.

She sailed lazily inland, on outstretched wings, following the shining course of the great river below her. Her bright eyes scrutinising the world beneath her. A verdant world of towering mountains clothed in impenetrable forests that tumbled down into rolling hills and further down into a vast rift that cradled the river. Strung out like pearls along the river's mighty course was a chain of lochans, each gaining in majesty until she reached the greatest of them all, a vast basin into which several rivers discharged their peat-stained waters.

Banking swiftly, she glided effortlessly around the circumference of the loch where small creatures crept down to the water trusting in the protection of the overhanging trees.

Nothing stirred.

With a gentle tilt of her primary feathers, she plunged through the thin morning mist to swoop low over the black waters and then, with a single flap of her mighty wings, soared up again. Her avian heart full of the joy and exhilaration of simple existence. She made another circuit before growing bored and then, with hardly a perceptible movement, turned steeply and struck out across the length of the lake toward her fledgling roost on the sheer escarpment that walled off the western shore.

Her eyes searched for signs of her dimly remembered fledgling nest amongst the cracks and galleries but saw nothing familiar or reassuring. A few smaller birds nervously broke cover as her shadow passed, but she did not pursue them. Instead, she reeled away again to gain height to avoid the colossal black granite spur that stood out from the cliff face. Up she flew until she surmounted even the towers that crowned its pinnacle.

Though she had been born and fledged here on this cliff-face, she still felt an instinctive unease about this strange tower, a thing neither fully carved by nature or by the hands of men.

She spiralled into the sky and circled the highest battlements. Though she was tired now, she did not alight upon the stones but cried out her defiance as she turned away towards the West again, where the primordial forest appeared to stretch on forever.

A great bronze bird catches the morning sunlight on its wings.
    As it soars above me.
        And burns its ghostly image into my vision.
        I reach out to it.
    Do you understand me?
        The whisperer in your head?
        I too have dwelt here too long.
          Take me with you.
    Oh, Beira!
        Spirit of the wind.
        Take me with you.
But she does not heed me.
    Her thoughts are set upon leaving this place.
    How I wish I could go with her.

I cast my gaze out across the loch.

From here I can see the dawn light dancing across the rolling mist giving life to its ghostly forms.

Beneath its pale shroud, I hear the slate black water that lies below.

A dark force.

Deep and fathomless.

A softly moving presence.

I tighten the shawl about my shoulders against winter's harbinger, but it has teeth of ice and bites deep into my soul.

Its power gives a low keening voice to the rocks and the water.

Down the length of the great loch, its voice carries to this high and lonely place.

Calling to me.

But I will not listen.

Samonios struggles towards its bitter end as now Samhuinn approaches.

This winter will bring no peace.

The Gaisgeich will not hang up their spears and swords in its darkest depths.

And the voice on the cold wind cries a lament for the dead and those soon to die.

From behind me, I hear him approach.

Heavy, measured footfalls and his laboured breath.

A gust carries his scent away, but I can still sense the mixture of smells that cling to him, wood smoke and ale, sweat, old leather and oil.

I no longer find the scent of him strange, as I once had, so long ago; it is a warm, comforting smell.

He moves quietly, closing to my right shoulder.

His mind is full of questions and doubts, but he does not form them into words.

Nothing, not yet.

His long sigh is like a furnace against my temple.

I tell him that we must continue to wait.

A few water birds take my attention back to the sky.

Flashing specks of silver against the pale firmaments.

Wan spirits ascending unto the heavens.

They circle lazily in perfect formation and then strike southwards, knowing instinctively the coming of the first of winter's snows.

Below us, the cruel wind is driving the last of the mist away. Back to the places it must go until the night returns when it can silently reclaim the water.

As the mist rolls back like a blanket, it reveals the loch and the mountains far beyond to the cold, harsh light of the new day.

Such a clear blue sky, as pale as my lover's eyes, but it holds no such compassion or warmth.

I can see the loch and the mountains clearly now, and the Coille Mhòr that covers the land beyond as far as my eyes can see.

An immense grey-green swathe of ancient trees, dark and impenetrable, crowding down to the water's edge on both sides and marching endlessly towards the far mountain slopes.

A breathtaking panoramic.

All laid out below us, high upon this crag.

I watch.

I wait.

I listen.

"What's happening?" demanded Ag, trying to push nearer to the tiny window.

"Nothin' yet." Kemble pushed the young boy's head away. "They're just standin' out there."

"She gives me the willies, Kem. Don't she you?"

"Aye, lad. Aye." Kemble turned back into the room, absently scratching at his cropped grey beard. "That she does. Though I'd rather have her with us than against us."

"Is she really magic, Kem? Like Rolf says?"

Kemble liked young Ag, but he was becoming more and more irritated by the boy's closeness with the clumsy oaf of a storekeeper. It was a relationship that crossed too many boundaries for his liking. Kemble, as the master of the gilles, stewards and slaves within the household, was responsible for the strict maintenance of such boundaries. Slaves were slaves but gilles, like Ag, were of the Clan, lowly servant lads mostly, but blood kin nonetheless, and it was not proper that Ag should be hanging on every word of a half-wit slave.

"What did Rolf say, boy?"

Startled, Kemble swiftly realised that her companion, Fyngard Kvällulf, must have been standing at the open doorway listening to their conversation about his mistress.

"Tell me that, then I will tell you the truth." Kvällulf stepped into the room, his gaze fixed on the boy. He was a big man, a Gothad, blond and bearded with cold, empty eyes. The kind of man anyone with an ounce of sense should be frightened of, let alone a lowly gillie.

Kemble opened his mouth to hush Ag, but it was too late.

"Rolf says she's a fairy woman," the boy blurted. "Not one of us at all. He says she can change shape an' put spells on you an' stuff."

Kvällulf's long face grew tight with anger, but the boy plunged on excitedly, almost in defiance of the glowering warrior. "An' that she can hear an' see thin's we canna, she can talk to ghosties and thin's you shouldn't have no business talkin' to. He says..."

"He's all piss and wind." The Gothad snarled through

clenched teeth, "Old women's tales to scare small children." He stepped closer to the boy. "You understand me?"

Suddenly Ag seemed to realise his mouth had put him in real danger. "Aye..." He stammered, "yes."

"Good. I will hear no more of it. She is not a Witch or damn Alf either. They don't exist." He lowered his face to only inches from the boy and growled. "Do you understand me? Or shall I show you something real to be frightened of?" Up close, the Gothad's unblinking grey gaze felt like a rope around Ag's throat. Unable to break it or find a way to operate his tongue, he mumbled something that sounded like compliance.

"The next time I hear you talking like that, I'll kill you and that slug Rolf." Kvällulf's hand snaked out so fast that the boy did not see him move; it caught him across the side of the head by the left ear, just hard enough to sting. "Förstår du? Understand?"

Ag's eyes filled as he nodded dejectedly.

Kemble sighed loudly and went back to watching the two figures on the parapet. "Though she is a strange one, Fyn. You must admit that. A Witch maybe not but as fey as any I've ever known or heard of for that matter."

Kvällulf gave a deep animal-like rumble, "Damn you people. She's here to give you what help she can. That's all that matters. Be grateful or tell us to go away." He stalked back to the door. "Myself, I don't think any of you are worth it. We should leave you all here to die." He strode out, slamming the door behind him.

Kemble turned back from the window to the young gillie, "I think yon man's more than a bit fond of that Lady. So, I think it'd be a clever thing if you an' old Rolf kept your tongues tied when you're around him, or he may just end up wearing them for trophies."

Ag had collapsed onto one of the benches and was rubbing his face sorrowfully. "But is she a Witch, Kem?"

Kemble paused and cast a glance at the two figures standing high up on the battlements. "Aye, lad. Of course, she is."

"Enough," he says, gently turning me to face him.
I look up into that great broad face, almost all of it lost in a mass of dark red beard and hair, and into those blue eyes.

So, kind.
"You must rest now. I will watch for a while. Go, eat, and rest."

He puts his huge hands on my shoulders, and the warmth from them flows into me. "Go on," he says softly.
I know that he is right.
I nod my compliance.

As I walk towards the stairwell.
I turn.

I love you.

I do.

I really do.

He says nothing; the only reaction is in his eyes.
I never thought I could love a man so much.

I pull the shawl tight and turn to descend the winding stairwell.

The stone is wet and treacherous underfoot.
I pick my way carefully down into the darkness.

At the bottom, Fyn stands, holding the small door open for me. He looks angry and sad.
I ask not why.

I know.

I know why they are frightened of me.
Men despise the things that they do not understand, and some would try to destroy me even now if their Laird did not need me.

Oh, Fyn, so angry.
I brush his cheek.

They are foolish, my darling, scared children.

They cannot hurt me.
It only pains me to see you so angry.

He smiles, but his thoughts do not change.
A good man, a good heart, but still that shadow hangs over him.
The Raseri.

A shadow of something so savage and unreasoning.

The Albans fear him, and so they should.

I wish I could make him understand that ignorance is one thing I know no spell or invocation to dispel.

Ag stood in the dark corridor shaking.

He had turned the corner and almost collided with the Witch. He had yelped like a puppy in surprise and dropped the lamp he carried. She had just smiled at him and glided past silently.

He tried to pull himself together, but it was of little use, his hands shook, and his heart pounded like a drum. He slumped against the cold stonewall and sighed deeply. She had possessed his dreams from the moment he had first seen her. Since then, he had spent numerous sweaty nights in his wooden cot fantasising about her. Part fascination, part fear. Adolescent dreams of the unattainable in which he was a man.

The dreams had abruptly stopped when Rolf had told him she was a fairy woman and that any man who fell in love with her would lose his soul and be damned.

Ag had pondered on this for a long time before returning to ask the old storeman if that meant those that travelled with her were damned as well?

"Aye." Rolf had sneered and spat to give emphasis. "May they rot in Hel's bosom."

Ag could accept that the Gothad was damned; after all, Gothads were a savage and wicked people, but he wondered about the Vör, Jacobis, because he seemed so gentle, softly spoken, and kind. He asked Rolf if the Vörish giant was also damned?

"The Vör has no soul to lose. He's damned anyway; they all are godless monsters, all of them." Rolf had turned over the lamb carcass he was preparing and selected another knife from the table, wiping it clean on his bloody apron.

"Are they all like that then?"

"Who?"

"The Vör... the giants, I mean."

"Aye, giants they are, all of 'em, as wild as wounded bears and twice as nasty. Don't you be fooled by that one's soft words n' clever ways. He'd cut your heart out as soon as look at you. They eat people." He held up the carcass. "Like you eat this lamb, he'd as soon eat you."

Rolf's words had sunk deep into Ag's thoughts and sprouted endless nightmares. He no longer pursued his sweaty little fantasies in the dark but found his dreams now full of menace and frightening images of painful deaths. Since then, he had tried to keep away from her. Hiding when he heard the Vör. He had spent almost a week creeping around in the dark, trying to avoid her. Now he had walked straight into her in the darkness.

She roamed through the Craig's endless maze of passageways and halls with no lantern or torch to light her way. Oh, no, not for her. She didn't need light, nor did she make a sound. Rolf was right, and so was Kemble; she wasn't right. She was not Human.

Something fluttered past his face, Ag's nerve broke, and he ran.

As Fyngard Kvällulf stepped up onto the parapet, the wind caught him, and he almost slipped.

"Be careful, Fyn," called Jacobis, though he did not turn to speak. "They're beginning to ice over."

Fyngard walked to where the Vör stood resting on his great spear and staring out over the loch. "They won't come in daylight, Jac."

"They may do as they wish. Come when they want. As you well know, there was a new moon last night, so tonight, we'll see the first of its waxing face. If they're coming, they'll be coming soon."

Fyngard looked up at the enormous Vörish warrior. It was like standing next to one of the stone monoliths the ancient people used to erect. Fyngard was a big man, taller than most Gothads, which meant he stood like a giant compared to the Albans that made up the castle garrison, but his head only came level with the big man's lower chest. Jacobis was a Vör, a giant. He was built like a bear and resembled one. He wore enough furs to make a bed for half a dozen men and enough iron and bronze to armour a horse. Fyngard admired Jacobis deeply for his plain honesty and his indomitable courage, he even owed him his life countless times, but he could not call him a friend. He could not be a friend to any man for whom he held such jealousy in his heart, and that was one thing he hated himself for. It was a betrayal in his own eyes. Bravery and fidelity were the currency of Fyngard's people, the values he had lived by since the day he was born. For any Gothad, to be a man was to live and die and be judged by the Gods on those values. Jealousy and covetousness were anathemas to everything he told himself that he still believed in. Yet deep in his gut, those feelings writhed and gnawed at him like maggots. He sighed and cast his gaze out across the loch.

After a long moment, he observed, "They'd have to cross the lake in daylight. To have any chance of getting off the strand before dawn. They hate bright daylight, and it would hamper them. They'll wait, at least until dusk."

The huge man nodded, "Ja, they prefer the moonlight, but they have slaves who will willingly bring them across the lake in the light. They could land at dusk. Or they will try to circle the lake by land, keeping to the dark of the forest for cover. If they came overland, they could be very near now. Either way," he patted the spear's haft, "we have a reception for them." He inhaled the air. "There's a fire somewhere off. Can you not smell it in the air?"

Fyngard sniffed, "Yes." He caught himself peering at the far treeline like a child scared by shadows. This was not a battle for a man like him. He was a Gothad, a seaman and a warrior of renown amongst his own people. He should be a heath-weru, a personal bodyguard to some King by now. Instead, he was standing here on an eagle's eyrie high above a land he hardly knew, waiting to battle what he could only think of as phantoms.

Why? What for? He asked himself repeatedly. Who for?

In his heart, he knew the answer, and it was what he hated himself for. He had fallen in love with her the first moment he had seen her, this strange otherworldly woman. He and his Ulvhinna brothers had been carousing in the hall of Jarl Turfeinar after a long winter's campaigning against Earl Fyrheard. With the Ulvhinna's support, Turfeinar had finally broken the wily Southron Earl's strength and scattered his army, leaving his lands wide open for ravaging. The takings had been good, but Fyrheard had had one final trick. He had secured the services of the dreaded Trollkvinna Kjerringa Angurboða-dotter, to lay a curse upon Turfeinar's only son. The Jarl had been desperate. There was nothing anyone could do, warrior, priest, or sorcerer, to stop the boy from wasting away in the grip of a violent burning delirium. So Turfeinar had summoned, he had beseeched, and he had eventually begged on bended knees, the Vörish King to send him the Völva Annis NicNevin.

That stormy night, as they dined in Jarl Turfeinar's hall, Annis walked in alone, unannounced, into the midst of the sullen and angry warriors with all the pride and arrogance of a Queen. She strode up to where the Jarl sat, her head held high and her eyes set upon him. There was no introduction, no speech, she merely told Turfeinar what must be done to rid the boy of the curse, and then she turned and left. In that moment, she was the most beautiful and terrible thing Fyngard had ever seen.

That should have been it, the one and only time he should have ever laid eyes upon her, but instead, abandoning everything in his life, abandoning even his Ulvhinna blood brothers, he had raced after her, and it seemed to him that he had been doing so ever since.

He spoke aloud to try to drown out the thoughts in his head. "Anyway, I came to keep you company. The Albans babbling gets on my nerves. All they do is whine all the time."

"They're nervous, Fyn," Jacobis sighed. "Nervous of us, nervous of Annis, nervous of the fight to come. Once the Isheen has arrived, you will see they are brave men. They are just anxious."

"I've fought them. I know they're brave, Jac. It's just ... They're so...."

"Superstitious?" Jacobis glanced down at him for a moment. "A very traditional people, superstitious too, but they can't help it. Neither could you; it is just that you know us well now, and they do not. When the battle is joined, they will understand us all better and then they will no longer fear us."

"If we live long enough."

"I have no intention of dying just yet. So long as Annis lives, I will live, so we'll have time enough."

"I think you're incredibly brave or incredibly foolish."

"My people have a saying, 'Að ég sé hræddur um að dauðadagurinn minn gæti verið á morgun,' I believe that the day of my death maybe tomorrow." He chuckled softly. "We Vör are not renowned for our wits. The intelligent thing would be to turn tail and run."

"We Gothads are not renowned for our intelligence either."

"Then we are both stupid," he laughed.

"And damned," the Gothad added sullenly.

Chapter 2

"Hateful to me as the gates of Hades is that man who hides one thing in his heart and speaks another."

Homer.

The Iliad

As the last gille left the butchery, Rolf sneered, waited for a heartbeat to be sure they had gone, then drove the carving knife almost through the oak worktable and let out a long, sibilant sigh.

His frustration was getting intolerable, two months in this mausoleum, in the middle of nowhere. With nothing to do but wait, watch, and hide from her. He felt as if he had been wrapped in chains and left for dead. In frustration, he drove his invisible talons into the wood, shredding the grain and tearing a sizeable piece off.

Oh, how he hated this waiting!

This physical form was good, and the glamour had worked well; she had no idea of his presence in the fortress. So long as he kept from her sight, she would not know until too late.

Far too late, he smiled.

Oh, how he yearned for the fight to come. This would be the best yet; the Albans, knowing their inevitable fate, would never yield. With her at their backs, they could hold this place for weeks, possibly through the winter, until the forces of their King could arrive from Ceanna-Bhaile to relieve them. That could not be allowed to happen. There could be no siege. He was here to make sure of that. When the time came, his task was to poison their food, then let down the barbican bridge and open the gate. The sport inside the castle would be wonderful; hunting through these corridors in his true form would be such a release.

Drool dripped from his mouth onto the table. He regained himself and wiped his chin with the back of his hand.

He had a personal score to settle with several Albans, but his masters would never let him near her, their prize. If he touched her, he would be made to pay, forever. No, he would have to be contented with that Vör of hers. Anything of hers would taste so good.

A strange sound filled the room as the thing that pretended to be Rolf chuckled childishly. In his mind's eye, he formed a picture; he would make his way through the castle picking off the Albans one by one, making them suffer for their stupidity. He'd have that snivelling brat Ag too, ooh yessss.

Then to confront the Vör. He would come in low and hard, not giving the giant a chance to use that accursed spear. Get in close, fight with bare hands and teeth, yes! He liked that idea; he was at least twice as strong as any damned Vör. He would smash the giant like a clay doll. Right there in front of the bitch and the whimpering Albans. That day they would know fear.

"Rol?"

Rolf spun around and snatched the Alban into the air by his throat before he realised who it was.

Ag must have walked in while he was daydreaming.

Rolf dropped the boy. "Damnú air!" he snarled. "You shouldn't go 'round creeping up on people."

Ag sat on the floor, rubbing his neck. He swallowed hard. "What happened to the table?"

The waiting is unbearable.

Here, in the dark, dark heart of this great stone monster, I long for an end.

A release.

Why do I have to carry this?

Oh, mother.

You never told me it would be this hard.

The midday meal was served to the Laird, Angus MacRoth, and his clansmen in the refectory; too small to be called a banqueting hall, it laid off to the right of the fortress' great hall. The walls were hung with heavy tapestries and bedecked with the brataichean of the Clan MacRoth, its septs and allies, coupled with the roaring fire in the great hearth; it was one of the few hospitable places in the Craig. It was here that most of the clansmen gathered to eat their meals and mingle during the day in vain attempts to keep their spirits up and to shake off the all-pervading cold. The Craig was always cold, even during the height of the short summers that came to the North. When other fortresses became hot, stifling, and airless, Eagle's Craig remained as cold as an icehouse.

Angus gazed at the food before him, unable to eat it; his appetite had left him several days ago. Now the lack of it was already starting to show. He was gaunt and was beginning to look as old as he felt. He was deeply weary, yet he could not sleep and wandered the castle aimlessly at all hours. Lying to his men, even to himself, telling all it was a leader's duty to be vigilant and prepared, but they all knew the truth as well as he did.

"I ate some bread this morning," he said to no one in particular as he pushed the trencher away, though none of his companions seemed to notice. He drained his tankard and refilled it himself before any one of the serving gilles could get to him. Angus was Chieftain of the Clan MacRoth and Laird of Eagle's Craig by birthright and election. Theoretically, the MacRoths had ruled from here since it was ceded to them by King Domnall almost two centuries ago. Though no Laird had spent a moment longer here than he had been forced to do by circumstances. The Craig had been a lefthanded gift that the MacRoths had been forced to pay for in continual blood and strife, a gift they had long ago learnt was not worth the price. A clever way of continually sapping the power and wealth of the Lairds of Cree'uch.

Angus had first seen this place when he was a small boy. His father had a berlinn sail them down the length of loch Racholl to see the Craig from the water. It looked like some great stone monstrosity perched high above them, a darkly brooding grotesque, staring out across the loch. Hewn from the cliff face and finished with black granite, the castle seemed to rise out of the living rock like a vast malevolent growth. The spur on which the Craig's fortifications were built was separated by a sixty-foot chasm from the land behind it on three sides. The highest battlements, the Tùr nan Iolairean, the Tower of the Eagles, was almost six hundred feet above the water's ice-cold surface. Eagle's Craig was the oldest and strongest fortification in the North. It was said that the Ancients had built a fortress here thousands of years ago to hold back some terrible threat, though the tales tell that when Angus' ancestor's people came to these lands, the days of the Ancients were long past. Only this colossal, ruined spire remained. A silent monument to the wars of a long-forgotten people. Successive Alban Kings had rebuilt and enlarged the defences, erecting the great watchtowers and tunnelling deep into the rock itself.

The sight of the place had frightened him as a child, and it still did not fail to raise a shudder each time he returned. Like most of his ancestors, he refused to live here, preferring to appoint his young cousin, Gabhran, as permanent Castellan.

Angus kept the castle's garrison at forty clansmen, all year round, plus a handful of gilles and a dozen slaves. Their task was to protect the border against Kern raiding parties or Gothad war bands pushing south. They could strike out at the raiders and spread the alarm through a string of beacons from here to southern Cree'uch and beyond. The cost of maintaining it all was ruinous and forced hardship upon hardship on the Clan MacRoth. Angus' father, Gallen, often muttered in his drink that the Kings of the Albans had lumbered the MacRoth's with this damn place so that they would never be rich enough to be of concern to them. That the MacRoth's, the most powerful of the border Lairds, would never have more than a cracked pot to piss in.

Gallen was a child when his father had died fighting Kern raiders along the river Aveeń to Cree'uch. In turn, Gallen had held Eagle's Craig against a Kern army and driven them back beyond the northern reaches of the Aveeń. Then, when Angus was still only a child, the Gothads had returned. Those had been genuinely dark days, the wild Northmen with their War Priests and shapeshifting warriors swept out of the northeast, burning what they could not loot, destroying village after village, putting all to the sword. The Craig had held against three sieges in less than five years. Angus had seen the last siege himself, though the eight days locked up here had been a party compared to this.

In those days, Angus had learnt much about the Craig as he explored the labyrinthine corridors and endless cellars that sunk deep down into the living rock itself. He firmly believed that the castle was a living thing with a temperament of its own, a black and primaeval nature, that affected everyone and everything that desired to control it or dwelt in it too long. The Craig had absorbed too much blood into its stones. It had witnessed too much misery over the long centuries, so much so that now the very air had become tainted by it.

My castle, he thought, looking around the table at his men eating their midday meal. These were his clansmen, big hirsute men, rough and indomitable, brothers and cousins and nephews. My people and my tomb.

One thing he knew was that he had never desired this place or wished to dwell here a second longer than he had to. He got up and walked to the window. It had been two months now in this tomb with eighty of his best warriors, all as bone achingly bored as he was. All this time watching for an enemy that he was not sure he even believed existed.

He raised his tankard and toasted his reflection silently. To enemies.

A commotion broke his maudlin. He turned to see the Grieve Kemble, hurriedly approaching. He had always been fond of the old man, though Kemble wasn't an Alban but a Gärian taken as a slave long before Angus was born. Angus knew Kemble was as loyal to him as any of his own kin. More loyal than most. Kemble had been his childhood tutor. Though now old, Kemble's knowledge was wider, and his wits were sharper than most men. The only pity was, Angus mused, watching the old man's swaggering gait, that he took too heavily to the drink these days. Still, Angus would have made the old man officially his privy-councillor long ago if it weren't for the bitter enmity his wife held for the old tutor.

"Laird!" There was fear in his face, apparent enough for

everyone in the room to read it.

"What is it, man?" Angus demanded more sternly than he meant.

Kemble caught his breath in heavy gulps and grabbed his master roughly by the elbow, turning him away from the watching clansmen. "There are Kerns at the Doolan Gate, Laird," he said close to Angus' ear before the Laird could react. "They demand to see you."

Angus stared at Kemble for a moment. "Kerns? Why?" Before the Grieve could answer, Angus pulled him closer. "How many?"

"About forty or so, a war band. They walked up all kind of casual like to the bridge and demanded to see you."

Angus found himself almost running through the labyrinth of dark passageways. His mind racing to catch up with his feet. Forty Kern warriors? Why come here? Maybe they'd been sent with a message or just had news. Bad news, threats, or an ultimatum – maybe the Druids were wrong; it was just another Kern uprising or some kind of feud. He could not afford to get drawn into a Kernach civil war, especially without the authority of his King, but King Cathail and the army may not have even left the safety of his palace at Cyann-Balu by now.

The massive Geural wall protected the western courtyard from the worst of the wind but not the breathtaking cold. Across the square stood the gigantic form of the barbican, known as the Doolan Gate. At the entrance to the barbican's defences stood Gabhran MacRoth, the Laird's young cousin and Castellan of Eagle's Craig, his usually grim face looking more alert than he had in the last two months. He grinned widely as Angus approached, "They're Kerns from Lya'ud, Angus. Armed to the teeth, they've got a Priest with them too."

"What do they want, Gabhran?" Angus pushed open the door and sprinted up the winding stairs to the ramparts of the barbican, forcing Gabhran and Kemble to run to keep up.

"The Gods alone know, Angus, but if they try anything, I have them covered from every arrow slit."

"Good." Angus reached the landing and stepped through the doorway out onto the rampart overhanging the drawbridge. Though the Doolan Gate faced almost due South, the turbulence caused by the Northwind as it swirled and screamed around the great towers made it almost impossible to stand upright. Angus grabbed the stonework to brace himself. "Bugger the archers, Gabhran!" he yelled, "They won't hit anything in this gale!"

"They'll bloody well try though!" Gabhran laughed.

For the first time in weeks, Angus' mood had lifted a little, and he was smiling as he glanced over the embrasure.

The Kerns stood opposite the barbican, the age-old enemy of his people, defiantly near the edge of the Dooglac, the vast chasm between the cliff face and the Craig. As if tempting the wind or the archers to test them. Angus counted fifty, all Kernach warriors,

'Caterans,' as his father used to call them. The old tales said that they came to this land in the age of the Gods and the Ancients and warred against both. Theirs was a brutal culture not given to farming or domestication but hunting and scavenging off their meagre homelands. A harsh, cruel people with a strange murderous religion. The sight of them standing so boldly at his gate was unnerving.

"See, Laird," shouted Kemble in his ear. "Savages!"

Angus nodded. Savages indeed. They looked every bit as ferocious as he remembered from his childhood. They stood taller than the average Alban by about two inches, lithe looking, often gaunt, as their diet was poor and scavenged, but they were as hardy as wild horses. Most were dressed in their traditional leno; knee-length, heavy, orange-coloured shirts, under thick padded leather gambesons, wrapped around with poorly made homespun cloth and furs. Their arms and faces were tattooed and painted with woad, ochre, and blood. Some wore their long red hair unkempt, others short and limed to stand up like a boar's back. Most wore long Alban style moustaches that hung from their chins, but others grew theirs into their side-whiskers, a uniquely Kern style, while others just let their hair and beards grow wild. Around every neck hung a heavy torc of gold or electrum. Around every bicep and wrist hung bracelets in a display of each warrior's wealth and status.

As Gabhran had said, they were undoubtedly heavily armed, with an array of weapons and their ornate square shields. The only visible armour was the helms that about half of them wore. Some wore their traditional tall, crested bronze helms, though some wore Alban style pot helms with their distinct long cheek guards. A couple even wore Gothad spangenhelms. A few carried short bows, but they were not truly warrior's weapons to the Kerns; they preferred their heavy gaesum spears, dirks, and their long, blunt-ended broadswords.

Amidst them stood half a dozen hounds, the Kerns used them for war and hunting; shaggy, ferocious beasts almost as tall as moorland ponies. Angus looked for horses. Had they come on foot? He doubted that, so that meant there must be more of them with their horses.

"What do you want?" He yelled to them.

One of the dogs yapped, and the men milled around for a moment. Finally, out of the throng stepped an old man with a mass of dirty white hair and an unkempt beard. He wore a huge white ox-hide upon which were tied an array of animal remains. His thin arms were covered in tattoos and paint; in one hand, he carried a roughly made bodhran drum, and in the other, a long staff topped with a deer's skull and raven's wings. He raised his skeletal body to its full height and announced, "A am the Tysher Mer MacLeech, these that follow A are the Kerns o' Lya'ud."

Angus' thoughts reeled, although he kept his voice firm, "Aye, I know you, Mer MacLeech. I'm Angus, son of Gallen, of Clan MacRoth, Laird of Cree'uch and Eagle's Craig. I'll ask you again; what do you want, old man?"

MacLeech's gaunt face was a horrendous mass of ritual scars and tattoos that spread out like a spider's web from his sightless left eye. He fixed Angus with his half-blind stare and grinned menacingly. "A have come to aid ye MacRoth. to partake o' the fightin' to come, to stand or to die with ye, whatever it is to be."

Stunned, Angus turned to Kemble and Gabhran, but they only looked back as shocked as he was. "What?" he asked them as if hoping his ears had deceived him.

Gabhran shrugged. "It's got to be a trick. Why would they want to help us?"

"More importantly, why would he want to help us?" sneered Kemble.

Angus had no idea; this was not what he had expected at all. Mer MacLeech was the stuff of myth; a Tysher, a warrior priest, feared for generations by the Albans in the North and Angus' father's sworn enemy. Angus grabbed Kemble's arm, "Get the..." he checked his words. "Get the Lady Annis and her men, tell her what has occurred."

I can feel them.

Though the Grieve tells me of them.

I already know them.

I know him.

An ancient and powerful soul.

I walk with the Grieve. He is a kindly old man, he talks hastily, too close to me, but the Kerns scare him more than I do.

Jac and Fyn do not like his proximity to me.

However, he is careful not to touch me.

The wind is not so bad in the courtyard, though it is now cold enough to freeze the small puddles between the cobbles. They crackle and crunch as the others step on them, though I am careful not to observe the patterns they leave.

A group of Albans are gathered in the courtyard; their minds are full of questions, their hostility to me clouded by a new uncertainty.

With gazes averted, they shuffle aside to let us pass.

None speaks a word.

The barbican steps are steep and winding. We climb in a single file with the Grieve leading the way.

Fyn keeps close behind me. He is full of anxiety; the Kerns stir dark memories in him.

Bad memories.

Pain.

Jac follows last, he finds these confined spaces difficult, but he keeps his thoughts deliberately calm and quiet so as not to trouble me.

The Laird awaits on the rampart, his face impassive, but his mind is in turmoil. He is a strong man, in body and in mind, though his heart is kind.

So kind that he doubts himself.

He does not doubt me.

He wants to be the warrior his father and grandfathers were, but he is a man unlike them.

He tries to smile.

He explains again.

I listen patiently.

"So, what I want to know is whether it's a trick? An' if not, why is he here? If you can really see into a man's heart and mind, Lady. Tell me what you see in his?"

He knows I can.

His words are for the ears of the others listening.

He knows much.

I smile at him.

Mer MacLeech is very powerful.

"Please try."

I close my eyes.

Jacobis steps past us and out onto the rampart.

I can sense the Kern's shock.

A wave of fear runs through them.

Even Mer is surprised.

While his thoughts are distracted, I reach into his mind.

I search, gently pushing at the edges of his thoughts. He talks to his warriors.

Though the giant on the ramparts alarms them, he is not frightened.

Because he knows I am here.

He knows I am here.

His mind snaps shut like a trap.

So fast.

Not fast enough.

The Laird listens to me carefully.

I explain as best as I can.

He wants to believe in what I tell him, so I am careful to tell only what I must.

Not all I saw.

I tell of ill omens and signs, of raided villages and dead children. Attacks that come in the dead of night. Of a terror that grips a people and a chill that touches even the heart of Mer MacLeech.

Of an enemy, as yet unseen, that knows no mercy, whose weapons are fire and sword.

I tell of a leader powerless to protect his people against the oncoming storm.

A proud unconquered old Warlock forced to deliver himself into the hands of his greatest foe.

So that what should be can be.

Acts of desperation by the proudest of men.

The Laird listens well.

Angus pulled his attention away from Annis. Everything about her scared him, but in this, he trusted her wholly. He turned to Gabhran, "Let them in."

"But..."

"You heard me, Gabhran. Let the Kerns in."

Gabhran stood still, his face white with shock and rage. "No, Laird. I will not!"

"We have no choice. We need the extra men, and the Kerns are good warriors. Now, Gabhran, go let them in."

"They're savages!" cried Kemble, horrified.

"No!" Gabhran looked flabbergasted, "You'd open the gates to them on the word of that whore?" He was screaming now. "She's a bloody Witch! Angus! She's probably in league with them. We should throw her to the bastards and be done with this stupidity!"

Out of the corner of his eye, Angus saw the Gothad move. His motion was smooth and fast. In the space of a breath, he had drawn the short sword he carried and placed himself between them and Annis. His gaze unfocused, and his body relaxed. The Laird quickly weighed the situation; he knew that Fyn could probably kill them all in this confined space, and he would readily do so if he thought she was in any danger. With mounting alarm, Angus also realised that with the Vör behind them, on the rampart, there would be no escape. The watching archers would have no clear shots, and anyway, he honestly doubted if they would have much effect upon these two. To die here of a misunderstanding would be as tragic as it would be ludicrous.

Angus turned and slammed his fist into Gabhran's face and then seized the younger man by the doublet and thrust him against the wall. "Gabh, you're my cousin, and I love you, but I am Laird, not you. Do as I say, or I swear I'll throw you off this wall myself." He shook Gabhran violently and roared. "Do you understand?"

"Aen…" Gabhran's protest began again.

Angus slapped him hard across the face. "Understand!"

"Aye, Laird," Gabhran sagged, "As you wish."

"Aye, as I wish." Angus shoved him towards the steps. "Now!"

31

The long narrow drawbridge slammed down the last couple of feet of its drop, revealing the raised portcullis, the lower stakes just visible in the roof of the entrance. To Mer, the whole thing looked like a colossal mouth beset with great metalled teeth, its huge black oak tongue lolling at his feet. The wind howled through the gap, giving voice to the monstrous maw. Mer took a long look into the mouth; beyond the gate, he could see clear across the courtyard to the steps of the keep. It occurred to him it felt like looking down the throat of some terrible beast. Mer had never feared death, least his own; if death herself awaited him here, then he would walk to meet her and look her straight in the eye.

So, this was the great, impregnable tower fortress of the Alban's, Eagle's Craig. Mer had walked its passages in dreams and visions, although never in all his long and hard life had he imagined that he would one day stand willingly before its open gate. He knew the history of this fortress intimately; the names of each of its towers, the wars it had seen, the deaths and the suffering. At his feet was the Glas a' Geta, the great drawbridge of the Doolan Gate. Almost a hundred and fifty years ago, Domnall, King of the Albans, had ordered Mer's great grandfather, Uist ru Mac Gurthinmoch, nailed alive to this bridge, a thousand nails to hold him there to rot until his body fell away piece by piece into the Dooglac, the vast chasm below. Beyond the Doolan gate stood the barbican proper, and soaring high above it all, the massive Dinah tower, the oldest part of the fortress, its glossy black surface had the strange seamlessness of a thing grown rather than built. From the top of that great drum keep, the Lairds MacRoth would hurl prisoners to their deaths on the cobbles below.

Mer's nerves were stretched out as tight as catgut, but he would not give anyone the satisfaction of showing it. He pulled his bull skin cloak tight around his shoulders, gripped his staff, and stepped purposefully onto the drawbridge and strode towards the entrance. As he reached halfway across the bridge, a dozen men and a woman came out of the shadow of the gate to meet him.

As they met at the threshold of the barbican, Mer took time to look carefully at the Chieftain of the MacRoths and pushed gently with his mind towards the man. MacRoth was a solidly built man about a hand span shorter than Mer; his dark ginger hair was long and tied back, his beard closely cropped, there was silver in it, he looked older than Mer expected, haggard. His appearance made Mer think of a dulled sword, but his slate-grey eyes showed no weakness. This sword still had its temper; his mind was keen and sharp, scrutinizing Mer and his warriors for a wrong word or action, studying them all closely, watching. Plans of action and questions ran through the Laird's mind, although Mer could sense no fear or vulnerability.

To the left of the Laird stood a younger man, too young to grow more than a ragged moustache and some fluff upon his cheeks, another Alban, he resembled his Lord but in a coarser, less refined way. Mer noticed there was a red mark on the man's cheek and blood in his mouth. The hate emanating from the young man was palpable; the hand that gripped his sword hilt was white at the knuckles. His mind was full of images of violence. Yet, he was doing a duty beyond his own prudence and was assuring himself with the knowledge of the presence of the archers behind every murder hole above.

Mer could feel their eyes too.

To the Laird's right stood a woman. Mer noticed how thin she was, how strange she looked, as strange as she was beautiful. As tall as Mer himself with dark olive skin and long hair as glossy and black as a raven's wing. Her features were angular and refined, her mouth thin but wide. Her striking green eyes, unnaturally large and deep, held him with a fearlessness and intent that warned of the power of the mind behind them. She held tight a pale fur cloak about her fragile body, little protection against the chill wind. Mer wondered if this was the fearsome wife of the Laird, Lady MacRoth, he had heard so much of.

Though the moment their eyes met, he recognised her for what she was. This was someone else, something else; there was enough power behind those eyes to sweep all these men away like leaves before the wind. This then was the Witch they had told of, the Fees'sacher, Annis NicNevin. She held his gaze for a moment and then smiled. At that, he realised there was more than one kind of power in those eyes. She made no attempt to shield her thoughts from him, but he decided not to reach out to her.

A Gothad stood behind her. He towered over the group, a tall and powerful looking blond man with tied back hair and a braided beard. He carried the air of an experienced warrior, but Mer could sense the trouble in the mind behind that iron façade. He returned Mer's gaze with the lowered brow stare of a wild animal ready to strike. There was passion there and a little fear, but also something darker, something barely human. Mer recognised that lupine stare. This one was an Ulvhinna, a 'Wolver' as his people called them. The thought sent an involuntary shiver down his spine. Mer had encountered such shapeshifters on the battlefield before. They sickened him. Only the Gothads would make a cult out of such abominations.

Behind them stood a dozen heavily armed Alban warriors, their hostility set like an invisible wall before them. They all hated him.

Mer relaxed, straightened, and smiled at the Laird.

This felt all so strange to Angus; he had no idea of what to do. There stood MacLeech, this wizened, gaunt, one-eyed old man that was so feared by the Albans. The great Warlock who had held the disparate tribes of the Kerns together against the Albans, the Gärian Hastions and even the Gothads. Warlord and Tysher. This man had been the stuff of nightmares for a frightened boy on lonely nights in dark rooms or huddled at his father's feet as the old warriors told their grisly tales. Angus was no longer a child, yet he had no idea how to speak to this man.

Kemble? Where's Kemble? Wasn't this what he kept the old fool for?

The Grieve arrived as if hearing his master's thoughts. He strode up to the gathering and bowed to both leaders, first to Angus then to Mer. "My Lord Mer, the Laird MacRoth of Cree'uch and Eagle's Craig welcomes you."

Angus sighed inwardly, he knew he kept the old drunk in his service for good reason, despite his wife's protestations, and it was times like this that he proved his worth. He let Kemble blabber on until he saw that Mer was getting bored with him, and everybody was getting tired of standing out in the freezing wind glowering at each other. Angus raised his hand to silence the Grieve. He knew little of Kernach customs, but he did know enough to remember that unless they were enemies, and thus at war, no Kern would enter a strange place uninvited. "Welcome, Mer MacLeech of Lya'ud, you are my honoured guest. Enter, please."

He sent Kemble to find the Kerns a place to rest while Annis and Gabhran led the Tysher up to the great hall, within the keep, to talk. Angus' father had told him once, so long ago, that the art of being a leader of men was to be prepared to deal with situations confidently, no matter how unusual or unexpected. If you have to seize burning coals, then do it, don't think about it, don't hesitate.

At least, Angus thought absently, try to look as if you know what you're doing.

As I turn away from the old man and step into the darkness.
I feel a new sensation.
They are near.
He can feel them too.
They are very near.

Ràrd paused her horse as soon as she broke into the clearing and lifted up her helm to rub carefully behind her left ear, where it was sore to the touch. The leather fittings and padding were fine, excellent workmanship, in fact. But why is this thing too tight? She examined the interior of the helm. Running her long fingers over the offending area, she discovered the problem, Ah, a dent in the dark bronze metal. Small but enough to press the leather against the back of her ear, where it was chafing. Sighing through her teeth, she put the helm over the saddle horn.

Carefully Ràrd looked around at the dense forest she had been pushing through for the last three days, but without the shade of the helmet's brim, the dappled daylight forced her to squint. The problem with a sealg during daylight was, she mused, that everything is so damn bright. It upset the natural balance of her senses. Ràrd, like most of her people, prided herself on her sensory abilities, and, as with most of the warrior caste, she had honed these senses to perfection; hearing, smell, touch, taste, and sight all in unison, balanced, but daylight forced her to rely upon her eyesight too much, and the brightness made her head ache. She absently rubbed at the furrows between her arched brows and the ridge of her short nose.

Ràrd scanned the clearing again, this time closing her eyes against the daylight, reaching out with her other senses, her hearing picking out every tiny sound, her sense of smell catching every scent upon the breeze. After a few moments, she was satisfied enough to relax, nothing unexpected. Thus far, so good. Though the scent of game made her realise how hungry she was.

Beyond the stand of trees, on the other side of the clearing, was a track. Ràrd went back to rubbing behind her ear. Something was wrong. She could feel it; something had been wrong for days, a sense of foreboding had settled on her, and she could not shake it. It was better out here on her own, but the feeling still persisted.

Maybe her brother Faylinn was right, this ride had gone on too far, and forces had begun to gather against them. The Alban's King would send reinforcements from his capital at Ceanna-Bhaile before winter set in. That would mean any strike further along the river Abhainn would meet heavy resistance, buying their King time to make whatever alliances he could before spring. Rànd didn't like the idea of any of it. A fast strike against the Daonna settlements in the North had been the original plan, as she knew it, and then, if all went well, a sortie beyond the forest into Crìoch. It was all diversionary, supposedly, while the Lord Cullach-Bàn struck farther north along the coast at the prominent settlements of the Gothads. There were to be no large-scale battles with the Albans, not this year. Mathan-Bàn, her uncle, was as devious as he was ruthless and often played games with rules known only to him. It was not for one as young as Rànd to question the wisdom of Warlords. Still, it seemed like madness to her. This was wrong. No one had mentioned attacking the Creag an Eagail.

Rànd spurred the horse into the clearing and onward across to the road, she had a task to do, and she would see it done.

Chapter 3

"Fair fellow deem I
The dark-winged raven,
In war, to a weapon-wielder."

Nikar Fjolnir.
Volsunga Saga.
Author unknown.

As the two riders dismounted at the foot of the hill, the wind tore at their heavy cloaks, causing them to billow like giant black wings about them. They preceded with an air of grim determination, their heavy boots crunching and skidding on the loose stones as they struggled to lead their skittish horses up the gradient to the top of the hill. The wind carried the bitter edge of winter, making this ordinarily harsh land even bleaker still. A dead land with only the freezing wind to wail its mourning. A desolate, cold, grey place full of nothing much.

The older man, known only to the other as 'Corvus,' wondered if the Priests of his people were correct, that lands had spirits of their own. If so, this place must have a genuinely hate-filled spirit; sick, old, and spiteful. A wretched spirit for a cruel land.

After a while, they crested the hill and viewed the forest that lay before them. The sight of it did little to lift their mood. The great northern forest lay like a solid blanket across the land. Ancient beyond reckoning, an immense primaeval wood of towering guibhas trees that marched steadily north from here to the ash forests of Lya'ud, only giving way grudgingly to the rowans that crowded the steep sides of the mountains and to the vast lochs that were strung through it like a necklace of precious stones.

Corvus found that often these past few days, his mind wandered to the warm, softly rolling hills of his homeland, the vineyards and tiny olive groves, the long summer afternoons when as a... He angrily shut out those memories. Increasingly these days, his thoughts kept escaping to find their way back to Aelathia, losing him in daydreams of his childhood, but for now, he had more immediate things to worry about.

Somewhere on this hillside, something was watching them with the intensity of a predator watching its prey. Corvus could feel their gaze burning into him, but he could not locate the vantage point from which they were being scrutinized. He silently cursed himself for being too old and losing the fighting skills that had once made him so feared. Time was when he could have beaten, in single combat, the very best of his own men, but now he was old and weak and worried that even his eyesight was failing him. He rubbed roughly at his face, snorted, hawked, and spat onto the icy ground. Turning casually to his companion, he spoke quietly in a measured tone, "Don't react. Keep calm. Slowly to your horse and get your sword. Do not look about you." The words barely reached his companion's ears before the wind snatched them and made off across the glen beyond.

Showing no other reaction, his young companion, Svein Jafnkollsson, turned to his horse and reached for his weapon amongst the pack. Corvus' eyes had still not picked out anything among the rocks and heather around them, but he knew it was there. Whatever "it" was. Svein had returned to leading his horse, one hand wrapped about the reins, the other holding the sheath and belt of his sword.

Corvus could feel the tension building up in the younger man. There was eagerness in him born of inexperience. He had seen the boy fight twice, once in practice back at Fluchtburgen and again four days ago against two ruffians who were attempting to steal his packhorse. It had been a good fight, an awe-inspiring display of the young man's swordsmanship, but he had not seen the third man with the cudgel that blindsided him.

Never one to feign modesty to others, let alone himself, Corvus had to admit that this boy was good with that strange rune carved sword, better than himself, perhaps better than he had ever been. He gave his companion a sideways glance, too clever with that sword and too pretty by half. Corvus had once been a beautiful youth too. His bright green eyes, olive skin and lithe young Aelathian body, had led him into more beds than he could remember or cared to for that matter. Lanista Leno Capua, the man to whom his captors had sold him, used him like a young stallion at stud. A plaything for bored, or barren, highborn women who had the money to pay Leno Capua for the chance to bed the last of the line of the Corvidians. However, his youth, along with the hopes and ideals his father had taught him, died a long time ago. Buried on a hundred battlefields since.

He cleared his throat and spat again. Most men's bodies would have broken an age ago, some better men in fact, but Corvus always had a solid motive to survive.

The years of war and disease, decades of hunger and foul weather had ravaged him, scarring him to the bone and deeper, creating a man far older than his years. The lithe and nimble body was now much slower, sometimes painful, but far more powerful, the smile now yellowed and seldom seen, the mass of raven black hair now cropped short, thinned and greying. Even his eyes had changed; they were still striking, the colour of emeralds in strong sunlight, but there was something else there now, something dangerously close to the surface.

"Talk to me," he said.

Svein habitually paused to check he had understood the man's odd accent. "What about?" he asked.

"Anything. Just talk." Corvus went back to scanning the area for signs of whatever it was that stalked them. An animal, maybe? As they descended the hill towards the tree line, there was barely enough cover for a child to hide, let alone a warrior.

Fyn sat down at the long table with the rest of them, always keeping as close to Annis as he could. To protect her, he told himself unconvincingly. At least the great hall was warm, unlike most of the rest of the castle, which was stark and unremittingly cold. The massive fireplace behind them now roared with life, throwing enough heat out to make even this tomb bearable. Gilles and slaves fussed, torches were lit and placed in their sconces, food and drink were hurriedly brought up from the kitchen. Smoke and voices swirled upwards to the rafters pushing back the veil of morbid dankness that seemed to pervade every corner. The flurry of activity diverted Fyn's thoughts as he watched the Laird offer the old

Kern a seat near him, then food and wine, and finally, as all settled, his attention.

Indifferent to the strained politeness going on around him, Fyn glared at the gilles until it prompted one of them to nervously approach him with a flagon of wine. He growled something and took the leather jug from the shaking hands of the young boy to fill his own goblet. The boy scampered away without attempting to retrieve the carafe.

Fyn lost himself in brooding silence, cradling the heavy glass goblet between his hands and staring at the wine's reflective surface. The dancing light mirrored in the warm blood-red liquid captivated his eyes, and his thoughts slipped elsewhere, to a moonlit night on a lonely moor in northern Gurvud twenty years before.

In those days, Fyn had been little more than a child, and all life seemed a great adventure to such a young boy. He had just seen his twelfth summer when finally his father had allowed him to see his first real action. Following his eldest cousin Nepur and his own brother Bjorn's friends raiding along the edge of the Kern territory, ransacking a few of their grubby little villages, and stealing whatever they could find. Which had not been much, so they had taken time to make sport of the Kerns that fell into their hands. Fun for idle young men who had not yet proven their manhood in any real battle.

Everything had gone well for a month until they blundered into the Kern war band that had been tracking them. Real warriors enraged by the despoiling of their homes and families and out for revenge. Through a series of savage running skirmishes, they had pursued the young Gothads back towards their own lands, but Nepur and Bjorn had lost their bearings. Somehow in the twilight and chaos, they had stumbled onto the Guh'ach Moor. The young Gothad's djärvhet, their bravado, turned to fear, as they staggered desperately onwards, they argued and fought amongst themselves like spoilt children. As night fell, a suffocating ground fog rolled in, and the moor quickly seemed to turn into a bog beneath their feet. Their ponies became exhausted, and they were forced to wade on foot through the thickening murk and the sucking mire.

Sounds changed, voices echoed, familiar noises twisted and amplified into a weird cacophony. The world became a strange place, dreamlike.

Separated from the others and bewildered, in his desperation, Fyn called out again and again into the milky darkness, but the answering voices seemed like distorted echoes of his own cries.

It was then that the ambush was sprung.

The Kerns, nightmarish in their full war gear, suddenly came howling out of the fog. The roar of the attackers, the baying of their hounds, mingled with the clash of swords and the screams of dying men, terrified him. Fog shrouded phantoms locked in struggles to the death, danced wildly about him. Frantically he slashed at those shadows, panic-stricken, striking nothing until his courage deserted him.

Fyn struggled against the mire to flee, but the Kerns were all around them. He had no idea where to go. He staggered a few yards before a Kern war hound brought him down. He tried to fight the massive dog off, but a spear point was driven into his shoulder, pinning him face-first into the mud. The pain was overwhelming as a deeper darkness swam up to meet him. He sucked a mouth full of water and silt into empty lungs and choked. Animal instincts told him he would die here if he did not get back to his feet and run for his life. His hands scrabbled madly for purchase on the thing he had fallen next to. He pulled himself up over the corpse of his brother Bjorn. As he fought against the pain and panic to get his body to work, the fog in front of him parted like a curtain, and a horseman thundered through. The enormous animal stopped and reared, kicking out at him with its iron-shod hooves, and high upon its back, its rider was monstrously crowned with the skull of some great-horned beast.

Annis' touch snapped Fyn back to the present, her eyes full of understanding and concern. He tried to return her gaze but could only look down at her hand on his. So delicate, with long fragile fingers and skin that looked so dark against....... Damn this! He thought. Where's Jac? He should be here. This is his place, not mine. I have no stomach for this.

Gabhran sat opposite, watching the Gothad over the rim of his own goblet. He could not say he liked the man, a Gothad in thrall to a Witch, but maybe Gabhran could understand how he felt.

It was there in his eyes whenever he looked at the Kern, hatred, gut burning hatred. Gabhran mused that if there was any trouble with these Kerns, at least he could rely upon the Gothad.

The conversation between the Laird and MacLeech was stilted and uncomfortable. Neither seemed to know where to begin; the Laird was gracious, the Tysher polite, the awkwardness was beyond words. Gratefully, all eyes turned as Jacobis entered. The red-headed giant had cast off his harness and furs, leaving only his breaches and a simple tabard. He carried no weapon with him into the hall.

Mer turned back to the Laird and asked, "Is yon Vör ceorl or tràill?"

Hearing the question, Jacobis answered, his deep voice, with its rich accent, booming out across the hall, "I am not a slave, I'm a Húskarl, a warrior, and my father was a Jarl, a noble."

Turning back, Mer fixed the man with his coldest one-eyed stare. "Whose service are ye in?"

Jacobis met the old man's glare and smiled back. He could feel MacLeech pushing at the edges of his thoughts, trying to find a way into his mind, so he blocked him out. To shield his mind from such intrusions was the first thing Annis had ever taught him to do; setting aside his surface thoughts and repeating old proverbs, Aldrei svo lítil kráka að hùn vill ekki maka... To emphasise his dismissal of the Magiker, he turned his gaze away and took a goblet proffered by an anxious young slave girl. "Like you, Magiker, I serve no one. Maybe you should ask me why I am here? Is that not what you want to know?"

Immediately MacLeech realised the Vör was blocking him out. He could only read the man's surface thoughts, a repeated verse, and the taste of the wine. Mer glanced at Annis. So, he is your man, Lady?

She tilted her head slightly to the left and smiled gently back at him.

Jacobis saw the realisation dawn on the old man's face and felt the probing withdraw. "I am Jacobis Arnflinsson, son of Jarl Arnflinn Jarnseaxuson of the Jötunn Vör." He walked towards the table. "The reason I carry no weapon is that it is our law not to when

44

at the Jarl's table, and, though I serve him not, I carry none here as a mark of respect for the Laird of Eagle's Craig." He stopped behind Annis, "There now, Magiker, is that what you wanted to know?"

MacLeech had seen only a few of the Vörish race before. They were huge men, giants, unstoppable in battle and insatiable in all appetites. It was said they came from the farthest north, the Windless Lands, so far that it was beyond the mouth of the great cave from which the North wind itself arose from the Earth. It was a vast white land where they lived in fortresses of ice and did battle with monsters in the snow-covered wastelands. A place where there was no day or night, and they worshipped fire that came down from the sky and the Great White Bear, Isborn. "Aye, A has met your kind afore, but A canna say it was ah pleasure. But whit brung you out from behind the North wind?"

Angus saw his opportunity and interjected; "Jacobis attends the Lady Annis as companion and guard, he also has experience in fighting the Sìthean, which is why King Cathail has sent him here. There have been no attacks so far south as yet, that we know of, but the King's seers believe the Sìthean are moving toward us." He watched the old Tysher's scarred face for any reaction as he spoke.

Mer smiled, not a pleasant sight, his crumpled parchment-like skin pulled tight, revealing a mouth full of broken and decayed teeth and a mischievous glint appeared in his remaining eye. "Though they cower at Cyann-Balu, your King's Druids are right enough for once. The Sithean are indeed mudgin aboot. They've burnt villages all thru northern Lya'ud, an' right down to Guh'ach Moor." He paused for effect, "They are workin' their ways south to you." He seemed to find pleasure in what he was saying, or at least in the look on Angus' face.

"So why are you here then?" Gabhran sneered, "Running away, are you?"

The old man's face hardened. "A'm no runin' awa. The Tigernonos, Talorgan, has gone to Gurvud to gather the Kerns o' Lya'ud an' Gurvud to face up to the Sìthean at Ben Doras. A, myself, know cowardliness when A smells it. Let him skook with his women an' bairns, blathering like a big yin but nae doin' nothing. At the hinner end, they're comin' down to here. This is where we put an end to them or no."

"We?" Gabhran's anger was visible on his face. "Who th..."

"Quiet," growled Angus.

Jacobis sat down heavily, the bench groaning beneath his weight. "They call themselves 'The Isheen.' They are a people of the Sìthean. They live in raths deep below the earth in the far reaches of the northern forests. They are of the Fey, creatures of magic. They call this a 'rade', but they seldom come this far into our territories."

"Ay, that A know, big man, but whit for this?"

The Vör shrugged his massive shoulders. "You're the Magiker, MacLeech, you tell me."

"But is she no the Seer?" Mer turned to Annis, "Whit say you, hen?"

Chapter 4

"Truly," said he, "it is a girl there, and Deirdriu shall be her name, and evil will come of her."

The story of Deirdriu.
Author Unknown

The thickening forest broke the force of the freezing wind, making the journey a little more bearable. The forest path flattened and widened enough to allow them to mount their horses again though they were still forced to pick their way carefully along the rutted track. Corvus pulled his scarf down under his chin and rubbed his hand across his face, wiping the running snot from his nose. Rain was coming; the sky was heavy with lead bottomed clouds boiling into grizzly thunderheads, all rushing southward. He knew the worst of it was probably passing over, but tonight it would pour down. If they didn't make Àth Clia, before nightfall, they were going to get a thorough soaking.

Finally, the sense of being stalked had passed. Corvus was sure there had been something up on the hill with them, but he was almost sure it had not followed them down into the forest. He had decided it was probably just an animal, a wolf maybe. Though for what use his companion had been, it could have been half the garrison of Cyann-Balu on that hill, and the boy wouldn't have had any idea. All the boy, Svein, was interested in was whinging about losing his packhorse and that Corvus hadn't stopped him from getting a beating by the horse thieves.

Why Corvus had agreed to escort this boy to Jarl Jergansson escaped him for the moment, the whole journey would take him at least twenty days and would take them too close to Lya'ud. The last thing Corvus wanted to do was run into Kerns, their memories were too long to have forgotten him so quickly, but the money was good, and from Noatun, he could buy a passage south to the coast of Gäria, and from there, home. It was not so much of a plan as a notion, but he was willing to follow it for now.

Let the wind and the barbarians have this frigid land. He should have left years ago when the last of the Gärian Hastions was re-called. Instead, he stayed, took an Alban woman as a wife, and became a farmer besides his remaining men. Corvus of Val Gär, a farmer, herding sheep! Sometimes he had a hard time believing the things that had happened in his own life, believing his own naivety. It would have been funny if it had not been so pathetic. His stomach groaned loudly, reminding him that he hadn't eaten since first light; in fact, he hadn't had a proper meal since they left Fluchtburgen ten days ago. Once, he could go days without food altogether; however that was a long time ago, now his stomach objected to this kind of abuse. He reasoned they should be at Àth Clia by early evening if the rain held off, where, with luck, they could at least get a hot meal. Even a bowl of the stewed slop the Albans laughingly called 'food' would be welcome.

Suddenly, with an ear-splitting scream, a horseman exploded out of the foliage at them. Corvus wheeled his horse, snatched his short flat sword from its sheath, and spurred the animal in between the onrushing attacker and the boy. Svein, shocked and bewildered, struggled vainly to control his horse and draw his own weapon. Corvus was too late to save him.

A long light spear thudded into Svein's chest, throwing him from the saddle as the attacker's horse ploughed into Corvus' shocked animal, rearing, kicking, and biting. A bronze shod hoof smashed Corvus' sword arm, sending his weapon flying through the air, as the attacker's long sword hacked down into his horse's neck, killing the animal with a single blow.

Man and beast crashed to the ground.

Reining her horse in tight, Rànd swung it around to face the fallen men. With no time to think, she urged the animal forward over the younger man's crumpled body and at the older one.

Corvus threw himself out of the path of the onrushing horse and into the bracken, desperately scrambling for the protection of the trees. Without a weapon and injured, his forearm probably broken, he knew death was only a wrong move away. He gained his feet and ran.

Rànd plunged her horse into the bracken after the fleeing man, single-mindedly pressing on her attack. The older man, a southerner of some kind, a Gärian maybe, was injured and stunned, but if he got too deep into the cover, it would be impossible to take him swiftly, and she had no time to play cat and mouse. She had to cut him down before he got too far.

Corvus' lungs felt ready to burst. His arm screamed with pain at every jolt as he weaved and dodged, throwing himself deeper into the thickening wood. He fell, rolled, and dived behind a large tree. Driven by instinct now, he snatched up the first thing that came to hand, threw his back against the tree, and froze.

Rànd pulled her horse up, she cursed through clenched teeth. She had lost him. Damn this day light, she couldn't see a thing. Her blood was up. All she could smell was the stink of her horse and her own sweat; she couldn't even hear a thing over her own heart's pounding and the animal's snorting breath. She tore off the ill-fitting helm, cursed and spat.

"Run home, old man!" she yelled, "Run all the way home! Tell them it is from I, Rànd Nic Fer Fí, that you run! It is from the Isheen that you run!" She sheathed her sword, turned the horse, and headed back to the road.

Corvus remained motionless. His attacker had shouted something in a language unknown to him and seemed to be moving away. It could be a trick. An obvious one, he thought, but they're the best. The voice was strange somehow. He considered it for a moment, a woman's voice, harsh and guttural but a woman's voice nonetheless! He almost laughed, by Mōmos' teeth! He'd been almost killed by a bitch in harness!

He looked at the stone in his hand, casually weighing it for a moment. Corvus, my boy, you are far too old for this; too slow and dull-witted, he told himself as he tossed the rock and caught it. Well, even if she was still waiting for him, he had to move sometime and now was as good a time as any. He also had to see the boy. Corvus had seen Svein take a spear full in the chest, although he had also seen many men survive worse, so he may still be alive, unless, of course, that bitch was going back to finish the job she had started.

Breaking cover, he ran, half crouched, back towards the road, the pain in his arm flashing through his body with every stride.

Leaning from the saddle, Rànd snatched up her spear, couching the weapon under her arm, and approached the fallen warrior carefully. Light enough to throw and long enough to be used as a lance, the spear's head was a long flat blade designed more for slashing and cutting than penetration. The Daonna lay curled up on the track, moaning like a wounded animal. She prodded the man's side. He moved, groaned, she thrust harder, he began to roll over. Rànd sat back in her saddle and waited. She was an Isheen warrior, not a murderer; she would not stab someone in the back, not even a Daonna.

When the stone ricocheted off the back of Rànd's head, her whole world turned black. Only her reactions saved her. Instinctively she grabbed for the saddle horn with both hands and slumped forward over the horse's neck.

Corvus ran and hurled his entire weight behind his left shoulder, impacting the horse's flank and sending them all crashing into the bracken in a tangled heap. Pushing himself backwards, he rolled away from the thrashing horse. His right elbow banged the ground sending pain like lightning behind his eyes, but he dared not stop. Lurching to his feet, he staggered back onto the path, grabbed his sword from the ground and turned to face his opponent.

The horse got up and bolted away, leaving Rànd to struggle to her feet. By the time she was up, her vision had almost cleared, though her head was throbbing savagely. There was blood pouring down the back of her neck. She chided herself for throwing the damned helmet away. Focusing carefully, as she drew her sword with as much feigned nonchalance as she could muster, Rànd studied the man awaiting her. He was old for a Daonna, older than she had thought he was, but still strong looking. It was unexpected for her to see a Daonna brandishing a weapon in his left hand like one of her own people. She had not seen that before. He held his right arm as if it were broken, but his stance was that of an experienced fighter. She knew she had underestimated him once; it was a mistake she would not make again.

Stealing a quick glance to the side, Corvus noted that the boy was trying to get up. That, at least, was as good as he could have hoped for. He turned to look at the woman as she advanced towards him with animal-like grace. She was unlike any woman he had ever seen before. She stood at least a foot taller than him. Her body, harnessed in dark leather, chain and green burrel, was lithe but powerful. Her face was pale and angular, the chin small, the mouth wide and thin, her nose, short and broad at the bridge, was set between two huge eyes. Her hair was thick and the colour of straw, tied back from her ears and braided. Her ears were long, narrow, and sharply pointed. To Corvus, they looked like horns.

"And from where did you crawl?" he asked.

Rànd could see the shock on the man's face, at the sight of her, all the Dhaoine she had encountered had that look, and most had died with that look still on their faces. Crouching slightly, she snarled dramatically, displaying her impressive teeth to full effect. She launched herself at him, hacking savagely, raining blows wildly. With her head still thumping and the sunlight too bright for her eyes, she needed to sap his strength and drive him back into the shade of the trees, but he was quicker and stronger than he appeared.

Sparks flew as Corvus parried frantically, trying to hold ground. She was too strong and too fast. Each blow hammered at him with incredible force, driving him a little farther back. Fighting left-handed and injured, Corvus knew he had to do something, or this dog-toothed bitch was going to cut him to pieces. Seizing an opportunity, he ducked instead of blocking and kicked as high and as hard as he could, hitting her on the right side with his heavy old army boot. She fell, rolled and was on her feet instantly, but Corvus had gained the advantage. He slammed his shoulder into her as she arose, knocking her back onto the corpse of his horse, where it sprawled across the road. Their legs tangled, and she stumbled, almost falling again.

He pressed his attack relentlessly now, thrusting and stabbing with his heavy short sword, no wild blows, everyone aimed to kill, driving at her, forcing her to defend. His blade sliced into her left upper arm just below the chain sleeve and grazed along the length of her arm.

Rànd spat through her teeth in frustration. He was too close for her to use the advantages of her superior strength and her weapon's reach. He was too quick, and it took all her skill and speed to avoid each of his lethally accurate thrusts. Trusting her instincts, she spun away from his attack, vaulted the fallen horse, and landed two paces away. He leapt after her, pressing on his attack, but now she had room to manoeuvre again; the swordplay became a contest of speed and agility between them.

By driving forward, he tried to deny her the advantage and forced her to keep moving in order to get a good swing at him. She, he reasoned, maybe very strong but, he had never doubted his own stamina, he had already cut her once, and that blow to her head would have killed a good-sized deer. If he only could keep the pressure on.

Instantly, dodging his thrust, Rànd stabbed her sword into the earth, sprang up, and kicked him squarely in the chest with both feet, sending him flying backwards over the dead horse. Corvus landed badly, striking his head and injured arm on the frozen ground. Unconsciousness welled up to meet him.

Rànd pulled her weapon from the earth and raced to the Daonna before he recovered; she felt sure to finish this now.

Corvus fought frantically against the oblivion, his mind struggling to focus. The world spun about him, and he was sixteen again. Laying in the saw dust and cattle shit of the Forum Boarium, injured and terrified, with a Retiarius' net tangled around his feet. He had been thrown into the makeshift arena to be butchered in honour of the Ephor Cephalus Modestus, the man whose treachery and betrayal had destroyed his family. The professional Bustuarii was closing rapidly, his spear held shoulder-high, ready to strike. Here the young Andreas Corvidious was meant to die. Here the very last of his family's blood would be splashed over the Modestus' family tomb. A blood sacrifice to celebrate the continuation of the family of the evil old bastard that had plotted to wipe the name of the Ephor Corvidious of Aeltha off the face of the earth. Andreas looked wildly about for help; there was none, only the black cowled figure of Leno Capua, dressed as the demon Charun, hammer in hand, patiently waiting to finish the job if the Bustuarii failed to make a clean kill. Screaming in terror, Andreas tried to claw himself away from certain death, suddenly a voice from the crowd shouted something, and a sword was flung down before him. As his hand fell upon the cold metal, it all instantly became clear. He knew exactly what he had to do; he seized the sword, rolled over, and threw it with all the force he could muster.

The sword hit Rànd squarely in the chest with the force of a horse kick, exploding the air out of her lungs and cannoning her backwards. Staggered and confused, she could not catch her breath. The world spun dizzily around her. Immediately a new sensation flooded over her; fear. Desperately she struggled to draw her dagger, clawing at the belt and sheath.

Corvus' mouth was full of the metallic taste of his own blood. Every movement hurt indescribably as he dragged himself to his feet and slowly retrieved his sword. He straightened up and took another long look at his waiting opponent. She stood awkwardly, one hand clutched to her chest, one hand unsteadily holding out a black stone bladed dagger in defiance. Blood splattered and dishevelled, she looked like a cross between a wild animal and an injured child. "Time to end this," he said softly.

Rànd could feel the blood pouring through the fingers of her hand clutched to her chest. Every time she breathed, something inside grated agonisingly. Her focus on the world around her swam in and out. He said something in words she did not understand, but she knew their meaning. He was coming, but she was no longer sure she could even fight him, let alone win. Rànd took one long, painful breath and screamed, "Skier!"

The ear-piercing screech froze Corvus for a second, a second too long.

"Corvus! Look out!" another shout: the boy's voice.

Corvus spun around in time to see the massive black horse

almost upon him. He threw himself to the ground as the great animal reared and lashed out. As bronze shod hooves pounded and tore at the frozen earth around him, he scrambled frantically away.

Rànd called Skier to her and clambered painfully onto his back. "Ruith!" she whispered into the horse's ear. Skier raised his head, sniffed the freezing wind, snorted loudly, and took off at a gallop.

Corvus pulled himself up and walked slowly over to where his horse had fallen. The boy stood over it, looking as if he was going to pass out.

"Are you alright?" he asked.

"I was going to ask you that, boy." Corvus bent and sat on the side of the dead animal.

"Yes, the hauberk, it was my father's, stopped the spear, but I think my ribs are broken. I can't seem to breathe properly."

Corvus laughed. "I'll wager she can't either."

Chapter 5

"Trickery and treachery are the practices of fools that have not the wits enough to be honest."

Benjamin Franklin

A wave of heat hit Kemble as he stepped into the cavernous kitchen. The coals of the enormous open hearth threw out a prodigious heat and deep red glow that gave the place a foreboding feeling, like the forge of some fire God, but the rich, warm smells of the food enticed him into this little kingdom within a kingdom. Here ruled Timmon the cook, a great stout man in his late middle age. Like Kemble, he had been taken as a slave almost a lifetime ago, and like Kemble, he now was one of the pillars upon which the household of Angus MacRoth rested. Timmon was the nearest person to a friend that the Grieve really had amongst the men of the household.

A young serving boy, who had been idling in a warm corner of the kitchen, scuttled quickly out of the room, trying unsuccessfully to avoid the old Grieve's notice.

Timmon turned from the bread ovens and grinned, "I thought it was about time you turned up."

Kemble ambled to the long table and sat down heavily. "Aye, well, Tim. I've had to empty the entire ground floor of the Tyeru Bàn tower. We've now got stores all over the place. There's no room to put anything."

The cook smiled at the old Grieve as he placed a bowl of broth in front of him. "How many is there?"

"I counted sixty-six, including the ones that came up with their horses and dogs." He shuddered dramatically, "I hate those dogs, great hulking beasties."

Timmon smiled and placed a platter of bread and meat beside the bowl. "How are we goin' to feed another sixty mouths?" He filled a tankard for Kemble and lowered himself gently onto the bench opposite. "We may well have to eat those horses."

"Oh, they sent the horses away, but they brought provisions, so at least we don't have to feed them for a wee while." Kemble ripped off a chunk of bread, dunked it into the broth, and stuffed it into his mouth. "Hmmm, good!"

The corpulent cook watched the Grieve eat for a while. "So, you've got 'em settled now?"

"Settled?" Kemble mumbled through a mouthful of soggy bread. "O' aye. Not that I care for it much. He should have never let them in. Gabhran tried to stop him, but..."

"I heard." Timmon cut him off abruptly. He did not want to hear another one of Kemble's tirades about "Kern savages." They often forgot that their kindly, fat, old cook was one of those 'savages' too. "Well, at least we could do with the manpower."

Kemble looked up from his bowl and caught the look on the cook's face. "Aye. I suppose so."

"Have they finished down on the strand?"

"O' aye, for what good it'll do. I can't see them being much use, no matter what the giant says." He waved a finger at Timmon, "I was here the last time the Gothads laid siege to this place, an' trying to hold the Trayad is impossible, mark my words. All that work has been a waste of time and effort."

"Ar' well, it kept the boys busy for a while anyway, stopped them getting' too bored."

Kemble finished his broth.

"More?"

Kemble nodded and watched as the cook took the wooden bowl and eased himself to his feet; the massive man always moved with such deliberate care. "Where's that clumsy dolt Rolf?"

"I dunno," he shrugged his doughy shoulders. "Skulkin' about somewhere. Probably heard you comin' Why?"

Kemble had not been able to put his finger on it, but recently he had begun to be uneasy about Rolf; there was something wrong. Well, more wrong than usual about that vile weasel of a man. Something odd that nagged at the back of his mind. "He's been filling young Ag's head with nonsense again, and if that bloody Gothad hears any more of it, he'll skin the pair of them."

Timmon grunted and shook his head. "He's just having a

little fun with the lad."

"No more, Tim. Tell him to leave the boy be, or I'll have him whipped or…." He wondered if he could have found a use for those damn Kern dogs after all.

"I'll tell him." The cook smiled.

"So, what's been going on up in the hall?" Timmon knew everything that went on in the household of MacRoth; every whispered conversation, illicit liaison, odd predilection, every piece of gossip and every true secret. Without moving more than a few yards from his kitchen table, he had dozens of almost invisible eyes and ears that heard and saw everything that went on in the Craig. Kemble relied heavily on what the old Cook knew, and what he did not know he could find out.

Timmon began ladling broth from the cauldron on the hearth. "They've been talkin' all afternoon. MacLeech reckons that we'll be attacked tomorrow night."

The tankard stopped halfway to Kemble's mouth.

"The Vör says they are probably here already. At least on this side of the loch." Timmon returned the bowl to the Grieve.

"Here already?"

"Aye. That's what he said."

"What does MacLeech say?"

"He reckons he has come here to fight because the omens say so."

"The omens?" Kemble snorted, took a long drink from his tankard, and burped loudly.

"Aye. He says this is where we must stop them before they move south into Cree'uch an' beyond."

"Why does he want to save the Albans from…"

"The Vör calls them Isheen'." Timmon poured the Grieve more ale. "They're from below the earth."

"Goblins! We're hiding here from goblins!" Kemble laughed. "You've been listening to that lazy fart Rolf too much."

Timmon looked at the Grieve thoughtfully. "They are real, Kem," he said gently.

"Stuff of children's dreams and old wife's tales," Kemble's face was reddening as his anger rose. "No goblins could put half of

Lya'ud to the sword! That one-eyed old bastard is trying to drag our Laird into a bloody civil war amongst those damn savages. That's what it is. Not goblins!"

"I sometimes forget, Kem, that you're no one of us," Timmon slowly sat down again. "Because you have nae seen them does nae mean they don't exist. My grandfather saw them when he was a young man. The warriors followed a trail of destruction into the heart of the Gothad kingdoms. They're no goblins, Kem."

"Bloody nonsense!!"

The cook smiled patiently and asked, "Tell me, Kemble, in all that learning you Gärian's have had ye ever seen a giant before?"

Kemble paused, unsure where this was going and surprised at Timmon's reference to his origins. "Once. When I was at Noatun. Why?"

"An' before that?"

"No, why?"

"Did ye believe they existed before you saw one?"

Kemble paused then looked down at his broth. "That's different."

"Is it? My father and uncles fought the Sithean. They are real."

The Grieve tried to change the subject. "What does the Witch say?"

"I dunno. I canna hear her words. I have nae the ears for it."

As they talk, I watch their faces.

The Tysher has gained confidence now. He eats heartily and talks loudly.

His skin is old and wrinkled like crushed parchment, his left eye is white and motionless, set in a mass of scars and tattoos, but his face is still full of mischief.

He constantly talks, although there is so much more he is not telling, things he hints at but never says.

He loves to play games, even now, though his coming here has cost him deeply.

Gabhran's anger has left his face, leaving only cold contempt.

His eyes flicker continuously from Mer to Fyngard and then to Angus.

Occasionally he speaks but only to spit out bitter words.

He neither looks at nor speaks to me.

Fear.

Fyngard's face is a mask, he says little, but the shadow of the Wodfreca hangs over him.

The Raseri is so powerful his conscious mind struggles to hold it back.

I can see its eyes.

Feel its insatiable hunger.

The Laird's face is stern, and he is quiet. He drinks but does not eat.

I hear the questions that chase each other around in his mind.

How do I tell him that the forces ranged against us hold court at Hel's feet and that it may cost all our lives and yet not stop them?

He knows without my saying it.

Jac's face has grown cold and brooding.

I touch his arm.

His thoughts flood into my mind.

Memories.

Memories of me.

Memories best forgotten.

I could chase them away.

Banish them forever from his mind, but they are part of him.

Part of what he draws his strength from.

I, too, have those memories.

The Tysher's question still hangs in the air.

I must answer him.

I lie.

I tell him that I do not know why they will come.

I only know that they will come.

Gabhran was growing impatient, the Witch's man and the Tysher both obviously knew far more than either would say, and they just kept playing at verbal cat and mouse, talking but saying nothing.

"Why here?" He finally blurted out, "What has this place got to do with them?"

"He who holds the Craig controls the routes North and South," answered Angus. "You of all men know that if they take this castle, then all of Lya'ud and Gurvud is cut off. The whole of Cree'uch and the South would be wide open to them."

"I know that, Angus, but why, if they're coming here, is the King of the Kerns going to meet them at Ben Doras?"

"Ay, at Ben Doras," Mer nodded. "There's a stone haffet at the foot o' Ben Doras, archaic even when the Ancients ruled these lands."

"A what?"

"Ah haffet, ae 'temple,' ye ken?" He gave Gabhran a sour look, "The Druids say that's where the Isheen will gather for the rites o' Flugh nan Marv, the Feast o' the Dead, in Oychu Savim. to celebrate their new Bànrigh, their Quean, in the blood o' the innocent."

"They are probably right," said Jacobis tonelessly.

"Ay, could be." Mer showed his broken smile to Annis, "But this place is the check to it all, is it nae?"

Annis closed her eyes and nodded slightly.

"Why?" demanded Gabhran.

Mer fixed Gabhran with his half-blind stare. "The 'temple' at Ben Doras exists as a focus o' the power that runs thru the earth, as the blood runs thru your veins. Such places are o' great power both this side o' time an other. Eagle's Craig is one o' those places, maybe the most important one in the North. Do ye no sense it? There's ae muckle o' power here. Can ye no feel it?" He paused, leaving his words to sink in, "Once, this fortress stood guard over ae vast city. Murias, the mightiest city of the Ancients, it's still down there, drowned, aneath the silt an' water o' the loch."

"So why do the Isheen need this place?"

"The Isheen do nae bide in this world as we do, they com'

from another place, an' they need this locus, this place, to find their way back."

"Why don't they just return the way they came?"

"Och, laddie. Would it was that simple ae thing."

The crannog stood out over the water, a huge man-made island raised on stilts. An immense squat structure fashioned out of earth and stone and defended by a palisade of enormous ancient timbers. From which, reached out to the land a narrow jetty and gate. The crannog's oldest pylons were sunk in the age of the Gods, long, long ago, and its massive old walls had seen aeons pass like rainwater. In the growing twilight, the light from the flaming torches set high on the palisade sparked and danced across the water giving the silent, brooding building a magical life against the deep purple of the sky. In the river valley, sheltered from the worst of the gale's force, the wind here only stirred the waters and whistled through the cracks.

It was Ker Diolain's turn on guard duty again tonight. Being one of the youngest and illegitimate meant that he was almost bottom of the pecking order, and thus the 'shite' jobs always fell to him. He knew that no one cared if he even existed anymore. At least when his mother was alive, she had looked after him, but she had died of fever last winter, and now he was on his own. Neither a man nor a child, and certainly not recognised by his father's family, he knew his lot would never change until he either left or proved himself. At times like these, he found himself nursing the hatred he had for those around him, nursing it like some precious flower that would one day bloom into revenge on all those who had made his life a misery, and there had been many nights like this.
Mostly these days, he amused himself with childish acts of cruelty, theft, and occasionally spiteful to his companion, Ned, and the slaves.

Although Ned was older and a nephew of the Chieftain himself, he was, as Meg called it, "Ah wee bit daft," which made the older boy a fine target for Ker's frustration, especially on nights like this.

Ker casually kicked Ned as he climbed past where he sat on the steps eating. Ned did not seem to notice. He just reached down and picked up the piece of pie he had dropped on the planking; not one to waste food, he brushed it casually and stuffed it into his mouth.

"Ned!" exclaimed Ker. "You're a damned animal."

Ned mumbled something apologetic back at Ker and reached for the jug of ale.

"Stupid ol' bouff…" began Ker, but his words trailed off as he noticed someone approaching. Jumping to it, he grabbed for his spear and knocked the ale jug out of Ned's hand.

"Wat?" Ned stared confusedly at the spilt ale.

"Someone's coming, ye daft bugger." Ker stepped up to the gatepost. Now with the torches on the palisade above him, he could see better, two figures approaching in the moonlight, one leading a horse. As they picked their way carefully down the shale beach towards the gate, the taller one occasionally reached out to steady the other, who faltered, almost stumbling on the loose shale. Ker watched them intently, trying to decide if they were friend or foe. Hard to say, he decided, but they were strangers for sure.

"Who 'a is it?" Ned struggled up to his side.

"How'd I know? Stupid."

"What t' do?" Ned did not like the idea of something going on that Ker did not understand, "What t' do?" He stood sucking the ale from his fingers and staring wide-eyed at his companion.

Ker sighed. Trouble always happened on his watch, and Ned was as good as a deaf sheepdog. He reached for the bell-rope but paused. No, he didn't want to raise a fuss too early, just in case. It was nothing after all. "Tell Big Wal." He shoved Ned roughly. "Go on."

Ned smiled at him meaninglessly for a moment before he seemed to understand. "Oh? Aye. I'll get Big Wal, then." Happy to do something, he climbed down and headed off back along the jetty.

Right, thought Ker, the bar's down, and the bolts are secure. I'll have to handle this myself until Big Wal arrives. If Neddy doesn't get lost or forget what he's supposed to be doing.

He watched as the strangers had reached the end of the strand and turned towards the gate. Ker took a long breath and, in his most authoritative voice, shouted. "Who ar' you?"

They stopped and looked at each other, the torchlight from the furthest posts catching their faces. Though the taller one tried to keep his face down and away from the light, the other one looked up so that Ker could see him clearly. It was a strange face, beardless, challenging, with cold deep-set eyes and a gaze that Ker could physically feel. A shiver ran down Ker's spine. He found his free hand grasping at the massive gate timbers for reassurance. The stranger's eyes glinted in the torchlight.

"My name is Corvidious. My companion and I were travelling to Noatun when we were attacked," he spoke in an odd accent but clearly and slowly, "We are now lost." He held himself awkwardly, holding his right arm across his chest.

"Aye? What of it?" Ker managed to croak out of a dry mouth.

"We need help, man!" shouted the other. "Let us in!"

Anger came all too easily to Ker, and this time he found his voice, "Ahhh, hech me ya...!"

"What's goin' on, lad?" Wal MacCoigruch and several of the men had arrived. He jumped up onto the guard's platform and strode to the wall behind the gate where Ker stood. Wal was taller than most of his kinsmen and built like a cart-horse, a blacksmith by craft, and a warrior by nature, his presence alone made Ker feel better.

"There's two of 'em. Dunno who they are."

Ignoring his answer Wal called out. "What do you want?"

The smaller one took another step towards the gate and answered. "My name is Andreas Corvidious. I am of the household of Jarl Jergansson. We are travelling to Noatun, but we were attacked, and now we are lost. We need only food and shelter for the night, we have a little coin, but we will gladly repay your kindness."

Wal looked carefully at the two. The smaller one was an Aelathian or a Gärian, middle-aged but hard looking, a mercenary probably, the other was tall but lightly built, probably a youth, a Gothad or Southron maybe. The Aelathian had mentioned Jarl Jergansson, Wal knew he should remember that name, but it escaped him for the moment. "I'm not Laird here, man, an' I'm sorry I canna help you."

"Who is master of this place then?" demanded the Aelathian's companion.

A voice behind Wal answered, "I am."

Jacobis and the Laird had been drinking alone since the others had retired. Gabhran had taken charge of the watch and was somewhere down on the Trayad, the strand below the Craig, inspecting the makeshift defences they had thrown up over the last few days. Angus knew that it was an excuse Gabhran used to get out from inside the walls. Fyngard would be asleep outside Annis' door until Jacobis retired. Of Mer MacLeech, neither knew nor cared. For the first time, the Laird of Eagle's Craig and the Jötunn Vör sat and talked as equals, telling tales, boasting a little, even joking. Angus sat slumped in a seat drawn up to the great fireplace for warmth. Jacobis sat on the marble hearth with his back to the wall. They had been drinking thick local meadh from a big leather pitcher that rested between them on the floor.

Angus felt relaxed and calm at last. Why? He thought it was probably the drink and the first proper meal in days, but it was also the quiet self-assurance and calmness of the Vör. They had talked about inconsequential things; the taste of the meadh, the weather. They had even talked about Gods. Was it true the Jötunn Vör worshipped a goddess? Jacobis had laughed and explained that a man's or woman's oath, their pledges and words, are sacred in his culture. They had to be when you lived in such a harsh environment, and so their Goddess was Vör, the Oath Taker, from whom they took their name. "You Albans take your name from these 'the white lands,' the Kerns from the rocky hills, those things define your peoples and your cultures, we take ours from what defines us; our word."

"And the Bear God?"

"Ahh, Isborn. Most of my people only venerate him out of fear. Few but the wildest would worship him; berserkir and their ilk. He is the fury of the Northwind, the raging voice of the storm, chaos and death." He laughed, "Not much joy at revels either." He chuckled at his own joke.

Angus had just decided he truly liked the Vör when his question came out of the blue.

"Why do you look at me that way?"

"What 'way'?"

Jacobis leaned forward almost conspiratorially. "Like... Like you pity me."

"Pity you!" Angus snorted. "Gods!"

Jacobis slouched back against the wall, his big face open and pleasant. "Well? If not, what is it?" A smile played around his eyes and curled the corners of his mouth just visible beneath his beard.

"I do not pity you, man. I just don't... Don't understand you."

Jacobis raised his eyebrows. "What is there to understand?" he paused. "I am only a man, like you, though not with such responsibilities. You have the lives of so many in your hands," he lifted own his huge hands, the great broad palms upward. "I have only one." The cobalt blue in his eyes flashed perceivably as a smile spread across his face.

Angus realised he was near the question he had wanted to ask since the Vör had first arrived with the Witch. He considered his words carefully and asked, "The Lady?"

"Yes."

"So, you are her protector?"

Jacobis' gaze drew cold for a moment. "You say 'protector' like others say 'thrall.' I am not her slave nor under any spell. I am her companion, occasionally her consort, not her guard dog."

Angus caught an unfamiliar tone in Jacobis' voice. "I am sorry if I..."

Jacobis smiled. "No, you did not." Then the smile was gone, replaced by something else, a look Angus had seldom seen. The silence hung heavy in the air between them, one man awaiting patiently what he knew instinctively was coming, the other man far away, lost in his own thoughts.

"I am a simple man, not educated or cultured like you. I can scarcely write the letters even of my own tongue, but I know what it is to love, and I love her beyond understanding. My people believe that few spirits are born into this world whole, and thus to be complete, we must find the missing part of ourselves. Every man and woman are two parts of one whole, not just in this life but in a thousand before and maybe a thousand to come. Maybe they are right."

"But she's not of your people."

"No, she is not. I found her. I do not know-how. It was as if she was calling to me, summoning me. I just awoke one morning, went out into the forest, and found her. I never took that path before and have not found it since, though I know those forests well, nor do I know why I chose that awful day to hunt." Jacobis paused as if trying to find the words to describe the indescribable. "She had been beaten and driven out of her home, accused of being a Sorceress by her local Priest, a Narbonensian fool. An idol worshiper who could not bed her and so turned the people against her." He grimaced as if the memory itself was physically painful, "They hunted her for days, driving her further into the teeth of winter, but she would not turn, she would not fight.

"So, I found her, a poor half-frozen creature, in bloody rags clawing at the frozen earth for roots like a starving animal. She was almost dead. I took her back to my father's hall and laid claim to her as was my right." He leaned forward again to explain. "Any foreigner amongst our people must either be a slave or under a Jarl's protection until he pledges himself to serve a Jarl. Otherwise, they are fair game for…whoever." Jacobis leaned forwards and reached for his tankard.

"It was five days sledging through the worst of mid-winter to find the men who had beaten her, raped her and hunted her like an animal." He examined the almost empty vessel, swilling the dregs absently. "Shameful deeds breed their own revenge." He swallowed the last of the meadh in a gulp. "My only regret is that we had not enough salt to seed the ground after."

"And the Priest?" asked Angus.

The giant put down the tankard and grinned wolfishly.

Angus decided not to push the subject further. He had heard of the terrible ferocity of the Jötunn Vör, tales of their unrelenting savagery was legend. They were said to live far beyond the northernmost reaches of the kingdoms of men, beyond the edges of the great forests in a land of endless wastes of snow, in a land the Gothads called Jötunheimar, the realm of the giants. Sailors and travellers told wild tales that the Vörs lived in great halls, the size of castles cut from the ice, and feasted on whatever they found to hunt, sometimes even men. Few dared to test the truth of those stories or wander too near to their lands; fewer returned. Angus shook the thoughts out of his head and tried a different tack, "What is she then if she is not a Narbonensian or one of your own people?"

Jacobis paused for a moment, and then he grinned broadly and said, "She's a Goddess." The big man's laughter suddenly filled the whole room.

Angus didn't quite catch the joke, but he found himself laughing too.

A woman stood on the rampart behind the palisade illuminated by the flaring torches, a tall figure in a long pale cloak with ashen hair flowing over her shoulders. "I am Jorunn Kolinka, Lady MacRoth. This is my home."

Corvidious bowed slowly. "Lady."

"Let them in, Wal. They shall be my guests." She turned and stepped down into the darkness.

Wal MacCoigruch barked orders to let the strangers in. As the gates swung open, he strode out to meet them halfway. Close up, he didn't like the look of either of them, but he had his orders and enough men to back him up. "No one's allowed to carry weapons beyond here, laddies. So, you'll hav' to give me your swords an' that," he said it confidently but as friendly as he could muster.

The Aelathian looked him in the eyes, a cold blank stare, a killer's gaze. Big Wal caught himself and stared right back. "No weapons," he said firmly.

The Aelathian smiled momentarily and then threw back his cloak, causing Wal to step back involuntarily. He wore a warrior's harness of boiled leather and chain, blackened through use, and the heavy buckled sword belt of a Gärian Fedorati, with a broad short dagger on his left and a heavy short sword on his right. His men, alerted by the sudden movement, brought ready their spears forming a hedge of blades between them. The Aelathian's smile twisted into a sneer. "I will surrender them to you only." The mirthless smile flashed again.

Wal didn't like that smile. "Aye," he nodded and waved the guards to relax. The youth was in harness too. Under his cloak, he wore a long Gothad style ring mail shirt over a padded jerkin and surrendered a simple dagger and a noble's broadsword, a heavy weapon sheathed in an odd-looking hide. Wal knew that such a weapon would carry more than just a fine edge and deliberately avoided touching it; instead, he let Ker put it aside. Wal was not happy. This felt wrong; these were killers, and she was letting them walk right in. They could be assassins or spies, but when she gave her orders, they could not be questioned. Once he had disarmed the strangers, he ordered Ker and five of the men to escort them to Lady MacRoth's presence. "Don't leave them for a moment, laddie," he added threateningly.

Ker, understanding the warning in Wal's voice, swallowed hard and, trying not to appear as nervous as he felt, began ushering the strangers towards the hall.

"Who 'a they 'den, Big Wal?" Ned asked as he struggled to hold onto the stranger's horse.

"I don't know, Neddy." Wal bent and picked up the Aelathian short sword from where he had propped it; it was a heavy thing, its edge chipped and scarred through recent use but superb quality steel and furnished with a finely decorated grip and pommel.

"Nice sword," said Ned.

"Aye," he weighed the weapon on the palms of his hands. "Nice sword indeed."

Jacobis climbed the stairs up to the Tùr nan Iolairean tower. The Grieve had roomed Annis on the first floor, as he claimed it would be the easiest for 'access.' Jacobis took that to mean it was one of the few places in the whole fortress where the winding stairs and doorways were wide enough for him to get through without crawling about on all fours or scrambling ungainly through portals like a dog trying to get through a hole big enough for its head but not its arse. Mannfólk scale buildings were a constant annoyance to Jacobis. Doors were too small, ceilings too low, and as for stairs! At the Alban King's castle, Cyann-Balu, negotiating every flight of stairs had been an exercise in contortion. He understood that these places were built by men who had never dreamt of someone his size having to negotiate their way through them, but the scale was all wrong. How, he wondered, could they live in such confinement? Cramped up cheek by jowl? And in such squalor? Manfólk, though they were mostly good at heart, and he did admire many, like Angus MacRoth, but most were grubby creatures that lived in damn tiny rabbit warrens. It only served to remind him how much he missed the space of his homelands and his own people.

Talking that evening to Angus had dredged up some old ghosts, which had not helped his mood. At times like this, especially when he had had his fill of good ale, he found himself maudlin on things he'd have rather thought dead and buried. Some things, some acts, were better forgotten and not revisited. There had been a lot of blood spilt on the snows of the past, and he feared there was a lot more to come. He knew that his people had a terrible reputation amongst the Manfólk for savagery, but no Vör was without conscience. In fact, they were afflicted with it more than most as a people, which led to the melancholic outlook that most Vörs shared. An old King of his people was often quoted as saying, "We Vör could rule the known world if only our consciences would allow us to." Conscience was a handicap to a people fashioned by such hardships and unparalleled in the arts of war. Some maintained that they all spent too much time around the hearth fires playing skáktafl and arguing philosophy in the long nights of winter when they should be out hunting, raiding, and making war.

As a race, the Vör had never numbered more than a few aetts, complex extended families, and the harsh conditions they chose to live in and their constant struggle with the brutal environment had always served to keep their numbers low. Jacobis had lost a sister to the perils of childhood and an older brother to warfare before he had even seen his own twelfth summer. Death was a constant companion for those that lived within the realms of the White Ormrs, the Ice Wyrms, and the great snow bears, the Children of Isborn.

Sometimes new blood entered their aetts when one of their kind was born into the communities of the Gothad or, very occasionally, other Manfólk societies. A jest by the Gods to remind the mighty Vör that they were no longer immortal, but that had happened rarely over the last few decades. Or, maybe, Jacobis supposed, fewer survived either being cast out or the journey into the far northern wastes. The 'Trials of Snær,' his people called it, for if the outcast endured, they had already proven themselves blessed by the god Snær. Jacobis could recollect the last one was a boy, born amongst the Gothads of Skjaldborg, who reached the gates of Gastropnir, struggling for weeks through the teeth of winter carrying two of his own people's arrowheads in his back. He had survived and grown into a fine warrior and lived to prove himself a true Vör.

Jacobis, like most of his people, was a natural hunter and an exceptional warrior, gaining honour and renown from the day of his rite of passage into manhood, and he carried the scars of a thousand battles and adventures to prove it. Tonight it was his shoulders that were aggravating him most; the scar in his right side where three decades ago a distressed ullar nashyrningur, massive shaggy beasts the Vörish warriors used for transport, thrust one of its fearsome horns deep into his hip as it tried to gore him to death. Sometimes he felt like nothing but a bag of twinges, aches, and niggling pains. Especially here in this dank, confined tomb of a place where the damp seemed to seep into everything, including his bones.

Jacobis reached the first-floor landing, squeezed through the doorway into the hall, and finally stood up fully, stretching his back and rotating his massive shoulders, feeling the muscles tug against scar tissue across his back. He sighed deeply and yawned.

The short corridor ended in a sturdy door of bronze bound oak against which was slumped the sleeping form of Fyngard Kvällulf. The Gothad had made an improvised bed out of his cloak and a couple of animal skins and dozed off with his head against the door frame. The Gothad's helmet was in his lap, and he was snoring gently. Jacobis took a close look at him. The usually carefully knotted tresses had unravelled and spilt across his face. For the first time, Jacobis noticed wisps of silver in Fyn's hair reflected in the flickering light of the ensconced torches. One hand was open on his lap, unturned, broad, and calloused, but with such strange conjunction of lines across the palm that Jacobis found it uneasy to look at. He liked Fyn; he was a stalwart and brave man who had given up so much to follow Annis. But he struggled so intensely with the power that he shared his body with that it made Jacobis wonder if the true Fyngard would be lost even to himself one day.

Jacobis stooped and patted the Gothad softly on the shoulder, "Fyn, time you were away to a proper bed, my friend." The Gothad simply grumbled something and tried to scrunch himself deeper into the recess of the door. Jacobis smiled and crouched beside him. There was something reassuring for him to know how devoted the Gothad was to Annis; such loyalty and love was hard to inspire in the hearts of such a man. Ah, my Lady, thought Jac. There is indeed a wolf at the door. Oh, but what a wolf!

He reached out and shook Fyn's shoulder firmly. "Fyn, come now. Off to your own bed. My friend."

Fyngard mumbled something incomprehensible and climbed unsteadily to his feet, clutching his makeshift bedding. His helm clattered onto the floor and rolled off to Jacobis.

"Good night, my friend." Jac stood up and placed the helm on Fyn's head, and patted his shoulder. "Rest well. She's my responsibility now."

I feel your awareness.
  I know you are there.
    Your softest touch.
No word can convey such meaning.
  I feel you beside me.
    Inside me.
Your warmth spreading from you into me.
  I float free on the tide of emotions and sensations.
    Away from this place.
      Away from this world.
Entwined like loving birds.
  Spiralling upwards into the brightest sky.
We are one again.
  Whole.
    And we are safe.
  At least for a while.

Chapter 6

Gáttir allar
Áður gangi fram
Um skoðast skyli,
Um skyggnast skyli,
Því að óvíst er að vita
Hvar óvinir
Sitja á fleti fyrir.

The man who stands at a strange threshold,
Should be cautious before he cross it,
Glance this way and that:
Who knows beforehand what foes may sit
Awaiting him in the hall?

The Hávamál
The Words of the High One

An old woman met them at the entrance to the hall; she was small, grey-haired and stern-looking. Her round, weather-beaten face was set with an expression that gave nothing away. "Com'," she said, turning to lead the newcomers into the heart of the circular building.

The inside of the crannog was a dark, cramped, smoky maze of curtains and wattle partitions, packed with people, animals, and the accumulated chattels of dozens of lifetimes. Only the rafters soaring above into the darkness gave an indication of the sheer size of the great round structure. The old woman pushed on through the chaos, shooing small children and roving domestic animals out of the way. She shoved a heavy curtain aside to be confronted by a startled young goat. It bleated noisily at her as she seized its scruff and dragged it out of the way. Stepping aside, she held the curtain in one hand and the indignant kid in the other. "Go in," she commanded.

They stepped through the opening into what was the heart

of the crannog. The central area was surprisingly spacious, easily ten yards across, with a big open stone hearth, a fire pit built of big flat stones, laid on the timber floor. A large group of men sprawled around the fire on furs, rugs, and cushions. They were Alban warriors, red and ginger-haired, stocky, sturdy-looking men, dressed in rough homespun plaid and dark leathers, their moustaches and long hair denoting their social rank. A couple stood up as the strangers approached, their faces betraying their suspicion. They all resembled each other, brothers and cousins, clansmen.

Corvidious had a fondness for the Albans; they were a dour, hardy people tempered by the harsh land they scraped a living off of and the demands of their traditions. Proud men, distrustful of strangers, blunt and quick-tempered, but beyond their grim facade, they were brave, loyal, and brutally honest, with a dark, sardonic sense of humour and a fatalistic resignation towards life's struggles that bordered on contempt. It was an attitude he admired. He took them all in with a slow, deliberate look, meeting each challenging stare for just a moment before allowing his gaze to move on.

After what seemed like an age, out of the shadows into the firelight stepped Lady MacRoth. Whatever authority she held here, she held it as much by her own force of will as by marriage or birthright. Corvidious noticed how some of these usually proud warriors appeared physically cowered in her presence as they cast their eyes down and away.

"Welcome to Crannag-mòr, my home." She was an imposing, tall and fine-boned woman with a mane of hair the colour of winter sunlight. Breathtakingly beautiful. However, something in the set of her mouth and the lines etched around her aquamarine eyes gave her an equally formidable appearance. Though she wore a flowing plaid cloak over a loose plain white tunic, fastened with simple broaches in the Gothad style, she looked less like an Alban 'Lady' and more like a Queen. Her height, skin and eyes confirmed she was obviously no Alban, a Gothad probably, a foreign bride to an Alban Laird, Corvidious supposed.

She smiled. "Meg, food for our guests." She waved her hand vaguely. "Sit down."

Corvidious lowered himself carefully onto a pile of furs that were pushed towards him, deliberately ignoring the helping hand of his companion. The warriors muttered and settled back to their positions around the fire.

Ker lingered with the guards by the entrance. Not knowing what to do, he could not sit down with the warriors, nor could he leave. Big Wal's orders had been specific. Desperately he tried to whisper a question to Meg, but she just tutted and pushed him out of the way as she went past. Sometimes he hated them all.

A young, willowy slave boy, sporting a large purple birthmark upon his face, appeared with a simple three-legged stool and helped Lady MacRoth to sit down upon it. Corvidious realised that beneath the flowing gown and cloak, she was heavily pregnant, her belly so huge that it could only be a matter of weeks until she gave birth.

"What is the matter with your arm?" Corvidious looked thoughtfully down at his right arm, which he held carefully across himself and then back to her. She fixed her gaze upon him, allowing the slightest indication of a gentle smile to curl the edges of her mouth.

"I was kicked by a horse." Someone to his left passed him a steaming goblet of honey mead. "It's not broken, but it won't be much use for a while."

"Where are you from?" she asked pleasantly.

Corvidious paused. "I'm from Aelathia, the city of Aeltha."

"Ah," she clasped her long hands under her chin and rested her elbows on her knees like a child. "And you?" She turned to Corvidious' companion.

The boy stopped rubbing at his chest absently and replied, "My name is Svein Jafnkollsson, of Fluchtburgen."

"Fluchtburgen, yes I know Fluchtburgen. Yes, I know." Her gentle smile turned to a grimace, then instantly, it was gone. "I lived there for a while after my father died. I cannot say that I liked it much, but then again, refugees can only take shelter where it is offered."

Svein tried to think of something to say; finally, all that came out of his mouth was, "Oh."

"The old Jarl of Fluchtburgen, Old Thorkel Bear-legs, was

my mother's uncle. He 'protected' us, or that is what he called it: we became his property. He was an evil old man." She almost spat the last words. The bitterness of her tone brought odd glances from the assembled warriors.

Anxious to find something to say, Svein opened his mouth and volunteered, "They say that Balor came for Bear-legs in the end because he insulted the Ginnregin."

For an overly long moment, she stared at the boy with an unfathomable intensity that left him feeling much as he would have imagined a rat felt confronted by an adder. "Enough with this!" She unexpectedly stood up, clapped her hands loudly, and shouted, "Out everyone! Go. Now! Out!"

Hands reached for Corvidious and Svein.

"Not them! Leave them!" she shouted threateningly. "You all, get out!"

The clansmen looked uneasy but obeyed. Others scattered and scurried away. In a moment, they were alone.

An overwhelming silence settled almost instantly, broken only by the sound somewhere in the darkness of a mother trying to hush an angry infant and the patter of rain on the roof shingles high above.

Corvidious remained seated unmoved. He had known something was wrong from the moment she had mentioned her uncle.

Svein stood looking at her, incomprehension written across his face, "If I hav..." he stammered.

"Quiet child." She turned her attention to the Aelathian, "I thought you were dead."

The Aelathian gave her a blank look, "Many have wished it."

"Do you know who I am?"

He took a sip of his drink. "You are Lady MacRoth."

She returned carefully to her stool. "My name is Jorunn Kolinka. My father was Jarven Olson. You remember him, don't you?"

Corvidious did not answer.

"Yes, you remember him. Don't you." It was not a question.

He took another drink. "Of course."

Svein threw his hands up in exasperation. "What? Who? I don't understand. What has this got to..."

Corvidious turned to him. "Jarven was governor of Northern Vanda, appointed by the Tyrannos Calticas Nefandous. He was the first Gothad Jarl to be made a provincial Governor."

"Oh," said Svein, none the wiser.

Jorunn laughed. "You didn't remember me, did you, Andreas Corvidious of Aeltha?"

I remember you, now, he thought coldly. "It was a very long time ago."

"Does the boy know?"

"Know what?" demanded Svein petulantly.

"Do you know who your travelling companion here is, child?" A look of triumph blazed across her face. "Do you know who this man is?"

The look had madness in it, and it made Svein suddenly feel very scared. Trying to maintain his wits and keep to the story he had been instructed to tell, he spluttered, "Yes, erm... His name is Ca... Andreas."

"Corvus," said Andreas the Aelathian. "They call me 'Corvus'."

"Yes, I mean... His name is Corvus. He's a Gärian."

Jorunn MacRoth shrieked with mocking laughter. It was not a pleasant sound.

"What!" The young Gothad's face grew tight, and his eyes glazed like a child who had been teased too much.

"This is Corvus of Val Gär. The great Corvus himself, the Emperor Calticas' most trusted Consul." She turned to him and added, "And butcher."

Corvus slowly rose to his feet, his face hardening with anger. "Lady..."

She did not stop. "What was the title the Emperor gave you? What was it?"

"Lady?"

She turned to Svein, "They called him the Torturer of Val Gär."

Svein looked at Corvus. "I don't understand?"

"It was a private joke," said Corvus tonelessly.

"Between him and the Emperor of the Gärians." Jorunn MacRoth added bitterly.

"Lady, what is your point?"

Her attitude abruptly changed as she glowered up at him. "If I call them, they'll drag you out, gut you and throw you to the gulls while you're still screaming."

"Don't threaten me," growled Corvus.

"We should leave," said Svein resolutely.

"Only when I say," she snapped. "Besides, it is raining, and there is nowhere for you to go." Her tone softened a little.

"What exactly do you want from me, Lady? Revenge? If so, then call your men and let's be done with it. It is late, I am injured and tired, and I have not the patience for your bloody games." And you'll be dead before they get to me, he added silently.

Lady MacRoth stood up again, meeting his gaze. "You murdered my father."

Yes, that was it. Corvus took another mouthful of mead. "I murdered a lot of people but did not 'murder' your father. He was a traitor."

"More lies," she sneered.

Corvus understood her hate, the burning desire for revenge, but he affected his most disdainful look and added, "Jarven died on his knees begging me for the knife to end his miserable existence." He lied.

"Bastard!"

He fixed her gaze and said emphatically. "He was a traitor to the Tyrannos. He deserved to die." That wasn't really true either, but it was what she expected him to say, so he said it.

Svein took an involuntary step back. The old man was taunting her! Did he want to die? Svein began to look around for a way out, as one hand clutched at the empty space at his side and the other to his chest. Panic was making him breathe harder, and the stiff pain in his chest was unbearable.

She was angry now, her face flushed and tight. "My father was a warrior, not a tax collector; he was loyal to his people, not to your half-Human Emperor!"

Corvus replied calmly and matter-of-factly. "There is no place for divided loyalties. He took an Imperial commission, swore loyalty to Calticas, then he stole revenues, murdered an Imperial Legate, and plotted rebellion with the Vanda chieftains. The very men he had been sent to keep in line. Your father, madam, was a liar, a thief, and a traitor. He died, as he had lived, without honour."

Her mouth opened, but no words came out.

Corvus noticed that there were now tears in her eyes, and her chin quivered. "He brought it upon himself," he added in a softer tone. "I took no pleasure in it."

"Bastard!"

"Yes, in that you are right."

"I should have you killed."

Corvus poured the last of his drink into the hearth. "Believe me, Lady, I do not care what you do."

She stared at Corvus for what seemed to Svein an age. "Meg! Meg!" she shouted. "Meg!"

The old woman appeared out of the smoky darkness like a summoned spirit, "Aye?"

"Get Tàmh."

"Aye, and the men?"

"Tell everyone else to stay out."

The old woman looked at them all curiously. "Aye," she said and withdrew. Svein wondered how much she had overheard.

"Sit down," Jorunn said softly, waving her hand at both of them. "If I were going to have you killed, I would not have bothered speaking to you. No, what Gods have delivered you here I know not, but here you are, and I may have other uses for you, Corvus of Val Gär."

Chapter 7

"May God not welcome you!
You do harm more often than you do good."
"What have you against me, black girl?" Said Peredur.
"You have caused the Empress to lose her board, and she
would not wish that for all her Empire."

The Magic Gaming Board.
Author Unknown.

The moaning of the wind around the Tyeru Bàn tower reminded Mer of the voices of the restless dead he so often heard crying out to him in his dreams. He pulled his bull skin taghairm tighter about his shoulders. This time, the wind, he knew, carried more than just the coming winter.

The room was small, dark, and cold, lit by a single large candle that sat in a cracked old goblet on the floor in the middle of the room. Mer sat on the floor, cross-legged, gazing at the glowing light. Through one eye, he watched the flame as it danced and spluttered, throwing eerie shadows on the walls, while the other eye, stolen by the lightning long ago and blinded to his world, looked upon another place, another world. A land of dreams and nightmares inhabited by things that had no place under any sun. No rain fell there, nor did the ground see sunlight save for one brief morning each year; no plant or simple beast lived in that vast miasma covered marsh.

The Tysher followed warily the fleeting feline shadow that was his guide through this unearthly realm. With each step and every movement, he had to be painfully cautious, for, in this place, the Dobhar-chú dwelt, and they could easily destroy a wandering spirit, even one as strong as his. And there were powers that, if they were to discover him, could reach across the gap between worlds to devour his soul. Resolutely he pushed on, clinging to his staff and his corrbolg, the bag of tokens about his neck, and whispering over and over the incantations that he believed were his only real protection in this dark and terrible place. Mer knew this realm well; he had travelled countless other paths through it and had come to know the bog's terrible secrets. In this land, you do not travel as you would in the world of the living. Here you journey but do not arrive. You may wander lost forever and never truly go anywhere. Mer was careful to focus on the fleeting phantom cat and refused to pause to look closely at anything or allow himself to listen to the voices that called him by name. Voices imploring him to tarry, begging him to stop just for a moment or to look at them. He did not dare. He sought one only in this other world, one who would aid him, but at a price.

Across an endless waste, the feline spirit swiftly wended its way, leading him onwards deeper into the mire to a place he had only visited in dreams. This was Tir Eile, the Other Land, a place no earthly road could lead to and from which few mortals ever returned. Tir Eile is at once both the domain of the Unseen, the Daoine Faoi Cheilt and the palace of their King, Finnvarra. Almost as he allowed the thought to coalesce in his mind, he came upon the palace of the King of the Unseen.

The walls of the palace were rough, gouged out of the fabric of the void as if by the claws of some almighty beast. Its roof was an immense thunderhead sheathed about in blue lightning. The floors appeared as pools of dark water that reflected not what passed above them but some other vista, as if they were windows through to other lands, each littered with precious objects and votive offerings. Around him, the cavernous halls of the palace, swathed in thick shadows, echoed with half-heard whispers, sobs and prayers, as if softened by some great distance. No mortal was meant to walk these corridors. No living thing disturbed the dust of ages, but the palace was far from empty, in every corner, in every room, the shades of the wretched dead and the eternally lost watched intently as MacLeech passed by.

In the great hall of his palace, Finnvarra sat in splendour, amid riches beyond the imagining of Emperors, engrossed in a board game laid out before him. A game MacLeech thought resembled brandubh or fidchell or the strange game the Gothad's played, skáktafl, but there were by far too many pieces on the board, each exquisitely carved from precious metals, ivory, or stone.

Finnvarra raised a silver piece and tapped it lightly on his lower lip as he surveyed the board, seemingly undisturbed by the presence of MacLeech. He exhaled dramatically, and a wry smile crossed his old face. His ancient blue eyes flickered from the piece to the board to his opponent, then to Mer and back to the unusual piece, an exquisitely carved figure of a Hag. "Mer Maqq Lighiche, welcome as you are. You interrupt my game."

Finnvarra's opponent, a beautiful looking maid in a warrior's harness, appeared totally unaware of Mer's presence. In fact, Mer observed, the girl looked unaware of everything but the game.

"Forgive me, Ardrigh. A did nae mean to disturb ye."

"Hmm." The King placed the piece firmly back on the board and reached for the goblet beside it. The young warrior's hand wavered between the ivory figure of a Bear and a Raven, unable to make a choice. Mer had never seen a set like it. Some of the pieces were so perfectly carved that they seemed to shimmer with life. "Well, Maqq Lighiche, have you found her?"

"Ay, she's at the Creag an Eagail ."

"Good," he took a long drink from the goblet. "And you?"

"A'm there too."

The King raised an eyebrow.

"A have spoken with her, an' with the Chieftain o' the Albans, they know what is ongoin', but they do nae know what for." Mer was making his pitch, he knew, and he knew the King knew. "They questioned me, but A know nothin' o' the Isheen's ways."

"Is that what you want of me? Am I to be your oracle, Maqq Lighiche? Is that what you ask of Finnvarra?"

The Tysher braced himself, "Ay, it is."

"Have not your King's Druids and soothsayers augured the reasons?" Finnvarra's words were full of mockery, "Seen the signs? Read the omens?"

"They scrabble aboot in th' goat's guts an' learn nothin'. Oncomes the festival o' Flugh nan Marv an' all the Druids can tell Talorgan is what the billy goat had for supper."

The King chuckled.

"The Druids could nae tell him the best time to take a shite, let alone what to do. Meanwhile, he hides in Gurvud with his bairns an' his women folk like a scalded wean, waitin' on his Chieftains to come an' save him."

The young warrior moved a White Queen two spaces forward.

The ancient King returned his attention to the game. "And you? Have all your powers fled you?"

"Nae."

"But you can't see what is happening, can you?"

"Nae, A can nae."

"Well, I'll tell you what you want to know, but there is a price."

"Ay, a have nae doubt aboot that."

Finnvarra lifted up another brandubh piece and casually examined it. It was a Black Queen, carved in pure jet. "The Isheen's realm is in flux. Their old Bànrigh is dead, and their new one awaits her consecration. She is young and potent, her blood is hot, and she is full of rage."

MacLeech found his attention drawn to the young warrior opposite the King. There was something strange about her. "So, what for this slaughter? Whit purpose does it serve?"

The age-old King's eyes turned to the Tysher. They were enigmatic and unreadable. "The Isheen must pay a tithe to their Gods at Oidhche Shamhna, and this year they must pay a heavy price. Her warriors feel their Bànrigh's mood, her appetite is whet, and she can only be sated with blood. They believe that such a Bànrigh is a gift, a portent of a new era to come. A great sacrifice must be made, a baptism of blood to consecrate and to satisfy their Gods." He held the black figurine up. "They are driven by her lust; until they share in her baptism, they will share her madness, and that is where the true danger lies."

"How do we put an end to this then?"

"You cannot defeat them on a battlefield, but there is a way to stop this insanity."

"How?"

"I cannot believe that you need me to tell you that, Maqq Lighiche. Tell me why you went to the Creag an Eagail ?"

"'Cause, Ardrigh, ye told me to get the Wutch. "

Finnvarra's face grew cold. "Humility does not suit you. Your games may astound others, but I do not find them amusing, nor do your lies wash here."

"Ye told me to find the Fees'sacher Annis," MacLeech insisted.

"You went to the Albans because you know what it will take to stop the Isheen, you know she awaits them there, and you know that he too is being drawn to the Creag."

"Who?"

The ancient King smiled facinorously as the brandubh piece in his hand transformed into the Black Raven. "One you fear. As evil comes to those who do evil, death is drawn to those who deal in it. Death walks with this one, and she is well pleased with her own begotten son."

Mer bit back his next question. Even if he asked it, he knew that the King would not tell him the answer; instead, he just watched as Finnvarra placed the figurine on the board. His gaze returned to the beautiful maid opposite the King who sat chewing her bottom lip, her attention fixed upon the board game as if her very life depended upon its outcome. Mer had no doubt that it probably did. "A must be awa now, Ardrigh."

"Not yet, Maqq Lighiche. You have not heard my price."

I lay here in the darkness.

Listening to the howling wind, screaming its unheeded warnings to us all.

They are near, close now.

I can feel them.

They must know I am here.

They must be able to sense me as I sense them.

Death's pale face has turned to this place fully now, and I can feel her attention too.

Blood is to be shed here and lives lost.

But there is something else, something more, something familiar, coming.

A memory I do not want to remember.

Something I do not want to touch.

It is being drawn here too.

I see an immense black carrion bird upon the winds of our destruction.

And suddenly, I remember.

I remember him.

Chapter 8

It is the green-ey'd monster which doth mock
The meat it feeds on.

Iago
Othello
William Shakespeare
c.1603

The labyrinthine network of cellars below the castle ran deep into the heart of the Craig, long torturous passages leading on to untold chambers and storerooms over a dozen levels, predominantly unused even in the upper levels and totally abandoned beyond the first sub-cellars. Rolf had spent a long time exploring down here in this cold, damp, rat-infested warren, and he loved it. There were a thousand places to hide himself and his work in this darkness. This had become his own little world over the last few weeks though even he did not like to venture too deep beyond the fifth level. There was something down there that uneased him. Down there where the rock walls started to become warm to the touch, and the shadows took on a life of their own.

The second sub-basement, with its enormous, vaulted rooms, was his favourite place, too damp and cold for storing much in the way of provisions, save a few bottles and jars, yet recently enough maintained to still have doors that were not rotted through and bolts that were not rusted solid. It was down to here that he had hastily retreated after the incident in the kitchen. It was down here that he had brought his work.

Rolf pulled the canvas back and crouched over the boy's body, tutting absently. He shook his head. Temper, temper, damn temper, he chided himself. Well, these things happen, don't they? He pulled the long carving knife from his apron and viewed its edge in the flickering light. He liked sharp things with fine edges. Turning his attention back to the boy, he ran his fingers along his belly, feeling for the soft area under the lowest joint of the ribs and sternum, the best place for the knife to go in.

As the boy moved and moaned beneath his hand, Rolf's mouth twisted into an obscene grin. In the lantern light, his bloated face and scraggy beard looked almost demonic. "Hush now, laddie, don't take on so, this won't take but a blink."

Ag's wide and glazed eyes flickered open as his consciousness came swimming back, he screamed, but the gag in his mouth stifled the noise.

Rolf watched with intense interest as the boy feebly struggled against the bonds. "Scream as much as you like, you wee bastart. No one can hear you down here," he prodded the boy's belly with the point of the knife.

"Just you and ol' Rolf."

Jorunn MacRoth had waited a long time for the moment when she would have the man she held responsible for her father's death at her mercy. She had spent most of a lifetime praying for this moment, willing it to come, but now that all that heart felt entreating to the Gods of her father was realised, it all seemed so empty. The last of the Gärian Hastions were long gone from the North. The Empire itself was in its death throes; the Vanda and the Rhos hordes had finally breeched the last lines of defence and smashed their way to the heart of the Empire. The once-great Imperial Consuls fought like vultures over a carcass. She had recently heard that the Vanda hoards had even attacked Gäria itself, Gardariki, the kingdom of towns as her father's people called it and burned the Tyrannos' own estates. They had brought their destruction to within sight of the walls of Val Gär, and there had been little or nothing the Gärians could do to stop them. The once almighty Empire continued to exist as little more than an idea. Now that idea was slipping rapidly even from the memory of even the Gärians themselves. This old man before her was a relic of that past age, few remembered him, and those who did would spit after mentioning his name.

She rested her hands upon her uneasy belly and comprehended how killing this old man would be pointless; it would achieve nothing. Moreover, there were more important things to consider. She observed him, this man who had brought her so much misery. He had grown old since she had last seen him; how long ago was that? He was greyer, and he seemed to have physically shrunk. This was not the proud General she remembered, the terrible destroyer of nations, the great hero who had been so good a friend to her father. The man who had talked to little Jorunn like she was a Princess and smiled upon her so kindly. The Imperial Consul, who returned from the eastern marches to imprison, torture, and murder her father, his friend.

Over the years, the hatred in her heart had grown to become a vast black hole inside her, but she could feel nothing now, only the weight of the emptiness. It occurred to her that he too had been made to suffer over the years, time had been a harsh judge, and the sentence of life was often more terrible than death. Maybe killing him would indeed be putting him out of his misery. No, she had something better than that, something of more use. She held power now and would make this celebrated Gärian hero work for her. Maybe he would die or maybe not. Either way, she would put him back into the hands of whatever Gods delivered him into hers.

When the Bard arrived, she waved him to sit. "Tàmh, do you know this man?" she gestured towards Corvus.

The Bard was young, little more than a youth; he was dark-haired, with clean-shaven cheeks and a little too thin, his face was narrow boned, and his long nose ran into high branched eyebrows. His clothes were simple but well made, the only sign of wealth being the heavy horseshoe-shaped broach pinning his short russet cloak at the shoulder. He studied Corvus for a moment before answering, "No, my Lady, I canna say I do. A traveller from the South, or so I heard."

Jorunn knew that Tàmh heard everything; however, she would not push him on it.

"His name is Corvus."

The Bard's open smile faded dramatically, and he turned to look at the man closely, "Corvus of Val Gär, the one the Gothads call, 'the Valravn'?"

Corvus did not react.

"Oh aye, I have heard of you. You're the one that put Mur Ollamhan and all the people there to the sword, burnt the fortress of Neroche and laid waste the Mide. Yes, I know of you."

"Well, it's nice to know I'm remembered." Corvus sneered and turned to Jorunn, "What is this all about?"

Jorunn rested a hand upon her big belly. "My husband, the father of my child, is at a fortress we call Eagle's Craig," she began. "He awaits raiders from the far north, which he believes are soon to strike towards our lands. I have messages and supplies to send to him, I intended to send Tàmh with thirty of the men tomorrow, but now I want you to go as well."

Corvus raised an eyebrow, "Why?"

"Because you know this land well. Because you are, you were said to be, one of the greatest warriors the Gärian's ever had." She smiled coldly, "And because if you don't go, I will have you killed. I give you a choice, go with Tàmh and the men to Eagle's Craig or die here."

"It's pointless to threaten me," he said tonelessly.

"Possibly," interjected the Bard. "Though my Lady does not issue empty threats. To provoke her would be to throw your life away, and only a man who has finally given up on his life would do such a thing. Have you?"

Good question, thought Corvus. Very good question. "What about the boy? He has nothing to do with this."

She turned to look at the boy. "He can go with you, or he can stay here."

"And if I refuse?"

"Then he'll remain here as my prisoner."

Svein turned to speak, but Corvus waved him silent. "His uncle won't like that. Jarl Jergansson is a very hot-headed man, I hear. He may not like you imprisoning his nephew. He might just come here and take him back."

"That's as maybe, but you'll never live to know."

Corvus rubbed his arm absentmindedly. "What 'raiders?'"

Jorunn put out a hand again, and the birthmarked slave boy appeared out of the shadows as if by magic to help her to her feet. "We don't really know. Gothads probably. Men out to gain a name or a place for themselves. They've attacked all across the North in the last few months, burning villages and towns, raping and murdering."

"Nothing unusual then," said Corvus sarcastically.

"We've had peace in these lands for more than twenty years, Corvus, ever since we drove the last of your people out." Tàmh pointed out.

"You may call it peace, boy, but you barbarians have never known real peace. You've always been too busy killing each other," he fixed his stare on the young Bard. "Don't fool yourself with tales of how you 'drove us out.' We left because there was nothing here worth keeping. The army was needed elsewhere, and this place just wasn't important enough."

The Bard met his gaze defiantly, "Then why are you still here?"

Corvus did not answer the question. He sighed and turned

to Lady MacRoth. "If I go to this fortress of yours, deliver the supplies, then I can go?"

"Yes."

"I have your word on it?"

"Yes, if I have yours."

"What makes you think I'll keep it?"

"Because you were once Corvus of Val Gär, you were once my father's only real friend and because, although I hate you, I know you are as good as your word."

Corvus stopped a habitual sarcastic reply just before it leapt from his tongue, swallowed it carefully and thought for a moment. "You say that your husband is at this 'castle'."

"Eagle's Craig."

"And he's awaiting raiders from the North."

"Yes."

"Gothads?"

"As I said, we do not know. My people called them 'vargr', wolf heads, brigands and pirates. We do not know who they are, but they have struck deep into the lands of the Kerns, and now they seem to be moving south. My husband has gone to Eagle's Craig. It over looks loch Racholl and controls the routes south. From there, he can strike out at them."

"Brave man, but what if they attack this castle of his, lay siege to him?"

"The Craig cannot be taken," said the Bard emphatically. "It was built by the Ancients long before my people came to these lands. It has held out against the Kerns and the Gothads for centuries. It is ancient and invulnerable."

Corvus shook his head slowly, "I have ruined too many fortresses to believe that any place is invulnerable. Given time and a good crew of sappers, any fortification can be reduced."

"Enough of this." Lady MacRoth folded her arms and stared down at Corvus, "Will you go or not?"

Corvus looked up into her strange pale aquamarine eyes. "I took your father from you, and now you want me to save your husband, a life for a life. But what about the revenge that you've spent such a long-time planning? All the things you suffered. All that hatred, am I supposed to believe that you'll let us go once I've saved his life?"

Tàmh and Svein opened their mouths to protest. Lady MacRoth silenced them both with a look that could have frozen water. "Yes. I swear upon the life of my unborn son."

"For what that's worth."

"You have my word before witnesses."

"He must mean a great deal to you."

"He is my husband and the father of my child, and I will not lose him. Not now, not after so long."

Chapter 9

For what is it to die but to stand naked in the wind
and to melt into the sun?

The Prophet
Kahlil Gibran
1923

Ag's mind fled through a dark and terrifying world of partly familiar places twisted into a bizarre nightmare landscape, fleeing from the rapidly diminishing awareness of the horror it had left behind. As the darkness became total, all sound and vision began to fade and with it the fear. Curiously, as he wondered further into the void, the fear itself was leaving him. As peace settled upon Ag, he began to understand that those strange images and places had actually been quite familiar really. They had just rushed by him too fast; they had merely been the places, sounds and sensations of his short life. He felt a little sad at the way they had just flown past him without a chance to stop and touch them. Just to see his mother again for one last time would have been enough. The blackness was closing now, and all he could feel was a tiny spark of regret as the image of his mother's face faded from his mind.

Just then, something touched Ag, like the gossamer wings of a moth, and a little of his awareness flowed back. He turned, and suddenly it seemed that the whole world was full of brilliant light, "Mam?"

The light appeared to coalesce before him into a woman's face.

"Mam, is that you?"

Deep within the tortuous passageways, caverns and sub-cellars of Eagle's, Craig Rolf hummed to himself as he began his task. It pleased him that the child had passed out again, that would make the work easier, this would need all his concentration. He took deliberate care as he sliced off the boy's clothes and shoes. He had a plan to use them later, something to spread panic and suspicion amongst the Albans.

Rerunning his hand over the child's soft belly, he selected the best point to begin, below the breastbone and down, remove the guts and offal first. Then get on with quartering the carcass. He would have it butchered, dressed, and hung with the rest of the meat in the cold room before anyone came looking for him or the missing boy. Rolf chuckled to himself at the idea of serving up the wretched child to the garrison, watching them chewing on the little runt's flesh and sucking the marrow from his bones. The thought of them made his mouth water in anticipation. Sometimes he really enjoyed his work.

Suddenly the lantern he'd hung on the wall guttered and died, plunging the cellar into darkness.

Rolf sprang to his feet, weapon at the ready. He had no idea what was happening, but he could feel strange forces moving around him. Forces like the ones that Gormul, the Seanghal of the Urisks, had used to mask his true form. Powers were beyond his understanding, but now the potent spells had begun unravelling. Colours beyond the spectrum of even his non-Duine eyes swirled about him like smoke, dissipating into the darkness.

"Múchadh is bá ort!" He cursed loudly, venomous saliva spraying from his lips, and spun around wildly, screaming his defiant challenges into the swirling vapours of magic. "Loscadh is dó ort! Damnú ort!" As his form slipped back into what he truly was, all reason deserted him leaving only animal fury. He screamed in frustration, "Go hifreann leat! Ciach ort! Ciach ort!"

Searing white light exploded in the room, shredding the last vestiges of the glamours about Rolf, blinding him painfully and throwing him to the floor. He roared and leapt back to his feet, tearing the remains of the clothes from his body and flinging them away. Ferocious and undaunted, he was prepared to face anything that would dare to confront him.

The Witch stood in the room between him and the barred door, a pulsating rainbow of nameless colours about her, her face expressionless, her eyes burning like bright coals.

Rolf snarled through a mouth that could no longer form words as the carving knife slid through his claws and clattered to the flagstones. Baring his vast array of teeth and flexing his great clawed hands, the ferocity and hatred in him becoming a killing rage, he crouched to hurl himself at her.

Before he could leap, she lifted her hand, and a rainbow of light flared out, hurling him against the far wall, the impact bringing a shower of dust down from the stone lintels above.

He crashed to the floor, thrashing and slapping at the residue of her touch as it skittered about him. He was not beaten. If that was all she had to throw against him, then he had little to fear; he roared again and pushed himself up. Before he could clamber back to his feet, she raised her hands again, and another blaze of light reached for him.

Rolf instinctively knew what was coming. He threw his arms up to protect himself from the blazing light, but it was pointless. Searing heat enveloped him turning his scaly flesh to ash, vaporising the fat beneath, and boiling the blood in his veins. His screams finally died as the air in his lungs turned to steam and his brain broiled in his skull.

"It's certainly dead," said Gabhran poking the charred remains with the pointed ferrule of his spear. All he had been told was that something had happened in the old cellars below the wine stores. When he had asked which one, he had been told the one with the big drain in the floor, it had been easy enough for him to find. Navigating his way about in the old cellars was simple for Gabhran; he had played alone for hours down here as a child. In his grandfather's time, they used to slaughter and butcher animals in this room.

When they had reached the sub-cellar, the door was still barred against them though it had been no match for Jacobis. With a single shove, the giant had torn the door almost out of the frame. They had burst into the cellar as one, lanterns held high and weapons ready but unprepared for what they found. The air was thick with smoke and the stink of burnt flesh. The young serving boy, Ag, was lying naked and unmoving on the floor. Across the cellar, in a corner, lay the smouldering remains of some strange creature.

"Whatever 'it' was." Fyn drove the point of his sword into the thing's neck just below its skull to make sure there was no life left in it.

Jacobis crouched beside the smoking mess and inspected the heavy flat skull with its huge teeth and large burnt-out eye sockets. "It's a Trow, a Sea Troll, by the looks of it."

"Gods! Look at those claws." Gabhran pried open the hand with his boot revealing a two-inch long claw on each finger.

"They can rip an armoured man to pieces." Fyn wiped the point of his sword clean on the thing's side and sheathed it. "My father and his brothers caught a Sea Troll once that had been raiding the village smoke houses, but it took six men with spears, gaffs and billhooks to kill it."

"But how did it get into the Craig?"

Jacobis scratched under his beard. "It's been here for a long time, my friend." He stood and watched as Kemble and a gille carried the boy out of the cellar.

"What do you mean?" Gabhran reached out to grab Jacobis' arm as he turned away, but Fyn seized his wrist. Immediately the two men were eye-to-eye, "Get your hand off me," snarled Gabhran through clenched teeth.

Fyn stared back blankly.

Gabhran threw down his spear and tried to pull Fyn's hand free. "Get fokkinge off me!"

Fyn growled something inaudible under his breath and seized the Alban by the throat.

"Enough," Jacobis wrenched them apart. "Enough!" he shouted, swinging his gaze between them, "Stop it! Now!" The men snorted and scowled at each other but made no attempt to attack.

"That!" Jacobis pointed at the charred corpse. "That is your enemy! Look at it. Look!" He waited until both men had made a cursory glance at the body. "There's our enemy, not each other; if we turn on each other, we have no chance against it. Do you understand?"

Fyn spat on the floor between them and stalked off. Gabhran made to follow him, but Jacobis stood in his way.

Gabhran realised that trying to get around the Vör would be pointless, so he just stood and glared up at him. "So how in Hel's name did it get in here, hmm? Tell me that?"

"It's been here all along," answered the giant softly.

"What does that mean?"

"That is one of your slaves, the one that worked in the kitchens, 'Rolf', they called him." He paused a moment for that to sink in. "They must have gotten him in here some time ago."

"But…" The look of disbelief on the young man's face was almost comical, "How?"

"Magic, spells or whatever you'd call it," Jacobis shrugged. "He's probably been posing as the real Rolf for months, and so long as he kept down here away from people like Annis and MacLeech, and so long as he didn't attract attention, he'd be alright." He relaxed a little and sighed. "I should have known they'd try something like this."

"That's my job." Gabhran picked up his spear.

"You're a good man, but you're no Magiker," Jacobis patted Gabhran absently on the shoulder, "You could never have seen through such glamour. You could have never known."

Gabhran felt the last of the anger go out of him. "One thing I don't understand."

"What's that?"

"Who killed it? The door was bolted against us, and that boy was in no state to even defend himself. And how did you know what was happening down here?"

Jacobis laughed gently and shook his head. "Annis. She sensed the boy's spirit wandering the castle and followed him back to here." He turned and walked towards the door. "When she discovered this thing masquerading as a Human, she destroyed it."

Gabhran had seen the Witch upstairs when the alarm was raised by Jacobis. "But she wasn't here; she was upstairs!" The giant stooped to step through the doorway and walked off without replying, leaving him alone in the sub-cellar with only his incomprehension and the charred remains of something he would rather not think about.

Gabhran MacRoth had never really believed in anything that he could not see for himself. He did what was required to observe religious rites and festivals but had never felt anything, never believed in Gods and spirits, and as for the works of Druids and Gutuatri, the Alban's Priests, they were all charlatans as far as he was concerned. He could remember as a child watching from the eaves of his uncle's great hall as the foreign Druid Tailginn had displayed his powers before the assembled household and warriors, turning sticks into snakes and making things appear and disappear. Everyone had been astonished and in awe of this great Magician's power, everyone, except for the young Gabhran MacRoth who, from his vantage point high above the audience, could see it all for the tricks and sleight of hand it all was.

He had tried to tell them all that he had seen, but no one would listen to a child's complaints. Finally, his father sat and listened carefully to him and then, when he had finished his tale, his father told him plainly: "Gabhran, never see what another man does nae, an' if ye do, then never say so. Some men hold their beliefs as close as their knives," he pulled his ivory-handled sciun du from under his jerkin. "And are apt to take offence. Just remember what you know an' keep your own counsel."

It had been good advice for the hot-headed young man that he had been growing into. Gabhran glanced at the still smouldering mess in the corner. It was still good advice.

The acrid smoke hung in the air like a billowing fog, fed by the smouldering thatch and daub of the ramshackle buildings and made greasy by the burning fat of Dhaoine and animal corpses. Silently through the haze glided wraith-like figures, macabre phantoms, lissom and ferocious, dancing effortlessly amidst the destruction they had wrought. The attack had come just before dark; towering warriors strode out of the forest bringing fire and death with them. Even in the grip of terror, some village men managed to rally against the attack, but it had been like fighting shadows that struck back with razor-edged steel. Ethereal ghosts that moved soundlessly, effortlessly destroying all before them.

Darkness was now deepening into night as the reavers slowly gathered about the granite outcrop on the east side of the village to await the arrival of their Lord.

Out of the darkness, as if through some secret door between worlds, stepped the warrior's master; the Àrd-dràgon of the Isheen, Mathan-Bàn, the Riaghladair of Dùn nan Làidir. Taller and broader than most of his kindred, he carried himself with the stately grace of authority and the dignity of one confident in his physical power. In human reckoning, he was a man in the latter end of his fourth age, wise and experienced but still a warrior and still strong. Only his great mane of silver hair that hung down to the small of his back implied his actual age. By counting seasons and years used by the Albans, Mathan-Bàn had ruled Dùn nan Làidir, the Fortress of the Strong, for more than a century.

Pausing at the top of the granite outcrop, he pulled his long leather gauntlets on and surveyed the magnificent scene that stretched out below him. The curve of the shoreline with its shale beach, arching itself into the grand sweep of the river bend and drawn off into the dark forest that blanketed the far bank. The mighty black forests of the North stretching out and away to the foothills of the distant mountains. He tightened the bear-shaped clasp that held his dark green cloak about him and yawned widely, ending with a tiny shiver. It had been a long time since he'd had any proper sleep. Preparations for tonight's assault had kept him awake all through the day, but he was not one to leave things to happenstance. Preparation was the only way to keep the hand of the

Morrigan tipped in his favour.

Below, moored at the shabby little fisherman's jetty, Jarl Olvarson stood on the prow of his longboat waiting for the Àrd-dràgon's signal to continue. The Gothads had drawn up their longboats onto the shore below the headland and were waiting to embark the Isheen. Already they were loading equipment and horses. Organised chaos. Everyone had a job to do and went about their task with resolute duty, they worked hard, and well, only the Southron mercenaries stood by, watching and chatting idly.

Mathan-Bàn found their casual arrogance annoying, though it was part of the price to be paid for their participation, that, and a sack load of silver. Daonna loyalties could be easily brought for material wealth; it was one of the things he despised the most about them.

Turning to the North, the fierce wind that had delayed his plans was lessening now, but it still held its icy edge. It was time to go.

He gave the signal and watched as his warriors filed down towards the ships, and the oarsmen began to drag and push the great longboats back into the water. It was essential to have them running before the wind as soon as possible. The journey, he knew, would take most of the night but would mean that they would reach the southern end of the loch an hour or two before dawn. This would still leave them time to run the longboats onto the shale below the cliffs and set camp.

Although the darkness would give him the cover he needed, he expected that the garrison from the castle would make a sortie against him as early in the morning as possible in an attempt to drive him back into the water. Although he knew his own warriors would hold their ground easily against the Dhaoine, he feared the mercenaries might break. If the Albannnaich managed to throw a large enough and savage enough attack against them before they could entrench in a defensive position and bring up support. That was the risk to be taken if he were to secure the Creag an Eagail before dawn.

Mathan-Bàn's musing ceased when he noticed a group making their way up from the shoreline towards him, the Galdràgon,

Sheela, and her attendants. He sighed inwardly; he loathed the stinking carrion crow and her miserable handmaiden's chorus of disapproval, a more tedious bunch of hags he could not imagine. The Galdràgon was a hoary, wizened old creature, a living mass of filthy rags that smelt like something that had not been buried properly, a vile harridan physically twisted by her own loathsome nature. They had crossed each other countless times over the decades, she delighted in taking every opportunity to meddle in his affairs, and he took equal delight in thwarting her at every turn. Until now, that is. Until she had outmanoeuvred him by using his own sister against him. He had found himself trapped like the King in a game of fidchell with no more moves left. Or, at least, that's what he endured the grizzled old crone to believe, but Mathan-Bàn had been playing games since he was a small child, games his grandfather had taught him, and he seldom lost.

He yawned again and stretched, flexing his powerful neck and shoulder muscles. Then went back to watching the commotion as they loaded the longboats.

The Galdràgon and her entourage reached the top of the path and stopped in front of the granite outcrop.

"You waste time," her voice was a rasping whisper full of unspoken malice.

Without looking down, he took a long slow breath and said calmly, "You're in the way, old woman. You spoil the view."

"Balor waits. The Lord of the Fomóiri is not to be trifled with, fool." A skeletal finger thrust out of the rag heap and waved up at him. "You will pay dearly for his displeasure."

Mathan-Bàn cast a glance down at her companions; they were a fine group of Isheen girls, all beautiful and bedecked in white, their golden hair braided and tied, their faces exquisite, their minds as black as Fuamnach's heart. "At least do me the small favour of standing downwind; your smell is nauseating."

The Galdràgon scoffed and then added, "You have failed Mathan-Bàn. You allowed that Maqq Lighiche creature to escape while you burnt villages. Now you waste more time here. The Witch Annis awaits us at the castle and the Bànrigh..."

"You forget yourself, you stinking hag, the Bànrigh is my

sister, and I know what my sister desires," he fought the rising anger inside him. "Now," his hand settled on his sword hilt, "Be gone, baobh!"

She spat on the ground, "You're damned, Mathan-Bàn."

"It would take more than your magic," he sneered. "Now get to the boats, hag, or shall I leave you here to chew on the corpses?" The Isheen's Àrd-dràgon stepped down and walked towards where his warriors awaited him. The old hag may indeed be right; he had to admit it, Maqq Lighiche, the Taibhsear of the Kerns, had escaped while his warriors had amused themselves, now the half-blood Witch was at Creag an Eagail awaiting them. He should be sitting in the hall of the castle, not messing about here, but his warriors were excited, and it was difficult, sometimes even for him, to focus clearly. Too much blood, he thought absently, this wasn't a war, it was a slaughter to satisfy the Gods, and my warriors are revelling in it. He sighed; Balor would have to wait. We have to take the castle first. The last thing he could allow was for that monster to seize the Creag an Eagail. Once the Fomóiri were in control of the castle, he would have to drive them out by force, and a war with the God-King of the Fomóiri could destroy them all.

Chapter 10

"I began to imagine, as always at my left side just out of sight, a brazen winged beast that I associated with laughing, ecstatic destruction."

W.B. Yeats.
Introduction to Resurrection.
1934.

The colossal black longship lay unmoving in the middle of the river. Though the wind howled around it and the current was strong, the determination of its master was stronger. Bigger than anything that human hands had set upon the seas, the vast dragonship, like the winds and currents, bent to the willpower of Balor Maqq Cenchos, God King of the Fomóiri.

Balor lifted his massive head up to taste the air. It was cold and sweet. The wind off of the freshwater was so much pleasanter than off the sea. They had come a long way, but he liked the smell of this place, the taste of it. He opened his remaining eye and looked around. Nothing, no welcoming delegation, not even a herald or messenger. Nothing.

He gave a tremendous fetid sigh; patience was not one of his virtues, and already he grew weary of waiting. They should have been here to greet his arrival. To pay respect and give homage. His temper was already rising at the idea that they had failed to show him the proper reverence, let alone the notion that they may have deliberately insulted him. If these hole dwellers thought they could treat him like one of their charmed slaves, he would make them think again. They had summoned him, and he had come; they were already in his debt.

The sound of movement disturbed his thoughts. Before him stood Morghath. "Son of mine." Balor's voice was little more than a whisper. "Where are they?"

"M'athair," Morghath Bres bowed. "I did not think to wake you, to disturb you from your slumber, for the Isheen are not here."

Balor regarded his son, tall and strong, fine-featured and powerful. A great warrior, undefeatable in battle and as strong as the leviathans of the deep. How any Duine womb had borne this child still surprised him. "They will be here soon; they will come. Rest now, great one." Morghath Bres reached out and stroked his father's cheek, his long fingers trailing across the glistening green,-black leather of Balor's skin. "Sleep. I am with you."

The huge yellow eye that floated like an egg yoke in a pool of bloody mucus slowly began to close.

"Sleep, M'athair, sleep well," Morghath Bres waited a few moments to check that the thing that had fathered him was asleep before going back out onto the deck. He issued commands to the warriors to gather their equipment and make ready to greet the Isheen. He wanted to handle this himself. It had been difficult enough to convince his father to agree to come this far, but now he was angry, and that could be disastrous for all concerned. If the Isheen upset him, then Hel herself would hear of it.

He walked to the prow of the longboat and surveyed the land. It was good to be back here again. This wild place was more home to him than the open sea, no matter who his father was. He smiled to himself. If this all went well, he would be King here before the month was out.

Below him, at the oars, the almost formless faces of those eternally damned to serve the longboat turned to watch him. Some had been Lords, even Kings, but for eternity they were chained here now, half-aware shades, in service to the greatest of evils. Somewhere deep down inside, whatever was left of their spirits, burnt the purest of passions; hatred.

He laughed and returned to his watch. Around him, the Fomóire warriors armed themselves and took their positions. Morghath Bres watched them grunt and grumble, lurching ungainly around the deck. Their coarse bodies and rough, ugly faces amused him; they looked almost comical, monstrous parodies of...of what? Grotesque caricatures of myself, maybe?

Oh, to be a King of a beautiful people, a people of magnificence, to be surrounded by delicate faces and smooth bodies. To be a King. To be served. To be loved. No longer to be just a thrall to an ageing monster. He rested his head against the carved prow.

To be free.

Mathan-Bàn took one last look at the night sky. The heavy rain-laden clouds hurried southward, obscuring the moonlight from the loch, blinding any Duine eyes from movement upon the water. The wind was with him, and the currents strong. The time had come, the moment of commitment. He took a long deep breath of the ice-cold air and gave the signal. The longships dipped their oars and pushed out into the slate black water. They would be across the loch well before daybreak, and then the work would really begin. He expected that the Albans defending the Creag an Eagail would throw everything against him as soon as they knew he had landed in an attempt to deprive him of any foothold on the shore.

He found himself almost looking forward to the fight; it would be the first real contest against the Dhaoine since this rade had begun. Numbers did not matter to him at this point. The defenders could have no more than a few dozen warriors, though, with a fortress like Creag an Eagail, they might as well have been thousands strong. Though in their desperation, they would undoubtedly strike at his landing site, and that would be their undoing. He took another long breath of the cold night air. He hoped for the wind to drop as the night drew on, the mist of the last few nights would have given much more cover for the landing, but there was no sign of the wind abating. He knew he could call upon the Galdràgon to turn the wind and call the mist from its hiding place, but he would not do so. Expending such power would be felt for miles, and he would rather eat dung than request help from the old hag. No, this would have to be done the simple way through stealth and brute force.

The Isheen Àrd-dràgon had decided to rely upon Strandwulf's Southron mercenaries and Jarl Olvarson's Gothads to counter any sortie by the defenders. The Southrons could at least earn their pay. He knew it was essential to get the measure of the Albannach before he had to commit his own warriors to the battle.

In single combat, no Daonna was a match for an Isheen warrior, but experience had taught him never to underestimate an enemy. Only three nights ago, the lesson had been underscored when a Kern village blacksmith had smashed the skull of one of his most promising young warriors with an iron hammer. There had been no way to save the youth, no matter how much the Galdràgon had wailed and chanted over her. Last night he had lost another good warrior to a lead shot flung from the sling of what was little more than a Daonna child.

As Àrd-dràgon, and father to his people, Mathan-Bàn felt each loss deeply, more so than Cullach-Bàn, the supposed Uachdaran of the West, who spent most of his time listening to the Galdràgon's ranting and whoring with her acolytes, the loss of Isheen lives seemed to matter as little to him as the loss of his wits. Mathan-Bàn dreaded to think too closely upon what Cullach-Bàn and the Galdràgon were plotting between them. The evil old hag was completely mad and Cullach-Bàn, who had no care for any living thing, was, in Mathan-Bàn's opinion, virtually insane. It had been Cullach-Bàn who had entreated with the Fomóiri, a move which Mathan-Bàn had strongly advised against. And it was Cullach-Bàn who had decided to split their forces and strike into the North at the Gothad settlements. It was all lunacy as far as Mathan-Bàn was concerned. The rade was simply to establish control again over the forest and its surrounding areas and to gather slaves and prisoners for sacrifices during the ceremonies; it was not to be a pretext to declare war upon the Daonna kingdoms of the North.

Mathan-Bàn harboured serious doubts that even now, the Isheen had the numbers and power to stand up to an all-out war with the Dhaoine. He had seen them at war and, no matter how powerful his warriors were, nor how confident his counsellors were, the Isheen alone did not have the numbers to withstand a prolonged and protracted conflict with the Dhaoine tribes. He had once watched the Kerns throw twenty thousand or more screaming warriors against a Gärian Hastion at Steidh-Dòchais, and that Hastion slaughtered them all. He had never seen such a battle before or since.

He pulled his cloak around his shoulders. Cullach-Bàn and the hag had no idea what the Dhaoine could do if they united against the Isheen. An awful image of Gärian Hastati with picks and shovels at the gates of one of the great raths flashed before his mind's eye. He shook his head to clear it, at least, thank the Gods, the Gärians and their Generals were long gone from the North.

Mathan-Bàn turned to find Faylinn, his nephew, the Marasgal of his personal guard, standing next to him, "Morair, may I ask you what we are to do about meeting the Fomóiri ?" Obvious, by his discomfort, he had been pushed to approach the Àrd-dràgon by the others.

Mathan-Bàn sighed and, after a long pause, finally replied, "Are we not of the Sìth? Are we not the Isheen?"

"Yes, Morair." The young warrior looked nervous.

"Then we shall have no truck with demons and monsters."

"But, Morair, the..."

"Do you fear the Fomóiri, Faylinn?"

"No, Morair."

"Good." Mathan-Bàn put his hand on Faylinn's arm, "We are Isheen, we are not afraid, we have nothing to fear. Now go back and rest."

"Yes, Morair." The warrior obediently turned to pick his way back down the length of the longship.

"Faylinn?" Mathan-Bàn called after him.

"Yes, Morair?"

"What of your sister, Rànd?"

The warrior's face grew grim, "I have heard nothing, Morair."

Corvus lay on a roughly gathered bed of furs and stared at the roof beams stretching away above him into the rafters as the flicker of firelight played shadows across their surfaces. He found himself listening to the sounds of the crannog; the wind outside, the water beneath, the creaks and groans of the wooden structure, the hushed voices and occasional snore or animal noises. Somewhere a mother was trying to hush a crying baby.

The place was warm, full of familiar smells, and a little smoky. It almost had a sensation of being a home. It was a strangely comforting feeling, a chance to relax, but he could not sleep. No matter how tired he was, his mind was too busy retracing the day's events. Everything had happened too fast, and as usual, he had reacted without thinking. It was one of many things about himself he hated, but now the situation was set in motion, and he had to think his way out of it. Which, he knew, was always easier said than done. Things had gone from bad to worse in a matter of half a day.

He found himself rubbing at his injured arm. The old woman, Meg, had examined it. The bones were not broken; they had concluded between them, but the tendons and the joint were pretty severely torn. She had given him something for the pain and strapped it well.

The attack on the road had taken him completely by surprise. Whoever or whatever that woman was, she had almost killed them both in a single attack and on her own. He knew that he had barely beaten her and that had been more by luck, and desperation, than skill. Although he felt no shame, it was exasperating; he was getting old and was making too many mistakes, there was no way that he would have been ambushed like that when he was younger.

"The great Corvus of Val Gär." Lady MacRoth had sneered. He had seen less hatred on the faces of men he had had publicly butchered or dragged away to be impaled. It was sad to see such cruel enmity etched so deeply into her face. He could clearly remember her as a child, a truly beautiful creature, dancing around the fountains in the collonaded gardens of the Governor's palace in Leucothea, like some ethereal golden sylph. Her eyes and posture were defiant when her father presented her to the great Imperial Consul, Corvus of Val Gär. She was the only one that had met and held his gaze, a child with a smile like a cross between a courtesan and a jackal. He remembered that smile well. There had been two sons as well, he wondered absently what had happened to them, but no matter, obviously the strongest of the litter had survived.

Jarven had sided with the wrong people, the losing side, not only in the field but in the Gerousia, the Gärian Senate, as well. The Vanda uprising had been crushed, and Corvus had been let loose upon the Gerontes to deal with the last of the conspirators.

"You, my most loyal man," Calticas had whispered in his ear, "Would you put the whole of Val Gär to the wrack to find a single traitor? Would you not?"

Corvus had just smiled and nodded slightly. It was the opportunity he had been waiting for, the moment he had thirsted for all his life. He was to be let loose upon the high and mighty like a fox loose in a hen house. What the Tyrannos had never fully understood was that destroying the power of the Gerousia had been his aim all along, the men who had devastated his family twenty years before. The men who had murdered his father and sent his mother to die in the quarries of Malus. The men who had sold his sister into slavery. The men who had laughed and applauded so loudly as he was thrown into the funeral arena to die for their amusement. The very same men who had forgotten precisely who Andreas Corvidious grew up into.

As the instrument of Calticas Nefandous' vengeance, the appointed Questor, he had sought them out, one by one, built a frame of lies and deception about them and denounced them as traitors regardless of their culpability in the current matter. He did only enough to protect the Tyrannos from the assassin's blade or the poisoned cup; that was all. He had never been interested in exposing the true traitors and conspirators that infested the Empire like termites; his mission was solely one of personal revenge. His reputation for pitiless brutality and fanaticism made even the Tyrannos's closest advisors fear him. Some thought him mad. Others believed he was evil. "The Torturer of Val Gär," they called him.

It had been a dark day for Corvus when the Tyrannos had demanded that he return to Leucothea. Jarven had been his friend, and he had tried hard to hide his complicity in the whole thing, but the proof of the Governor's involvement in the murder of an Imperial Legate and theft of taxes had been handed directly to Calticas by Jarven's enemies. Men outside of Corvus' immediate reach or control. It took all Corvus' influence and guile to prevent Jarven's family from being put to death as well. Instead of through various intermediaries, he had had them spirited away to what he had honestly believed was safety. It was the last promise he had made his friend... the last promise he had made his friend before he crucified him.

It was hard to believe how it could have been so long ago. That did not make sense. Now fate had delivered him into the hands of the woman the wild-eyed child had grown up into, and all she wanted was revenge. Revenge, like the revenge he had taken on those that murdered his family. Cold-blooded, cruel, brutal revenge. Corvus understood her; she had grown up into a beautiful woman, proud and strong, in her heart though there was a black void where only a child's screams of incomprehension and terror still echoed. Corvus knew those feelings all too well; little Andreas had grown up with the same anger, the same hate, the same need for revenge eating away his soul until there was nothing of him left until there was only Corvus, the Torturer of Val Gär.

The sounds of the night interrupted his thoughts, bringing him back to the reality of the crannog. Beside him, Svein was murmuring in his sleep. Corvus turned to watch for a moment the regular rise and fall of the furs covering the boy. Two or three cracked ribs and a big bruise all across his side where he had landed on the frozen ground. Corvus allowed himself a smile. Well, at least it had stopped the boy from whining; now, he had a better idea of what real pain meant. He had found himself liking the boy much more since they were attacked. It had changed him a little, quieted him, not just through the pain, but almost as if it had knocked some sense into him. On the other hand, maybe it just knocked some of the arrogance out. Corvus laughed to himself.

Nevertheless, what am I going to do with you now? He thought, I can't leave you here, and I don't think taking you to, wherever this bloody place is, is much of an idea. I can't get you killed fighting someone else's war, and, knowing your uncle's reputation, I would be probably starting another.

Corvus turned back to stare at the roof beams. He wondered what agency of what God had delivered him to this place? And which mad God was it he could hear laughing?

Chapter 11

There's nothing certain in a man's life except this:
That he must lose it.

Agamemnon
Aeschylus

Angus stood by the window staring out into the night, seeing nothing but his own candlelit reflection distorted by the ripples of the thick glass diamond-shaped panes. He had tried to drink himself to sleep after Jacobis had retired, but just as he felt he could relax enough, the alarm had been raised. He knew that it would be yet another night without sleep. So now he just stood and stared out of the window of his solar, awaiting the dawn and whatever that would bring with it.

There would be few who would have much sleep tonight, not after what had happened, not after discovering that one of them, whatever one of them was, had been here all along. A spy, an enemy, walking amongst them. No one could imagine how that thing had managed to get into the castle masquerading as Rolf and how it had managed to fool everyone. Jacobis had simply said, "Spells, a glamour, to make you see what you expect to see."

However, that was not enough. There were other questions such as when and how? It was frightening to think that that thing had been living with them in this tomb for the last two months, pretending and waiting. Angus concluded that it must have either been during their journey up from the crannog, or it had been hiding in their midst for several weeks, possibly months. Angus had had to go down to see it, this thing. Partly out of duty, to be seen to be in control by issuing a few orders about getting rid of it, and partly out of his own morbid curiosity. He had never seen anything like it before.

On his return to the hall, Kemble had informed him that the child, Ag, was not seriously hurt but seemed to be in some kind of deep slumber that they could not wake him from. At least it was good news that the boy was alive, but when Angus had asked who had discovered the thing and killed it, Kemble had just mumbled and deferred to Gabhran.

Gabhran's eyes refused to meet his, and all he would say was, "The Witch did it. I don't know how, you'll have to ask the boy," before walking off.

Angus had let him go. He knew his young cousin well enough to sense that this had troubled him deeply. It would be useless to push him for any further answers; Gabhran had always feared the things he did not understand.

Jacobis had been no more forthcoming; all he had said was that Annis had discovered the creature in time to save the child. She had dealt with it. He had then begged his leave, promising that he would explain things more fully in the morning.

Angus had decided to leave it at that; he would not question them further in the morning. In truth, he knew the answers to his questions; he had smelt it in the air when he had gone to see the remains of the thing that had pretended to be Rolf. Above the acrid smoke and the stench, there was a familiar metallic tang; the air seemed charged, as it is before lightning stalks the skies. The others seemed not to notice it, but Angus had recognised it immediately. It was how the air used to smell after the Druids and Gutuatri had displayed their powers. It was strange how that smell in the old cellar had brought back so many memories.

He could remember the smell of the saturated air over the battlefield of Achagh nam Muc, the day Drust Feallsanach, King of the Albans, had finally destroyed the power of the Gothads and killed their King, Gothorm Landeythan. Angus could remember riding across the battlefield, hanging on to the cantle of his father's saddle after the slaughter. The air had been so charged with power that it had drawn raging thunderstorms for days.

Angus had always been more sensitive to such things than most uninitiated. His father's Druid, Erbin nam Ban, had suggested that he teach Angus so that he could become like the Druid Kings of old, but his father had refused to allow it. He would not afford to have his heir spend twenty years, or more, training to be a Druid; he needed Angus to grow up fast and learn to be a leader of men.

Gallen MacRoth had set about grooming his son to be Chieftain from the moment he was born. There would be no place for the Druid's arts in Angus' life; instead, Gallen sent his daughter, Morath, to the Druids. Angus' mother had never forgiven Gallen for sending her daughter away, and, in some part of him, neither had Angus. Not that he really missed his older sister; he could hardly remember her. He could not forgive his father for denying him the chance to go with the Druids, train and learn, and not be the Chieftain of the Clan MacRoth.

Gallen had been a good Chieftain and a good husband and father, Angus admitted to himself, well 'good' by Alban standards. He had been strict and quite fierce, but he mainly had been fair and, more often than not approachable, and munificent. He had never been harsh to his clansmen or brutal to his family; in fact, he had been quite a kind man. But rulership calls for harsh judgments, even of the most thoughtful men.

Angus refilled his mazer from the jug he had perched on the window ledge and silently toasted his father. After all, this would have been what he wanted; his son, another MacRoth of the MacRoths, cooped up in this tomb, waiting to fight yet another pointless battle against yet another enemy.

Enemies.

That made him laugh almost out loud. His father's and grandfather's greatest enemy, the Kern Tysher, Mer MacLeech, now slept peacefully in one of the watchtower rooms. Even for Angus, it was hard to believe that he had allowed 'the auld bastart,' as his father called him, into Eagle's Craig, let alone allowed him to stay. He had even allowed MacLeech to bring Kern warriors and their hounds into the castle! War, it was true, made for strange alliances, and it is said that it is better the evil you know than the one you don't, but Angus worried whether all this was only proof that he was really losing his grip. Angus knew the answer his wife would give if she were here.

MacLeech was an evil that could not be controlled by a man like him. No number of spears and brave warriors could be protection against such a man. Angus knew he had only one guarantee, one assurance, against the Tysher, and that was possibly an even greater danger to them all; the Witch Annis.

And that was like keeping a cave lioness in your home to keep the wolves at bay.

Fyngard sat on the floor of the tiny cell allotted him in the Tyeru Du tower in almost complete darkness, his hands busy sharpening the edge of his sword with a whetstone that had once been his father's. Even in the darkness, he could see the gleam of the edge and the occasional spark of the stone against the steel.

As he had climbed from the cellars to his room, his mind had been racing, conflicting emotions welling up in him, a strange sense of hopelessness mixed with the blind anger that made him feel as if he was ready to explode with frustration. He was not handling this situation well; he knew it. The animosity and the constant provocation from the Albans was driving him mad. Amongst his people, they called it 'snömara,' an insanity that affects people who have been snowed in for weeks or trapped somehow for months unable to get out. He had once seen it himself on board the ship. They had been blown off course by a storm and had been thrown so far out into the Northern sea it had taken nearly four weeks to make land. By which time some of the younger men were going mad, driven beyond all reason, one had even jumped overboard. Another had to be restrained from attacking the other members of the crew. Another time Fyn had come upon a wolf that had chewed its own hind leg off to escape a snare. He now clearly understood what had driven it to that.

Once in the cold, dark little room, he had stripped naked, pulled his wolfskin cloak around his shoulders, and carefully tied his hair into an elaborate knot above his right temple. It was the style of the oath takers who had sworn the blood oath of eternal allegiance to their Jarls or Kings. Out of his old leather kitbag, he took all his trophies and charms; the torc of Kernach gold he had been presented after his first real battle, the hammer-headed amulet his father had given him, the necklace of wolf's teeth and claws his Ulvhinna brothers had presented him, the rings and bracelets that had been bestowed upon him by his Lords. He put them all on. He drew his father's sword from its sheath and took up the axe he had taken from a dead Southron Huscarl. These were the things that defined him for what he was; Fyngard, son of Bådebyggar the Boatwright. These were the symbols of his status as a warrior and as a man.

He stood in the darkness alone. Fyngard Kvällulf, the 'Evening Wolf,' the war name he had carried since his initiation into the Ulvhinna, the Wolfcoats. The Ändring had been the most terrible and thrilling experience of his life, the first time he had felt the Wodfreca take hold of him entirely, the first time he had shed his physical bounds to join his brothers and sisters in the Jaga, the hunt. Striking out at the enemies, ranging far and wide in the night, bringing terror and destruction deep into the lands and hearts of all those they were set against. Nothing was as feared as his Wolfcoat pack, his syskon, as they prowled the night, rending with sword, teeth and claw. Nothing could stand against them, and no one was safe, especially nights like this one when the moon was up. He could feel her pulling at his blood, even beyond the stone of the walls and the thick cover of the rain clouds. Last night had been worse; he had had to drink himself into a stupor to sleep. Even then, the dreams came unbidden, and the Wodfreca rode his soul.

His Ulvhinna syskon had served Jarl Turfeinar Longrkyrtill proudly for six years; he had even taken the Högtidligt Löfte, the oath of unswerving loyalty, to his Jarl, in life, death and beyond.

Then three years ago, he had abandoned everything, and in doing so, he had brought disgrace upon himself, his family and his syskon. He had thrown away all that he had once held dear. He had broken his sacred oath and had silently, passionately, undertaken another to follow the Völva Annis. It was an oath he could never break; he would not fail, for to do so would be to fail her.

Now, as he sat in the darkness, wrapped only in his pale silver-grey wolfskin cloak, grinding at the edge of his father's sword, the sound and the rhythm allowed him to reach an almost meditative state, calmness, a sense of purpose he had nearly lost.

I can feel you.

Your pain.

The raging anger and the frustration.

Inside of me.

Absorbed.

Foolish creature, but who is the greater fool?

You or I?

Did you not know? Did you not understand?

My wrath, the Nàdur inside me, is more powerful than I.

Beyond my understanding. Beyond my control.

My mother's gift that I can still not comprehend.

I could wish that I had not destroyed you, but I cannot wish you back to life.

Can I?

So, your masters draw near, and their time shall truly come.

But you shall not greet them.

You shall not return to the sea again.

You shall not see the sun.

I must send you on now.

Time to go.

My sweet child.

Into the welcoming arms of Death.

For She who waits.

Awaits us all.

They are here.

Chapter 12

"Gemunan þa mæle   þe we æt meodo spræcon,
Þonne we on bence   beot ahofon,
Hæleð on healle, ymbe heard gewinn;
Nu mæg cunnian   hwa cene sy….."

"Let us remember the speeches which we often uttered at the
mead, when we, on the bench, heroes in the hall, raised up
vows about harsh battle; now it will be possible to prove who is
brave…."

The Battle of Malden.
Aspr.vi.

The first longboat ran silently up onto the shale propelled by
its own momentum. The second and third boats drove up almost as
far, their ash hulls cutting deep furrows into the narrow strand. The
other longboats drew into the shallows but did not beach
themselves. They were to wait until the Southrons and Gothads had
secured the landing site.

Mathan-Bàn, watching from the prowl of his own longboat,
was impressed with how swiftly and efficiently they worked: even
though the darkness was not their natural element. Dhaoine could
still surprise him.

The Gothad crews secured their longboats and began to
unload the equipment and ponies while the Southrons, already
heavily equipped, formed a semi-circular defence line on the shale
and began to push out as quickly as they could. Nothing, not a rock
or bush, between the water and the cliff face, was left unchecked, no
stone unturned. Once they had reached the base of the Craig, the
semi-circular line split into two groups, one to the North and the
other to the South. Mathan-Bàn had planned this stage meticulously
with the Southron's leader Earl Strandwulf. It was difficult for the
Dhaoine to work in the darkness, but Strandwulf had trained them
well, and their discipline was impressive, even to the Isheen Àrd-

dràgon's eye. On the northern side, the path leading up off the beach to the forest tracks was difficult. To the south, the beach sloped gently up and around the foot of the Craig to finally lead them up to the castle itself. The Àrd-dràgon and the mercenary leader knew that control of both accesses would be vital. The northern climb was faster; however, only the southern route would allow for any significant numbers, and both knew that the Albans would try to deny them control of both.

Mathan-Bàn knew that if his forces were pinned down here on this narrow strand of beach, they would never be able to break out. If they were driven off the beach, then they would have to sail back across the loch and attack the castle from the landward side. To attack the Creag an Eagail from the land would be almost impossible. Impossible without the aid of the Fomóiri, that is.

In council, both he and Strandwulf expected the paths from the beach to be defended, but it was a calculated risk. With the element of surprise and weight of numbers, the Southrons should be able to clear any obstacle before the Albans had time to react. The Àrd-dràgon knew it was a gamble, even more so without the mist of the last few nights, but it had to be this way. The Albannaich warriors were not known for planning strategic defence. Their battle plans habitually hung solely upon the old axiom of attack being the best form of defence, often attacking as one cohesive mass. Mathan-Bàn knew such tactics would fail miserably against his own warrior's superior strength and skills.

For now, things seemed to be going well, almost too well. The Southrons had not yet encountered any resistance. The nagging fear of entrapment crept into the back of Mathan-Bàn's thoughts even though he tried to dismiss it. It was irrational, but he could not shake the sense that something was not as it should be. He summoned Faylinn and told him, "Take your Companaich and go ashore." Faylinn led some of the best of the Gaisgich an Taighe; there should be little or nothing that could cause them difficulty.

Calum knew that he was not much of a warrior, too small and prone to a weak chest, but the Gods had given him a good heart and exceptional hearing, and even though the others made gentle fun of him by calling him Calum of the Ears he did not mind. Over the last few nights, he had been set the task of watching the strand of shale below the Craig from the makeshift defences that the Laird had ordered thrown up, and it made him feel like he was important. "The best man for the job," Kemble, the Grieve, had told the Laird.

This, Calum knew, was probably true. Few of the men had Calum's patience, and few would enjoy such a task; just sitting watching, well listening really, to the sounds of the water and the animals scurrying about in the darkness and the fog. He had particularly liked the mist; it amplified and distorted sounds in strange and unusual ways that he found fascinating. Tonight, though there was no fog, just the bitter wind and the cold coming off of the water, he had wrapped up well, his cloak tight and the bonnet his mother had made him pulled down hard on his head. He had snuggled down between the earth rampart and the sleeping bodies of his two fellow guards, and he was safe and warm enough. He liked to let whoever was on duty with him sleep, although he had to listen to their snoring. At least this way, he did not have to listen to their complaints or make conversation with them. Calum had never been very good at small talk with his own family, let alone others and preferred the silence.

In the silence, he could listen, for he knew it was useless to watch; it was too dark to see anything out on the loch. The heavy clouds blanketing the moonlight from the water's surface turned the water into a black void that would not abide a man staring out at it for too long. It could send a man insane or at least make him feel as if he were being drawn into madness. So, all Calum needed to do was listen to the water on the shale, the wind in the crevasses of the rock face, and the occasional sound of the birds crying or small animals moving in the darkness. He played a game in his mind, trying to identify each creature by its slightest sounds; mouse, bird, even the insects that had taken up home in the timbers behind him.

He had heard the approaching longboats long before they had landed. Listening intently to the sounds of the riggings, the creaking of the hulls, and the movement of the men and animals aboard. Trying to gauge the number of boats and men. Once he was satisfied, he had heard enough; he shook his fellow guards, Seumas and Wrad, awake. He told them to climb back up to the castle and raise the alarm but to do so softly so as not to warn the invaders. Once they had gone, he loaded his crossbow and crept closer to the beacon stack and waited. There was nothing for him to do now but wait and listen again, hoping that the others would raise the alarm before the invaders discovered him.

The Gesith, Eanwind, was the first to reach the obstacles that barred the track up from the beach. As Gesith, and thus one of Strandwulf's most experienced men, it was his task to lead the vanguard of the Southron strike force sent to explore the southern path up from the strand. As he had expected, the way was blocked by some sort of earthen rampart reinforced by logs and boulders. Crude, he knew, but effective. He allowed his men to catch up while he studied the defences. There were no apparent signs of life, they seemed abandoned, and secretly he hoped they were, but he had to find out. Crouched below the edge of the rampart, he gestured to the others to follow him.

The Southrons pushed forward as stealthily as they could, shields and spears at the ready, expecting the worst, but the defences remained silent. Once they had climbed as far as they could reasonably expect to without detection, he gave the signal to rush the defences, but no resistance was met. He stood for a moment on top of the timber rampart. The defences were indeed wholly abandoned. Casually Eanwind leapt to the ground behind the timber rampart, but almost as soon as his feet hit the ground, he knew he had made a terrible mistake. There was an overpowering smell of lamp oil. The earth was soaked in it.

The first arrow hit him in the chest, just above the heart, sending him reeling back against the logs. The second nailed him through his linden shield and his arm to the oil-soaked timber revetments.

The first wave of arrows took the Southrons by total surprise, downing several of them instantly. As the others turned to flee, they realised the trap they had walked into. The earthworks they had scaled were false. They were trapped in the open space between them and the real defences. Realising everything soaked in oil made it impossible to climb the bulwarks; in sheer desperation, the Southrons charged the real defences. It was to no avail; the Albans had been schooled hard and long, their discipline was good, and their aim was excellent.

Angus watched as the Southrons ran back to the beach to raise the alarm with a sense of relief mixed with sadness. There would be a great deal of blood spilt tonight, and many a good man would die for a few feet of earth. The trap Jacobis had set seemed to be working well. The vanguard had blithely walked straight into it and had been cut to ribbons. Now it was Angus' task to hold his clansmen back, for sensing an easy victory, they would have instinctively charged after the retreating enemy.

"There will be no time for pride or honour here," Jacobis had warned. "You must hold your men firm, keep their nerve and hold their ground." And so, Angus held them back from the pursuit by firm words and the force of his presence amongst them. He found the waiting as difficult as his men did, but he knew the value of defence over the attack, and they had arranged at least one more surprise for the invaders before they could abandon these positions either to pursue the enemy or withdraw to the castle.

As Angus stood with them, he noticed how the weight of the weeks of waiting had suddenly been lifted. They were in good spirits now, laughing and joking, as they crouched below the defences. They busied themselves checking their bows and preparing the little clay pots of what they called 'draigon's blood.' It was an alchemist's mixture of viscous oils and exotic compounds, that when exposed to the air, would blaze and burn with the ferocity akin to the blood of a fire-breathing beast.

Angus began to pace the bulwarks, using movement to relieve his own frustration. Some men looked up and greeted him with wry comments; others barely nodded in acknowledgement of his presence as he passed by. He knew they did not need words of encouragement or speeches; after so long, they only needed an enemy to fight. He found Gabhran and stepped up onto the rampart beside him. "How does it feel?"

Gabhran turned. "What?"

"To finally see the enemy."

Gabhran thought for a moment. "Good. Well..." he shrugged. "I didn't expect Southrons."

"Mercenaries. We haven't seen these 'Isheen' yet."

"If they exist."

"Hmm. We'll see. Let's deal with these first." He leaned over the rampart and stared into the darkness below, it was impossible to make out much detail in the dark, but he could hear the moans and cries of the injured and dying.

"How many?"

"The Gods only know. A dozen or more, plus those we hit who managed to climb back out. You were right. The Vör knows what he's talking about…it was as if they couldn't see us at all."

Angus did not answer; he just smiled and put his arm around his cousin's shoulder. "You've done a good job here with the earthworks and training the men. Your father would be proud." Gabhran made no attempt to reply, and the two men just stood watching the darkness and awaiting the inevitable onslaught.

The Southron leaders managed to swiftly regroup their men and throw them into the first assault on the beach. They came in three waves; the first launched their spears and dropped back to protect their archers, forcing the Albans into an exchange that was to give cover to the rush of the Southron's main force. They leapt the false earthworks and raced for the actual defences. Well trained soldiers using well-tried tactics that needed little instruction from their commanders in the field, perfectly timed and carried through even in the darkness of the night.

Angus watched patiently as the first Southrons reached the true earthworks and began to clamber up towards the palisade. He flourished his sword in the air and shouted with all his might, "Fire!"

As one, the Albans threw down their bows and snatched up their small pots of volatile oil and threw them into the mass of the attackers. A deafening roar swallowed the sound of the shattering pots and the cries of the Southrons. The oil-soaked killing ground and the false defences exploded into flames. The men trapped between the defences were instantly incinerated or turned into ghastly screaming manikins that stumbled and thrashed wildly as if in some horrific insane dance.

Angus stood dumbstruck at the sight, unable to think or react. His sword fell from his hand.

Gabhran seeing his cousin's shock shook him. "Are you hurt?"

For a second, Angus looked into Gabhran's face, but all he could see was the face of a demon, some great salamander staring back at him.

"Are you alright? Angus?"

"Aye, I'm alright." He turned back to the fiery pit below, where men were still screaming and thrashing about in the dying flames. "Kill them, Gabhran, in the name of mercy, kill them."

Gabhran reeled and shouted the order to the archers.

Fyngard Kvällulf watched the sky light up from his vantage behind the logs and rocks piled precariously amid the trees high above the northern path. The firelight threw the profile of the cliff and all that was on the beach into strange silhouettes, bizarre capering shadows cast upon the sands, otherworldly and unreal.

Jac's plan seemed to have worked well; the enemy was now streaming back onto the beach in disarray, some with their clothes and armour still on fire. As quickly as his eyes would allow, Fyn surveyed the landing force, five big longboats beached upon the shore, their Gothad crews milling around them as yet uncommitted to the fray. There was also another large group of Southron men and horses that were standing by. Fyngard guessed they were reserves for the main attacking force, but it was hard to tell numbers. A charge of horses would be almost useless on the strand.

Below him, a force of about a hundred men was making their way up the steep incline towards his position. He recognised them as more Southron heavy infantry by their chain hauberks, spangenhelms, and kite-shaped shields, with a vanguard of lightly armoured skirmishers carrying short bows.

Fyn knew what he had to do; it was a simple plan, though Jacobis had promised it would be effective. The invaders would expect a fight on the beach, and that is precisely what they would get, at least on the northern side of the strand. The north path up from the beach was steep and barely wide enough for three men abreast, and the ground was slippery underfoot, difficult terrain at the best of times, worse when there was a reception waiting at the top.

Turning, he surveyed the line, twenty Albans lay amidst the rocks and trees, well-skilled archers, and behind them, in the darkness, patiently stood MacLeech's Kerns and their huge war-dogs. Across from where Fyn stood, he could just make out the figures of Kemble and his gilles among the trees, not much good as fighters but strong enough and disciplined enough for the task Jacobis had set them.

Fyn allowed the Southrons skirmishers to reach the foot of the defences before he gave the first signal. Almost lazily, the Albans began to pick off the vanguard, one by one, their deliberate unhurriedness belying their numbers. The surviving skirmishers fired a few arrows in return and fled back to the safety of the ranks of the heavy infantry.

Fyn then watched as the soldiers did exactly what Jacobis had predicted. They formed up tightly in the confined space, the front line wedging their big shields together to form a wall before them, with the others holding their shields high to protect them from high arched arrows. They began to trudge slowly up the slope again in their close ranks as behind them, their skirmishers continued to provide cover.

Fyn smiled to himself and shook his head solemnly. He knew that, as Jacobis had said, being predictable on the battlefield was as good as sealing your own death warrant, and these men were all too predictable. Pushing the thoughts from his mind, he turned and waved his sword at the men above him on the path. At the signal, the Albans let fly with volley after volley of arrows into the front ranks of the infantry below. The route was too narrow to allow the Southrons to use their weight of numbers and they had become almost standing targets for the Albans in a bottleneck of their own making. At this distance, even their heavy shields and armour were little defence against Alban arrows.

Men screamed and fell under the feet of their comrades as they struggled forward over the dead and dying, only to be cut down by the relentless hail of missiles.

Fyn wondered just how long it would be before they broke ranks and tried to climb up the steep banks on either side of the path when the first Southrons did precisely that. It was a brave but futile attempt; they only made themselves easier targets for the archers. A couple even struggled to the top of the banking before they were shot down. With two dozen or more of their men dead or dying and their way blocked by their own casualties, finally, someone gave the order, and the retreat began.

For an instant, the cloud cover parted enough for a shaft of moonlight to penetrate through and fully light up the strand below him. Fyn knew that this was his moment to turn a retreat into a rout. He pulled his wolf's head cowl over his naked shoulders, gripped his weapons and bounded high up onto the rocky defences. Thrusting his head high, he let out a terrible howl and bound down towards the retreating Southrons. The Kern warriors behind him answered him with a thunderous blast on their war trumpets and charged after him. Like a murderous wave, they came leaping over the defences and down onto the retreating infantry.

As Fyn ran howling down the path, he could feel his consciousness slipping away as his instincts took over, his mind melding, changing, reforming into something else, something beyond human. The Ulvhinna called it the 'Wodfreca', to be in possession of the wolf spirit, to become one with it. Fyn could feel its power flowing through his veins into his heart, joining with him, transforming him. He was no longer human, no longer a disciplined warrior; he was an animal, a ravenous wolf. In this frenzied screaming rage, he leapt onto the hastily thrown up wall of shields and battered his way through to the terrified men beyond. All thought was gone, all trace of humanity abandoned, leaving only his heightened instincts and the insatiable need to kill. The screaming and the stench of blood drove him deeper into the knot of infantry, hacking furiously at bodies and limbs. Shields splintered, helmets smashed, and blood splattered to the wind as Fyn carved a lone bloody swathe through the Southron infantrymen.

Seconds later, the Kerns fell upon the front ranks of the Southrons, their heavy blunt-ended swords cleaving through shields and armour, cutting men down like saplings, driving the front ranks onto the rear, making any organised defence impossible in the crush of bodies. The fighting raged for only a few minutes before terror seized the Southrons and panic erupted. The retreat became a rout; the infantry turned and fled back down to the safety of the beachhead pursued by the baying war-hounds of the Kerns.

In the chaos, it took some time before the Kerns found Fyn. He had lost most of his equipment and was hunched over the body of a Southron Gesith trying to rip the man's heart out with a broken knife and his teeth. The Kerns formed a circle around the raging Gothad, and, on the orders of their Tòshuch, they rushed him using their square shields and broken spear hafts as staves. Still screaming and fighting, the blood-soaked madman was beaten semiconscious and dragged back up to the safety of the defences.

Earl Eadric, known as Strandwulf, sat astride his warhorse shouting orders to his men. He was trying desperately to organise his soldiers into a counterattack against the Alban's defences when a giant appeared to walk out of the thin air right in front of him. Shocked into silence, Strandwulf could only gape in disbelief as the huge figure lunged for him.

Seeing his Lord in peril, Heca, one of the best of Earl Strandwulf's Hearthweru and a loyal man of excellent reactions, spun his horse and drove it between his Lord and the giant. The giant hardly paused to bat Heca and his mount aside like a child on a hobbyhorse.

Strandwulf's astonishment suddenly gave way, and he frantically tried to goad his horse into movement, but it was too late. The giant seized him and his charger, lifting them both clear above his head and threw them at the prow of the nearest longboat, smashing the beast's spine and shattering Strandwulf's shoulder. The great Southron Dryhten, Strandwulf, fell onto the shingle like a discarded rag doll.

It was all that the stunned Southron warriors could do but to stand open-mouthed as the giant reached into the nothingness and drew forth a great bronze bladed spear. An evil-looking weapon with a long, broad leaf-shaped blade that seemed to sing as he began to spin it about himself. Three of the stunned Southrons and their beasts fell dead before the spell of shock was broken, and the rest even tried to defend themselves. It was futile. The strange weapon ripped through shields and armour-like parchment, unerringly gutting and beheading all that came within its terrible reach. As the Southrons tried desperately to rally and fight back, the giant only seemed to grow greater in height and more frightening.

Suddenly their courage broke, the Southrons scattered to safer distances screaming for the Gothad archers to cover them, but no aid came. Jarl Olvarson had seen enough, and his men were already busy dragging their longboats back into the water.

As the giant strode down to the waterline, nothing stood in his way. The few arrows and spears that were launched at him clattered harmlessly to the shale, apparently losing their energy in mid-flight, before even reaching him. A few brave Southrons mounted a desperate charge, but their light lances were useless, and the giant's terrible spinning blade cut them to pieces.

When the last of the Southrons gave up and ran from him, the giant turned and continued his steady walk to the shore where a small boat had been beached, and seven warriors stood as if awaiting him. Tall and beautiful, they showed no sign of the awe-struck horror of the Southrons, only the patient indifference of the genuinely fearless.

The gore-splattered giant stopped a few yards from their leader and rested the ferrule of his great spear upon his boot, and firmly announced, "I am Jacobis Arnflinsson of the Jötunn Vör, and I deny you right of entry, you may not pass. Be gone."

Their leader, a tall, thin, and unearthly beautiful youth wearing archaic bronze armour under a voluminous dark green cloak, stepped forward determinedly. "You mistake us for wraiths? You cannot forbid us to enter upon this place or any other."

Jacobis grinned wolfishly. "Then welcome to Eagle's Craig."

The Isheen inclined his head in acknowledgement. "I am Faylinn Mac Fer Fí of the Isheen of Dùn Nan Làidir," he announced in lisping Alban through ferocious looking teeth never designed to pronounce such words. "These are my Companaich."

The giant cast a glance over them. "Very pretty." He snorted dismissively, "I cannot say I am pleased to meet you this day."

"You're the giant in thrall to the Fees'sacher, the Witch, Annis."

"I am her 'companion'. Yes."

"She has an exceptional talent for a half-breed, but her magic will not protect you against us."

Jacobis ignored the insult and answered with a casual shrug. "Maybe, maybe not."

Faylinn had never confronted a giant before, and this one was every bit as intimidating as the stories foretold; he was almost twice the height of a Daonna and resembled more a giant red-maned bear in armour than a man, but, as Mathan-Bàn had reminded Faylinn, he was an Isheen warrior, and he would not be afraid. He gave his voice its most indifferent tone and said, "Depart now, giant, while you can, for this is not your fight."

The Vör scratched his beard and seemed to contemplate the idea for a moment before replying, "Listen, little Elf. My Lady's fight is my fight, and to get to her, you must go through me." He sighed exaggeratedly and hoisted the great spear, "Have your masters not seen enough bloodshed tonight or do I have to kill you as well?"

Faylinn looked closely at the aura sheathing the spear, it had a strange luminosity that he did not recognise, but instinctively he understood what it was. He had heard tales of such weapons, but he had never seen or encountered one until now. It took a physical effort to pull his eyes away from its radiance; dry-mouthed, he forced himself to answer the giant's jibe. "That is a mighty weapon, but you are alone, and you alone cannot stop us."

The savage grin again spread across the giant's face. "This is the spear of Samildanach, the balu-gaisos, known to all the peoples beyond the North winds as Gungnir. The Gothads say that the smith, Volund Allwise, forged it, and the All-Father decreed that every blow from it shall kill." He lifted the rune carved blade and casually inspected it, "And so far, I think they're right."

"Your threats do not impress me, I am Isheen, and we are immortal," Faylinn lied.

"No one is truly immortal, my little pointy-eared friend, nothing, not the mightiest oak, or the mountains themselves, or the Gods, can withstand the weight of time. Your people are no more immortal than mine; it is tales you spread to frighten the gullible. You may be great warriors and live far beyond the ages of men, but this weapon was blessed by a God and has killed better than you. Now scurry off back to your masters and tell them that I, Jacobis Arnflinsson, deny you passage and, as you have seen," he gestured vaguely behind him, "I am not alone."

On either side of the strand, the gilles from the castle ignited large beacons that roared into life, illuminating where the Albans and Kerns were dug in to defend the routes off the beach. The defenders cheered wildly and beat their weapons upon their shields. From the northern side of the strand came the ear-shattering cacophony of the Kern's war horns with a great chorus of howling of war dogs and vociferous warriors. Jacobis noticed how the Isheen warriors visibly cringed at the level of the noise.

Irritated into action, one of Faylinn's Companions drew his sword and thrust forward. "Enough! Step aside, monster, or I will destroy you."

Before Faylinn could intervene, the blow had been struck, and the balu-gaisos had split the Isheen warrior from shoulder to belly. Faylinn snatched his own sword but froze as he found his chin resting upon the giant's spear point.

"Well now, he wasn't quite so immortal, was he?"

Faylinn threw himself backwards as his Companions launched themselves at the Vör in a furious assault. Like a graceful yet deadly dance, they spun around the giant, lashing at him with their swords. A thrust buried itself into the Vör's side as another slashed deep into his thigh and yet another across his back.

The giant roared like a wild animal and seemed to warp and grow even bigger, though his movements were as the lightning. The merciless blade of the balu-gaisos sang as it sliced through the night air. The spear embedded itself into the belly of one Isheen and carved him in two as the giant flicked it clear. Another warrior instantly lost the front of his skull as the weapon spun around to take a third full in the chest. The Vör hoisted the skewered Isheen high into the air and tossed him into the loch.

The remaining warriors saw their chance and hacked for all their worth at the giant's sides and arms, but the work of the terrible balu-gaisos did not stop. The great Vörish warrior drove the pointed ferrule through the eye of one Isheen and gutted another, a perfect backstroke beheading him before he hit the ground.

Finally, only Faylinn remained standing against the giant, though faster and more agile than his dead Companions; the young Isheen fought with all the desperation of one facing certain death for the first time in his life. He concentrated on trying to avoid the balu-gaisos' hungry blade rather than try to attack the Vör, who seemed incredibly huge and totally invulnerable. In a flash, he saw his chance, an open space, and stabbed for the giant's chest, but it was a trap. The shaft of the spear cracked down on his wrist, and the ferrule slammed across the side of his helmet, sending him sprawling to the shale. Before he could leap back to his feet, the bloody steaming spear point was once again at his throat.

"It would seem that your people are not as immortal as you thought, my friend." The Vör's huge face glared down at him. "Now crawl back under whatever stone you crawled out from under," he picked up Faylinn's sword and tossed it away.

Faylinn sprang to his feet. "You are a mighty warrior, Jacobis Arnflinsson, but are you so mighty without that accursed weapon?"

Jacobis' face grew angry. "I was my father's champion. Undefeated in battle or trial of honour. I took this weapon in single combat from the man who wielded it before me." He levelled the point of the spear at the Isheen's chest and said, "Now, little Elf, I said; be gone!"

The souls of the dead are darker shades against the darkness.

Confused, they wail and claw at themselves in terror.

Some are drawn unto the flames of the beacons like strange ethereal moths to a flickering candle.

For fire is the only earthly thing that is tangible in their state of limbo.

They are trapped between.

Some wander pitifully amongst the dead and the living.

Pleading to be heard

Some cry out for their friends.

Pleading not to be abandoned.

Some cry out for their mothers.

Pleading not to be dead.

Lost, fearful children, bewildered and alone.

I reach out unto those who will listen to me and send them on.

She is near now. I can sense her watching.

Go now.

For She is waiting.

Always waiting.

So patient is Death.

Still, a few shining souls remain.

Unheeding.

The Isheen and those who in life never knew their gifts.

Mer stands beside me. He understands what I am doing.

Later he will do the same himself.

For his warriors and kin.

He has a strange expression on his face. I cannot tell what he is thinking.

He is always careful to guard even his surface thoughts against me.

There is a flicker of anger across his face, just a tiny movement in his white eye and a dark thought, the echo of it too strong for him to hide completely.

I smile.

He turns and gazes back over the parapet down onto the strand below. His sight is almost as clear as mine is in the night. "They will no take kindly to yon big man slaughtering their kith an' kin. ye can nae stop them on ye own."

I am not on my own.

Am I?

Did you not promise the Laird to help him?

Or was that a lie?

He flashes a look back at me, his face a mask of hate, both eyes burning with ferocity.

"A'm nae coward, Wutch."

I return my attention to the horror below us.

The rage of the Síth is palpable.

It flows upon the wind.

They are baying for revenge.

As they draw their powers together to strike.

To strike at Jacobis.

To destroy the one I love.

MacLeech can sense it too.

He is eager to see what I will do.

He wants to know the extent of the gift that my mother bequeathed me.

Oh, my beloved mother.

Am I a woman, driven by the loves and emotions of a woman?

Or am I just the mongrel creature that he thinks I am?

Black Annis.

He thinks that if I am a woman, I am weak.

He thinks that if I am one of them, he can destroy me.

He is wrong.

I tell him.

Do what you can, and I will do what I have to.

Let him see.

Let them all see.

Mathan-Bàn found himself astonished by the events on the strand though it had started off much as he had anticipated. The Albans had planned their defence well and fought admirably using every advantage the terrain offered. Then, just as he had feared, even though the Southrons had far greater numbers, they were unable to bring their traditional tactics and full weight to bear and so had lost their discipline, and thus their nerve, in the darkness and the mayhem. They were mercenaries, and mercenaries have little true stomach for a desperate fight; that was to be expected. The Southrons were, after all, only the vanguard to his main force, their task being only to test the strength of the Albans before he would decide at which point he would commit his own warriors to the fray.

What he had not expected was the giant's attack on the Southrons. The giant had been clouded by a fith-fath, a spell powerful enough to protect him from even the eyes of the Isheen. That was something Mathan-Bàn found troubling. He knew that the Witch was supposed to have a giant in her thrall, but he had not expected her hand to reveal such a warrior. He had watched with mounting anger as the Witch's thrall had marched down to the water line and slaughtered Faylinn's Companaich. Some of the very best of his own household warriors. If he had not seen it with his own eyes, he would have believed it impossible. Neither man nor monster had stood alone against seven Isheen warriors and defeated them since Dubhcheilg himself, and he was the son of a God. This giant, protected by the Witch's hand, seemed invulnerable to even the weapons of the Isheen.

Worst still, Mathan-Bàn could already hear the Galdràgon hopping about on one foot, and screeching curses from the other end of the longboat, the hag and Cullach-Bàn would, he knew, make significant capital out of the slaughter of his warriors, accusing him, before the Bànrigh, of being weak and foolish. The whole assault plan appeared to be falling apart, and he knew that he had to be seen to act before the hag and her acolytes started to wildly throw their powers about.

Blocking out the commotion about him, he studied the shoreline carefully. The fighting was over, and the giant had picked up the head of one of the fallen Isheen warriors as a trophy and was sauntering back up the beach. Faylinn was returning with the bodies of his Companions. The Southrons were crowding around the Gothad's longboats, confused now that their leader was probably dead. There was nothing Mathan-Bàn could do about that; if Strandwulf was dead, he had little use for such a leaderless rabble of Dhaoine.

However, there was something he could do about the Witch's giant. He drew his long bow, nocked an arrow, and aimed. "I give wings of wrath to you, my flightless bird, fly true and strike down my enemy." Mathan-Bàn's arrow flew instantaneously and unerringly to strike the giant high in the back. He then watched, almost emotionless, as the giant staggered on for a few paces before he slowly collapsed to the ground. The Isheen on the longboats and the mercenary warriors on the beach cheered loudly. At least, Mathan-Bàn thought with some satisfaction, this is no son of a God.

Suddenly a tremendous scream went up from the rear of Mathan-Bàn's own longboat. The Àrd-dràgon spun around to behold an arrow, his arrow, thrusting from the chest of one of the Galdràgon's acolytes. The girl, with pallid face and wide eyes, clawed wretchedly at the small black stone arrowhead, as bloody foam spluttered from her mouth onto her white vestments, then, as a bloom of dark red appeared on her bosom, she silently crumpled.

The Galdràgon stood frozen to the spot, her vicious gnarled face stuck in the blank expression of shock. Instantly, she flung her arms skyward and began screaming with rage, calling on all the powers she could summon and hysterically beseeching them for bloody revenge.

From someplace far off across the water and the mountains, as if in answer to her pleas, came a tremendous low roll of thunder.

Mathan-Bàn turned away furiously, shouting his orders to the warriors on the awaiting ships. The oars of the longboats smashed down into the icy waters, lifting the vessel's prowls high off the surface. They sped towards the strand like great wooden fish intent on beaching themselves upon the shore. The Àrd-dràgon immediately regretted so rashly committing his Gaisgich an Taighe, but it was too late to call them back. His hand had been forced, and it was with shock that he realised how easily it had been done.

The defenders knew they would have to face the full ferocity of the Isheen that night, but still, for all the Vör's warnings, few were truly prepared for the speed and savagery of the assault. The Isheen's ships seemed to be ashore, and their warriors charging into the fray almost before the defenders had time to realise the attack was coming.

Far taller than Dhaoine and bedecked in archaic armours, with their beautiful faces twisted into animal-like masks of rage, their eyes glinting eerily in the dying light of the beacons, the Isheen were a truly terrifying sight. They launched themselves at the defences in a display of extraordinary courage and strength, some able to leap the revetments in a bound or two to throw themselves onto the defenders.

Gabhran's disciplining and drilling of his warriors paid off, though, and his men, once jolted from their disbelief, met the onslaught with a merciless hail of arrows cutting down the attackers at close range and driving them back off the earth works under a constant rain of death. "Push them back!" Gabhran kept screaming as he and those without bows hacked at the injured and threw their corpses back over the revetments.

On the northern side of the strand, the Kern's Tòshuch let the attackers rush to the very top of the stone piled defences before he signalled the castle gilles to do their duty. Screened from the fighting by the trees, the gilles took up their ropes and hauled with all their strength.
Pulling away the lower supports of the walls sending tons of rock and logs crashing down onto the Isheen and Southrons below. Elated by the sight of the mighty Isheen in disarray, the Kerns blasted their war horns, released their war dogs, and charged down upon the stricken enemy with merciless glee. The fighting in the freezing dark was savage and brutal. The Kerns fought with unparalleled ferocity, using every advantage their tactics had given them, while the taller and faster Isheen warriors relied solely upon their determination and skill.

Ultimately, as all the defenders had been so carefully warned, their initial successes began to turn. The Isheen were more than a match for the Kern warriors in the manic struggle of close quarter combat, and, on the northern defences, the Isheen's spears and vicious black-headed arrows slowly began to drive the Albans from the ramparts. The Southrons too had rallied and were now able to bear their disciplined ranks and weight of numbers in support of their Isheen masters.

The Kern's Tòshuch gave the order to retreat as soon as he sensed the tide of the mêlée turning against his warriors. Though they had inflicted more damage upon the enemy than he thought possible, he could not risk losing good men in a rout. The remaining Alban archers now high above them on the castle ramparts began to provide cover as the Kerns withdrew back to the top of the steep path and made the frantic dash to the barbican's drawbridge.

Angus was not prepared to see a single one of his warriors needlessly injured or killed. As soon as he considered that the Isheen had rallied, he gave the signal to set fire to the remaining defences and withdraw to the safety of the castle. The original plan, he had devised with Jacobis, had never been to fight a protracted battle upon the trayad, the strand itself, only to maul the enemy sufficiently to test their strength and to raise the morale of his men.

As his father had once said to him, "The fortress is our strength, Angus; trust in it. It will not fail us."

Chapter 13

"Gnothi se auton."

"Know thyself."

Inscription.
Temple of Apollo.
Delphi.

Corvus awoke startled by the first rumbles of thunder. He hated storms. A long time ago, the palace guards had come for his family during a summer thunderstorm, and he had never been rid of that nightmare. Now though, as he lay awake listening to it, he knew this storm was different; someone, or something, had summoned this one. He could tell; he had seen it done several times by the Imperial Magi and the Druids of Mur Ollamhan. There was something about summoned storms, something more savage, more intense. The roar of the thunder sounded like some tremendous elemental beast awakened and tormented into action, screaming its rage across the sky. Even deep inside the crannog, he could feel the force of the winds slamming against the outer walls and catch glimpses of the cobalt blue lightening as it tore across the night sky.

Corvus could never have been a Magi, but he had known enough of them to know their ways and powers. It took immense ability to summon even a mild change in the weather, let alone a thunderstorm. In the whole of the Gärian Empire, there had only been a few individuals reputedly powerful enough to do such things on their own, frail old men and women who could summon the limitless forces of nature at their will, but they were all long dead. As far as Corvus could recall, there had only ever been a handful in the North with that kind of power, and he had killed most of them at Mur Ollamhan. All the storms, wind and lightning in the heavens had not protected them.

So, who, in the name of Charun, was left? He rubbed his hands across his face and tried to think. Some Gothad Priest, maybe? Or a coven of… A name leapt out of the dark corners of memory. He swore through clenched teeth, threw off the skins and blankets, and struggled to his feet. Finally, it all made sense to him; there could only be one man left in the North with such power; Mer MacLeech.

So that was it; the Albans were at war with the Kerns again, and he was getting drawn right into the eye of the storm. A storm that the Warlock MacLeech had summoned.

Corvus shoved aside the cloth partition and almost stumbled over the dozing young clansman set to guard him. He quickly regained his balance and stood silently, unmoving until he was sure the guard was undisturbed. Once he was confident that the guard slept on, he picked his way past the youth and headed towards the centre of the crannog where Lady MacRoth had held her audience. Another two guards sat dozing by the entrance, probably set as a second line of defence if he should try to escape in the night. He gently relieved one of them of a dagger and slid carefully by into the main chamber.

"Ah, you're awake."

The voice froze Corvus to the spot.

A silver-haired old man sat by the stone hearth in the centre of the room. He lifted up his head and smiled warmly, "Come, sit down," he patted the pile of furs and blankets beside him.

Corvus took a long look around the room before he moved. "The storm woke me."

The old man's attention seemed to have turned to the contents of the bronze bowl nestled in his lap, though he did not stir it or drink from it. "I thought it might."

"And you?"

With a long bony finger, the old man gave the contents of the bowl a stir, "I seldom sleep."

There was something familiar about the old man, though Corvus had not seen him in the crannog that evening. "Who are you?"

The old man looked up again and smiled broadly; bright eyes sparkled under his bushy white brows. "A friend."

Corvus squatted beside him. "Do I know you?"

"We met once briefly, a long time ago, but we were never introduced."

Corvus' blood ran cold. Maybe he had been right; his hand tightened around the hilt of the dagger in his belt. "Are you MacLeech?"

The old man's eyes twinkled with mirth, and he chuckled. "No, I'm not."

"Then…" Corvus seized the old man's sleeve and pulled him close, shouting over a great roll of thunder. "Then who are you?"

His eyes were as blue as daylight reflected off ice. "I am Finnvarra."

Corvus let him go. "What are you then, a Druid or something?"

Finnvarra shrugged, "Or something."

"Where is Lady MacRoth?"

"Asleep. They are all asleep."

"No one could sleep through a storm like this."

"Some have not the sensitivity of you, nor the bad memories." The old man went back to staring into his bowl. He had a strange, almost unearthly look about him; behind his long white beard, his features were stark and sharp, emaciated, elongated by the shadows of the dying firelight. For a moment, Corvus thought of the woman in the woods but dismissed it immediately. He slipped the dagger beneath the furs and seated himself carefully opposite the old man.

Without looking up from the bowl, Finnvarra asked. "Tell me, Fitheach, why did you come back to these lands?"

Expecting an insult, Corvus demanded, "What did you call me?"

"Fitheach? 'Raven.' Is that not your name?"

Unsure of how to respond, Corvus simply grunted.

"I ask again then, why you have returned?"

"What?"

"After such a long time. Surely you should have gone home, back to your people, where you belong."

Corvus thought for a while, the concept of exactly where he 'belonged' was one that he had spent most of his adult life trying to comprehend. Where did he belong? Gäria? An empire in the midst of its death throes? Aelathia? The Aelathia of his childhood and memories was long gone. So long that even in his dreams, he could no longer speak the language.

"I stayed because I chose to."

The old man looked up again. His eyes were like huge pools reflecting the light, not from the fire but a light emanating from the bowl. "But it has been so long, Fitheach. Why so long?"

Why so long? How long had it been? It was hard for him to guess, five years, maybe? At first, he had stayed to oversee the withdrawal. Later, after Calticas' assassination, he stayed because it was safer to be in this barbarian wasteland than the cesspit that Val Gär had become. They had summoned him, the new Tyrannos and his court, but he had refused to return. Instead, he had taken an Alban woman for his wife and set down amongst his old soldiers to become a farmer. He found himself shaking his head in incredulity. Lunacy! A ridiculous idea! But why could he not remember his wife's name?

The old man smiled again. "You don't remember, do you?"

"What do you mean? It's only been three summers since…." Since I buried Móraig and my unborn child.

Immediately the memory rushed back in a wave of pain and despair. Corvus drew his hand to his face to stifle the strange sound coming from his mouth and tried to focus on the old man, but tears were welling up in his eyes. How could he have forgotten? How could a man forget such pain?

The old man's face was stern and grim. "No, Fitheach, it has been much longer. Three decades, thirty years, since the Tyrannos Ekraun Porsenna summoned you. Thirty years since you buried your wife and child."

The Bard said thirty years since the Hastions had been re-called, but that was impossible. He had ignored it as a poet's exaggerations. Impossible! Corvus' mind reeled. "No," is all he could say.

"Where have you been, Fitheach?"

What could make a man forget such pain?

The memories were flooding back. Dark things, frightening

things, memories of things, impossible things. Corvus seized the old man by the throat and hauled him to his feet, sending the bowl clanging to the floor. "No!" he shouted into the face before him, "NO!!!"

Finnvarra rested his hands lightly upon Corvus' and lowered them. "It is true," he said softly.

Corvus stared at the old man in disbelief, but he could now clearly taste the coin in his mouth and feel the wet earth on his face. He had welcomed death without fear, embraced her like a lover, an old mistress well known and comforting. He had walked in her shadow for so long it was like returning to his mother's womb.

"How?"

The old man picked the bowl up off of the floor and inspected it for damage, "The 'how' is easy," he flashed a sly smile at Corvus. "It's the 'why' that I do not know."

A spark of rationality flared in the darkness of Corvus' despair, "Why should I believe you?" He stiffened, "You're a Magician. This could all be some trick or a hallucination."

Finnvarra drew closer. "How is your arm?"

"What?" Corvus looked at his bandaged arm.

"Did you always heal so fast?"

Corvus was about to protest, but it was true. He had used it to haul the old man to his feet. There was no throbbing, no stiffness, no pain. As the thunder roared out across the darkness again, Finnvarra leaned closer and whispered, "Men do not hallucinate their own deaths, Corvus."

Chapter 14

"Heaven is not what it is said to be;
Hell is not what it is said to be;
The saved are not forever happy;
The damned are not forever lost."

Attributed to
St. Oran
Iona

The rain beat down with a vengeance as if the sky itself had something against those foolish enough to venture out into the steel-grey dawn. Everything was sodden, and the mud churned up by boots and hooves began to spread to anything anyone touched. Saddles, cloaks, and packs became caked with muck as men and women struggled to load pack ponies and mules. Hunched warriors sheltered in the lee of their horses and muttered sullenly amongst themselves, cursing the weather and the delays. The icy rainwater found its way down necks and through seams. Mud stuck to boots and made the act of walking even a few feet treacherous.

Corvus sat on the horse they had provided him and watched with growing apathy. He had seen this acted out before, sometimes by small groups like this but often by Hastions, tens of thousands of spear men, struggling to pack and ready for the day's march, but it was always worse in the rain. The whole thing took far longer, and much more effort, and, correspondingly, tempers wore away faster. Even the mules protested.

The whole show was being organised by the big Alban warrior they called Wal. He was an impressive sight, built like an ox and a head taller than most Albans and swathed in plaid and furs. He wore his mass of grey hair tied back in Gothad fashion and one of those long drooping moustaches that the Albans affected. He strode about waving a claymore like a walking stick or an Ouragos' baton. Corvus summed him up as a good organiser and probably a good leader of men; he was firm, calm, and good-humoured. He spoke to everyone and double-checked everything himself. The kind of experienced and careful man you could rely upon and on whom the men could trust. The sort of man that would have made a good Ouragos.

Corvus studied the others preparing for the journey. Most of the warrior's faces were familiar; he had seen them around the hearth last night, heavy set men with grim, expressionless faces. All, like their leader, were wrapped in yards of homespun plaid with heavy furs over their leather and chain armours, some wearing their great swords slung across their backs. Quiet, stern clansmen, all related by blood, marriage, or both, some so wild looking and heavily bearded that it was hard to tell where their furs ended, and they began. Corvus smiled. What a shock they had been for the Gärians when they had first met them in battle, though not as shocking as the Kerns.

Corvus found his attention drawn to the youth that had met them at the gate, a sneering rat-faced boy with a long nose and sharp, darting eyes. He always stayed close to another youth, a big, heavily built boy with almond-shaped eyes and the open flat rounded face of the permanently innocent. While Rat-face did nothing but complain, the other diligently harnessed horses and packed. Corvus recognised their relationship, the mocking bully and his easy-going permanent victim. He made a mental note to watch the pair of them.

Apart from himself and Svein, he counted thirty clansmen, ten youths, gilles and slaves, big Wal, the Bard Tàmh, and twenty pack animals, not counting the dozen or so extra horses. Every available space was packed with provisions for the journey and supplies for Eagle's Craig. It would be a slow hard trudge in this weather, moving at the best speed of the slowest man or animal. It would be dangerous, especially if they were going to have to push through areas that may already be in the hands of these 'vargr', as the Bard called them. Corvus had no doubt that 'they' were probably the Kerns, but he had not pushed the point with Lady MacRoth. The strange dreams of the night still haunted him, and he had no wish to avoid the inevitable. As she wanted, he would go to this 'Eagle's Craig', wherever it was, and try to save her husband, because maybe it was fitting that he owed her that much.

This morning it had been enough to reiterate the agreement and collect his things. Though he could feel her eyes on him, he would not look back. He would not look back at her; to him, she should still be little more than a child, but that was thirty years ago.

The Bard was plodding towards him through the quagmire. He stopped and wiped the rainwater and mud from his face. "Ah, my Lord, I hope you're well this fine morning."

"I'm not your 'Lord'." Growled Corvus without looking at him.

"Ah, err…. Aye. Lady Jorunn said…."

"Said what?"

"That you were to be treated with proper respect."

Corvus shook his head and laughed.

"Did I say something funny?"

"Respect? Do you have 'respect' for me?"

Tàmh looked thoughtful for a moment. "Aye. I do."

"Why?"

"Because you were a … great leader."

Corvus leaned down in his saddle until his face was almost level with the Bard. "I was a great butcher; that's all I was. I destroyed everything I touched, and I revelled in it. It is easy to destroy things, very easy." He pulled back up in his saddle. Since last night he had felt nothing but horror as one memory after another unfolded before his mind's eye. He felt like a dying man reliving his past in flashes, but every new memory was worse than the last. He shook his head, trying to physically remove the images. "Tell me about this place, Eagle's Craig?"

The Bard's face brightened. "It's said to be the oldest fortification in Tir Mór, built by the Àrsaidh, the people we call the Ancients, just after the great flood. It's huge and primordial, actually carved out of the living rock. It sits at the southern end of Loch Racholl, guarding the river and the roads South through to the Collie Mhòr and the whole of northern Reeachca."

"Collie Mhòr?"

He made a broad gesture at the dark sweep of the forest that surrounded the lake. "This; the Great Forest."

A defensive fortress guarding the routs north into the lands of the Kerns and the Gothads beyond. "And this fortress, it has never been taken?"

"Never. Though the Gods alone know how many times the Kerns and the Gothads have tried. Some say even the Àrsaidh when they were at war with themselves tried to, but the Craig held out."

"That's hard to believe." What was harder to believe was that he had never heard of this place in all his time in the North. He had campaigned deep into these lands with the Seventh and Ninth Hastions after the battles at Mur Ollamhan and Sh'tey-Dochas, decimating the countryside and pursuing the Kerns back into their own kingdoms. He knew the Great Forest and of the vastness of Loch Racholl beyond, but he had never heard of this so-called impregnable castle.

"Aye, well, you've never seen it," Big Wal interrupted. "When you see it, you'll understand. It's a haunted and eerie place. No one in their right mind would want to stay there long." He began to check Corvus' horse's harness and pack.

Tàmh continued, "It sits perched on a Craig hanging out over the Loch like some ancient beast. There is no connection to the land on three sides and no way to get up to it except form a small strand, the trayad, at the foot of the Craig, but the up paths are dangerous enough in daylight on a peaceful day. If the defenders wish to stop you, you'd be trapped at the foot of the rock, prey to anything they'd throw down at you and the tide. The Craig is only near enough to the cliff face at one point to allow for a drawbridge, but once the bridge is withdrawn.... Well, you'd have to learn to fly."

Wal stopped what he was doing, looked gravely at the Bard, and said flatly, "The Seelie can fly."

They set off about an hour later and headed north at a walking pace. There was very little talking amongst them as they trudged miserably along the shore towards the dark line of the forest edge. After what felt like an age to Corvus, they finally reached the big trees. The guibhas, great pines that towered over them like ancient sentinels breaking the ice-cold wind and sheltering them from the driving rain. The mouth of a broad, rough track opened before them, leading deep into the heart of the forest.

The Albans seemed to relax now, and their speed picked up though it was still much slower going than Corvus was used to. These men did not march; they ambled along as if they had all the time in the world. Once he had been grateful of that fact, as he had raced them to Mur Ollamhan, but now it was annoying and time-wasting. A Hastion would have covered twice the distance already.

Corvus wondered why he had spent most of the morning thinking of the past, of his men and the extended campaigns in the North against these people. Against the fathers of these people, he corrected himself. Thirty years ago, that was impossible. There was some trick to all this, he was sure. He shook off the wondering and daydreaming like the rain from his face; if there was a trick to all this, it would reveal itself in time. Better to deal with the here and now, one thing at a time. Careful, he had always been careful, and that had paid him well in the past, always methodical and cautious. He knew that it was the only advantage he had at the moment, and so he had to rely upon it.

By midday, some of the younger warriors, the mule packers, and others began to complain to Wal about stopping for a break. Wal dismissed them gruffly, telling them that if they wanted to stick their arses in the mud, go ahead, but no one would be staying around to pull them out. They would stop when he said and not before. The complaining seemed to focus upon the fact that they were forced to walk while Wal and the older warriors had horses, and some had spare mounts. Wal's reaction was precisely what Corvus expected of the man. He got off his horse and began leading it. Corvus was interested to see that most of the older warriors did the same.

By mid-afternoon, the rain had abated, but the ominous sky

with its dark clouds and purple lustre promised much more. Wal called a halt as soon as the rain stopped and told them all to take their much-requested rest for a while. Everyone struggled to find a spot to sit on the damp earth or amongst the bracken. Wal commandeered a lump of fallen tree where several of the older clansmen quickly joined him.

Corvus climbed down from his horse and looked around. Svein was strutting around stiff-legged like a chicken about to lay an oversized egg. Cramp probably. Tàmh had found a dry spot under the trees and was beckoning them over. Corvus ignored him and carried on surveying the others. They had formed into roughly three groups; the younger warriors, the mule packers, and the older warriors grouped around Big Wal. By the look of them, the half dozen clansmen around Wal were what the Hastion would have called 'veterans,' the fiercest men of the Clan; the others were experienced but not battle-hardened, possibly they had seen some cattle raiding but little else. Of the rest, the mule packers as he thought of them, Corvus had not taken much interest, save for the one marked badly with a birthmark on his face and the rat-faced boy and his companion. Birthmark, he estimated, was no more than a youth and very quiet, tall, but lithely built, he kept his head down and his face covered as much as possible; he worked hard and seemed to be in charge of the horses. He made a mental note to change his designation from 'Birthmark' to 'Horse-boy.' Corvus had always named people like this; it helped when dealing with groups. It was something he had learnt as a child, a way to remember faces in a crowd. Rat-faced boy and his companion kept away from the leading group of mule packers, keeping themselves to themselves. Ratface's eyes were everywhere, and he had a permanent vicious sneer on his face that he dropped only when the warriors looked directly at him. It was a dangerous look; Corvus knew it meant the boy was trouble. Ouragos were trained to recognise that expression on the faces of new recruits. People like that spread dissension, disobey orders when no one is watching, thieve and lie. It can lead to a Hastion being decimated or, worse, failing in battle. Ratface's presence worried Corvus, but he was also aware that Wal watched the boy closely too.

"Corvus!" the Bard called loudly. "Come, it's dry here."

156

Corvus shrugged and walked over to Tàmh and sat heavily down beside him. "Bannock?" the Bard offered a chunk of rough-looking dark cake. Corvus waved it away, but not put off, the Bard proffered a wineskin next. "It's good. Not as good as you're used to, no doubt, but reasonable."

More to quiet him than out of thirst, Corvus took the skin and drank. It was good indeed, and he quickly had to force himself to stop drinking; it felt like he had not tasted wine in years. He took another mouthful, swilled it around, and spat it out. He shoved the stopper back and handed it to the Bard. "Who is that boy?" Corvus gestured towards Rat-face.

"Who? Oh, Ker is his name."

"Ker!" Corvus chuckled, "Do you know what that means in my language?"

"No? I think it's an old word; it means 'fastness,' or something. His mother was from the South Islands. They speak an old tongue there."

"You'd not want to call a child that in my homeland."

"What does it mean?"

Corvus shrugged, "No matter. Who is he?"

"Ah, he's..." He leaned forward conspiratorially and lowered his voice, "He's Big Wal's nephew, but how would you say illegitimate?"

"A bastard."

"Yes. His father was betrothed to another, and his mother was only a serving girl."

"A slave?"

"No, a servant."

"And the big lad with him?"

"Ned. His father was the Chieftain's brother, Kinart; he died about twelve years ago, caught a terrible chill in the lungs and wasted away."

"And the boy?"

"Oh, he's harmless, simple, touched by the Gods, as they say, but a good lad. They'd have either killed him for being different or thought he was a God in the old days. Why?"

Corvus thought for a moment. Because Rat-face is trouble,

because I don't like the look of him, because the last time a man looked at me like that, I had him broken upon a wheel. He took a piece of the bannock, pulled off a bit and chewed it. "The boy, the one with the mark on his face, who is he?"

The Bard lowered the wine skin, paused, and wiped his mouth. "Him? A slave, his name is Nissien, he's of the Setantii. I think."

"Setantii?"

"Strange people. Live on floating houses in the marshes and estuaries."

"He doesn't speak?"

"Dumb, he makes noises," the Bard shoved home the stopper. "Good with horses, though. Why are you so interested in the gilles and slaves?"

Corvus took a moment to think whether he would answer the Bard's question. The Bard had lied about Horse-boy; he could smell it on the air, but was it important? Let them keep their secrets. "Sevius Mastarna," he said finally.

"The Gärian General?"

"Yes."

"What about him?"

"Sevius Mastarna was murdered by a slave, a girl, she put broken glass in his food, and when he'd eaten it and was screaming in pain, she stabbed him in the throat. Just enough to stop him screaming, but not enough to kill him quickly."

"A slave?"

"Little more than a child, daughter of a Southron Chieftain, but someone forgot and took their eyes off of her. Why? Because she was only a slave child." He bit off another chunk of the bannock. "It pays to know who is passing you the cup." And who gifted you the slave, he added silently.

"The histories told that Mastarna was murdered by Porsenna."

"Porsenna? No, Porsenna never got the chance. The girl beat him to it. Sometimes you don't even have to utter a word or pick up a knife to effect the destruction of another. An act of generosity, a gift, can be as deadly as a viper in a box."

The Bard shook his head and sighed. "You Gärians are mad. No wonder your Empire collapsed."

"I am not a Gärian," he said softly.

"Tell me, Corvus, was the Emperor Calticas really a monster?"

"What?"

"Calticas, it is said that he was a monster, a man with the head of a beast, a uilebheist."

Corvus laughed, "No."

"Oh, it was…."

"He had strange eyes like a cat and hair that grew out from his head and neck like a lion's mane, but in other respects, he was normal. I have known a stranger."

"Really? I once saw a uilebheist, a Fomóire, I think, but I was only a child, I didn't really understand what it was."

"There are stranger things. Porsenna had a Hastion of women their skins the colour of jet, and Maxim had a cohort of Cynocephali as personal guards."

"Cyno…"

"Men with fur on their faces, they looked like hounds. They come from the deserts beyond Keme, savages, but they were loyal to Maxim."

"Vargr?"

"That is what you called these raiders last night." Without waiting for an answer, he pushed on, "'Vargr,' that's a Gothad word, it means; Wolfheads. Does it not? But today Wal called them 'Shee,' and you said they were an archaic race of men from the time before the Great Flood. Which is it?"

The young Bard paused for thought and then said, "Lady MacRoth prefers to think of them as 'Vargr' because to accept them for what they are is too frightening for her, werewolves and wild men she can understand."

"Why, what are they then?"

Wal began loudly issuing orders for the men to pack up again; Tàmh saw the opportunity to excuse himself from the conversation. "I must go." He almost leapt to his feet, "We'll talk later."

Corvus watched him go. He knew that there had to be more to this than the usual casual raids by yet another tribe of barbarians out of Mōmos knows where, but the Bard was studiously avoiding explaining precisely what was going on, and Corvus could feel his own anger rising. He hated playing games and being lied to, but the feeling that someone or something was having a great joke at his expense had grown since yesterday. At some point, he would have to push the Bard into answering his questions, whether he wanted to or not, which could lead to a difficult situation. The Albans were hot-headed and quick to take offence; if things got heated, he knew that the warriors would not be slow to come to their Bard's aid, and things could get out of hand very quickly.

Corvus smiled to himself. Was he really worried if 'things got out of hand?' Strange, he thought, am I honestly concerned whether some hairy arsed Highlander would pull a sword on me? Surely not, he chided himself. Well, Corvus, you are getting too old for this life. Maybe farming is about all you're fit for. Are you now so slow and stupid that these hairy windbags actually intimidate you? He dismissed the thoughts as nonsense. He had never really cared if he lived or died since the palace guards took his family away, so why should he begin now. Anyway, according to the phantom in his dream last night, he was already dead. Perhaps the Bard was correct; there were uilebheist walking the world. Maybe he was the monster. A monster that was afraid to fight.

No, he decided; he wasn't a monster, only a man. A man driven by hatred and rage that had twisted over the long years into a pitiless thirst for revenge. A thirst he had sated with the blood of every fool that had crossed his single-minded path of destruction through their damned Empire. Many had called him a monster, and possibly they had been right; he had become a demon, a uilebheist more terrible than the Bard's fantasies. Once, he had been just a simple boy growing up in a world of safety and kindness, a world of bright days and long cool nights full of music and laughter. It was the Gärian Empire that had taken him away from that world and made him into what he was. It was the Gärian Empire that he had made pay a terrible price. He had brought it to its knees, but at what cost to himself?

Still lost in thought, he went through the ritual of checking the horse's harness and climbing aboard. He did not even notice it had started raining again until a stream of water found its way down his neck and spine to pool in the seat of his breaches.

Daydreaming again, he scolded himself but continued anyway to let the real world slip a little. Trying desperately to think of better things, things no less painful, but at least without the terrible sense that he was being forced to review his past as a drowning man does before the darkness swallows his soul. He forced the dark images out of his mind and went back to the vineyards and olive groves of his childhood, long hot summer days running wild with his sister, Malina. Spending a whole childhood doing nothing much at all.

Abruptly a memory flashed into his mind. Light hazel eyes, smiling eyes, set deep in a knot of wrinkles and creases, a dark brown face, skin like saddle leather, such kind eyes, always smiling. He fought to find a name for that face, searching the corners of his memories. The tutor, my 'Mu'adib,' what was his name? He came from Keme, the Black Land, across the Middle Sea. What was his name?

The old Kemenite had been an excellent teacher, a man who let his charges think they were doing exactly what they wanted to do while all the time they were learning. Only now, looking back, could he really appreciate how carefully planned were all those seemingly aimless days. The old teacher made it so simple; a walk in the woods or a day at the market would become a chance to learn something new. Corvus realised he had been teaching all the time; he never stopped teaching. But what had been his name?

"Andreas listen to me," the tutor said one day, unexpectedly quite stern. "Whatever happens in your life, always remember who you are and from where and from whom you came. Be true to those things no matter what happens. Men may exult you or try to break you, but never forget, never forget who you are, and never forget those you love and who love you.

"The praises and curses of men are as fleeting as leaves in the breeze, riches come and go, and so does power. The only thing you must hold onto is who you are."

Strange, he had never really thought about what the old teacher had told him that long afternoon by the river. Corvus had always believed that it was the sight of the thunderclouds in the eastern sky that had depressed him, but that night's storm had brought more than wind and rain. Had he known? Had he sensed it? Had he overheard something?

The image of the old Kemenite lying dead at the feet of the palace guards shocked Corvus. Had he really forgotten? The tutor had tried to stop them from taking Malina, he had fought them with a ladle from the kitchen, and the soldiers had jeered as they hacked him down. However, he had marked one of them badly, badly enough for Corvus to recognise the scar on the man's face fifteen years later. That mark had been the man's death sentence.

Corvus pulled the hood up over his head and wrapped the great cloak tightly around him. There once was a time when he could use the memories of his revenge like a candle flame to warm his heart, but now all they did was make him feel colder inside than he did out. That palace guardsman died as painfully as Corvus could arrange, but only after he had seen everything stripped from him, his family scattered and destitute, his home destroyed, and his name reviled publicly as a traitor. Then death, but not the sweet kiss of swift death, but the terrible death of the traitor. Blinded and gelded, broken on the wheel and then impaled, done properly a man could last a week, the man had lasted three days, three days in a market square while people gawked, laughed, and spat on him. Finally, Corvus watched him tarred and burnt. He wondered why he had never felt pity until now, a twinge of regret? He dismissed it, too late for guilt, and as for pity, he had spared the lives of the man's family, and that had been enough compassion for him.

"Nebti!" That was it. He realised he had spoken aloud, and several faces were now watching him.

"Corvus?" Svein pulled up his horse side him. "Are you alright?"

"Fine, I'm fine." He looked around quickly, trying to gain his bearings. They were deep into the forest now. The dense ancient trees crowded around them, and the track had degenerated into little more than a muddy trail through the bracken. Above them, the light was waning. Corvus looked up to check if it was the time of day or just the canopy's shadow that formed the great green vault high above them. From what he could see, it was late; he must have been daydreaming all afternoon. At least the rain had stopped, he thought; small mercies.

"Wal says we should camp soon."

"Camp?" he cast his gaze about. "Where?"

"He says there's a clearing a mile or so ahead."

Corvus subdued the instinct to lecture the boy on the indignities and dangers of camping in the forest; instead, he just pushed back his hood and rubbed his face. Svein was watching him closely, intently even. "What?"

The young Gothad pulled his horse nearer until the two animals trotted side by side, leaned even closer and said quietly, "I don't understand what's going on, Corvus. I mean, what are we doing here, and why did you agree with what Lady MacRoth wanted? I think she's insane; my father said that pregnancy sends them mad sometimes. We should have slipped away in the night." His young face was full of confusion.

"And have taken our chances, hmm? Running in the dark?" Corvus smiled sadly. "Good plan. Even if we could have made it off the Crannog alive, which we would not have, then found our weapons and stolen fresh horses. How long do you think we would have lasted out here? In the dead of night and in the middle of a thunderstorm? How far would we have got?" He did not wait for an answer. "Oh, and you're still in pain from yesterday, still finding it hard to breathe, and your muscles are as tight as rigging. So how long?"

Svein looked like a scalded child. "Not long." He said softly.

"Not far either."

The young Gothad's face brightened and as his hand fell to the pummel of his sword. "But we would have given them a good fight, err Corvus?" Corvus had seen the boy wield his broadsword with its strange designs and razor edges. It was quite a weapon and, though young and still fine-boned, he had the strength and speed of a warrior but not yet the instinct to kill.

"Don't be in such a hurry to die, boy. All those heroic sagas by the fireside have softened your wits. Death is not heroic; the only heroes are the survivors." Svein tried to protest, but Corvus talked over him. "There is no Valhöll, no hero's hall, no heaven. Guard your life well, boy; you'll be a long time dead."

Svein found it impossible to argue. Corvus' tone was as hard as his stare. His eyes were like emeralds; they glittered unnaturally. It was like catching the gaze of a basilisk. For the first time since they had met at Fluchtburgen, Svein felt afraid of the man; there was something terrible just behind those eyes, something inhuman. The Gothad King Faresheued had called him 'Valravn', Raven, and he strode through many of their sagas dispensing death and destruction to nations. But Svein had always thought of him as a myth until his uncle had summoned him to meet the stranger who was to take him to Noatun. He had wondered why everyone had seemed so on edge that morning. The old Völva, Gyrd, had been in hysterics outside the hall, but Svein, like most of the men, took no notice of the old crone as they shoved past her. Maybe, he thought, I should have listened. She had been screaming something about a 'gjenganger', a spirit that had returned.

"I..." his mouth was too dry to form words. He swallowed hard and tried again. "I just don't understand."

"Be calm, boy," Corvus leaned closer, "None of this makes much sense to me either. We'll talk later tonight."

Svein tried to relax a little and let his horse drift from Corvus' side. In truth, he knew he understood little of what had happened last night or why they were going on this insane march into the North. Every time someone told him why, the reasons changed. Even the names and the nature of the raiders had changed overnight. In the last few days, he had been beaten unconscious by a group of thieves, attacked, and almost killed in the forest and threatened with death by a mad woman; now, he was being dragged into someone else's war. He did not like Albans anyway. They were a dour bunch, sullen and miserable. Corvus was wrong. If they had managed to get their weapons back, the two of them would have easily fought their way out of the Crannog. These Albans were not real warriors, all noise and showing off, up close they had no real stomach for a proper fight.

Corvus watched as the young Gothad, lost in his own thoughts, drifted away. He was a good lad, a reasonable companion and brave. Like most Gothads, Corvus had known. Svein was full of bravado and willing to fight anything, a willingness not often matched by skill but full of passion and hot-headed eagerness. Those, though, who matched skill with bravery, were formidable warriors and terrifying in battle. Men like Jarven Olson. A tremendous hulking barrel-chested bear of a man. A good friend and a brave warrior, Corvus caught a fleeting memory of Jarven's booming laughter. Yes, he thought, this would have surely amused him.

Corvus and Sevius Mastarna had campaigned for nearly a decade beyond the northern frontier before an uneasy peace could be imposed. Sevius Mastarna had always blamed the land; the terrain was impossible, wild, rugged, and cold, always so bloody cold. However, as Corvus had identified it, the problem wasn't the terrain or the weather; it was the people. The Empire could never fully conquer the northwest because it was made up of people like Jarven Olson, Mer MacLeech, Big Wal, and their like. Fierce, rugged men who owe no allegiance to anything more than themselves and their Lords. Even the Southrons had a single King that commanded loyalty from all their tribal leaders, not so with the Albans, the Kerns and the Gothads. They followed no single leader; each tribe or clan or war band seemed to do as they pleased. That is until they all come together to unite against some common enemy, as the Albans and the Kerns had united against the Gärian Empire.

In the decades past, other kingdoms had fallen before the Gärian's might like wheat before the scythe. Ancient Aelathia, Ghalia, Narbonensis and Keme all capitulated in less than fifty years. Parthia and the nomads of the Rhos soon after. The Flamen Martialis, the Cabiri Priests, they had turned Val Gär from a stinking cesspool into the heart of an Empire in a hundred years. Gäria had seemed invincible. But when the Priest King's eyes turned to the northwest, beyond the Spine of the World to the lands beyond the North wind, only failure followed.

The last of the Flamen Martialis, the Lars Maurcus Marcellinus, had died at Malum fighting the Vanda tribes, plunging the Empire into chaos. It took a brutal civil war to drive out the Lars, the Priest-Kings, and throw off the yoke of their tyrannical theocracy in favour of the ideals of true Empire. The Gerousia and the Ephors elected Calticas Nefandous, the richest, most powerful, and most feared man in Gäria, as Tyrannos, and immediately he set Corvus and Sevius Mastarna to quell the northwest tribes once and for all.

Corvus had broken the Vanda at the second battle of Malum, but never in all his time in the North had he believed the Empire would indeed rule here, and it had not. Beyond the Vanda stood Èathel, the kingdom of the Southrons. They defeated Mastarna at Saenaessas and again at Rofene, butchering the Seventeenth and Nineteenth Hastions and driving the Gärians out of Èathel.

It fell to Corvus to meet the Southron King, Anwealda, on the field of Heolfre, with two Hastions and eighteen thousand Vanda and Rhos auxiliaries. He could remember the way the Southron army had marched out onto the field, clad in heavy chain and scale armours, banging upon their long shields. They were the best standing army in the North, proud and undefeated, a magnificent sight, frightening even. The battle had raged for the whole day. The Southron's army was easily a match for the Gärian Hastions and held together with equal discipline; breaking their formations had been impossible. The two armies had spent the day slogging it out eye to eye while the allies and auxiliaries skirmished around them.

Corvus had known that there was no chance of withdrawal or allowing the battle to draw to a stagnant end; he had to win. He had to destroy the enemy, or he would pay the price of defeat with his life. He had no powerful patrician family to protect him like Sevius Mastarna, only the fickle favour of the half-human Tyrannos, Calticas Nefandous; if he had failed, he would have lost everything.

He pulled together the Gärian cavalry and the Rhos heavy horse in a mad gamble and threw them in a single mass against the rear of the Southron's right flank. Meanwhile, he personally led a small force of his best Hastati in a lightning sortie deep into the heart of the centre block. Distracted by the impact of the cavalry, the Southrons hesitated. The right flank almost broke, and confusion reigned just long enough for Corvus to get to the shield wall of Huscarls around the King. Huge men wielding great axes, they fought like devils, but in close combat, it was not enough to stop the Hastati.

The death of Anwealda caused panic within the Southron's ranks; the army splintered and broke, some tried to withdraw, some fought on, others scattered and ran. The battle was over; the butchering had begun. Corvus ordered that no Southron should be allowed to escape and pursued the survivors for days before reforming the Hastions and marching into the Mide, the heartland of Èathel, to lay waste the land by sword and fire, destroying everything in his path.

The campaign gave him the status he built upon and used to exact the revenge that had raged inside him for a lifetime. So long as he gave the Gärian's their bloody victories, he remained a hero, showered with accolades and gifts, untouchable. Unquestioned even by the Tyrannos Calticas himself, though Corvus knew that Calticas had always had suspicions of Corvus' intent. Calticas would allude to things, deliberately vague, make jokes and veiled comments, but never truly question Corvus' actions.

Calticas Nefandous was as cunning as a fox and as treacherous as a snake. Corvus could still clearly remember his strange cat-like yellow eyes watching him. It served Calticas well to use this ex-slave, the son of a fallen Noble, as a weapon against all those who opposed him. The Ephors and Gerontes feared Corvus because they did not know what drove him or how to corrupt him, so they were powerless against him. Calticas rewarded Corvus' victories by appointing him as the Tyrannos's Questor, judge and executioner. With free reign over the Empire, no one was beyond his grasp, no matter how powerful or high placed. For Corvus, the exhilaration of revenge itself had been matched only by the thrill of having to watch over his own shoulder. It became a bloody, flagitious, but intoxicating game.

Calticas' enemies waited a long time for their chance to act, plotting their treason in dark corners, waiting for their time to strike. Waiting for Corvus to be called away so that they could take their opportunity, and when the chance came, they were ready.

Sevius Mastarna had not been much of a General, and he was even less of a politician; as Governor of the Northwest Provinces, he let them slip through his fingers like a child dropping a glass bowl. He appointed idiots and thieves as regional administrators and surrounded himself with sycophants, catamites, and fools. The lowland Alban tribes saw their opening and rebelled. Emboldened by their actions, the Kerns took their chance to exploit the chaos, and the whole of the northwest exploded into war.

Corvus had known the threat to the Tyrannos but had returned to the northwest immediately. Why? He could not say why had he not refused or exposed the plotters? Why had he not warned Calticas? The man who had taken him out of slavery and given him power beyond belief? There were a dozen other Generals who could have taken the Hastions back into the northwest provinces, but it was he that returned, leaving Calticas exposed to the assassin's blade. Why? He had wondered for years over that; maybe it was his final act of revenge against the Empire. The assassin's blow that struck down Calticas left a wound through which the Empire would eventually bleed to death. Corvus had known that even before he had set out for the northwest.

When, as he had expected, the news of the death of the Emperor reached him, he was at the gates of Mur Ollamhan facing the most significant provincial rebellion the Empire had ever known. He had used it as a reason not to go back, promising the Gerousia that only after the Albans and Kerns had been smashed would he return with another victory in his bloody hands. Though even after he had destroyed the massed hordes at Sh'tey-Dochas, he continued to make excuses, time was needed to secure control, time to hunt down the last leaders, time for this, time for that.

Until the summons came, the new Tyrannos, Ekraun Porsenna, commanded him to attend an audience before the Gerousia and the Ephorate. It was a death sentence in the form of an invitation, an invitation he had no choice but to accept. Corvus returned to Val Gär for the last time. Insane though he had been at the end, Corvus had liked Calticas; even in the darkest of days, he had always kept a bleak sense of humour and a sharp wit. Ekraun Porsenna had no sense of humour at all, a dull little man, a common soldier with a common soldier's mentality. Pragmatic and unimaginative, Porsenna was led by the ear by anyone who could get close enough to whisper into it, and Corvus knew all too well who had gotten close enough to do so. Men of wealth and power, who hungered only for more, corrupt men who put gain and pleasure before all else. Petty men with petty concerns, each with an axe to grind and a gut full of venom. Porsenna was willing to give them what they wanted, and they treated him like a Tyrannos, although they tried hard to stop him from ruling like one.

Corvus returned to a Val Gär grown sick and debauched, her streets full of whores and hawkers, where rich men's slaves flaunted their wealth and garrison soldiers openly caroused while on duty. People petitioned him to act, restore order, and bring his loyal Hastions out of the northwest and into Val Gär itself. He only found their begging pathetic. They showered him with gifts and the promises of anything he wished so long as he would remove this dull-witted Soldier Emperor. One group of Ephors and Gerontes even offered him the throne! He had made them squirm for a week before he refused. He had set the wheel in motion as if he had struck the assassin's blow himself, and he would not do anything to stop the Empire's spin into destruction.

Corvus knew Porsenna feared him and that those around him demanded his death, but Porsenna had learnt fast. Dull he was, stupid he was not. For once, Corvus was taken totally by surprise when instead of being given the choice of the dagger or poison, the Tyrannos welcomed him, hailed him as a hero and called him brother. He was presented before the shocked Gerousia and Ephorate members hand in hand with the Tyrannos. It was the only clever act Porsenna did, by affirming Corvus as a trusted Consul and the new Governor of the northwest, he assured his own position. For an oath of loyalty to the Tyrannos, he was to be sent back to the northwest as one of the most powerful men in the Empire with five Hastions under his command and the vast riches of the north western provinces at his disposal. Moreover, Porsenna thought he would be secure in the knowledge that the Raven of Val Gär always stood ready to defend him. Corvus made the pledge, swore the oath, kissed the Tyrannos' ring, and left Val Gär forever.

The horse stopped, jarring him back to the real world; Wal had called a halt at the mouth of a large man-made clearing. The trees around its edge were now so dense it probably remained dark on the forest floor for most of the day. The Alban warriors collapsed into the bracken, rubbing tired feet and legs, while the mule packers unburdened their animals and began to make camp.

Corvus climbed down and led his horse into the midst of the activity, looking for someone to give the animal to. Horse-boy approached, smiled shyly from behind the edge of his hood, and took the horse's reins from him. Looking around, Corvus noticed Wal striding about issuing commands to the mule packers and the young warriors, the young men were surly and tired, but they obeyed his instructions. Wal kept good discipline and delegated well; Corvus admired that, maybe with more men like him, the Albans would have won at Sh'tey-Dochas.

Svein was walking around rubbing his side; he looked grey and ill. Corvus guessed that the pain was getting too much for him by now. It reminded Corvus that the old woman, Meg, had given him a pouch of herbs last night to relieve the pain of his arm. He flexed it quickly, it was healed completely, and he resolved to give the pouch to the boy later. Tàmh was already making himself comfortable on the ground near where some of the mule packers were building a fire. The Bard noticed his gaze and smiled timidly.

Corvus ignored him and walked across the clearing to where a huge deadfall lay; its moss-covered trunk looked like a giant's arrow pointing to the heart of the clearing. Time and travellers had stripped it of its branches and foliage, but the mass of its body would provide an ideal sheltered place to sit. It would be a good site, as it was the only blind spot in the clearing; from here he could see most of the area, but in the dark, he would be out of the firelight and shadowed by the body of the tree trunk. Anyone approaching from behind would not see him tucked in here until it was too late. As he kicked back the bracken around it and cleared a space to sit, he noticed that Horse-boy was approaching, bringing his bedroll and blankets. Struggling to balance them against the weight of the saddlebags slung over his shoulders as he picked his way unsteadily across the muddy clearing.

The youth arrived and almost reverently laid down the equipment before Corvus, gave another half-hidden shy smile and headed back to the horses. Strange boy, Corvus thought as he wadded his sleeping gear into the lee of the deadfall and sat down with his back against the soft moss, strange boy indeed. He registered a thought to make sure he asked the Bard more about that one.

He sat quietly for a while watching the mule packers and younger warriors going about their assigned duties, tending horses and mules, unpacking, collecting wood, building a fire, and preparing the meal. As soon as it was fully dark, they would light the fire but not before, because the smoke would be too easily seen from a distance, but they had to balance the need for light, heat, and hot food against the chance of the firelight and the smell attracting danger. Corvus knew the tactic, considered risk; need weighed against need. Wal made the choices and would carry responsibility.

They all left Corvus alone as the darkness drew in; only Rat-face approached and asked, "Are ye alright?" Corvus only nodded his reply. "Aye, Wal says to bring ye some food later." Rat-face scurried off, and Corvus made a mental note not to eat anything the boy brought him.

The food arrived after dark, but it was the Bard who brought it. "It's not particularly appetising, but at least it's hot." He handed Corvus a deep wooden bowl and a chunk of dark bread. "May I stay and talk with you?"

Corvus was about to say 'no' when he realised he had quite a store of questions of his own for the young Bard, so he just nodded and chewed on the bread. Tàmh swung his wineskin off his shoulder and sat down. He was even younger than Corvus had thought last night, an angular face with large dark eyes and a square chin; with long delicate hands, he unstopped the wineskin and took a drink.

"It's the Kerns, isn't it? Call them whatever you like. You're at war with the Kerns, again, aren't you?" Corvus was surprised how well Tàmh held his best intimidating stare, but the young Bard looked uncomfortable and stumbled to find an answer.

"Ah, I…well…." Tàmh tried to gather his thoughts quickly. He had been caught off guard, it was an old trick, but he had not expected it.

"Well?" Corvus demanded.

"Well, what?" asked Svein as he approached. He was carrying a small lantern and another wineskin. When he received no reply, he asked, "Should I go away?"

"No." Corvus put the bowl aside. "Sit down. The Bard here is explaining a few things to me."

Svein sat slowly down, "Like what?"

"Like why the Albans are at war with the Kerns again."

"Do they need a reason?" asked Svein wryly.

"No, we are not at war with the Kerns." Tàmh plunged in. "The 'Vargr', as Lady MacRoth calls them, are what we call 'Seelie'. They are ancient people of great power. They attacked the Kerns of Mahir-ushcu, and we hear tales that they have crossed the Guh'ach Moor and attacked the Gothads at Skjaldborg. Now they are pushing south, towards Reeachca, towards us."

"And the Kerns?"

"They have not been able to stop them. Their Overking Talorgan is a weak-minded man, and their tribes have fragmented."

"What of the Warlock, Mer MacLeech?"

The Bard's brows wrinkled. "Long dead, I should think."

"Like me." Corvus smiled, "So who are these 'Shee', as Wal called them?"

"The Sidhe, the Sìth. They are of the Tùsanach, the First People, the Daoine-Sìth. It is said they were driven underground after the Great War that ended the age of the Àrsaidh. Some tales say they were of the Àrsaidh too; maybe they are the last of them."

"Ar-see?" asked Svein exaggerating his own inability to pronounce the words.

The Bard shot him a disdainful look. "The Ancients who built Eagle's Craig and the great stone circles. They passed away long before your Empire crawled out of the mud." He moved on quickly before Corvus could react. "It is said their tribes made war upon each other and even upon An Talamh, the Great Mother, herself. They were great Magicians, powerful but Godless. Some tales say they destroyed themselves in a Great War; others say that the Gods struck them down."

Svein turned to Corvus and said, "Have you noticed how he never answers a question directly? Ask him a straightforward question, and you get a walk in the woods." Corvus nodded but without taking his eyes off the Bard.

Tàmh sighed loudly. "These are the Isheen. They came from the far western isles; we call them Sìth." He turned to Svein. "Your people call them Huldufolk, the Hidden People, I believe."

Corvus noticed even in the poor light of the lantern that the boy's face paled. "The Dock-Alfar," Svein replied slowly, "the People of the Mounds...."

Tàmh made an expression, Corvus was unsure if it was a grimace or a quickly subdued grin, but it was gone in an instant. "Aye, them."

"Troglodytes?" Corvus sneered. "People that live underground. You talked of them as some archaic race of powerful Magicians, not cave dwellers."

"They are powerful," said Tàmh earnestly.

"Oh yes? Then if they are so powerful, why have I never heard of them? I marched an army through these lands, remember?" He leaned closer to the Bard, "Your people have never forgotten, have you?"

"No."

"If these Sìth are so powerful, where were they then? And, if they are so powerful, why do they live in holes in the ground?" Before Tàmh could reply, Corvus thrust on. "If you expect me to swallow these fantasies of yours, then you had best learn your craft better. I'm not some superstitious child frightened of the dark and shadows." He deliberately glanced at Svein, "Or gullible enough to believe all the shite you would feed me."

Tàmh stared blankly back at the old warrior and said slowly, "I know they're real, Corvus; I was held prisoner by them for a year and a day. Why they live underground, I don't know, but, whatever you think, I swear to you they are more powerful than you can imagine."

"They released you?" asked Svein.

"No, I escaped."

Corvus took one of the wineskins and drank long and slow;

when he had finished, he passed it to Svein and then turned to the Bard. "If I am to believe you, then these 'people' have been around since the fall of the Titans. Why should they show themselves now? Why did they not march out against the Empire or against the Gothads? So why now?"

"I don't know. They usually shun the worlds of men. The Druids and Seers have no idea either."

"My people have warred against them," added Svein. "It is said that the Gothads of Hauge fought a blood feud for a hundred years against a tribe of the Dock-Alfar."

"Who won?" asked Tàmh.

"Neither, the saga tells that eventually, when all the warriors and men on both sides were dead, the women took up their swords and spears, and they were more terrible than their menfolk. No one won because no one survived."

"What were they fighting over?"

"A tree."

"Now that sounds more like the Kerns." Corvus laughed. "So why do you need me? If these troglodytes are so powerful, what am I supposed to do? Make up an extra number in the body count?"

Tàmh smiled slightly. "You are Corvus of Val Gär, the greatest warrior to set foot on our soil; you defeated our Kings, broke our armies, crushed the Southrons and the Kerns and..."

"Enough," snapped Corvus. "I had three Hastions; sixty thousand men, double that in auxiliaries, and the resources of an Empire behind me then, boy. I did not come alone."

"You'll do." Tàmh stood up. "The Seers foretold your return, 'the great Raven will return from the East,' they said." He picked up the bowl and wineskin. "You are the Raven; you will stop the Sith."

Before Corvus could say anything, the Bard turned to walk away. "Damn! Damn, damn, damn!" Corvus leapt up, hauled the young Bard off his feet, and dragged him back to the shadow of the deadfall.

For a moment, Tàmh thought the hand that was wrapped across his mouth was going to rip his head off. The old warrior's strength was astonishing. He was down and in the cover of the tree trunk before he could even think to struggle. The Gothad had covered the lantern, and all Tàmh could make out was the silhouette of Corvus above him, the vice-like grip slipped instantly from his mouth to his throat pinning him down against the damp earth as the other hand clamped onto his wrist, wrenching, and twisting his arm like a spring sapling, the pain was unbearable. Desperately he managed to choke a few words out, "Please, please don't.... kill me."

Corvus glowered, "By Mōmos' teeth, boy, I'll gut you right here and feed you to these damned heather eaters."

A wave of horror paralysed Tàmh as he realized he could still make out Corvus' eyes against the darkness; they gleamed like an animal's. A cold reflected green against the blackness. Long forgotten nightmares flooded back as absolute panic gripped him. He began to fight with all his strength, kicking and thrashing about with his free arm. It was pointless, Corvus' grip only tightened, but now the Gothad was on him too, pinning his free arm and his legs down.

Corvus released the Bard's wrist and slammed the palm of his hand hard up under the young man's ribs, driving most of the air out of his lungs and all the fight. Pushing his face as close as he safely could to the Bard's, he whispered, "If I wanted to kill you, you'd be dead already. Now, be quiet and listen to me; I am no longer going to play your game. You either tell me the truth, or I will kill you, right here right now, and then I'll slip back to the Crannog and slit Jorunn's throat. Do you understand?" He took Tàmh's trembling as acknowledgement, "Good." Corvus pulled his long knife and held it close to the Bard's face. "Now you're going to answer my questions and...."

Suddenly someone screamed, and the clearing exploded into activity. Svein swore and grabbed for his sword, "Shut up," growled Corvus and thrust his hand back over the Bard's mouth, "Wait."

All three lay motionless, silent in the dark until it became apparent they were not the focus of the alarm. Something was happening on the northern edge of the clearing, and now the warriors were plunging in after whatever it was. Corvus released the Bard, jumped to his feet, and went after the Albans without a word.

Svein looked at Tàmh, shook his head, and got up. "Here,"

he dragged the Bard to his feet.

"I thought he was going to kill me."

Svein laughed, "So did I."

Corvus reached the edge of the clearing and pushed through the bracken. Beyond it, there was a small animal trail leading away northwards down which the Albans had gone. In the distance, he could see their torches guttering in the darkness.

He quickly caught up with them by the bank of a small stream, they had formed into a semi-circle with their backs to him and their torches raised. They all seemed frozen, like statues of men, transfixed by something. Corvus shoved his way through them until he could see the thing that was holding them spellbound.

In the centre of the semi-circle, half crouched to the ground, was a warrior. He recognised her instantly; it was the woman that had attacked him the previous day. She was at bay, like a wild animal, holding off her attackers with a strange black bladed dagger in one hand and a struggling boy in the other. Her head snapped up, and by the look in her eyes, he knew she recognised him too.

Corvus saw it was Rat-face being swung about by the scruff of his neck like a mannequin, a human shield. The boy's eyes were wide and glassy, and he was covered in blood, but from the soft whining coming from his throat, he was still alive. Apart from the boy's whimpering only the strange bestial growling coming from the woman's throat broke the deathly silence. Corvus raised his free hand, the palm outstretched and, keeping his sword down by his side, lowered himself to her level. She snarled like a wolf and shook the boy vigorously. Corvus tried to weigh up the situation as fast as possible. He could see she was wounded; her clothes and armour were soaked with blood, there was also a fresh wound on her scalp. She looked weak; in fact, she was shaking violently. Fear or tiredness, he did not know, probably not fear, he decided.

"Corvus, leave it," warned Wal.

Corvus hushed him and slowly inched forward, keeping eye contact with the woman. She backed a little, and the Albans surged forward. Corvus angrily waved them back. When he felt he was near enough, just outside the arc of her knife, he stopped and waited, watching her intensely, waiting for her to act. Her eyes kept flickering from his to the Albans, to the stream and back to his. He realised something about the water scared her; she was more concerned with it than with him or the Albans. Fear of drowning?

He dismissed it instantly; it was barely deep enough to reach her waist, superstition probably.

Suddenly something in her eyes changed, decision, but she moved so fast that he almost missed it. With a considerable thrust, she flung her prisoner at him and leapt towards the stream. Corvus dodged the boy and threw himself after her. Grabbing wildly, he caught little more than a few strands of her ragged cloak, but it was enough to bring her up short.

His own momentum slammed him into her back, and they both went sprawling into the stream. Hitting the water was like smashing into a wall of ice. The shock of the cold burst the air out of his lungs, and it was only the frantic struggling of his captive that kept him from blacking out completely. He threw his arms around her and held on, but she was incredibly lithe and strong, twisting, kicking, and punching him with all her might; it was like trying to hold onto a tiger in a snowdrift. He immediately realised she was slipping away from him. Where were the others? Why weren't they helping? She managed to get an arm completely free and slammed her fist into his face; his head flew back and cracked against the stones in the stream bed. Ice water filled his mouth, and the world abruptly went black.

Then in that instant, he saw it; a hand was laying silver coins on his eyes, in the distance the sound of wailing, lamenting, they were wrapping linen across his face. Corvus screamed and fought against it, clawing at life, dragging it back. He would not die, not here, not again.

As his head cleared the surface, he began to hit out madly, something was in his hand, and he struck again and again with it until she stopped fighting, stopped struggling, stopped moving.

"CORVUS!" Wal was screaming at him, his face only inches away. "Stop! In Bel's name, stop!"

Corvus froze.

"Stop," Wal put a hand on his shoulder, "Easy now, man. You're alright."

"Am I?" Corvus looked at the blood-covered rock in his hand and dropped it.

Chapter 15

"O wad some Power the giftie gie us
To see oursels as ithers see us!"

To a Louse
Robert Burns

Awareness slowly crept back into Rànd's mind, but she knew enough not to move. She just remained still, listening and sensing her surroundings. Her hands and legs were tied, even her ankles and her head hurt, her whole body hurt, and she was wet. She remembered the water and tried to suppress a shudder; she hated running water, rivers and streams. Her people had always taught her to fear running water, it was the lifeblood of An Talamh, the Goddess, but it can carry away your life as easily as it sweeps away the autumn leaves. The Isheen had many sacred pools, but few ever dared to swim in them.

Putting the memory out of her mind, she concentrated on what was going on around her. She was near a fire, she could feel the heat and smell it, and when she turned her head slightly, she could make out the flickering shadows cast across her eyelids. Food, she could smell food, or what to Dhaoine passed as food. There were voices, dozens of them, Albannaich, males though, no women, A war band, warriors going where? She wondered how far into the South Mathan-Bàn had reached, had he taken Creag an Eagail? North probably.

She could not understand the language of these Dhaoine, she had never learnt; even though her brother had always insisted on trying to teach her a few odd words, she had actively refused. Stupid, she chided herself, but she had never dreamed she would fall into their hands. Anyway, they had too many languages, and they were cumbersome and difficult to speak, little more than guttural animal grunts. Dhaoine were children of the soil, mud grubbers and despoilers; she despised everything about them.

Amid the noise, a voice caught her attention. Him, she

recognised the tone and sounds of his speech, the Old Warrior. She fought a rising panic in her breast; whatever he was, he was not one of them. He looked different, dressed differently and even smelled different, but it was his eyes that gave it away. His eyes reflected in the darkness; they shone, bright and green, like her own. He was not a Daonna, but she could not believe that he was of the Sìth; she tried to calm herself and think. A changeling, maybe? Something masquerading as a Daonna. A Galioin possibly or worse; a Fomóire. He had defeated her in the woods, fighting like she had never seen a Daonna fight, too strong for a Daonna, too fast, and then tonight, he showed no injuries from yesterday at all. Though after a day of rest, she had barely begun to recover, yet he was as strong as a bear and fast enough to catch her.

Rànd chanced, turning her head a fraction further and opening one eye a little. From what she could make out, she was amid their encampment; there were dozens of them milling around a massive fire, a cauldron and spit had been set up near it, and one of them was dealing out food to the others. They were all far too interested in filling their stomachs to pay her much attention. They were rough, ugly, and dirty, with little intelligence and no skills. They ate like dogs, and they stank of the awful brews their kind regularly drank; it oozed out of their skins and made them smell like rotten sheep's carcasses.

She heard the Old Warrior's voice again, nearer, but behind her now. Closing her eyes tightly, she feigned a moan of pain and tried to roll onto her left side. A sudden real pain almost ruined her act. The ribs in her left side felt like they were broken and ground together as her weight moved onto them. The pain was intense, but she kept her eyes shut and tried to will it away.

Slowly as the pain subsided, she opened her eyes again. He was standing nearby talking to two others, a big hair covered Albannach warrior and a smaller young Daonna, who for a moment she mistook for one of her own. Behind them hovered another youth, tall and blond; Rànd recognised him from their encounter yesterday. She could tell by the way he held himself and moved that he, too, was still in pain.

The Old Warrior and the big Albannach were arguing over

something, probably what to do with her, she guessed, and the young one was obviously trying to mediate between them. She was surprised to see that the Albannach, probably their Chief, was not in any way awed by the Old Warrior's presence. They were standing close, staring into each other's eyes and shouting, while the young one tried to keep his place physically between them. Obviously, she concluded, the Albannaich knew nothing of the Old Warrior's true nature.

She watched for a few moments trying to concentrate upon him, to try to see through the fith-fath that clouded his real nature, but the glamour was too powerful. She could make out almost nothing through it, only the vague aura around him and possibly another presence close to him, something as insubstantial as a shadow in the moonlight, but there nonetheless. Rànd tried harder to focus on the shadow form, to centre her perception on it, and see it with her mind instead of her eyes.

Slowly the shadow form became clear, but as it did, it shifted, flowed, and changed. For a moment, she recognised the God Crom Cróich, wrapped in the feathered tuigen cloak of a High Druid; about his goatlike head hung a bloody red crescent. Then the form flowed to become an old man, old but straight-backed and proud. For a second, Rànd was confused; he looked harmless enough, but then she saw his eyes; they were ancient beyond imagining and as cold and pitiless as the Northwind in winter. Then it transformed again, and for an instant, Rànd saw Death herself. The eternal grinning skull of death, a figure clothed in burial shroud with ashes upon its brow, inevitable, unforgiving, unrelenting, Death.

Wal thrust his face forward to as near as he could get to the Gärian and growled through teeth covered in foam, "That "thing" almost killed Ker and Ned, and I say we kill it now."

Corvus stood his ground impassively against the sprayed onslaught. "I said, no."

Wal shook a bawled fist at Corvus and roared, "You! You don't order me about. You almost killed two of my boys yeself!"

Tàmh, who had been trying to stop Big Wal from physically attacking the Gärian, abruptly realized his presence between them was probably not going to solve anything. "Wal, calm down, please. It was an accident." He said, stepping aside.

"They shouldn't have got involved," sneered Corvus.

"Accident! ye almost drowned them, ye mad bastard!"

Corvus snorted and turned away. "She's awake."

"What?" barked Wal.

"She's awake," repeated Tàmh.

All three stared across at the female warrior. "What do you want to do with her, Corvus?" asked Tàmh.

"Well, if she is one of these 'Sìth' or 'Shee' or whatever you call them, then she may be able to help."

"Help us?" Wal spat. "That "thing" will not help us! Don't you know what that is? Anything it does or says will be lies."

Corvus turned back to the young Bard. "You said you spent time with them."

Tàmh nodded, "Yes, as a prisoner."

"So, you can speak their language."

"Aye, a little, yes, but..."

"A little will do." Corvus grabbed Tàmh by the arm and dragged him over to the Sìth warrior.

Wal glared angrily at Svein, who merely shrugged and followed.

"Ask her name."

Tàmh crouched down and asked, "Dè ant-ainm a tha ort?"

Rànd cleared her throat and lied, "Is mise Sradag nighean Seileach, De na sìthichean Isheen. Cò th 'annad?"

"She says she is Sradag, daughter of Seileach of the Isheen."

"Isheen?"

Tàmh looked up at the old warrior, "A tribe of the Daoine-Sìth."

Corvus ignored the look of triumph on Tàmh's face and asked. "Can she understand us?"

"Is mise Tàmhasg MacKeelta, tha mi `nam Bàrd. Am bheil thu a' tuigsinn Albannach?"

Rànd shook her head slowly, "Chan eil Albannach."

"She says not."

Wal shook his head disbelievingly.

Corvus crouched beside Tàmh. "Translate what I say exactly. No embellishments. Understand?"

"Yes, but..."

"No 'buts'."

"I'll try."

"Good." He fixed his gaze on the Isheen. "Now tell her this; My name is Corvus. Yesterday you tried to ambush us, the boy and myself. Tonight, I could have killed you, but I spared your life." Corvus paused to allow Tàmh to catch up. "These are Alban clansmen, and the one behind me is their leader; he wants to cut your throat right now, do you understand?"

Rànd fought the impulse just to snarl and instead nodded her head slowly, never taking her eyes of Corvus. He was cunning, trying to gain her confidence, but she had seen what walked in his shadow, and it chilled her to even look at him.

"I am the only thing between them and you," he paused again for Tàmh. "Now I want you to answer my questions, no lies, I'll know if you lie." He turned to Tàmh, "Does she understand?"

Rànd understood. She had no doubt that even though he said he could not speak her language, he had the power to know if she lied. "Innis don Galioin; Dèan na tha thu ag iarraidh. Chan innis mi dad dhut."

"She says she will tell you nothing."

Corvus didn't need the translation; what she meant was written all over her face. Up close, she had a strange animal-like beauty that reminded him of something he couldn't quite remember. Her eyes, though held something else, a tint of fear or maybe a gleam of knowledge, secret knowledge. Instinctively he seized the

Isheen by the hair and dragged her head forward until they were almost eye-to-eye. "What do you see?"

She could smell him, taste him even, the air from his lungs, and feel the heat of his breath on her skin. It was as if he was trying to stare into her soul, and it took every ounce of control she had to stare right back, unflinchingly. Looking, though desperately trying not to see, it was of no use.

The Bard repeated the question.

Was that it? Was he looking for his own reflection in her eyes? She deliberately drew her gaze away. "Nothing. I see nothing," she lied.

He shook her head, brutally snarling something vituperative that she did not need any interpretation to understand.

"Don't lie. He can tell when you lie."

Rànd looked up into the Bard's open, gentle face and said, "Tell him; I saw nothing."

Corvus swore and shoved her back onto the ground; by the time she had managed to regain herself, he had stalked off. She watched him go, wondering if his anger was because he didn't believe her or because he did.

Ker sat upon a log near the fire; he had been placed there by Wal himself and wrapped in one of the other warrior's cloaks. Someone, he could not remember who had given him a drink, not of rough mead but of mulled wine and spirit. He sat gazing into the maser, lost in thought. He was amazed; for the first time in his life, they actually seemed concerned about him. Even the older warriors seemed to care. They patted him on the shoulder and murmured reassurance as they passed. For Ker, it was strange but exciting. He began to daydream about how their faces would change with wonder as he told his story.

The Sentatii mute was looking after Ned, although they had not been able to wake him yet. Big Wal and the others were tight-lipped and grim-faced about it. Some of the younger warriors cast dangerous glances at the Sith woman and the foreigners, mumbling about revenge if Ned died. Ker secretly hoped Ned would.

Ker would tell them a fantastic tale of how he was a hero, how he had discovered the Sith woman, how he had saved Ned, and they would accept him at last as a man, as a warrior. Here was his chance. Then Ned would open his eyes and his great big stupid mouth and ruin it all. Whatever he said, they would ask Ned, and Ned, being Ned, would tell them the truth. Ker swilled his drink around in the wooden cup. Damn Ned.

Well, Ker thought to himself, better get the story straight, something believable. Close enough to the truth to fit in with whatever the idiot will say when they wake him, but also something that will make me look good. Ker hoped that with a bit of luck, Ned had taken enough of a whack on the head that he'd forgotten most of what happened. Ned was never very good at getting any story right, so he'd probably only confuse things, but all the same, Ker knew Ned was going to tell them things that would drop him in the shite, well and proper.

It had been after the camp had begun to settle down, and everyone was more interested in filling their bellies when Ker had slipped away. He had done it before when he had gone out with the clansmen hunting or chasing raiders. He had slipped away as quietly as possible into the forest edge and begun to circle the camp. It was fun, and nobody ever missed him, let alone caught him. It seemed to be a rule that if no one could find him, then no one worried about him or tried to find him work to do, out of sight, out of mind.

His plan was to wait until the camp fully settled down, then sneak back in to see what he could steal. Mostly it would be a few mouthfuls of wine or something insignificant, occasionally something personal, but seldom anything really valuable or noticeable. Small annoyances. He would then hide it in the bracken, under a distinctive rock, or by a tree and return to his bed. Ker understood that it wasn't the thing he stole that mattered. Sometimes he wouldn't even bother to retrieve them; it was the act of stealing that he enjoyed. The fact that he could get as close possible to these big tough, hard men and take from them anything he wished, and they never knew a thing about it, was where the fun in it was.

The following day they would wander around stupidly searching for their missing possessions; occasionally, they would even mount a search of the camp, even searching the gilles and slaves, but they never found the things he had taken from them. That was really amusing for him, as he would enthusiastically help in the search.

Once or twice, he had gone so far as to plant his loot on one of the others, it was dangerous, but the trouble it caused was wonderful. He had gotten the Sentatii mute, Nissien, whipped like a dog for stealing a ring. Serves him right though, he was that Gothad bitch Jorunn's favourite, and he had it coming to him. Ker loved to dwell on the havoc he had caused. However, his best was when he had stolen the jewel from the pummel of Big Wal's dirk and planted it on Hamish MacReul. The result had caused real trouble because the MacReuls were a powerful sept, twenty cousins and brothers sworn personally to Angus MacRoth, and Hamish was their leader. Accusations were made, knives were drawn, and blood would have been spilt if that Gothad bitch had not intervened again. The MacReuls still carried the injustice though Hamish had died a year ago in a skirmish with Kern raiders.

It had been Ker's intention to have some such fun tonight; his target was to have been the foreigners. First, he wanted to see what he could pilfer from the warriors, then he would have raided the foreigner's belongings, taken anything of interest and planted anything he had taken from the clansmen. He had snatched a small bronze covered lantern and had been trying to slip away into the shadows when Ned, the big lumbering ox, had spotted him and decided to follow. That was going to make things impossible for Ker, so he had to get rid of him fast. Earlier, while looking for water for the cauldron, he had found an animal path outside of the clearing that led to a burn, so he led Ned down it.

Ned had caught up with him as they reached the stream. "What ye doin'?" Ned's big soppy face loomed out of the darkness at Ker as he knelt to light for the small lantern he had 'borrowed'.

"Shut up. Stupid!" The ember he'd brought caught quickly, and the lantern sprung to life.

Ned's expression dropped at Ker's tone. Trying desperately to understand what his friend was doing, he decided to point out, "Ya should nae' be out in the dark, ye could get lost an' eaten by beasties, and anyway they'll be lookin' for ye ta clean up soon."

"No, they won't," Ker jumped to his feet. "Unless you've told them." He thrust his face towards the bigger youth's.

Ned's eyes blinked innocently, "No'wa, I did nae' say...."

"Nothin', right?"

"Aye."

"Better not have."

Ned fell silent as Ker held up the lantern and looked around. The cow horn cover of the little bronze oil lantern had a small hole in it that threw out a beam of light into the darkness.

"What ye lookin' for?" asked Ned.

"Something." True enough, he thought, in fact, I have no idea.

"Ho," the bigger youth gazed around intently. "What?"

Ker sighed; the night's fun had been ruined, he couldn't do anything with this idiot following him, anyway, he decided, there'd be tomorrow. The thought of the castle at Loch Racholl cheered him a little. Ag was there, and Ag was even better sport than Ned, not as much of an idiot, but gullible and a cry baby to boot. Yes, he decided, tomorrow would be better. He gave Ned his most malevolent grin, turned, blew out the lamp and walked off.

"What ya, eh? Ker, where ye goin'?" Ned panicked by the sudden darkness grabbed him.

"Get off!" Ker fought himself free of the big youth's hand. "Ge....." It was then that he saw it.

A huge figure silently arose from the bracken behind Ned like a coal-black shadow against the dark of the night. Ker froze.

"What?" Ned just about noticed something was wrong before it hit him. Ker guessed it used the pummel of its dagger by the sickening sound it made as it slammed across the back of Ned's head. The big idiot went down without a noise. Ker was sure he was dead. Suddenly the ability to move returned to Ker. He flung the lantern at the shadow and ran, but he was too slow; he made only four strides before he was snatched off his feet and dragged backwards. At that point, he could remember, with shame, that his bowels emptied themselves, and he screamed at the top of his lungs. His struggling took the creature by surprise as he managed to get a couple of good wild punches and kicks at it before it spun him around and seized him by the throat. He couldn't remember much more. It hit him around the head and drew him near. It had a terrible vulpine face with eyes that shone in the darkness like a wild animal's. He was sure he was about to die. It was about then he passed out.

The next thing he could remember was Wal trying to make him drink water and asking him if he was all right. He could remember the terrible fight going on in the stream, the creature that had attacked him, and several of the younger clansmen and the old foreigner were fighting in the water. The foreigner beat the beast down with a rock from the stream bed, but he would not stop. He started on the young warriors around him until they overpowered him. Other warriors bundled Ker and Ned away back to the camp as Wal tried to calm the foreigner down.

No one had really spoken to Ker since they had just put him here, wrapped him up and given him a drink. He was still shaking, and he realised his breaches were still full of his own excrement. They were his only breaches, the last pair his mother had ever made for him. He realised nobody really cared and he began to cry.

Chapter 16

"I'll go no more:
I am afraid to think what I have done;
Look on't again I dare not."

Macbeth
Act II, Scene II
William Shakespeare

"Well, Fitheach?"

Startled, Corvus spun around to find the Magician, Finnvarra, by his side. "You again."

"Aye," Finnvarra smiled. "Did you not expect me?"

Corvus shrugged, "I thought you were little more than a badly digested meal."

Finnvarra chuckled. "No."

"So, what now?" Corvus looked around the camp. No one seemed to have noticed that this stranger had appeared in their midst.

"It is one of the great gifts of mortality that one can live a lifetime yet learn more in a single day than one has learnt in all those years."

"So?"

"What has this day taught you, Fitheach?"

Corvus was in no mood to answer that question. "I have no intention of debating philosophy with you, old man. What is it you want from me?"

"I called you here, summoned you, because of a debt you owe me."

"What?" Corvus snorted loudly. "I owe you? I owe you nothing."

Finnvarra's face darkened. "Think back, Fitheach, when you destroyed Mùr Ollamhan, you took a prisoner."

Ah, thought Corvus, that would be it; he was an escapee from the Druid fortress, after revenge. "I took hundreds of prisoners."

"This one was different."

"I have no recollection of any prisoner." He folded his arms and returned the Magician's stare.

"Think Fitheach, think."

Corvus thought.

He had struck at the Druid's fortress of Mur Ollamhan to end their continual agitation against everything the Empire had established in the North. They would seldom come to battle, preferring to organise resistance, and spread dissension. Time and again, pacts made and allegiances sworn were deliberately undermined by the Druids of Mur Ollamhan. The final straw was the murder of Conor MacCaladh, the emissary between Corvus and the Alban Lords. A man of peace and a man Corvus actually liked. The High Druid, Mac Cathbhadh, dragged MacCaladh before the Alban King and butchered him like a sacrificial goat and prophesied doom from his entrails.

Blind with fury, Corvus swore to fulfil that prophecy by striking fast and with utter savagery. He wrought a swathe of destruction through the Alban's Kingdom, the likes of which they'd never seen before and was at the gates of Mur Ollamhan before the rot had time to set into MacCaladh's corpse. Taken by surprise, the Druid's had little time to prepare for the onslaught. Though they tried desperately to bring to bear the full force of their sorcery against the Gärians, Corvus' own Battle Mages were more than a match for their magic tricks. Regardless of their powers, Corvus knew that surprise, ferocity, and fire were greater weapons in the assault than any cantrip or spell. The sky rained black blood, and the Druid's fought with the desperation of the damned, but all the wizardry in the world could not save them once the Hastati had breached the walls.

Corvus had come in search of retribution and showed no mercy. Mur Ollamhan was to be a warning, a salutary lesson, to all those who would dare to defy his power. He set about slaughtering every living thing in the fortress and burning the remains. He ordered the High Druid dragged to his own altar and butchered with all the ritual ceremony he had used to kill MacCaladh. Then the altar was smashed, and the temple torn down. It was Corvus' avowed intent that nothing but a pile of ashes and rubble would remain as a testimony to his wrath.

Nevertheless, such things take time, and even the most savage and battle-hardened men quickly become sick of the carnage and the stench of death. The temple resisted its destruction, and the storm rains dampened the pyres into stinking, choking smoke. Corvus saw it in their eyes; even the half-savage Rhos warriors had grown sick of murdering prisoners after two days. They had all had their fill of this orgy of death, but Corvus had not.

Roaring and berating his men for weakness, Corvus took up an Alban battle-axe, dragged the last of the Druids to the ruins of their temple and began slaughtering them himself until his arms became too tired to heft the bloody axe. He could remember the faces of each of them as clearly as if they were before him now. They were nothing but a few young neophytes and cantors, terrified children. Cold dead eyes caught his reflection like a thousand shards of glass.

"What did I become that I should war upon children?"

The sacking of Mur Ollamhan was the biggest mistake of his command; he wasted too much time. In the evening of the second day, outriders brought news of a vast hoard of Kerns and Albans only a day's march away. He was trapped, ensnared in an indefensible fortress he had reduced to nothing but a smouldering, corpse-filled ruin.

That second night had been full of horrors. Talk of the walking dead and vengeful spirits started amongst the Rhos and the Vanda light cavalry, who were as skittish as their highly strung horses. Dread spreads faster than winter flu, and soon even the veterans of the Hastions were frightened. Fear led to chaos, Battle Mages and Gärian Priests pursued phantoms amidst the dark ruins. Corvus knew all that would soon bleed into panic.

Physically it was rest they needed, but morale needed discipline and activity. Corvus ordered the last remains of the fortress burned and marched his men out of Mur Ollamhan and down onto the flood plain of the river Sruth Fool below the fortress to meet the enemy head-on.

Attack was the last thing the Albans and Kerns expected

from the Gärians; it wasn't in the Empire's rule book. Gärian soldiers stood firm on the field of battle, a solid wall of shields and thrusting spears, and held the line against the attack. Corvus did not draw up lines or entrench to await the assault; he drove his men headlong into the oncoming hoard.

The Albans fought well, quickly forming a disciplined resistance, but the vast majority of the Kerns were too disorganised to pose any real threat. Confused and ill-disciplined the Kerns routed quickly, leaving only the Albans and the few Gothad allies to put up any actual fight. Though still outnumbered, Corvus knew this tactic favoured his auxiliaries more than his Gärians. The Vanda cavalry easily negated the few chariots the Albans managed to get into the fray and scattered the fleeing Kerns. With their bows of sinew and horn, Rhos horse archers wrought devastation on the close-packed Albans, managing to cut off almost a third of them from the main force and hold them at bay. Still, the Albans fought with all the ferocity they could summon.

Most of the Kerns had fled, but their Warlock had not, and he unleashed every terror he could upon the Gärians; black lightning walked amidst their ranks, and the rain turned to fire when it touched Gärian skin.

Meanwhile, the Gärian's own magicians stood by, seemingly powerless to combat him. Screaming with rage, Corvus pushed his way through to the knot of Gärian Battle Mages, where they cowered at the centre of the Hastion's square. The Primus Magus' acolyte saw Corvus coming and tried to intercept him, but he died with Corvus' knife in his mouth before he could utter any excuses. Two more quickly died before Corvus' hands were at the Primus' throat. He dragged the old man down into the bloody mud and beat and kicked him like a dog. Before the rest, Corvus swore if they would not fight, then, before the Gods of Battles, he would kill their families, wipe their kin from the pages of history, root out and crucify everyone; men, women, children and burn the infants. There would be no mercy. He then cut the Primus' throat before them and drank from the spurting wound.

Corvus could still taste the hot blood.

The remaining Battle Magicians chose to fight.

With their Magicians support and Corvus at their head, the Gärians rallied and drove a wedge through the Alban's centre. Rhos horse archers smashed into the remaining Kerns and chased their antler wearing Warlock from the battlefield under a hail of arrows.

Now came the slaughter of battle proper. The Rhos and Vanda had secured the field, and only the Gärians and Albans stood toe to toe and fought. Bravery and ferocity were no match for discipline and training, the Albans fought, and the Gärians slaughtered.

When finally, the battle haze cleared, less than half his Hastion were left standing amidst carnage as far as the eye could see.

It was horror beyond comprehension, and even the great Corvus, the most feared man in the Gärian Empire, stood alone in the ice-cold rain and cried bitter, bitter tears.

Sick of killing, he spared the lives of all prisoners and had them sent south to Mastarna to sell on. All the prisoners save for one.

"I think there was one, a woman." A strange woman, not Kern or Alban. A tall, proud silent woman, pale-skinned and green-eyed. "The Ouragos brought her to me thinking that she might have been an Aelathian or Gärian noble woman held as a slave by your Druids."

Anger flashed across the old man's face. "You raped her."

"I...."

"You raped her, Fitheach."

"She..."

"She was my granddaughter."

Corvus' mouth went dry. No, that had to be wrong. Gaining his composure, he said flatly. "I neither remember nor care. She was a prisoner, a slave, nothing of worth." He turned to walk away.

Suddenly Finnvarra was in front of him, towering and formidable. "Do not turn your back on me, Duine." His voice rolled like thunder.

Corvus' hand went to the hilt of his sword, but he had no idea who this Magician was or how powerful, so instead of drawing the weapon, he asked calmly, "Who exactly are you?"

"I am Finnvarra, King of Tir Eile."

A King? One of the old Alban Druid Kings. Thought Corvus, that would explain a lot. "What do you want from me? If it's revenge, then it seems Jorunn MacRoth's beaten you to it."

"Revenge? No, Fitheach, I do not require revenge upon you. It was I who delivered you into Jorunn's hands, and it is my council that stayed her anger. She is strong, but her loyalty to her kin has always been her weakness."

"Then what do you want from me?"

Finnvarra smiled slyly and said softly, "I want your daughter."

Corvus laughed and shook his head. "I have no children. Save a still born infant, and you can go dig in the frozen earth for that."

"Yes, Fitheach, you do. The bastard you shamed my granddaughter with. Deliver that child to me, and your debt to me shall be repaid."

"No. I don't know who you are or what you want, but if there was a child, I never knew of it. Anyway, if there is a child, I have no idea where she would be, and, even if I did, I certainly would not hand her over to you."

Finnvarra smiled his nefarious smile again. "But Fitheach, you don't understand."

Chapter 17

"May I be an island in the sea, may I be a hill on the land,
may I be a star when the moon wanes,
may I be a staff to the weak one:
I shall wound every man, no man shall wound me."

A Charm with Yarrow
Traditional Scottish
Folk Charm

Oh, mother, forgive me for what I have done.

You who bore so much with such patience and strength.

I am ashamed.

Ashamed of my weakness.

Weakness they see as power.

They genuinely fear me now. They are terrified in my presence.

But they do not understand it is weakness that drives me.

Frailties.

Anger is a weakness.

Rage is an indulgence.

Such terrible things.

You taught me never to let go.

Never to release control.

I have.

I am sorry.

I am so ashamed.

And I cannot drive the sound of their screaming out of my head.

Fyngard pushed back hard against the wall and flattened his shoulders, then began rotating them, trying to exercise the ache out of the joints. Something in his right shoulder popped loudly, and his elbow clicked, allowing a little of the pain to flow away. He knew it would be like this for days; every joint and every muscle ached as if he had been stretched on a rack. The minor wounds and the bruises were almost healed, but the dull cramp would take much longer; even his teeth ached. Breathing exercises next, in slowly, deeply, and out fully, and again. His breath caught, and he began to cough. "Damn."

"Take it easy, relax into it." Jacobis looked up from keening the edges of his spear. "Slowly. That's better."

Fyn slid himself down the wall into a crouching position, wincing at the audible cracking sound from his kneecaps. "I feel like I've been frigged by a bear."

"Rough love?" Jacobis laughed. "Well, if you hadn't had lost control so completely this time, MacLeech's boys wouldn't have had to beat eight bales of shite out of you."

Fyn laughed. "But it was fun, wasn't it? To see the bastards run…."

Jacobis paused again for a moment and smiled at his friend. "Well, not actually. I was rather indisposed if you remember."

"How long are we going to have to wait here?" Fyn sighed loudly and looked around. They were ensconced at the mouth of a shallow cave offset to the main tunnels somewhere deep in the bowels of the Craig.

Jacobis reached over and offered Fyn a chunk of dark bread. "These things always take time."

They had been skulking in this little cranny for at least five hours, waiting for Annis and the Tysher to return. It would have been a tight fit for three or four healthy youths, as it was there were five of them crammed uncomfortably into the tiny space around the massive frame of Jacobis.

Fyn shoved aside an elbow that had come to rest on his thigh and cast his best disdainful look at the others. The smallest Alban sat clutching a crossbow. He was an intense-looking young man known as Calum, wiry framed and beset with the most oversized ears Fyn had ever seen on a man. They stuck out from his head like a pair of jug handles. The other's said Calum could hear a spider weaving its web and, with ears like that, Fyn could believe it. He seemed to be the companion of Seumas, owner of the wandering elbow, who was about the same age as Calum but heavier set and bearded. He had the typical bravado of a young Alban, hard-eyed and apt to swagger, but it could no longer cover the smell of fear emanating from him. He stared back at Fyn and mumbled an apology; whether it was for the elbow or for falling asleep, Fyn could not make out.

The other two were older, experienced Alban warriors, dour quiet men with grim faces behind bushy beards and knitted eyebrows. Fyn had not gotten their names and, in truth, didn't care. They huddled together in swathes of homespun plaid, hardly speaking, but their eyes, permanently fixed on Fyn's every move, said more than enough. One hugged his huge two-handed sword like it was his woman, and the other nursed a battle-axe like a mother with a newborn, stroking its blood-spattered haft as if cooing it to sleep.

Some way farther back, another dozen Albans were lodged in a little storeroom with a door too small for even Fyn to fit through. Though they had had some macabre fun shoving the old cook through it.

Other warriors were scattered throughout the tunnels and passageways of the Craig. The Isheen and their allies had tried to pursue the fleeing Albans into the bowels of the fortress, but the defenders had fought a desperate rear-guard action in the cramped subterranean labyrinth. After hours of savage fighting, the blooded pursuers withdrew to the upper levels of the cellars. Amongst the defenders, there was much speculation as to what would come next as they barricaded their positions and settled in for the siege.

Fyn knew all too well what would come next. Once the Isheen and the monsters they'd summoned had rested, they would attack again, this time using whatever they could to drive the defenders deeper into the tunnels, like a cork being driven into a bottle; eventually, there would be no place left to go.

Angus stopped at the bottom of the narrow, roughly cut stairway and held up his lamp so the others could see ahead. "There."

MacLeech hobbled down the last few steps and peered beyond the glare of the lamp. The short corridor ended abruptly in the face of black rock. "Ay." He glanced back at the woman as she stepped carefully down behind him. "There, hen, is it nae?"

Angus caught the lamplight in her eyes; it shone back with an unnatural intensity.

She nodded.

"My grandfather had these tunnels cut in hopes of getting low enough to burrow through to the landward side, but then they hit this." Angus walked down the short corridor and placed his free hand on the rock; it was warm to the touch, hot even. "The Silurian stonemasons called it 'Galon y Graig' the Heart of the Craig. Their tools couldn't make any effect on it. Nothing they tried would even mark it," he ran his hand over the smooth glassy surface. "They don't even know what kind of stone it is."

MacLeech reached out tentatively to touch the stone. "It throbs!" he gasped and dropped his staff.

Angus instinctively stepped away. "Aye, it vibrates. And sometimes it's so warm down here that a mist rises into the passages above." And the dreams it put into the mind of Erbin nam Ban drove the Druid insane until he threw himself from the tower of Tùr nan Iolairean, the Tower of the Eagle's, the highest battlement in the Craig, to escape them. Angus added silently, I remember those dreams too. "Well, Lady, can it be done?"

They look at me like lost children.

What do they expect of me?

I, too, am tired and frightened.

They bring me to this rock, and yet they dare not ask.
Can I?

Will I?

MacLeech knows the answer.
He fears it.

He fears me.

They all fear me now.
I, whose wrath is as the lightning and as swift as…
… a raven's wing.

Annis Nic an Neamhain.

The Cailleach Dubh.

Am I not revealed to them now?
I see how they revile me as clear as the lamplight reflected in their eyes.

But their need for me now is greater than ever.

I tell them that it can be done but not yet.

I must rest, regain my strength, calm myself, for this day has taken a great toll on me.
MacLeech sneers, but the Laird understands.

He pats the great black stone that is the Heart of the Craig and smiles.
"Aye, Lady, if you can do this, then take as much rest as you need."

We return the way we came.

I walk ahead for here. I need no lamp.

Down here, the living rock itself radiates enough light for me to see by. Though I know not to dwell here as this kind of light would soon sicken me, and many strange things are dwelling here desirous to be seen.

I cast my gaze from them and block out their voices, their pleas, and their cries.

We pass back up into the tunnels below the storerooms and the cellars now far above.
The Laird's mind is full of reservations; he is uncertain what MacLeech says can possibly be so, and he dreads the coming

onslaught. Myriad battle plans race through his thoughts; each thought is quickly examined and disregarded in favour of the next.

In truth, he knows it will be no contest, only a trial by ordeal, a test of how long he can hold back the tide of death. Strangely it is in that that he finds solace and peace. It is the true strength of the warrior.

Yet, he still fears the sorcery of the Isheen.

In that, there is the taint of hopelessness; how can a sword defend against such an attack?

MacLeech is careful to keep his mind closed to me now, but I sense there is much more to his insistence than just the aim of escape.

He is lying to us.

I know that.

And he knows that I know.

Above us, other awarenesses try to seek us out, scrying and seeking.

Groping blindly for us here in the dark below. They have passed over us again and again, for down here, it is easy to meld into the aura of the living rock.

I can clearly discern them, the Àrd-dràgon and the Galdràgon of the Isheen, I can even perceive their hatred of each other, but there is a darker presence now.

An ancient evil has entered the Craig.

He must have only recently arrived, as I could not sense him before we went down to the Heart.

I reach out to the walls.

The Craig knows the hunger and malevolence of the creature.

It's aware of...

It's aware.

I did not realise.

Mathan-Bàn stood passively watching as the Fomóiri hauled the gigantic bulk of their God-King into the Great Hall. He had kept them out all day, though they angrily demanded to enter the castle. It was against Mathan-Bàn's better judgement, but the Galdràgon and her chorus had flown into screaming hysterics, so tonight, he had relented.

As he watched the little entertainment show, he mused on the events of the previous night. Things, he found, always had a way of finding their own balance. The battle had gone badly on the strand, the Southrons and the first Isheen had suffered terribly at the hands of the defenders, and there had been far more of them than he'd expected, but his own warriors, the Gaisgich an taighe, had swept the Dhaoine off the defences.

In all that had gone well. Part of him had been pleased to set his Isheen against truly worthy opponents, though there had been a few surprises. Then the Galdràgon, in her grief and madness, had summoned the storm that brought the Fomóiri . Even in the eye of the tempest, they had scaled the walls of the Craig like ants and fallen upon the Daonna defenders. The mad old hag had given the Craig to the Fomóiri ! It was at that point, in his rage, he had come near to having the Galdràgon thrown from the cliff face. He was forced to watch as the Craig slipped through his fingers. So much of what had gone wrong since they had begun this campaign lay with the Galdràgon, but that is when the hand of fate had rebalanced the scales.

The hag had wholly underestimated the powers of the half-blood Witch and the Taibhsear of the Kerns.

It was with no little relief that he watched the Fomóiri that had scaled the wall annihilated before the astonishing power of the Witch. He had had to restrain himself from laughing openly as the monsters fled from the Craig in screaming panic. The Witch's stand was a rear-guard action giving time for the defenders to make good their withdrawal into the keep, and as soon as they were safely away, she had walked calmly, serenely, back to join them.

Mathan-Bàn found himself admiring her; she was awe-inspiring even for a half-blood, magnificent, beautiful, everything the Galdràgon was not. Everything his sister was once. Maybe that instant of admiration was why he let her go unassailed, why he had stayed his hand for that moment before sending his Isheen into the killing grounds beyond the barbican.

The Craig was in his hands now, and he had insured it would stay that way. A whispered command to Faylinn and the Gaisgich an taighe had fallen upon the remaining wounded and dying Fomóiri butchering them where they lay.

The battle for the castle proper had been savage, but he had again been surprised by the tenacity of Strandwulf's Southron soldiers, they were far more experienced in this kind of fighting than his Isheen, and they had proved invaluable. Overall, the abilities of these Daonna warriors on both sides were beginning to concern him. Once, he would have believed his Isheen were invincible, but now the Dhaoine, with their iron swords and pragmatic determination, were exacting a heavy toll in lives and limbs. A toll that he was no longer sure his warriors, let alone his race, would always be able to pay. Since his youth, the Dhaoine had bothered him, and now a taint of doubt for the future grew in his heart.

The hulking thing that was the God-King of the Fomóiri seated itself into the enormous ironbound thrown its attendants had hauled up into the hall. The cradle-like 'thrown' groaned alarmingly as it settled under its massive weight but held.

Mathan-Bàn, standing on the great hearth with his back to the roaring fire, took time to assure himself of the situation. With his beloved Faylinn by his side and his Gaisgich an taighe, invisible in the dark shadows lining the walls, the Isheen outnumbered the dozen Fomóiri three-fold and outside awaited reinforcements. The great white Àrd-dràgon seeing nothing to fear, smiled benignly down at the creature and its attendants and began. "Welcome Balor MacCenchos, King of Tir fo Thuinn, Lord of the Western Seas, welcome to Creag an Eagail, the Rock of Fear."

Above its gaping maw, Balor's one remaining eye glared menacingly at the Àrd-dràgon. It was said that Balor had lost the other in battle with the Magi of the Àrsaidh, the Ancients. Some even said that this abomination was once one of the Great Lords of the Àrsaidh. Mathan-Bàn doubted that. Balor looked more like some obscene cross between a vastly bloated man, a frog, and some salmon in breeding season. When he grew angry, he flapped his useless appendages furiously and gaped like a floundering fish. He was angry now.

"Where is the Banshee, the half-breed Witch?" gurgled Balor.

"The Witch Annis has fled," replied Mathan-Bàn.

"Escaped?"

"Aye," the Àrd-dràgon sneered. "She sprouted little wings and flew away."

"Amadán!" Balor thrashed wildly. "Fool! How could this happen? Your promise, your oath, was to deliver her to us."

Mathan-Bàn stepped down from the hearth. "I did not promise you anything, uilebheist."

The Fomóiri stiffened and nervously closed around their master.

"You struck a covenant with Cullach-Bàn and the Galdràgon, but I am Mathan-Bàn, Riaghladair of Dùn nan Làidir, Àrd-dràgon of the Isheen, brother to the Bànrigh, Fearchara Nic Darach. And I do not truck with monsters."

"My Lord…." Out of the small group of Fomóiri pushed a tall, hooded figure, "May I speak?"

Mathan-Bàn waved his hand permissively.

The figure stepped forward. "I am the Prindsa, Morghath Bres, the seventh son of my father, Balor, Ardrigh of the Fomhórach." Morghath pushed back the cowl from his face. "It was I that struck the accord with Cullach-Bàn. It was I that sealed the contract."

Mathan-Bàn gaped at the Fomóire, he was tall and fair, and nothing about him betrayed his origins, the Àrd-dràgon suspected a trick until he saw the creature's eyes; they were slit and yellow like some water living reptile and brimming with malice.

"You must blame me. Hold me responsible."

The Àrd-dràgon was taken aback. "I…"

"But believing it true, the Uachdaran of the West and the Priestess did offer this treaty. We did so in good faith, with an open hand."

Mathan-Bàn regained his composure and resolve. "They do

not speak for me."

Morghath Bres smiled sadly and nodded. "So is obviously true. For who dares speak for you, without your permission? Nevertheless, we were summoned, and we fought for you well. So how are we to be repaid for our strife, rewarded for our endeavour?"

"I owe you nothing."

"Truly? The contract may have been a conniving lie, a deceit, but they were only words spilt into the air, the blood of my father's warriors is not spilt so cheaply, spent so wantonly." Morghath Bres drew himself up to his full height and added a harsher tone to his voice. "You are the master of this battlefield. It is to you we now come to receive our due, collect our reward. Regardless of the lies of others, it is you we hold to account. This debt you owe us."

Mathan-Bàn glared at the Fomóire. "As I said, I owe you nothing."

Balor growled deeply.

Morghath Bres glanced at his father and smiled wolfishly. "Think again carefully, oh Great One. To anger my father is to anger a God. To insult my father is to insult us all, and we are many."

Mathan-Bàn raised his right hand, and the Isheen warriors lining the walls nocked their arrows and drew their bows. "I fear no one, man, uilebheist, Sìth or God."

"Enough!" roared Balor. "Is this truly how you intend to honour your debt, to repay me?"

Mathan-Bàn held his breath for a moment allowing a deafening silence to fill the great hall. He would have so dearly loved to have simply answered, 'Yes,' and to have dropped his hand. He knew he could not; it would plunge his people into a war the likes of which none but Balor himself had ever seen and from which few, if any, would survive. So Mathan-Bàn held his breath until the silence became unbearable and then answered, "My Lord Balor MacCenchos, most ancient Ardrigh, forgive me if I offended you. Of course, you shall be rewarded for your toil, but I cannot deliver the Witch unto you as she has fled. As you witnessed, she is far more powerful than we expected, and those around her are formidable warriors. In the chaos of the battle, they made good their escape. I know not where to or how. I will be pleased to provide you with the pick of the captives and anything you wish to take from this place." It was a strain to keep the contempt out of his voice.

Morghath Bres grinned again and cocked his head to one side in a mock obeisance. "Gratefully, we thank you, a grand offer, but we shall tarry a while, linger here until we have what we have come for until the Witch is delivered to us."

"Why are you so intent upon this Witch?"

"Our kind, our people, have met her before, she is our enemy, an old adversary, and we shall have revenge upon her. It was part of the pact, the pledge made to us, and we will see it honoured." Morghath's grin grew wider. "Or we shall stay; take this place, as payment."

Mathan-Bàn stared into the Fomóire's reptilian eyes. This game of brinkmanship was going nowhere, the Fomóiri were used to getting exactly what they wanted, and they had no intention of backing down, and he had no intention of giving into them.

"Morair," interrupted Faylinn precisely as planned. "Forgive me, but I am to remind you that the Bànrigh Fearchara's emissary is waiting."

Mathan-Bàn nodded thoughtfully. "My Lord Balor, I must see the Bànrigh's emissary and take her counsel upon this matter. If you would return to your ship, I will send word as soon as we have spoken."

Morghath Bres stared at the Isheen Àrd-dràgon, his expression was a mixture of contempt and utter disbelief, but Mathan-Bàn ignored him. "It would not be safe for Your Majesty to remain here while there are still defenders at large in these halls, let alone the Kern's Sorcerer, the shapeshifter, a Vörish giant and, possibly still, the Witch herself." He let that thought sink in before adding. "I cannot guarantee Your Majesty's safety."

Balor knew it was a clear warning, almost a threat, but caution was called for here; he glared coldly at this posturing Isheen coxcomb for a moment before nodding his consent.

Mathan-Bàn could easily read the thoughts of revenge running through the monster's fishy brain. They were simplistic and brutal, totally lacking any subtlety or finesse. With a few moves, he knew he could counter anything Balor tried to throw against him. He smiled widely at the ancient Ardrigh of the Fomóiri and bowed courteously.

Chapter 18

**"I know indeed what evil I intend to do,
but stronger than all my afterthoughts is my fury,
fury that brings upon mortals the greatest evils."**

**Euripides
Medea**

The weak northern winter sun feebly tried to penetrate the blanket of rain clouds that had rolled down off the mountains to cover the vastness of the Collie Mhòr. The Great Forest stood silent and brooding in the watery, cold dawn. From its trees rose a mist, like the sight of warm breath on a cold day, forming an opalescent layer that hung just below the treetops, obscuring the daylight even more.

Corvus had not slept. He sat in the lee of the deadfall and watched those around him as they dragged their selves into the new day. The rain started as the dawn broke, compounding everyone's discomfort as they shook off the night's sleep if sleep they had. The younger warriors had found it hardest, unused to sleeping out on the ground at this time of year. They complained to each other and swapped stories of discomfort as they tried to warm themselves and pound blood back into cold limbs and feet. The older men, with more resolution and the benefit of experience, better equipment, and preparation, ignored their younger clansmen's whining or simply made fun of them.

Since before dawn, the slaves and gilles had been up breaking the camp and struggling to load the animals.

Tàmh sat on his horse watching them and singing softly into the morning air, he sang surprisingly sweetly, but no one seemed to take any notice except for the Horse-boy who stood gazing at him from some way off. Corvus registered that look, its intensity, almost wistfulness; there was great sadness in that damaged face.

"O mhàthair uile-choitcheann,

a bhios a 'cumail
Bho shìorraidh do bhunaitean gu domhainn,
An rud as sine de rudan,
an Talamh Mòr,
tha mi a 'seinn bhuat!
A h-uile cumadh aig a bheil an taigh aca sa mhuir,
A h-uile càil a tha ag itealaich,
no air an talamh diadhaidh
Beò, gluais, agus tha beathachadh ann - is iad sin thusa;
Tha iad sin bho do bheairteas a tha thu a 'cumail suas; uaibh
Tha babes cothromach air am breith, agus measan air a h-uile
craobh.
Màthair, maighdeann agus cailleach mhòr."

Wal, who had been up most of the night watching over Ned,
now prowled the camp like a disgruntled bear, growling orders and
dragging stragglers out of their beds.

Corvus had been drinking all night, and when he drank
heavily, he could not sleep. Actually, he had drunk to make sure he
would not. Instead, he had forced himself upon a journey of his own
making. He had been plagued with memories of the past all the
previous day, fragments like the shards of a broken glass bowl. As if
they were slowly revealing themselves deliberately, trying to tell him
something, warn him, admonish him, and shame him. Why? He did
not know, but last night had been different, worse.

The Magician had appeared right in the middle of the camp,
and no one had seen him. That, as Corvus reasoned, clearly meant
he was not real. Though if he was an illusion or a trick, then who
was perpetrating it and why? There had to be a reason, a purpose to
it.

What had shaken Corvus the most was the accusations and
demands that the Magician made. He was quite willing to accept that
this was trickery or illusion, possibly just his own fevered
imagination. What he was not prepared to do was accept it as truth.

And in that was the problem.

"My people believe that every man has to pay the price in the
next world for his actions in this one. He is judged, his soul weighed

against a pure white feather, and if he is found unworthy, he is damned. Emperor or slave, Magi or brickmaker all will be judged." The voice was so clear in Corvus' head that he found himself instinctively looking over his shoulder, but it was Nebti's voice, and Nebti Alem was long dead. "But, Andreas, the Gods give every man one chance in his life to atone for all the wrongs he has done before he dies."

"Have you had that chance?" Andreas had asked as they sat on the marble steps outside the village temple.

The Tutor had smiled, sadly, it seemed to the boy. "No, I don't think so, not yet. Though when it comes, I hope I'll be wise enough to know it for what it is and brave enough to seize it with both hands."

Corvus knew that Nebti had found his opportunity for atonement only a month later and had seized it. He understood now why the Tutor had been so unafraid the night he died.

Well, was that it? Is this my last chance at redemption? Corvus swilled a mouthful of wine, spat it onto the ground and wiped the rain off his face. Redemption for what? He thought, I made my pact with Death, and I never flinched from it. I never regretted a thing. But as soon as the words formed in his mind, he knew they were a lie. He regretted many things; the countless deaths, the destruction, the waste, and the misery he had visited upon so many. All the lying, the plotting, and the betrayals. Like some vile carrion bird, he had fed for decades upon the hate-filled carcass of the past. The shadow of his wings had brought devastation and death to all it touched. Yes, he regretted it, even then, but it had never stopped him. He had never wavered, never faltered. He had betrayed his Tyrannos, Calticas Nefandous, and murdered even his own best friend and...

She, the prisoner the Ouragos brought him, the prisoner, the Magician, talked about, had been the most beautiful woman he had ever seen. Tall, pale, and as silent as the stones. Her hair was the colour of polished silver, her skin like translucent alabaster and so finely boned she looked as fragile as Aelathian glass. She wore a simple emerald robe and carried herself with the bearing of one who had never known fear, and she had shown no fear of him at all. No dread of the great General from the East. Conquer, destroyer, butcher. She had just reached out and stroked his face like one would stroke that of a child or a lover. Although silent, her eyes, the colour of emeralds on fire, spoke clearer than any voice. They spoke of sadness, compassion and understanding, and they spoke so clearly, he could almost hear her inside his head.

That night something deep in him had broken, and he had cried in her arms like a child, cried in a way he had never cried since that night long before. In the morning, she was gone, as if she had never been. The Ouragos looked at him dumbly when he questioned them; they had seen no such woman, prisoner or not. In fact, he had almost dismissed it as a dream had it not been for what she had stolen from him that night.

She had taken from him not only the will to fight on, but the will to live. It was the greatest of punishments; his life should become meaningless at the moment of his greatest victory. She had taken the thorn out of his heart and the poison out of his soul; everything that had driven him he lost that night. By the time he was finally forced to return to Val Gär, even the desire for revenge had died in him.

Had they killed him, it would not have mattered, but they did not. He patiently watched them play their power games, paid homage to their new Tyrannos and returned here to this harsh land.

For what? To become a fat lazy provincial Governor. To take a wife, build a villa and breed children? It all seemed insane now, but it was true. He had watched as the Empire slid into anarchy and as his soldiers were re-called. Though the summons had never come for him. He had been grateful, for now; free of the hate and the rage, he was slowly freed of the power and responsibilities too.

He could remember Móraig's beautiful face clearly now, soft, round and gentle, so young and so kind. No noble blood or Chieftain's daughter, just a simple Alban slave girl, yet she had loved him, and he had known love too, if only for a short time.

Corvus sighed. Was that Mōmos' greatest jest? The Laughing God's best trick, at the end of his life, to rob him of even her? To bury the only person he had ever let himself love. To lay her down beside his stillborn son and to carry on, to die, as he had lived? Alone? However, he had robbed Mōmos of his victory. He had died as he had lived, in defiance of the Laughing God and in the service of another.

Or had he? What was he doing here? That was the question. He had felt the steel and tasted the earth in his mouth; the memories were clear now.

So, what was this? He chuckled to himself; if this was the 'afterlife' the Narbonensian priests preached about, then life was indeed not worth living. Or was this just another of Mōmos' games? Punishment for trying to cheat the God of his entertainment or for trying to find refuge in the arms of Death herself.

Andreas Corvidious, the man known as Corvus, began to laugh loudly, his voice ringing out across the clearing. Everybody else stopped and stared.

Wal pulled everyone together in his inimitable rough, cajoling way and had them all ready to go in short time. He knew that travelling would be even more difficult with Ned unconscious and a prisoner to guard, but they had to move on whatever. He had made the decision last night not to send Ned back to the Crannog, and Corvus had stopped him ordering the death of the Isheen warrior, so he had to improvise as best as he could. A litter of sorts was arranged for Ned, whose care had been given over to the slave boy Nissien, though to Wal, there seemed little to do other than watch the boy die.

Wal admitted to himself, the prisoner was not in a much better condition after being beaten senseless and half-drowned by Corvus, so he had her hands bound and leashed to the bow of his saddle. It would have been an act of punishment if Wal had believed that this little procession could have moved at anything more than a walk, though he doubted they would even make that amount of progress today. Also, three of his younger warriors were still nursing themselves after the battering the Gärian had inflicted on them when they had rushed into the water last night to help him subdue the Isheen. No serious injuries, but they hurt, and that too would slow things down.

Wal then climbed up onto his own horse and made another quick inspection of the party, checking things against his mental notes, and once he was fully satisfied, he gave them the order to move off.

As the morning progressed, the Isheen warrior trudged silently beside Wal's horse with her head down, seemingly unconcerned about her predicament or the weather. The big Alban warrior took the opportunity to take a long look at her for the first time. Although dishevelled and bruised, she was still an impressive creature, long-limbed and muscular; she moved with an animal grace that he found almost attractive.

When she finally noticed his staring, she returned it with defiance. So, Wal thought, this was the fabled Isheen? The Sìth, the stuff of legends and nightmares. He could understand now how many lost their hearts and lives to such fey creatures, but the look in her eyes and the strange proportions of her face and ears reminded him that she was no creature of his world. Beautiful, but as deadly as henbane.

Rànd had been trying to keep her eyes down and sheltered from the daylight as the brightness made it almost impossible for her to see. The assault on her senses was coming from all directions; the stench of the Dhaoine and their animals stunned her sense of smell, and the cacophony of their every movement hammered inside her head.

The Bard had brought her water to wash her face and get some of the blood and mud out of her matted hair at dawn. He had been surprised that her wounds had already begun to heal; she was a fast healer even for one of her kind, but she was still sore, and her head ached savagely. The Bard had given her willow bark to chew and more water to drink. He seemed kind enough for one of them, but she knew he was only trying to gain her trust, and she had no intention of giving that to any of them.

As she trudged on, she tried to reach deep inside herself, searching for her own focus; àite. The centre of her own being. Blocking out the noise and smells, giving her movements over to pure instinct. She regulated her breathing and closed her eyes, centring herself, shutting the material world out. It was difficult but worth trying as the concentration helped block out some of the noise and the pain in her head.

As she closed out the physical assault on her senses, she became more aware of other things; the strange lustful thoughts running through the Albannach's leader's mind, the fear in the minds of the others, the hate from all sides directed at her. She quickly pushed on deeper inside herself, blocking the other's thoughts out. She could sense the evil around the Old Warrior and was desperate not to attract its attention. She pushed on deeper inside herself, but there was something already there.

She could feel it, waiting for her. What do you want? She demanded of the presence.

As it became clearer, it answered.

Wal was still watching Rànd closely when she collapsed, so he managed to catch her before she fell. As he hoisted her onto his lap, he was surprised just how little she weighed and how pleasing she smelled.

The Trow observed the Dhaoine trying to count numbers, though counting wasn't his greatest strength; he'd got to eleven-eight but had lost count again. Anyway, he thought, what did it matter? They're only Dhaoine and nothing to be feared. He let out a long low whistle, more like a hiss, a signal to the others scattered amongst the bracken. He steadied himself, clutched his battle-axe tightly, and crouched down. On his shout, they would attack and destroy the Dhaoine, kill them all, and feast on the corpses.

He waited until he could see the entire column of riders and stragglers, warriors, and pack handlers. He knew his masters would be pleased with supplies and provisions, and if he could see to it that some of the younger Dhaoine would be taken alive back to his masters, they would appreciate the delicacy.

Once he was satisfied that there was no more of the Dhaoine to come, the Trow stood up, roared his order to the others and charged as fast as his stubby legs could carry him towards the enemy.

The Albans hardly flinched. Wal had signalled them minutes before that they were being stalked, and as the ambushers broke cover, the warriors drew their weapons, wheeled around, and charged with practised ease. For most, the sudden relief and exhilaration of the fight blocked out any shock or fear at the sight of the attackers. And for those who felt the pangs of apprehension, there was no place or time to show it. They met the Fomóire's charge with a savagery that the creatures did not expect. Driving home spears with deadly accuracy, using the combined weight of man and mounts to offset the creatures' size. Behind the mounted charge came the younger clansmen on foot using their axes and huge two-handed swords.

The Fomóiri were massive and heavily armed but slow and cumbersome, though they roared and slashed at their enemy; their lumbering gate was no match for the horsemen's speed and agility. Wal yelled orders to the packhorse handlers as they grabbed their bows and crossbows and followed their clansmen into the bracken.

Svein sat on his horse in the middle of the path, his mouth open in a soundless shout and his eyes wide in shock. Out of the woods had burst monsters, giant, misshapen scaled creatures, with enormous barrel chests and great toad-like heads beset with dagger-like teeth. They shambled forward, snarling and flourishing their massive weapons. Svein had only heard of things like them in the terrifying tales of childhood. These were actual monsters.

Corvus seized the young Gothad's arm and shook him. "Don't just look at them! Draw your sword, boy, or those things'll make a meal of you."

Still, Svein dragged his great grandfather's sword from its sheath in a half daze and stared at it. Fredsmäklare, was its name, 'the Peacemaker', the runes carved into the heavy blade seemed to shimmer and writhe as they caught the sunlight.

"Attack!" Corvus shouted as he slammed his boot into the side of Svein's horse. The animal reared and thundered forward into the chaos.

A Fomóire lunged at him with a wicked-looking mace. Svein managed to shy away and bring his sword down with all his might on the creature's skull. The blow clanged off of bone or iron. He had no idea which, but the beast faltered for a split second and Svein, seeing his chance drove his sword point into the thing's chest. The Fomóire dropped its mace and scrambled to get at the Duine, but Svein was too fast. Dragging the sword free, he drove it hard as he could into the thing's unprotected throat; as the point hit what he presumed was bone, he slammed his boot into the creature's face and wrenched the weapon free. For what seemed an eternity, the creature just stood there before him, dumbly patting at the blood gushing from its throat. Svein steeled himself and reined the horse to attack again, but the creature had slowly crumpled to the ground by then.

Amazed by his own good luck, the young Gothad searched around for another. A creature stood over the bodies of two fallen Albans bellowing defiance at the men who had brought it to bay. It was massive, much bigger than the one Svein had just killed, but it had its back to him, and Svein could see the opportunity. Goading his horse fiercely, he charged the creature from behind, sending it sprawling under his horse's hooves. As the monster tried to scramble to its feet, Svein and the Albans were on it. One drove his spear into its side, up under the strange breastplate it wore, while the other took a wild hack at it with his claymore and took the

Fomóire's arm off at the elbow. The blows staggered the monster long enough for Svein to take time to find his point at the top of the creature's neck, urge the horse forward once more and rammed home his sword. The Fomóire stiffened and then collapsed, writhing into the bracken.

Svein pulled the horse up hard and tried to gain some sense of how the fighting was going.

The thick bracken was now devastated, trampled in the struggle between men and monsters. All about lay the dead and dying. Several of the creatures had been cut down, but a dozen or more clansmen also lay amongst the twisted carnage of horses and monsters. Ten or more of the Fomóiri fought on, although numbers were against them.

Wal was on the edge of the road hacking viciously at one of the creatures while the pack handlers enraged and weakened it with a hail of crossbow bolts and arrows.

Corvus was on foot in the midst of the worst of the fighting. Trading blow for blow with a hulking thing even bigger and uglier than the others.

Svein was amazed that the old man seemed to be winning. The monster dwarfed him as it loomed over him, raining down blows with an immense hatchet. However, Corvus was driving it back, dodging its blows and relentlessly stabbing deep into the thing's gut. Svein was shocked to recognise the look in the creature's eyes; it was afraid. Blows that should have shattered the Duine and driven him into the ground seemingly had no effect. Corvus just kept attacking. Finally, a carefully aimed stab folded one of the creature's legs, and it fell to its knees; another perfectly aimed slash disarmed the beast, and Corvus closed in for the kill, each debilitating stab driven home with incredible precision. The creature was screaming now, not fighting but trying to fend off the relentless stabbing of the short heavy blade, like some wretched victim caught by a maniac. The final blow went in under its desperately flailing arms deep into its maw and up into its brain. Corvus paused only to kick his weapon free before turning to locate another victim.

The fight was going out of the Fomóiri; with the death of their leader, the Trow, and the determination of the Duine's counterattack, some of them began to look for an escape route.

A few saw their chance and began to fight their way to the safety of the big trees but only to find their way barred. With a loud roar and deafening cacophony, another wave of Dhaoine burst out of the tree line.

The fight was now a slaughter, the Fomóiri struggled on desperately, but even their massive size and power was useless against the Duine's spears and arrows. Once down and injured, the Dhaoine butchered them like cattle, rejoicing in the pitiless slaughter.

The last Fomóire made a valiant stand, but it was of no use, for everyone he batted aside two or three took its place, and now armoured dogs ripped at his legs and arrows rained down on him. He roared, hit, and struggled, but it was pointless, too many spears, too many Dhaoine. And then he saw it, there beyond the line of his attackers, the Death God of the Dhaoine laughing at him. Of course, he understood now; it had been a trick, a trap! In frustration, he pulled himself up to his full height and threw his weapon at the God in one final act of defiance before he was hacked down.

As the last of the monsters died, the warriors began to take stock, helping the wounded and counting the dead. Others just collapsed to the ground, exhausted as a stunned silence fell over the battle scene, broken only by the baying of the dogs and the cries of the wounded.

A warrior grabbed Wal's arm and pointed to the newcomers. "Kerns," he laughed. "Wally! Bloody yellow-backed Kerns!"

Wal wiped the blood and sweat from his eyes and squinted. True enough, amidst the Albans that had come to their aid were the orange-yellow shirts of the Kerns. He searched for a face he could recognise amongst his own people until one of the older MacReuls, Taran the Red, stepped forward out of their midst. Whether it was the look on the man's face or the way he walked told Wal something was very wrong.

"Taran Roou?" called Wal.

"Aye, Wal."

"What happened?"

"It's lost." Taran MacReul threw his sword down angrily.

"The Craig is lost."

Chapter 19

All concerns of men go wrong when they wish to cure evil with evil.

Sophocles
The sons of Aleus

Kemble lifted Gabhran MacRoth up a little so he could take another small sip of water. Kemble had learnt a lot about dealing with wounded men in the decades he had served the MacRoths, and whether Gabhran wanted to or not, he made him drink regularly. He hoped it would help to keep the young man's fever at bay. The wound in Gabhran's side was deep but clean and no longer bleeding; however, the one in his back worried Kemble. An Isheen arrow had struck him high in the left shoulder blade as he led the Geural wall defence. Kemble had dug the small black stone head out and cleaned the wound, but it was still angry, a raw colour, and hot to the touch. Poultices and clean dressings helped, though Kemble feared his knowledge would not be enough. He felt that the young MacRoth, whom he had helped bring into the world, was slipping away from him into a dark fever little by little. For now, Gabhran had to answer the questions of the Gaisgeach, Wal MacCoigruch, and the strangers he had brought with him.

It had never been Kemble's way to question too closely the elder warriors of the Clan at times like these, let alone to issue demands, but he made his anger about the whole business as evident as he could. There had been no introductions and no explanations as to who these strangers were, though Wal had demanded to know why there were Kerns with Gabhran's warriors, the explanation had left mouths open and eyes wide in disbelief. The older stranger, a man that Kemble found disturbingly familiar, took over the questioning, demanding answers like an interrogator. The stranger wanted to know everything about the Witch, her consorts, the castle, but especially the Tysher MacLeech; he seemed to want to know every detail about him. When he appeared finally satisfied, he began to ask about the Isheen and the battle for the Craig. He listened intently, questioning each aspect, teasing out every single detail.

Kemble kept looking to Wal with his most pleading expression, but the man seemed oblivious to him.

Gabhran sipped carefully and relaxed back. "Well," he tried to smile though it looked more like a grimace. "We withdrew to the Craig, letting them have the damned beach."

"You fought well," Corvus prodded the fire with a stick. "The Vör's planning was sound."

"Aye, I suppose it was the only thing we could do."

"How did they get into the Craig?" Tàmh had a strange sense of morbid curiosity. He had to know people he loved, friends and relatives, had been in the Craig, but more importantly, he would have tales to tell and poems to compose.

"We got the bridge up and the gate down and let them have everything we could throw at them from the battlements." He stopped and looked at Wal intently. "We made the bastards suffer."

"Aye, good," said Wal.

"But then the storm hit. They summoned it."

"Who summoned it? MacLeech?" asked Corvus.

"No. I don't know. The Isheen, I think, they're all sorcerers."

"What happened then?" pushed Tàmh.

"Sheet lightning struck the battlements a dozen times, the sky opened, and it rained black ice, hail the size of your fists, and then the wind took up. We couldn't remain on the ramparts; our men were being blown to their deaths. So, we took shelter, but it must have been worse for those in the open."

"Such things are too unpredictable," Corvus observed. "Not any real use in battle, too indiscriminate."

Gabhran took another sip of water but choked it back up.

Kemble glared at the others as he wiped the young man's brow. "He's running a fever, and we need to get him to Crannag-mòr." Facing the Laird's wifee was not something Kemble particularly looked forward to, but Meg was there, and she was the best healer they had.

"No," Gabhran pushed the Grieve's hand away. "They used the storm to summon a monstrous black dragonship... It was Balor himself, Lord of the Fomóiri. Those monsters," he gestured towards the battle site. "We never stood a chance against them; they climbed the bloody walls like spiders! Before we knew it, the bridge was down, and the Isheen poured in." He winced against the stabbing pain in his back. "It was madness, horrific madness."

"And MacLeech?" asked Corvus.

"I don't know. We retreated into the keep and the towers, but we couldn't hope to hold them off. I thought we were all going to die. Then the Witch appeared among them, in the courtyard, and struck them down."

"With what?"

"Lightning. She struck them down with strange lightning from her hands; it was incredible. They just burned up like dry tinder."

"On her own?" asked Corvus.

Kemble answered. "She had a huge grey wolf, the size of a horse, with her. Those she didn't kill; it tore to pieces. The Isheen fled like startled children." Kemble re-soaked the cloth he'd been using to wipe Gabhran's forehead. "After Gabhran was injured, the Laird ordered us to use the Jeevir door to get out while we could. I tried to argue, but he insisted we make for the Crannag-mòr and send warning to the King."

"The Jeevir door?" asked Corvus.

"There's a secret door that leads out to steps on the sheltered side of the Craig. Only the Laird of Eagle's Craig and the Castellan know of its existence."

"An' me," Wal reached for a wineskin. "The others?"

Gabhran struggled to sit up. "Angus would not leave; they went further into the castle."

Corvus took the wineskin off Wal. "They?"

Kemble scowled at Corvus. "The Laird, the Witch, and the others. They followed that madman, MacLeech, into the old tunnels below the castle."

"Why?"

Gabhran shook his head slowly. "I don't know."

"Where did the wolf come from?" inquired Tàmh.

Wal walked back towards the road. As far as he was concerned, Gabhran was of no use as a leader, wounded or not, and the Grieve was nothing more than an over-indulged house slave. He understood it had come down to himself to take charge. After finding the Kern's Tòshuch, a burly, softly spoken man named Drust Mac Mailcon, and agreeing on what to do, Wal issued his orders.

They would bury the dead here; the Fomóiri could rot where they lay. He would then move everyone, wounded and all, onto the next clearing to make camp.

Once he had the burials organised and gotten everyone moving, he finally would have time to think about what to do next. Things had radically changed; this was no longer a relief caravan taking supplies to the besieged; the siege was over, and as far as anyone knew, the Laird himself could be dead. Things had to be rethought and fast.

The idea of returning home with unanswered questions held no appeal to him at all. There were few people that Wal had ever feared, and Jorunn MacRoth was the one he had learnt to fear the most. But he couldn't go on with all this stuff and dragging the wounded. A split had to be made, some to go on and some to turn back. The big questions were who and how many. He found a stump to sit on and began to make his calculations.

Chapter 20

"Sna coilltean a siar
Chan iarrain fuireach gu brath
Bha m' intinn 's mo mhiann
A riamh air lagan a' bhaigh
Ach iadsan bha fial
An gniomh, an caidreamh 's an agh
Air sgapadh gun dion
Mar thriallas ealtainn roimh namh…………."

"In the woods of the West
I would not want to wait forever
My mind and my wish
Were ever in the little hollow by the cove
But those who were gracious
In act, in friendship and in mirth
Are scattered without protection
Like a flock of birds before an enemy…………."

Donald MacLver
"An Ataireachd Ard"

Wal had made the necessary decisions; Gabhran, Ned and the rest of the wounded would have to return to the Crannog on Loch Tymor, along with as many men as he could dare to spare. Most of the younger stewards and packhorse handlers would have to go back as well. He put Kemble in charge of the whole thing, he was a drunk, but at least he was an officious old bugger and could be trusted to do this. Wal wanted to send the Bard back as well, but he would refuse to go, so he had left it unspoken. That left him with the strangers, Corvus and Svein, as well as the prisoner and twenty-two Kerns and their war dogs. The Kern's wounded would go south with the rest under Gabhran's protection.

On the headcount he had now; he would go on with twenty of his own lads he'd brought up with him plus Taran Roou and his kin, another eleven, four stout gilles who he had armed to fight, the twenty-one Kerns and their leader, the two strangers and Tàmh, the Bard. Not including himself and the three remaining slaves, which made sixty fighting men, forty-two riding horses and ten pack animals. He had spared as much as he could for those going back, but he had to weigh his responsibility to his Chieftain against all else. Nothing was more important than to get to the Craig as fast as possible and find out for himself what had truly happened.

He sent Nèill, the youngest of the MacReuls and the best horseman in the Clan, ahead of the rest to warn those at Loch Tymor and spread then news of what had happened. He was relieved that it would be the lad rather than himself that broke the news to Lady MacRoth. She favoured the younger men over the older ones, and he had no wish to face the full force of her rage. Wal had never been Jorunn Kolinka's friend, but he had never seen himself as one of her enemies either; he had simply always kept his respectful distance from her personally. She, like him, was a 'coigreach,' an outsider of Gothad blood and even after two decades or more, she still felt the older clansmen's unacceptance. For Wal it was different; he had made them accept him, it had taken almost four decades, but he was now Gaisgeach, armour bearer for the Chieftain himself, Wal MacCoigruch, still the bastard son of a Gothad, still looked on as different, but more accepted than Jorunn MacRoth would ever be. When she had first come to the house of the MacRoth's, an exquisite, delicate, golden girl child, he wished he could have reached out to her, as a friend, a confidante or ally, but, even then there was something about her that worried him. She was Jarven Olson's daughter, and she had inherited much from the old Jarl, his wealth, his bearing, and a good portion of his insanity. Kemble had been against the marriage from the first mention of it, and his opposition had seen him banished to Eagle's Craig for years. Others, like the Chieftain's brother, Kinart, had come to more unfortunate ends. Jorunn MacRoth was not one to oppose lightly.

"You've done well."

Wal looked up, startled. "What?"

Corvus had drawn up his horse beside him and now sat with one leg thrown casually over the bow of the saddle, Rhos style, chewing at a chunk of black bread. Wal took a good look at the Gärian. He looked in better health and vigour than any of the rest of them. The rigours of their journey seemed to be agreeing with him; he looked almost younger. "I said, 'You've done well,' with the arrangements, I mean." He lent towards the horse's head and fed it the last of the bread.

"It had to be done." Wal stood up.

"Hmm, but is not the task of the Chieftain's cousin or the Grieve to organise such things?"

Wal felt a rush of anger at being questioned. "I do not answer to you."

Corvus held up a hand. "True, but I wondered why you took over so fast. Are they both that useless?" Reading the answer in Wal's eyes, Corvus pushed on. "Are you sure of the wisdom of taking those," he gestured towards the Kerns, "back with us?"

Wal glared at the Gärian, but he was only asking the question going through his own mind and almost every other Albans present. He answered truthfully. "I donna have any other choice, do I?"

Corvus nodded sombrely.

Wal hauled his swathe of plaid onto his shoulder and swung his claymore across his back. Letting the irritation he felt clearly into his voice, he demanded, "Do ye have any other questions?"

"One"

"What?"

"The Isheen woman." Corvus straightened up in the saddle.

"Aye?"

"Why, when you were so intent on killing her earlier, have you chosen to keep her with us?"

Wal felt like he was being played with, Corvus seemed to be trying something on with him, but he couldn't quite understand what. "We may be able to use her." Wal was quite pleased with that answer even though it just popped into his head, so he pursued it. "She's one of them, so she may be of use even if only to trade."

"A hostage," Corvus seemed to accept that but then added quietly. "But you must tell your men to be careful, Wal. If what the Bard says is right, she has more power than just in her sword arm. She may try to influence one of them to…shall we say, aid her?"

Wal stiffened, so that was it, the Gärian was insinuating that he'd fallen under the spell of the Isheen woman. He grinned coldly at the ridiculousness of the idea. "I do not need ye to warn me aboot the Sìth." Wal swung around and began to walk away, adding loudly over his shoulder. "Until today, you didnae believe they even existed."

They pushed on through the remains of the day as the forest grew darker and more primaeval. As the grey, rain-laden clouds closed in, a solemn hush descended over them.

Svein pulled his horse up alongside Corvus and leaned closer to the Gärian. "Is this really a good idea?"

"What do you mean?"

"This," he gestured around him at the column of warriors and at the forest. "Those creatures, they were, we were... lucky. There could be an army of them waiting for us or worse." He jabbed a finger towards the prisoner, "An army of them."

"Aye, there no doubt is." Corvus pulled his hood up over his head to fend off the light drizzle coming in with the approaching darkness. "Listen, boy, we don't have much choice here." Well, at least I don't, he added silently. "We're going along with this as long as we have to, and that's all," he lied. "Whatever awaits these people at the castle, it is not of our concern; it's their war."

"Shouldn't we try to..."

"Quiet, boy," Corvus growled.

Svein swallowed the question and looked around nervously. About midday, they had left the main path, for a more direct route to their destination, through fear of another ambush and had started following this forest track. At first, it had been almost as easy going as the road, but the wood had been getting denser and more oppressive all afternoon and the dirt path, now little more than a game trail, was so overgrown that they were having to push on in single file, with those at the front slashing their way through the bracken and overhangs. Now, to add to his misery, the sleety rain was returning. Svein hated all of this, it was cold, miserable, and he felt lonely. The fighting this morning had cheered him up a little, but his ribs still hurt from two days ago, and he was tired. Corvus was only supposed to escort him to Noatun, not drag him into someone else's war. Anyway, what did he care about Albans and Kerns? If the Dock-Alfar rose up and destroyed them all, then they'd be doing the Gothads, in fact, the world, a service. As soon as that idea entered his mind, he knew it was wrong, he was no lover of the Albans, Kerns, or any of the other peoples for that matter, but he understood there was one truth behind all this; if the Dock-Alfar,

228

Isheen, or whatever they called themselves, defeated the Kerns and the Albans then they'd most probably turn their attention towards Noatun and even the Kingdom of Skjaldborg itself. Svein had heard the legends and knew the tales, but that had always been in the long-ago mythical past of the skald's stories. Most of his generation didn't even believe these creatures existed. How could his people defend against something they have never seen? The question scared him; worse still, what terrified him more was how they could fight something they didn't even believe in?

Fluchtburgen! What if they struck further south through Eathel to Fluchtburgen? His whole family, brother, mother, sisters, all of them were at Fluchtburgen. A rising tide of panic suddenly choked him, and his heart began to pound.

Corvus seized his arm. "Steady boy."

Svein looked at him, his eyes wide with fear and realisation. "We have to get word to my uncle. They have to be warned."

"Calm down," Corvus released his arm. "I doubt if your people are under any threat."

Rationally, Svein knew, it was a true enough observation, but it may be only a matter of time. Whatever had happened to start this war, it looked like both the Kerns and the Albans were no match for the Isheen and their monstrous allies. The Alban's so-called impregnable castle had fallen in a night, and the enemy was moving South fast enough to strike them this morning. Possibly that was only a group sent out to pursue and destroy, but it would be foolish to think it would have been the only one. Corvus had said that Wal had made the right choice to take them off the main drag towards the castle, but this turned out to be costly in time and nervous energy. Wal had had the Kerns set loose their hounds, and they were doing an excellent job of sweeping the area as the column moved on, but they were causing too much noise for Corvus' liking and unsettling some of the packhorses. Everybody was jumpy, and tempers amongst the men were getting frayed. That could lead to mistakes or worse.

"Just keep your head and stay close to me whatever happens." Corvus patted the young warrior's shoulder. "Keep calm."

Corvus, though felt calmer in himself than he had done for

some time, the strange visitor had not appeared since last night, but he was now more open to accepting that the old Magician was in some way real, deluded, or deranged, but probably real. He had also accepted that somehow the old Magician was orchestrating this, at least in part, which meant he may be as powerful as he intimated, but that didn't concern Corvus overly. He doubted whether the old Magician could control all the forces involved in this chaos, and certainly, this was not all for his benefit. Not even the most insane Tyrannos would cause a war just to trap one transgressor, whatever the transgression. So that meant there were forces at large that were beyond the old Magician's control, and that, for Corvus, was a comforting thought. No, Corvus decided that the old Magician was not omnipotent, which meant he could be tricked, outmanoeuvred, and defeated. All he had to do was wait for him to make his move.

Corvus felt that the accusation of rape was a bluff; there had been no rape, there was no child, but the old man wanted him to believe it like he wanted him to believe that he had been dead for years. Corvus knew it for what it was; a mind game, a play to make him feel isolated, to keep him off balance. Wrong footed, so he would do things without seeing the real consequences. Whoever this old Magician was, he was ingenious, but Corvus could now see right through his game.

He had noticed that the old Magician resembled the prisoner, the long face, the ears, even the teeth; his look was subtler, softer, but it was there nonetheless. That answered many questions; if these creatures, these Isheen, were as powerful as the Bard and Svein said, then one of their Magicians would be a true force to be reckoned with. Probably far more potent than the old Imperial Magi, but just as arrogant and vulnerable to cold steel.

Deep within his thoughts, Corvus made his last dark little pact with Death herself. He would give unto this Magician whatever he wanted, whatever it took, whatever it took to get close enough to strike. Whatever it would cost him, he would thrust this spell weaver into Death's embrace even if he had to drag him there by the throat.

Corvus found his hand had come to rest on his sword hilt, his fingers caressing the familiar form of the grip and the heavy pommel, still, in part, tacky from the Fomóire's blood. Old friend, he thought, you've never failed me yet.

Something disturbed his chain of thoughts, an odd sensation, an overpowering feeling of being watched. Pushing back his hood, he turned to look straight into the eyes of the Horse-boy, Nissien, the mute Sentatii slave. He had one fine-boned hand holding together the bottom of his cowl, but his aquamarine eyes were clear, bright, and unflinching. I thought you'd gone back to the Crannog with the others. Corvus caught himself instinctively raising his hand in greeting, embarrassed. He slapped his hand back down, but the slave acknowledged him with a gentle nod and pointed off to the distance.

The path opened out a little and then fell steeply away on the right side down towards the surface of a vast, steel-grey lake. As the little column moved out of the protection of the trees, they came into the full force of the driving rain. Exposed on the path, the horses became skittish as their hooves slipped on the mud and shale. As men climbed down off their mounts, Corvus took the opportunity to walk to the edge of the ridge and gaze out across the lake.

Tàmh joined him and pointed to the steep escarpment on the other side, jutting out from the cliff face, like a colossal talon, was a massive pinnacle of dark rock, upon which sat a brooding fortress of black stone towers.

"Creag an Eagail," said Tàmh, "Eagle's Craig."

Corvus looked at the young Bard. "I know enough of that language to know that is not what it means."

Chapter 21

"Ac hēr forþ berað,   fugelas singað
Gylleð græghama,   gūðwudu hlynneð,"

"Ymbe hyne gōdra fæla,
Hwearflīcra hræw.
 Hræfen wandrode."

"But now starts war, the carrion-birds shall sing,
The grey-cloaked wolf shall yell, the spear resound."

"And round him many noble heroes fell,
The corpses of the brave.
The raven circled."

The Fight at Finnsburh
ASPR .VI

I lay my hand upon the black stone.
    That is the Heart of the Craig.
       Ancient thing.
          A living thing.
Warm.
    A beating heart.
       Trembling under my touch.
       I concentrate.
Drawing the warmth into me.
    Don't be afraid.
       Taking the rhythm into me.
Breathing, carefully, slowly.
    My heart, my rhythm.
       I close my eyes and rest my forehead against the
soothing surface of the stone.
    Don't be afraid.

Now I can see it clearly.

The light that burns within the Heart.

I concentrate.

I focus upon the light.

A light older than time.

A splinter of the First Light.

I draw it into me.

Carefully, slowly.

My light.

My rhythm.

I can feel the surface of the Heart change beneath my fingers.

It reaches out for me.

Its warmth envelops me.

It welcomes me.

You are so beautiful.

I step into the living light at the Heart of the Craig.

The shock wave of light, heat and noise was so intense that several men in the tunnel stumbled, stunned by its physical impact. Angus shielded his eyes behind his arm and steadied himself against the wall. Others turned away, swearing and cursing, covering their eyes and ears.

Angus heard Calum's cry above the noise, and someone at the back collapsed. As his eyes began to adjust, he risked squinting into the light. Annis was gone, but now MacLeech stood before the stone holding forth his staff and drum and chanting, almost screaming, at the top of his lungs. His words were nearly lost in the deafening roar that filled the tunnel.

"You have to go now!" Jacobis yelled close to Angus' ear. "There's no time to waste! They can't hold it open for long." Jacobis shoved him roughly, "Farðu núna!"

Angus staggered forward under the outstretched arms of the Tysher and threw himself towards the light. His whole body tensed at the impact all reason told him to expect, but it never came; there was only the blinding flash of light, the searing heat, and the strange sensation of falling.

Jacobis swung around and grabbed the next in line, "Farðu núna!" One by one, he thrust the warriors and gilles towards the blazing light. Some faltered and hesitated, but the Vör gave them no choice. As he shoved and cajoled, Jacobis could hear the snarls of Fyngard at the back of the queue, driving the stragglers forward with the flat of his sword.

Once the last of the Albans, the fat cook, had lurched into the light, Jacobis turned to Fyn, who was now carrying the unconscious body of the young serving boy, Ag, over his shoulder. "They'll be right behind us."

"I can hear them," Fyngard replied. "Well, after you," he gestured towards the light.

Jac glanced at the light and smiled sheepishly. "I insist, after you."

Fyngard laughed, sheathed his sword, and stepped into the light.

Jacobis turned to MacLeech; he had fallen quiet, but the continuing strain was written on his face and running in rivulets of sweat down his forehead. Jac noticed that the old Tysher's blind eye appeared to be pulsating with the same strange radiance emanating from the Heart. Suddenly MacLeech turned to him, his face now little more than a skull mask, and whispered, "Awa with you, big yin!"

Jacobis nodded, picked up his backpack and spear, turned, and stepped into the Heart.

With a few mumbled incantations to close the gateway, the Tysher summoned the very last of his strength and took the three steps into the roaring light.

The Galdràgon lifted the hound's lung out of the way and inspected the heart. She sighed unhappily; it was large, firm, and unblemished, still hot with the fresh blood it had only just stopped pumping. A healthy heart, a strong heart. She lifted her hands out of the animal's rib cage and watched the steam rising from her fingers into the cold air. Forces were working against her, and now she found that even her own powers were weakened by this accursed place. The half-breed Witch must still be in the castle, but no matter how hard she tried, she could not locate her or those around her. It was as if the castle itself were shielding them. In desperation, she had been forced to try other methods. Simple scrying had failed miserably; she could not even locate Mathan-Bàn, let alone the Witch. A spell of summoning had had quite an effect but not the desired one. A fuath, the spirit of a recently dead Trow, appeared and became so wild with fear that it tried to attack her when she had questioned it about the Witch. She had been forced to resort to this haruspicy. She was tired, near to exhaustion, and this digging about in the entrails of a cur made her feel increasingly desperate. Something was blocking her, a profound darkness at the edges of her consciousness, but she knew she must keep on.

She looked around at the solemn faces of her acolytes officiating in the divination, the purest of all Isheen maidens, high born and proud. Her handmaidens, handpicked, but the certainty in their faces was gone, and she could feel their anxiety; they were frightened. The Galdràgon could understand their fear; they had lost one of their sisters and seen their own brothers slain by the hands of the Daonna. However, more unsettling was the unnatural strength of the half-breed and the casualness of her display of power. Few of them had seen such raw cumhachd before, and it frightened them.

It is not her that frightens me, she added to herself.

She washed off the blood in a bowl proffered to her and ran her hands over her face letting her fingers follow the lines and scars running down her cheeks to the point of her chin.

Mathan-Bàn's lackeys, the Gaisgich an taighe, the young men of his Household, were growing bolder in their contempt for her and the Fomóiri now sat on their ship sulking like petulant children, even the Daonna mercenaries were beginning to show disrespect.

How, she wandered, they dared to show anything other than fear and awe to me, Sheela na Cìoch, the Galdràgon of the Isheen of Dùn nan Eilean? It's astounding. She would see them pay for their insolence, but they were not the real problem; the real problem lay where the contempt stemmed from; Mathan-Bàn. That stupid, prideful, ignorant, weak-minded fool. He had allowed the Taibhsear of the Kern's to escape his clutches a dozen times by dallying around in the countryside burning villages and collecting slaves, and then he had made a mess of the battle for the Creag. He had wasted the lives of dozens of Isheen warriors when he should have used the Daonna mercenaries; now, he had not only lost the Taibhsear but also the Witch. She sighed again. Damn him!

If he were not Fearchara's older brother, the Galdràgon would have rid herself of him a long time ago, but the Bànrigh had always been so loyal to him. Even now, the Bànrigh, at the height of her ascension, would never allow anything said against her beloved brother. Sheela knew that even if he lost this whole campaign, the Bànrigh would still side with him. Fearchara had the stamp of a good Queen, a Bànrigh that could lead the Isheen, possibly the whole of the Sìth, back into the light of the upper world and thus beyond the powers of Finnbharra of the Daoine Faoi Cheilt. Mathan-Bàn was her weakness, an 'Àrd-dràgon' with no actual stomach for the fight. Sheela had always pinned her hopes for her people on her nephew Cullach-Bàn, he was young, strong, and virile, and without Mathan-Bàn's influence, she would have been able to marry Cullach-Bàn, Uachdaran of the West, to the Princess Fearchara and create a bloodline the likes of which had not been seen amongst the ruling houses of the Isheen for ten generations. The possibility of a lineage of Queens of one House, one bloodline ruling for generations, made her almost weak with the heady scent of power. She would be the midwife and High Priestess to generations of Isheen Queens. Mathan-Bàn had thwarted her at every opportunity; he had poisoned Fearchara's mind against Cullach-Bàn by spreading lies and innuendoes. Now Fearchara was Bànrigh, bright, youthful, and potent, and without a consort to temper her, her desires had become a lust for blood and war. Mathan-Bàn's stupidity had brought them to this, to this point, to this place, and his continuing actions were in danger of allowing even this to slip through his fingers.

The Galdràgon knew how important it was to secure this place, locate the gateway that existed somewhere in the castle, and capture the Taibhsear and the damned half-blood Witch. Fearchara needed to make a great blood sacrifice on Oidhche Shamhna, a powerful tribute to the Gods, but Mathan-Bàn was only interested in holding onto the castle. As if that were important and playing games of brinkmanship with the Fomóiri. Stupid, arrogant, fool, she cursed again. Damn him!

She returned her attention to the dog's entrails; the signs were ominous, she knew, but maybe the liver would hold the answer she was looking for. She reached for the knife again.

Suddenly the whole castle, the very stone of the walls, seemed to suck in a deep breath. Then came a tremendous low resounding thud, like a great strike upon some massive drum, held down deep within the castle. The Galdràgon froze as panic seized her. She could feel the power of life flowing through the veins in the living rock around them. It was as if they were in the chest of some primaeval stone giant that had just been startled awake. Then the beat struck again, shaking the very floor and walls of the room. Again. Like the thumping beat of some great heart, deep within the Creag.

In that instant, she realised what was happening. "No!" she shrieked as she flung the knife across the room. "No!" The Witch must have found the portal, the gate deep within the rock, and was trying to open it.

"Stop them!"

She flew from the room with her acolytes frantically chasing after her and ran down the winding stairs towards the Great Hall. "Mathan-Bàn!" She threw open the doors and screamed into the Hall,   "You   must   stop   them!"

The Southron mercenaries had grown exhausted and wary of the catacombs; for a whole day now, they had been fighting the defenders room by room, cellar to cellar. The Albans knew these tunnels and passageways by heart, and it was easy for them to waylay their pursuers and escape into the darkness. Every doorway, every opening had become a trap, every room an ambush, but still, the Southron's had pushed on. This was the kind of work they understood well; they were trained and experienced in such fighting, house to house, room to room, they had sacked towns, cities, castles, and fortresses, and knew what tactics to use and what to expect, but down here in the darkness, things had rapidly become nightmarish.

Earl Eadric, known as Strandwulf, had done his best to allay their fears, but a leader cannot truly lead from a sickbed. His left shoulder and collarbone had been shattered, and even with the ministrations of the Isheen Galdràgon's handmaids with all their skills, the pain left him swimming in and out of consciousness. In his stead, the Gesith, Heca, had now assumed command down in the tunnels and was trying his best to hold up the men's morale, but like his own, it was flagging.

This was like no other place they had fought in, and there were things down here that truly unnerved even the bravest of them. Occasionally they would hear the cry of things in the darkness and the baying of the terrible war hounds of the Kerns, but far worse was the tension of listening for the howl of the great wolf that attacked them on the beach and the fear that at any moment the Vör would step out of the darkness spinning that awful spear.

Heca knew the Isheen's superior capabilities well, but they still kept back, never genuinely engaging in this guerrilla fighting, willing only to follow up and shoot a few arrows. Heca didn't care what they did so long as they kept their distance from him; they were Ælves and evil, born of lies and treachery by their very nature. What Earl Eadric was doing treating with such creatures was beyond Heca's understanding. Every simple goodwife knew that it was courting doom to strike a bargain with Ælves or their kind.

For now, none of that was his concern. His men were doing a good job of driving the Albans down into the bottleneck of the tunnels, and soon the defenders would have nowhere left to retreat to. Then Heca could hand it over to the Isheen, who would finish the job if they had the stomach for it. He had just made himself sure of the security of a long section that included an enormous old wine cellar when one of his comrades approached him.

"Heca, com' see this." Jaenberht, a big solid man, veteran of a dozen campaigns under Strandwulf, looked drawn and tired. His face was ghostly in the flickering torchlight.

"What is it?"

Jaenberht turned away. "Som'thing you must see."

Heca followed the veteran warrior out of the cellar and down a small corridor. Jaenberht stopped by a door and held up the torch. "Here."

The door was gone, wrenched off its hinges by the looks of it; Heca peered through the empty doorway into the room. It was an odd room, square, but the walls were curved, and there was a slope to the floor with a drain in the centre.

"Look." Jaenberht gestured to the far corner.

In the corner was what appeared to be one of the sea monsters the Ælfen witches had summoned, but it was burnt black, its skin blistered and cracked, like pork rind held over a fire for too long. Its head, or what he supposed was its head, looked as if it had exploded from within. "Scite!" swore Heca.

"Is the work of the Witch again, No?"

"Yea, she must have caught one down here."

Jaenberht looked at him sternly. "When we corner them, she'll use this kinda magic on us, you know. She killed scores of them with a wave of her hand. What use are spears against that?" There was no hint of fear in the older warrior's voice, only cold pragmatism.

Heca shook his head. "When it com's to that, the Ælfen will have to do their own bloody work."

Jaenberht nodded slowly, "Yea. We should have never...." He let the thought trail off.

Heca looked the older man in the eyes. "We did not choose, old friend, but it is too late to change what is past."

"I am tired, that's all."

"I too. We'll have to..."

A sudden clamour in the tunnels cut him off, the sounds of panic, shouting and running. Heca, fearing a counterattack ran back to the cellars to find his men now gathered in a large group in the middle of the vault. "What in Hel's name is happening?"

Ingeld, Heca's cousin, pulled off his helmet and shouted back. "The Ælfen, they have decided it is time they did som'thing!" he laughed. "They've gone rushing down there like hounds after a hare."

"Why?"

Ingeld shrugged. "I could hear some drumming, I think. Maybe there's merrymaking." He laughed at his own joke.

Several of the others sniggered.

Heca suppressed his own laughter and took control. "Well, we wouldn't want to miss a gebéorscipe, would we?" He drew his sword. "Send word to the others," he slapped Ingeld on the back hard. "We're going to finally have the chance to see how good these cifesboren Ælfen are at fighting."

The Southron mercenaries all looked at him as if he were mad.

"Move!"

They grabbed their long shields, drew their swords, and trotted off in the direction that the Isheen had rushed.

The corridors and cellars wound down further than any of the marauders imagined. Passages became steeply sloping tunnels that ran into barred doorways that opened onto narrow stairwells that plunged further down into the living rock. Tunnels ran into tunnels that grew narrower by the yard or opened unexpectedly into vast pitch-black cellars before dropping again down winding stairwells. Torches guttered as if starving in the oppressive darkness, adding their smoky fumes to the choking humidity of the labyrinth. As they pushed on downward, they came across corpses of hounds, Dhaoine and Ælfen, Albans and Kerns, all butchered and discarded, left where they fell as the fighting passed over them. The stench of blood and spilt guts adding to the sickening claustrophobic atmosphere.

Heca's men picked their way past the dead and on down into the warm, dank darkness. Ahead they could hear the terrible clamour of fighting and the strange steady drumming, like a heartbeat, pounding in the darkness. Catching the nervous glances of his comrades, Heca grinned assumingly back and joked, "Well, som'thing seems to have woken the sons of whores up!"

The fighting was raging around a massive iron portcullis that barred the way. The defenders on the other side were holding off the Ælfen's frantic attempts to assail the doorway with a hail of bolts and arrows. The mighty Isheen, it seemed to Heca, were being sent insane by the terrible drumming to the point that they were simply throwing themselves at the gate, wild-eyed and baying like enraged animals. It was a massacre, packed together in the tunnel mouth and driven to lunacy. The Ælfen were being cut down with callous ease by the efficient and delighted defenders.

Dead and dying sprawled everywhere. Hacked limbs and ripped bodies spilt blood and entrails into a growing lake of gore now so deep that some of the fallen were struggling not to lose their footing in it. The whole scene was one of bloody chaos as if Hel herself had thrown open her gates and all her horrors were pouring out into this sickening slaughter.

Suddenly more Isheen poured out of the darkness and shoved past the knot of Southrons to throw themselves, howling, into the fray.

Stepping neatly back beyond arrow range, Heca untied his chinstrap and pulled off his helmet. "Scite! Have they gone mad?" he said, pushing back his sweat-soaked hair.

"Nā," Jaenberht rested his shield on the floor and lent on it. "Look. The gate is made of wrought iron, and there," he pointed at the bottom, where parallel iron bars, rusted red with age, were inlaid in between the flagstones. "Som' one built this geat to keep the likes of the Ælfen ūt. It's sapping their scinnlāc. Weakening them." It was said that Jaenberht's mother's father had been a Gothad Gothi, a war priest. She had passed down to him a wealth of knowledge that often caused others to wonder whether he was more Gothad than Southron. "They're never going to get past that, Heca. Not without help."

Heca glanced back at the two dozen men behind him. "Well, we'd better help them then," he said fatalistically.

Jaenberht grinned and reached for the water jack hanging on his belt. "But not just yet, a' Heca?"

Behind Heca, the Southron mercenaries laughed mirthlessly.

Faylinn led the forty strong contingent of the Gaisgich an taighe down into the labyrinth below the castle keep. With every step further into the bowels of this great stone monster, his senses screamed louder for him to turn and run. Something was going terribly wrong, and it had fallen to him to deal with it.

If the Witch had succeeded in finding and opening the gate, then she and the Kern's leader would have escaped, but there was more to the Galdràgon and Mathan-Bàn's fears than that; if the Witch had the power to pass through the gate, then she could seal it behind her for a thousand years. The Isheen would be trapped in this place and forced to withdraw back across the lands they had ravaged.

Faylinn knew the dangers all too well; spies had told them that the Kings of the Kerns and the Albans were already amassing armies for their counter strikes. Caught out in the open and with numbers heavily against them, the Isheen would suffer heavy losses. There was no thought that they may lose such a battle, but any substantial losses of Isheen lives would be disastrous. Sìthean blood was far too valuable to waste frivolously.

The nature of the differences between the Sìth and the Dhaoine had always intrigued him; the strangeness of the Daonna's psyche and their bizarre behaviours, greed and belligerence, everything about them.

He had studied them as best as he could from the safety of the great libraries, second-hand stories, and the occasional encounter, but as he had learnt about them, yet more questions had arisen. The one thing that interested him most was why they aged so fast. Their lifetimes were, on average, he supposed, about a fifth of that of his own people, and they were subject to so many illnesses and diseases. It was incredible that they managed to survive as a race at all, as they in the majority lacking in any real powers other than hedgerow Magicians and the occasional Seer. Nevertheless, they had advantages; they multiply like rats and inhabit Saoghal Solus an Latha, the World of the Light of Day, which gave them vast advantages. Faylinn didn't like broad daylight, few Isheen did, and fewer ever spent any length of time living in that world or desired to. But it benefited the Dhaoine immensely; their pitiable hearing and inadequate sense of smell coupled with their lack of any true powers meant that they relied heavily on their eyesight. Their eyes were far better suited for the world of daylight than the eyes of the Isheen. Though the Isheen were much better able to endure sunlight than some of the other great races of the Sìth.

Faylinn had lived all his life in the vaulted halls of the great rath of Dùn nan Làidir, far below the roots of the most ancient trees at the heart of the Coille Mhòr. In the opulent splendour of a subterranean world that hardly any Dhaoine ever saw, and none ever escaped to tell the tales of. You could ride four abreast through the avenues of Dùn nan Làidir, armies of hundreds could parade in its plazas, its squares could hold thousands of merrymakers. All far below the ground, hidden from the blinding sun. It was a timeless world of beauty, a place of safety and wonder, unsoiled, ordered, gorgeous and spacious, where the Isheen ruled seemingly untouched by time or the affairs of other races.

Faylinn was very proud of his home. In his own lifetime, he had seen Mathan-Bàn shape the city into the most beautiful in the North, second only in magnificence to mighty Slievenamon, the seat of the Lord of Tir Eile, Finnvarra, King of the Daoine Faoi Cheilt, the Unseen, in the far distant West. However, Finnvarra was insane, and Mathan-Bàn was not.

To be home again, to be a child again, chasing through the Temple precincts with Rànd, Faylinn sighed to himself. Where are you, sister, my love? Far below this Daonna fortress, all thought of such happiness died in his heart, consumed by the Creag. Here there was no art in the work of Dhaoine, no beauty; their work was brutal, cold, and stark. They had hacked these tunnels out of the living rock, boring their holes down into the earth like ants. There were no fabulous vaults or spacious avenues, just these squalid little burrows going ever deeper. At home, Faylinn loved the earth and the warm feeling of the safety of the living rock around him, but here it was hostile, malevolent, and cold to the touch.

The others could feel it as well, this was no place they would ever want to be, but here they were and here they would be trapped if they didn't get to the gate in time.

He could now sense the heat rising to meet them on the

stench laden air as they pushed on down into the depths of the Creag and the dreadful rhythmic throbbing of what sounded like some great heartbeat in the depths. As they plunged further, they could hear that somewhere below them, a terrible mêlée was being fought. Voices, Isheen war cries mingled with the roar of Dhaoine and the sound of clashing of arms, the screams of the dying mingled and dulled by the pounding beat.

Faylinn could feel gnawing pangs of fear in his gut; somewhere down there was the Vör with that dreadful spear, or worse, the Witch herself whose powers made those of the Galdràgon look like a child's conjuring tricks. He had seen Mathan-Bàn's arrow strike the giant and seen him fall with his own eyes, yet the same arrow had struck and killed Kyla where she stood not five yards from Mathan-Bàn in the very same instant.

Nevertheless, Faylinn had a charge to carry out, an order from his adored master, and he would under no circumstances let fear cloud his judgment or turn him back. He was Isheen, the Marasgal of the Gaisgich an taighe, trusted and loved by his master, whom he could never fail.

Abruptly the sounds of fighting coming from ahead stopped.

Fear seized Faylinn; he drew his sword and ran, throwing himself heedlessly down stairwells and running wildly through the tunnels.

The Gaisgich an taighe shoved past a knot of Southrons to burst onto a scene of carnage, a horrific tableau, frozen motionless in the moment. A massive portcullis guarded a huge opening at the far end of the tunnel; it was half raised, the lower spikes looking like the great iron-bound teeth of a monstrous yawning mouth. Before it, as if vomited forth from the immense maw, lay a host of dead and dying. Shattered bodies, Isheen and Daonna, were piled upon each other, some still locked in deadly embraces, teeth bared, hands still clawing at eyes and throats, white-knuckled fists still clenching weapons, frozen in the instant of death.

For a split second, Faylinn thought himself insane; madness must have seized his mind as he froze and almost slipped in the pool of blood. Steadying himself, his reason returned, and he found himself staring into the eyes of his sister.

Rànd stood beneath the teeth of the portcullis, her hands unseen and her head held back, behind her, at her shoulder, stood a big Alban, with a knife at her throat.

Faylinn cast about frantically. Around him, Isheen and Southrons stood transfixed. Some shot him nervous glances; others looked away.

In front of Rànd stood another Daonna, shorter than most, heavily built, an old man, but hard looking. He wore a dark, studded leather harness, a small Alban buckler hung loosely from a strap off his left arm and in his right hand, he held a heavy short sword. He was blood-soaked, and there were five bodies at his feet, yet he stood with an air of casualness that was almost offensive.

Beyond the portcullis stood a knot of Albans and Kerns whose faces shared none of the casual distance of the other man; they looked scared and confused. Their eyes were like those of a rabbit caught in a hunter's lamplight.

Faylinn stepped forward.

Chapter 22

"Her eyes were as blue as bugloss; her lips were as red as vermilion; her shoulders were high and smooth and soft and white; her fingers were pure white and long; her arms were long; her slender long yielding smooth side, soft as wool, was as white as the foam of the wave."

Édaín the Fairy
Irish
Author Unknown

Rànd looked into her brother's eyes and bit down hard on the gag in her mouth to stifle the instinctive cry that leapt from her heart. She had to warn him, but first, she had to think.

Think! She demanded of herself, Think, damn you!

The thing they called Corvus was waiting for him, ready to play with him and then kill him, and there was nothing she could do about it. Her hands were tied behind her, and the one called Wal had a knife at her throat. She could still fight him, though she knew she would die in the act. She couldn't let Faylinn die, not at the hands of this monster, not in this forsaken place. It shocked her to find hot tears running down her cheeks.

She shook her head. Stop it!

I am Isheen, I am strong, and I have no fear. She knew it was a lie even as she told it to herself; she was more frightened than she had ever been before.

Despite her almost day-blindness, the first sight of the Craig had been enough to put fear into her heart. It seemed like some vast black beast perched high above the loch; it reeked of evil. An enduring, patient evil, waiting and watching. It felt like the creature's attention had turned towards her as she had laid her squinting eyes upon it.

In that instant, she had tried to escape, more through alarm than planning. She screamed and rammed her entire weight against the neck of Wal's horse, hard and upwards. The horse stumbled and panicked, throwing its rider violently to his left. Rànd hit the ground and bounced back up again with all her strength, aiming her shoulder into Wal's chest. The impact threw him back over the right side and clear out of his saddle. With a single movement, she had the leash off of the saddlebow and was running as fast as she could back along the narrow path towards the protective darkness of the trees.

The first Alban tried to stop her by unthinkingly throwing his arms wide to catch her as she flew by. Aiming low, she slammed her shoulder into his chest and kneed him in the groin. The next one was too confused to act, and she took him down with a vicious head butt that exploded his nose across his face. As he fell, she threw herself over him and took another few strides towards the gap of freedom.

Another Alban jumped into her way with his spear held level across his chest; like a quarterstaff, she deliberately faltered for an instant. He feinted to his right, she went with it as if fooled, he swung hard with the left. She leapt, pirouetted, and hammered her right boot into the side of his head. Landing cleanly on both feet, she launched herself into a dive and roll that took her past the next two men before they could react. The leather leash around her wrists snapped with the impact, and she was up and running again.

Just as Rànd thought she might make it, the tow-headed youth rode his horse into her path, she screamed her most harrowing war cry at it, and the terrified beast reared wildly. Ducking under its flailing hooves, she launched herself towards freedom, but as she came up, the youth caught her across the back of her head with the hilt of his sword. The blow sent her senses reeling, and as she stumbled, a warrior slammed his shield into her side, knocking her off her feet onto the muddy bank. Though dazed, she managed to turn and kick out with both feet sending the Alban reeling, but by the time she was up, a dozen spears were pointing at her chest. She swore, spat and bared her teeth at them in defiance.

Rànd consoled herself with almost breaking the arm of the first one to try to lay a hand on her and forcing them to overpower her by weight of numbers, though she still managed to bite a few.

What came next had surprised her though, she expected a beating or worse from them, but Wal protected her from the warrior's rage and quelled any talk of revenge, even though one of their own, the one she had head-butted, still lay unmoving on the cold, wet ground. The big Alban seemed to want her unharmed; she had no idea why, she could undoubtedly sense his desire for her, but there was something else to it unless she decided, he was merely acting on the orders of the thing they called Corvus. And she dreaded to think what purpose it had in keeping her well and unmolested.

They bound her more securely, threw her unceremoniously over the back of a pack pony, and started off towards the castle.

They seemed to know the woodland margins well and camped deep in the shadows of the forest's edge. There was some discussion between Wal and Corvus, and then orders were passed to the men. She could not tell the words, but they seemed to be organising the place as a fall-back point before pushing on. The serfs or slaves were left to secure the camp and tend the still unconscious warrior, while the others ate a little then armed and prepared themselves.

The Bard approached her and had them lift her off the pony's back. Once she was securely tied to a tree, he offered her water to drink, she sneered and spat at him.

"Please," he held out the mazer again. "Please, you have to drink."

She knew she had to but to accept it from the hand of her captors was too disgraceful. "Let me go, you stupid sheep farmer."

"I can't," he crouched down beside her but just out of range of any sudden movement. "But I'll try to protect you as best as I can," he glanced across to where Corvus stood.

Rànd's eyes followed his gaze. "Who is he?"

The Bard seemed to stifle a shiver. "He is Corvus of Val Gär, a Gärian General. He used to rule these lands a long time ago."

"Long ago?"

"Before I was born."

Confusing, she thought, they age so quickly. It had never occurred to her that they may all be of significantly different ages, the Bard looked younger than the others, true, but that was only because he had no real beard, only a few wisps, and none of the stature of the others. And some amongst the slaves were obviously children.

"He was once the most feared man in the world." He offered the cup again. Rànd nodded and allowed him to pour a little into her mouth. "Now he has returned, as prophesied, to lead us."

"Lead you where?" she sneered sarcastically.

The Bard smiled sadly. "In our war against your kind. He is the one who slaughtered the Great Army at the battle of the Sroo Fool, the Stream of Blood, and destroyed Mur Ollamhan, Fortress of the Learned, the greatest Druid Fortress in the North." The words from his mouth seemed oddly contrasted to the sad tone of his voice. "He is the Raven of Battles, the Torturer of Val Gär, the most feared of men."

Rànd knew Corvus was no ordinary man, for she could now clearly see the sinister cowled, shifting thing that walked in his shadow, the Lady in Darkness, Death herself. The image had been made clear for her earlier in the day when to gain some relief and solace, she had tried to escape into her own àite, her inner sanctuary. Only to find the shade of the Great King Finnvarra waiting for her. He had explained it all to her and had lifted the glamour that clouded her eyes from truly seeing the Lady in Darkness. Now she understood, though it made her more afraid than ever; if the One Who Stands Alone walks beside this Corvus, what terrible purpose does he have? The Bard's words bit deeply, "To lead us in our war against your kind." Against the armies of the Daonna Kings, she had no doubt of victory, but against an avatar of the Goddess of Death?

What, she demanded of the Ardrigh, had happened to turn the Goddess' anger against the Isheen? The ancient King had merely smiled knowingly, shook his head, and departed from her inner place.

Since then, she had watched Corvus with growing fascination; he stood aloof from the others, ate alone, and spoke only to the Alban's leader and the younger tow-headed Daonna. She surmised by their actions that the Albans sensed something very wrong about Corvus; they avoided his presence and even tried to avoid looking at him. They whispered and huddled away from his sight. She had thrice noticed them make strange gestures beyond his notice, passes to ward off evil, and other times even shunned walking in his tracks.

But they followed him. Rànd had no doubt that the balance of control in this little mob had shifted from Wal to Corvus as the day wore on. The shadow of the Goddess was waxing darker, and his presence was growing stronger.

The warriors had assembled in tight knots at the edge of the forest line awaiting the signal from the scouts to show them the way up to the covert entrance into the Craig. Rànd had noticed with dismay that she could no longer see the Goddess in the shadow of the man. The shadow now hung about Corvus like a mantle, and as the wind billowed his cloak, the shadow mantle appeared to stretch and flex about him like great black wings; it now seemed that they were one. As if sensing her watching him, Corvus had turned and stared at her. There was a cold green light in his eyes that chilled her to the bone. He suddenly barked an order, and hands checked her bonds and roughly gagged her.

The troop clambered down into the chasm that separated the Craig from the mainland; the colossal body of the granite spur shielded them from the strand. The trees and bracken, still resplendent in their full autumn colours, camouflaged them from those watching from far above on the ramparts. The descent had ended in a treacherous scramble that saw several men stumble and slide painfully to the chasm floor. After a short ascent, another scramble up loose shale, through bracken and gorse, they came upon a well-concealed entrance. It was not the Jeevir door they talked of but a low cut and steeply angled tunnel that ran two hundred yards through the side of the rock. Rànd had sensed the strange magic of this place. Old magic; if you were not absolutely sure it was here, you would never find the entrance. It emerged into the open again at the foot of a narrow stairway cut into the exposed granite, weathered and ancient. The steps led straight up the steep face of the rock. The climb up them was even more precarious than the descent to the chasm floor. Rànd watched with some amusement as the Dhaoine struggled and clambered up, often on their hands and knees, while she did her best, under the restraints, to spring lively from one step to the next. A dozen times on the ascent, she had had the opportunity to send one of them plunging to his doom, but she waited instead, they had given the leash around her neck to the Bard, and that alone was an advantage she did not want to waste for a simple kill.

The steps had ended on a tight little landing that opened into another narrow tunnel running deep into the darkness. Rànd's moment of relief for her eyes was quickly ended as the Dhaoine struck flints and lit torches. There was power here, the sense of entering the beast's lair, the overpowering feeling of its awareness, flooded over her. She hesitated, but they simply bundled her along the passage.

The Jeevir door was only a few yards farther in, a small, thick, heavily bound oak door silvered by time and locked tightly against them. There had once been marking upon it, ogam or runes, but they had been hacked away a long time ago. Rànd was about to make a scathing comment and laugh at them when Wal turned away from the door and ran his hands along the seams in the left-hand wall until his fingers seemed to find something. "Caraid," he shouted, and the door clicked open.

The strange pounding started at that moment; at first, Rànd thought it was her own heartbeat, but quickly it became a distinct resonance, something emanating both from some point within and throughout, the Craig. The oppressive feeling of the living rock, its powerful awareness, grew stronger with every beat and every step they took into the tunnels beyond the Jeevir door. Rànd noticed that the Dhaoine were growing nervous too; she wondered if they could yet hear the pounding as clearly as she could.

Wal led them through the maze of twisting tunnels and passages with apparent familiarity. They began to climb again, seemingly endless little spiral stairwells one after another until the pounding noise was clear to everyone. Some of the Dhaoine muttered and questioned each other, but Wal kept them moving with shouts and chides.

When finally, they could hear noise above the thumping, the noise of battle, Wal had pulled them all together. He explained something quickly to them, fighting orders Rànd expected, and then they all set off running. They kept her at the rear guarded by the young Bard and three older warriors, but they all had to keep up with the rest.

After another short climb, they came out into a wide corridor that ran for several hundred yards in either direction; one end seemed to narrow and divide into three tunnels, from one of which was coming the now deafening throbbing noise. The other end of the corridor was barred by a great iron grating. A fierce mêlée was raging around the gateway as the Alban defenders tried desperately to drive back a force of Southrons from the portcullis. While the Southrons used their big kite shields and spears to hold off the defenders, others were trying to lever the gate up inch by inch, and they were succeeding. Behind the Southrons, Rànd could see Isheen warriors striving to strike with spear and bow over the heads of their Daonna mercenaries.

Wal bellowed an order, and his men threw themselves into the fray, leaving only himself, Corvus, and the tow-headed youth with her and the Bard. They stood in a huddle discussing what action to take; Rànd couldn't understand their words, but Corvus' intentions had been easily read. He had already formed a plan and was telling the big Alban what to do. What surprised Rànd was how readily the Alban leader accepted it and began walking towards the portcullis, shouting instructions at the top of his lungs.

The tow-headed youth had cast a glance at her and whispered into Corvus' ear; he nodded and replied softly. Rànd felt a burst of anger at herself for never bothering to learn their languages. For a moment, she wished she were more sensitive like her brother. If only she could understand just a few words or have learnt more from the Seers than simply reading the thoughts of animals by their movements and sounds. If only she had been more adept at learning subtle things, like languages and draoidheil, the craft, but she had never had the tàlann, the talent, to learn. Rànd's father had once told her that he had met Trows with more magic in their souls than her. She had hated him for that remark, but it was self-evident, and she had learnt to accept it. She had always been a warrior, and that was all she had ever wanted to be, but what use were those skills now she was bound and in the hands of this monster? She looked about for a means of escape, but the whole place seemed to be a trap. She had missed her chance upon the stone stairway, Stupid.

The fighting at the portcullis was becoming desperate for the Albans. The Southrons and Isheen now had the grill up to almost three feet and were bracing the gap with a heavy old table and benches they had found.

Suddenly Corvus and the tow-headed youth lunged for her, knocking the Bard almost off his feet. She tried to struggle, but it was too late. Corvus had the leash strap tight, and the tow-headed youth was behind her, his hands wrapped around the ties binding her wrists. She was dragged forward towards the gate with Corvus waving his sword shouting at the top of his voice. The fighting paused momentarily, and immediately she knew what his aim was, to use her as a hostage.

As the men on both sides stopped struggling, the portcullis mechanism sprung into life, and the grill slammed resoundingly up into its home in the tunnel roof.

In the shock of it, Rànd tried to escape again, but it was the wrong time. The Albans leapt back, the Southrons and Isheen surged forward, and Rànd threw herself towards them, ramming Corvus aside but tangled with the tow-headed youth and a body on the floor. A shout went up and hands, Daonna and Isheen grabbed for her, she kicked out at the towhead and tried to roll to safety, but it was too late.

Corvus was amid the scramble, snarling like an animal and lashing wildly about him with his sword. A Southron, his neck split through into his chest, but still writhing and gurgling, crashed down onto Rànd. An Isheen, taken by surprise, lost the outstretched hand that still clasped the green burrel fabric of Rànd's jerkin and died instantly as Corvus' heavy short sword swung back to smash into the middle of his face. Another Southron tried to leap clear of the swinging blade but slipped on the bloody flagstones and died as Corvus' blow severed the back of his neck and spine. Another Isheen, a face that Rànd knew, lunged his sword at Corvus' flank, but the buckler in his left hand deflected the thrust, and he brought the heavy blade down on the outstretched arm. As the warrior's hand fell freely to the floor, Corvus' back swing sliced through his throat.

Rànd was hauled to her feet by Wal and a knife thrust under her chin. "Gonnae-no!" he roared. "Stop!"

Everyone froze as if a spell had been cast, leaving only the pulsating sound still issuing from the depths.

The Daonna, with the short sword, raised a finger to his lips and cocked his head to the side as if listening.

Faylinn froze.

The pounding had stopped.

"I think whatever you were so desperate to prevent is over." He smiled a vicious smile, a wicked smile that did not reach his glittering green eyes.

Faylinn knew he was right. The Witch had escaped and probably sealed the portal behind her; now they would be trapped here, in this hole, hiding from the daylight world, or they would have to travel back through the lands of the Dhaoine to the safety of their home. The thought was nauseating.

Faylinn nodded gravely though he could barely take his eyes off his sister's face. Rànd, my beautiful Rànd, how could they have brought you down to this? Something was faintly itching at the edges of his awareness, but he brushed it aside and deliberately turned his gaze to the old Daonna warrior. "Who are you?"

There was a startled murmur from the Albans at the shock of their own language issuing from the mouth of an Isheen, but the old warrior seemed unsurprised.

"What does it matter who I am?" He shrugged, "I am here, and I am in your path. To pass, you will have to go through me."

"I have heard such said before, and still we prevailed." Faylinn tried to push away the prickling at the limits of his consciousness and stepped forward. "I am Faylinn Mac Fer Fí of the Isheen of Dùn nan Làidir. I am Marasgal to my Lord Mathan-Bàn. I ask you again, who are you?"

"Titles! All you people are all so impressed by titles, Lord of this, Master of that, I learnt a long time ago that titles are meaningless."

"Who are we if we are not known by our prestige? I show you the respect of giving you my known name, lineage, titles of honour, and the name of the one I serve. That is far from meaningless, Daonna. Have you no name?"

The same cold smile flashed across the warrior's face. "My name is Corvus; it means Raven. Fitheach, in your tongue."

"Step aside, Fitheach, and I will…."

No, Faylinn! No. He isn't... You must not challenge him!

The words burst into Faylinn's mind with painful clarity making him take an involuntary step backwards. In his confusion, he did not recognise the voice and instinctively reached for his sword.

No! Listen to me!

Rànd? It was impossible. He stared into her eyes, it was truly her voice, but she had no tàlann, no abilities. How...?

You must not fight him; he is not a Daonna. He is a reaver, an avatar of the Lady in Darkness. You must not challenge him!

I must. My Lord...

PLEASE! Faylinn, no! He'll kill you! I could barely fight him, and he was much weaker then. Let him pass; you cannot withstand him.

"Err, hmm?" Corvus cleared his throat loudly. "I don't wish to interrupt your moment, but presume by the look on your face that you know this...woman?"

Faylinn turned back to him. "Yes, she is my sister."

"Sister? Now that is fortuitous."

Faylinn regained some of his composure. "Why 'fortuitous?'" With his free right hand, he signalled his warriors to prepare themselves to strike.

Corvus, who recognised the pass, ignored it. "Because you and I both have something the other wants, and you want this...sister, of yours and I want something from you."

"Ransom."

"A fair trade."

"What is it you want?"

"Two things. One, I want you to let these men withdraw under a promise of safe passage."

Faylinn raised an eyebrow. "There is nowhere to withdraw from here, and you may surrender, and I will give you my word for your safe passage."

Corvus seemed to consider it for a moment. "No. I just need your guarantee of safe passage, and how we make our way is none of your concern."

"And the other thing?"

"I want the Witch, the one they call Annis."

Chapter 23

"And, as Echo far off thro' the vale my sad orison rolls,
I think, oh my love! 'tis thy voice from the Kingdom of Souls,"

Thomas Moore
At the Mid Hour of Night

This place is like no other.

As the light fades from their eyes, they can now see.

This land is no place for the living.

They stumble about, awestruck, uncomprehending, terrified.

A thick miasma blankets the sodden earth that clings and sucks at our every step.

Flat, like the surface of a mirror, the plain stretches as far as their eyes dare see.

A marsh, a moorland, with no beginning and no end.

Còmhnard Mòr, the Great Plain of Tir Eile.

A realm of neither the living nor the dead.

Some gasp and point.

Behind us, a mile or a thousand stands a Dark Tower.

A single black talon tearing at the belly of a sky that is not there.

A sentinel.

Creag an Eagail

The Rock of Fear.

As it was, as it truly is.

A living thing.

They gather around me now, my frightened children.

Demanding explanations or reassurances.

I have none.

I have brought them here.

Now I must find a way back.

Quickly.

"Stay together!" roared Jacobis. "Stay together, don't stray! The ground is not safe!"

"Keep together!" echoed Angus, more out of the need to make his people feel he was in some control than out of any real thought that anyone would be stupid enough to wander off. The ground beneath his feet had the consistency of a week-old porridge covered with chaff, and he had already realised that if you stood too long in one place, you began to sink. "Keep moving! Follow the Vör!"

Jac gave him a look of incredulity.

He added quickly, "We must keep moving until we find firmer ground!"

Jac nodded slightly and strode forwards with apparent great confidence and absolutely no idea of where he was going. The entire plain was so featureless that every direction, but backwards, looked exactly the same, and it was difficult, if not impossible, to even tell where the horizon ended and the sky, for want of a better word, began. Angus was right; staying still was not an option; they had to get moving even if there was no 'firmer ground' to find.

The demand to know where they were, grew out of the general mumblings of the men, finally finding the voice of the fat cook Timmon who was now carrying the unconscious boy; Ag. "Where are we? What is this place?" They all looked to Angus for an answer. Angus looked to Jacobis, and Jacobis looked across to the distant figure of Annis, her head bowed and her thoughts far away; there would be no answers from her.

At least not yet.

"Niflhel," Jacobis answered. "The realm of mists and fog. This is no place to dawdle. There are things that live here!"

"If you can call them living," grumbled Fyn.

"What things?" demanded an Alban.

Jacobis paused.

What do I tell them?

The truth, my love, always the truth.

"This is the realm of the lost, the place in-between. These are the marshlands where forlorn spirits wander. Beware, it is also home to other wandering things; Ironwooders, Trollwitches and the Draugr, and those that just won't die. There are doppelgängers here, too; they may try to trick you into following them or straying into the fog. Stay close together and follow me."

The few mumbles of dissension were silenced by Angus shouting, "Do as the Vör says!"

Jacobis set off after Annis, and the nervous little troop of Albans and Kerns followed.

"Where is she going?" Angus whispered to him.

"I don't know. She's looking for a ley stóð."

"What?"

"A path, a track out of here."

Angus looked uneasily around." Have you been here before?"

Jac shook his head. "No, but Fyn has."

Fyn looked up at the mention of his name but said nothing.

"Is that true?" asked Angus.

"Yes, once. We, my brothers and I, we strayed into this place."

Angus was amazed." How?"

"Because this is Conurd Mòr," MacLeech interjected. "The marshes o' Tir Eile, the Land o' the Deid, an' at certain times an' certain places the daftlike can gainder unknowingly from the world o' the living into the world o' the Deid. Where were you, laddie? Raiding, no doubt."

Fyn turned and growled deeply at the Tysher. "Guh'ach Moor, killing Kerns."

MacLeech stepped closer. "Aye, lad, but ye got more than ye bargained for, didn't ya?" He grinned widely. "Ah? Cost ye dearly, A think, No?"

"Yes. It cost me dearly." Fyn answered bitterly.

MacLeech laughed hollowly. "Aye. Two brothers and half ye war band."

"No, my brother, Bjorn, and my cousin…." Fyn abruptly realised what the Tysher was telling him. "It was you."

"Oh aye, laddie, but was it no you that came intae my lands an' attacked my kin?"

As rage flooded over him, Fyn lowered his head and growled deeply.

"Ye dinna frighten me, wolfy. A know ye still carry my spear point in ye back." For a brief moment, the old wound in Fyn's shoulder screamed with pain, almost knocking him off his feet. "Does it no hurt ye still?"

Jacobis stepped quickly between them and lifted MacLeech's chin with the point of his spear. "Stop."

Before the Kerns could spring to the defence of their leader MacLeech waved them back, his blind eye glittering with mischief. "Aye, big yin. We were just gettin' reacquainted." He grinned. "An' you there leading us to nowhere fast. What use is it to follow you, to follow her?" He turned to the others. "Tae, where? Do ye trust the Wutch? Look at her; she does nae know where she is, an' neither does he."

"And you do?" asked Angus.

"Aye, A do." He was yelling now. "I know this place, A've been here before many times. I know the way out, back to Guh'ach Moor, back to our world."

"How?" demanded Angus.

"There are paths, trackways. A have the sight, and A can see them."

"We follow Annis," Jac said firmly.

"Tae where? She's lost, and she'll lose us too."

"That is not your choice to make, Magiker."

"No," agreed Angus. "It's mine."

It is true; he knows this place well.

    Too well.

        He wants them to follow him.

          Why?

There is something he is hiding.

    Deep within him.

        Somewhere he wants to take them.

    Us.

        Me.

Is he right?

    Am I lost?

        I raise my hands to show them.

    Let them see.

Ahead of them, Annis suddenly threw up her arms and, though she did not speak, they all heard her voice. She cried out an invocation; in words, none of them understood. Strange words that rang in their minds like the strikes of some great temple bell. Words that seemed to change the very air about them. Words that blocked out all conscious thought, leaving most of them unable to do anything other than to stare mindlessly as the sky, if it was a sky, began to boil and roll with thunder. The mist covering the boggy ground began to disappear like ice from red-hot coal, and the sticky marshland heaved and shuddered under their feet like a writhing, living thing.

Around the frail figure of the Witch, a blinding rainbow nimbus flared, and as she lowered her hands, the corona discharged to the ground leaping and dancing across the marsh like lightning born sprites.

Some of the warriors shouted excitedly and pointed at the places where the lightning flares struck the ground, revealing lines and tracks on the soggy surface. As the burning sprites disappeared, paths began to reveal themselves, glowing with an eerie jade iridescence as if some Goddess had thrown down her weaving upon the boggy earth. The trails crisscrossed the weird landscape in endless straight tracks from far horizon-to-horizon, intersecting at all angles but never deviating or terminating,

"Leys," mumbled MacLeech. "The paths o the dead an' the Fey."

"Look." Jacobis pointed off to their left; a glow was dimmed by the distance but discernible now on the far horizon. "A beacon."

"Och, ye don't know what it is, man," MacLeech responded dismissively.

Jacobis turned and smirked down at the Tysher. "No, but it's the nearest thing we can see, and there's a path heading straight for it. It could be the nearest way out of this forsaken place." Jacobis reached out and patted MacLeech patronisingly on the shoulder. "You can go where you wish, Magiker. I'll follow whichever way she decides." He motioned towards the still figure of Annis.

MacLeech tried to quell his fury and keep his voice level. "Ye don't have any idea, big yin. The Gods have far from forsaken this place. A know ae sure way outta here, ae safe way, not one that'll have ye wonderin' about like cattle in ae fauld."

MacLeech shook Jacobis' hand off angrily and turned to Angus. "Laird?"

Angus looked from MacLeech to the lonely figure in the distance. "As I said, we follow her."

MacLeech was furious. They had now spent hours trudging after the Witch through this acrid bog and were getting nowhere. He had always hated this place and only visited it in physical form when it was unavoidable. To spirit walk here was bad enough, but to have to actually trudge through it was sickening and dangerous.

As they had been travelling, the ground fog had begun to roll in again, and with it, MacLeech could sense the attention of the denizens that made their homes on this endless moorland. Things neither alive nor dead crawled and slithered in the murky fog, just beyond the edge of visibility. Things that were growing bolder the longer they remained in this netherworld.

Some of the men had already heard voices calling to them from the miasma, and some had seen glimpses of things that reason told them could not possibly be out there; lovers and friends, the long lost and the spiteful dead. Angus and Jacobis tried to hold the men together with stern warnings and reassurances, cajoling them onwards. It was even becoming difficult for MacLeech to ignore the things that called to him from beyond the mist, friends and victims, enemies, and kinsfolk, all were out there, and they knew him.

For the Gothad, it was harder. Fyn was like an irritated guard dog straining at the leash, his countenance now more lupine than human. MacLeech feared the Gothad was unnerving the warriors as he snarled and growled at shadows, though Jacobis appeared to have enough control over him to stop him looping off into the murk. Gentle words and the repeating of his name seemed to help him maintain some measure of control.

MacLeech dearly wished that the Gothad would lose control, for if Fyn fled off into the murk, then the Witch and the Vör would surely follow, and then he could lead them to the place he wanted them to go. However, it seemed no use, the Ulvhinna was maintaining just enough self-control, and his baying was helping to scare off all but the bravest of the shades that congregated in the fog. The Tysher knew that those denizens of the mist could sense clearly that Fyngard's nature could do them great harm even here in this place. There was little he could do as they continued to plod onwards along the strangely glowing path towards the nimbus on the horizon, every step taking them no nearer their destination but further away from the place he had sworn to bring them to.

There would be a reckoning, MacLeech knew it; he had promised Finnvarra, and if he failed, then there would be a heavy price to pay, but he had, at least, brought her here. It was just that getting her to do what he wished was harder than he'd thought. She was potent, and controlling her was virtually impossible, and all his attempts at persuasion met with the stonewall that was the Vör, her bodyguard and lover. Finnvarra had been wrong, or at least ignorant of how powerful she really was. But surely, MacLeech reasoned. The Ancient One had felt her presence here in his realm?

Has he not felt mine? The idea chilled him, and he quickly uttered a few words of warding, made a sign to protect from Finnvarra's scrying, and a few passes of his hands to cloak his presence in that of the others.

He knew it would not be of use if the ancient Ardrigh truly sought him out, but it would, at least, shield him from the attentions of those things in the mists, many of which had good reason to hate him. Normally they could only note his passing, but this time was different; he knew he was vulnerable, and so did they.

Something blazes upon the horizon.

    Another portal?

        A way back to…

    Somewhere.

Would anywhere be better than here?

    The men are frightened.

       And Fyn.

          My Fyn.

This is a living nightmare.

        He is taking refuge in the Wodfreca to avoid the things he sees in the mists.

       He must not know.

          For they are indeed there.

His kin's spirits.

    Condemned.

        Ensnared here by this place.

By…

    Mer MacLeech.

       Half a lifetime ago.

          I reach out to them.

    Nepur is here.

Still proud and tall.

    His anger is strong, but his understanding is clear.

       Björn Eigi Einhamir is here too.

    Fyngard's brother.

        Though he is almost consumed by his rage.

          Still trapped, as he died.

    In between.

Neither man nor beast.

    Berserkr.

       Others follow them.

          Spirits that are drawn to Bjorn's spirit force.

Only the living are enemies here.

    I try to reach out to them all.

       Touch them.

    Soothe them.

Talk to them.

Tell them.

Only Nepur will speak to me.

His heart is full of despair.

Was he not worthy?

Was he not a warrior?

Did he not die well?

"Where are the Valkyrie?"

He cries.

"Where is the Valhǫll? Death's great prize?"

I calm him.

I promise him.

I promise them all.

I will set them free.

"Why has she stopped again?" Angus whispered anxiously to Jacobis.

Jacobis took a long breath and sighed. "She is...she's auguring the way." He was not about to tell the already anxious Laird the truth, so he lied. "Taking her bearings."

Angus exaggeratedly looked about. "From what?" The sky was again a featureless blanket, the mire below their feet was re-covered in a thickening fog, and everything appeared bathed in the sickly green glow of the leys. He looked back to the willowy figure of the Witch a furlong ahead. "She seems to be talking to someone."

Jacobis looked at Angus with surprise. He liked the Laird, but he hadn't suspected that he had an iota of ability outside those of ordinary men. Was it a guess? Exceptional observation skills? He doubted it. "She is." He answered softly.

Angus took note of Jacobis' tone and decided not to pursue the point. "We have to find a way off this moorland; the men are hungry and tired." He cast a glance over his little troop of followers. "Is this twilight or dawn? Is there no day or night here?"

The giant shook his head desolately, "No."

"We must have been walking for most of a day; they need to rest."

Jacobis nodded.

"And there ar...."

A terrifying scream rang out from the rear of the little troop as something dark and ragged leapt out of the fog onto one of the Kerns. The men froze in horror as the screeching thing tore at the fallen warrior with long talon-like hands and savage teeth.

"Hvað i nafni Hel!" Jacobis hoisted his spear and turned towards the fallen warrior. "Draugr!" cried Jacobis. "Draugr! Kill it!" His warning seemed to break a spell of fear over the men, who now rushed to aid their companion. Though it was too late, as the Draugr had already ripped out the Kern's throat and was gulping down his blood. One of the Kerns, enraged by his friend's death, bravely launched himself at the monster, hacking madly with his heavy blunt-ended sword. The blows rained down upon the thing's back and head, but the creature seemed undaunted; it merely looked up to snarl its defiance and went straight back to feasting on its still struggling victim. Unwilling to back away, it crouched over its kill and batted away their weapons with ferocious boldness.

It looked little more than a short, ragged Wildman, but instead of fingers, it had claws and its eyes burnt with a bright yellow intensity. Abruptly it leapt to its feet, raised its shaggy, gore-splattered head, almost proudly, and began to let out an ear-splitting howl.

"Hlandbrenndu!" Jacobis shoved through the ring of shocked men and thrust his spear deep into the Draugr's chest.

The impaled creature clawed frantically at the spear shaft as if it could not quite understand the idea that a weapon could harm it.

"Farðu til fjandans ljóti rassinn þinn!" Jacobis wrenched the spear out and slashed the creature's head from its shoulders.

Suddenly another screech went up as a second Draugr launched itself out of the fog, this time straight at Angus.

Fyn caught the creature in mid-leap and slammed it to the muddy ground. The Draugr struggled frenziedly, snapping and tearing at the Gothad with its ferocious teeth and claws, but it was helpless as Fyn relentlessly beat upon its chest until the bones shattered, and he could drive his hand through to rip its black and rotting heart out.

"Gods!" cried the Cook. "There's more of them!"

A boiling bank of fog was rolling slowly towards them. Inside it, formless shadows with eyes like burning coals seemed to writhe, sometimes coalescing vaguely into the shapes of great, snarling animals before flowing back into the mist.

"Run!" ordered Angus, pointing towards the light on the horizon. "That way. Now!" He grabbed and shoved the first man he could. "That way, follow the Witch, Now!" Dreading what might next emerge from the miasma, the men did not need further encouragement. Some paused as they reached the place where the Witch stood, while others, driven by fear, kept running on towards the light on the horizon.

Jacobis cursed loudly, raised his spear, and took a step towards the fog.

MacLeech held out his arm to stay Jacobis' progress. "Ye no wantin' to go lookin' for what's in there, big yin."

"What is it?" demanded Angus.

"Trouble," said Fyn grimly.

Nepur warns me.
　　　We have dwelt too long in this place.
　　　　　　We must go.
Another voice calls to me now.
　　　　From the light on the horizon.
　　　　　　We must go.
　　　　　　　　　Before it is too late.
　　　We must go.
　　　　　NOW!!

Chapter 24

Whoever fights monsters should see to it that in the process
He does not become a monster.
And when you look into the abyss,
The abyss also looks into you.

Friedrich Nietzsche
Beyond Good and Evil.

Mathan-Bàn watched as the mercenary leaders paced about
the hall like caged animals. He knew their loyalty was being tested to
the limits, but it was essential to keep them here longer than they
had agreed and far longer than he had ever envisioned. To balance
the threatening presence of the Fomóiri, he needed every able-
bodied warrior he could muster, even if they were only Dhaoine. It
all felt like he was playing some immense esoterical game of
brandubh against an opponent he could not see. If, as the Galdràgon
feared, the Witch had escaped through the gate and sealed it behind
her, then he was going to need every advantage he could gain until
he could make his move. His grandfather, Shardik, the first to wear
the ring of Lordship over the great rath of Dùn nan Làidir and fly
the standard of the White Bear, had loved to play board games.
Brandubh, fidchell, even the strange game of the easterners so loved;
chess, and he always won. His secret, he once told his awestruck
grandchild, was, "If the game goes badly, Ogha, then change the
rules!"

Now from his vantage point in the shadows of the minstrel's
gallery, he watched and considered how to change the rules of this
game. The Gothad, Jarl Olvarson, a barrel-chested bear of a man
with a huge shaggy grey beard, and his captains, cast about angrily.
They were demonstrative men full of bravado, though, even high
above them, Mathan-Bàn could smell their fear. Five Southron
Gesiths stood in a tight knot at the other end of the hall, they
masked their unease behind impassive faces and ice-cold stares, but
Mathan-Bàn could read it clearly. The most senior Gesith, Eanwind,

had been killed on the beach, and although Earl Eadric lay in another chamber not a dozen yards away, he may as well have been already dead to these men. Decisions would have to be made, and they knew they would have to make them.

The two groups eyed each other with thinly veiled hostility. The fighting had gone badly for the Southrons; they had suffered heavily at the hands of the Albans, while the Gothads had done little else but guard their boats and shoot a few arrows. What enraged the Southrons most was that when the giant attacked Strandwulf, the Gothads did nothing, not even going to his aid after he had been injured. They just left him to die. The hatred emanating from the Southrons was palpable.

Mathan-Bàn climbed down the little staircase behind the minstrel's gallery and spoke to them. It was hard, neither group wished to stay a moment longer, and their hostility threatened to explode into violence at any second. It took all of Mathan-Bàn's skills and persuasion to gain their agreement. He promised them more gold, cajoled them, rebuked them, he even resorted to charming them. His tàlann and skills in these matters were second to none. Though Dhaoine could be difficult and unpredictable, in the end it was by appealing to their greed that he had gained their agreement. The Southrons would stay to help defend the castle and flush out the last of the Albans, while the Gothads would take over from them on the strand and keep the longboats ready. So long as they did not have to deal with the Fomóiri, who they feared and loathed.

The agreements were struck, their oaths given, and words accepted, and they left none the happier but resigned to the situation. At least, Mathan-Bàn was relieved to discern, no longer ready to kill each other. He sighed and flexed his shoulders. "Cathadh!"

"Morair?" Cathadh, in her full armour, appeared instantly out of the shadows, where he had stationed her earlier in case of trouble. Though now, she had relaxed enough to remove her helmet and allow her snow-white hair to flow down over her shoulders. A true Isheen beauty, marred only by the scar that ran the length of her cheekbone to the corner of her mouth and on under her chin. It gave her lip a permanent merciless curl belied only by her bright green eyes, shot through with flecks of gold; they always seemed to dance with irreverent humour.

Exquisite eyes, Mathan-Bàn stilled the thought quickly, though the hint of a smile in those eyes told him she had already heard the thought. "What news?"

Cathadh shook her magnificent head slowly. "Nothing yet, Morair. Though the drumming still continues."

A voice like the rustling of autumn leaves. Mathan-Bàn caught himself again. "Bring me word immediately Faylinn returns."

"Gun dàil, Morair." She bowed, stepped back into the shadows, and was gone. She had always been his favourite amongst the warriors though she was older now than most of them, not only for her looks but for...What? He pondered; that look in her eyes? It always made him feel like a blushing child. He knew one day he would marry her. She was of high enough birth, but she would not easily give up her sword for the trappings of an Àrd-dràgon's Lady.

Mathan-Bàn often marvelled at the complexities of his status and position, he was the ruler of the Isheen's greatest rath, Àrd-dràgon of the Isheen, older brother of the Bànrigh, and yet he was never free to act as he wished. He could bed any he wanted, but to take a wife, he would have to ask permission of his own sister, and that wife would have to be of the right noble birth, to be able to bear him children and to be willing to be 'a Lady at Court', to attend upon the Bànrigh. He laughed and shook his head; Cathadh attending upon anyone would be a miracle, and as for children? She had all the motherly instincts of a snow cat.

"She is fine-looking. A beautiful creature."

Mathan-Bàn instantly seized his sword and spun around. "You?"

The Fomóire Prince stood only a few paces from him. He was wearing heavy armour, with a tuigen, a big feathered cloak, over it. The hood was pushed back, and his head was bare, save for a small circlet of silver to denote his rank. "It is I, yes. Me." Morghath Bres raised a hand and gently pushed the point of Mathan-Bàn's sword aside. "A fine weapon, an ancient weapon, but what good would it avail you against I?"

"How…?"

"You are not the only ones with powers, 'tàlann'. Yes? Abilities. I am, after all, my father's son." Morghath Bres smiled widely. "I too can walk through stone if I wish."

Mathan-Bàn suppressed a shudder. This creature's powers were a matter of course, but what chilled him was that it had been able to pass so close to him without his notice, without him sensing its presence. Gods! How long has he been there? Keeping his voice level, he asked as calmly as he could. "What do you want?"

"Want? Desire, yes, I desire something." He stepped forward.

As Morghath Bres drew closer, Mathan-Bàn fought the instinct to back away; instead, he levelled the sword point at its chest. "No further."

"Indeed." The strange reptilian eyes narrowed. "I want, there is a need in me, I crave, something you can help me obtain. Freedom."

Mathan-Bàn could not understand what the Fomóire meant, "Freedom from what?"

"Freedom, to be free from he who holds me in thrall."

"Balor?"

"Balor. My father."

Mathan-Bàn struggled to keep from laughing aloud. Does this stupid sea troll think I would fall for such a preposterous ruse? But he held back. Do they underestimate me so or, maybe, I have overestimated them? "You seek freedom from your father, from Balor?"

"From Balor. I will offer you this thing in exchange for your aid."

"What thing?"

"I will send the Fomhórach away, back to our realms under the western sea, if you will aid me and grant me sanctuary when the deed is done."

"What deed?"

"I will kill my father; I will do murder unto him."

Mathan-Bàn was stunned, it was a trap he knew, but it was too ludicrous to believe even for a moment. "Nonsense! Balor is a

God, as old as the oldest tales of our people; he cannot be killed!" Or my people would have done so a long time ago and been rid of his stinking fish gut presence for good.

"The Balor of your archaic tales is not the one that awaits at the shore, though he is powerful, he is no God, and though he is age-old, he is not immortal. No one and nothing lives forever."

Too engrossed in the conversation, Mathan-Bàn did not notice as someone else slipped quietly into the room and into the shadows behind the pillars.

Morghath Bres noticed though.

"How?" asked Mathan-Bàn incredulously.

Morghath Bres edged closer and whispered. "Fire. That element opposite of all he is. Fire, the thing he most fears." He reached out and grabbed Mathan-Bàn's forearm. "Will you aid me, help me? Please, my Lord?"

Immediately Mathan-Bàn understood that the Fomóire was not lying; he meant what he was saying and really intended to murder Balor. "I must think." He whispered back. "I must...think on this."

"Is not this what you seek, desire? Pray for? To be rid of him once and for all? Such victory would make you as a King! Such renown!" The nictitating membranes in Morghath's eyes flickered, and his grip grew tighter. "Do not expose me, betray me, for you will suffer more than I."

Mathan-Bàn pulled his arm free and glared back into those terrible eyes. "Do not threaten me."

The silence between them was electric; neither backed nor blinked until Morghath Bres finally spoke. "Decide soon." He stepped neatly aside and strode purposefully out of the hall.

Almost before the door had slammed shut behind the Fomóire, the whispered voice of the Galdràgon echoed out of the shadows.

"So, my great Lord, how low have you come? Is this it? In the final act, betrayal?"

Mathan-Bàn glared into the unnatural darkness that cloaked the High Priestess. "Be still, harridan, harness your tongue, or I will..."

"You will, what?" She shrugged off the spell and stepped out of the shadows. "You will do nothing."

"Why?" He inquired softly.

"Because you are weak, and I am strong, stronger than you. Traitor!" There was obvious glee in her voice. "I heard everything. Damn you! You plotter and betrayer, you would plot against Balor himself!" She cackled wildly. "For so long have I waited, waited for you to finally go too far. Your weakness sickens me, you are nothing but a grovelling coward that hides within the folds of his sister's skirts, but she will not protect you now. 'Àrd-dràgon', ha! Stupid, prideful, ignorant, weak idiot. What use are you?" She was almost hysterical now. "You've tried to thwart me at every turn and to humiliate me at every opportunity. You have wasted the lives of our warriors, our own blood, Sìth blood, upon the ground, upon these very stones! For what? You have lost the Taibhsear, you let them kill my beautiful Kyla, my Thurifer, and now you have allowed that riataiche that abomination to escape! The Bànrigh will not shield you this time, not from Balor's wrath; you are doomed and by your own actions!" She clapped her hands delightedly. "My Great Lord, I will be rid of you at last! I will marry our Bànrigh to Cullach-Bàn, and I shall establish a dynasty worthy of our people." She laughed as something occurred to her. "I shall give Cullach-Bàn your rath, Dùn nan Làidir as dowry, while you rot in chains praying for your death."

"You will do no such thing, Hag," he assured her.

"Fool!" she jabbed a blood-stained, gnarled finger at Mathan-Bàn. "They'll be no lies to save you this time, no escape. That ancient monster will eat your flesh and suck the marrow from your bones, and when he spews forth your skull, I will gild it and give it to Lord Cullach-Bàn as a wedding gift!" She was really enjoying herself now, almost dancing on the spot with delight.

Mathan-Bàn realised that the sword was still in his hand and that his grip was so tight it was making his hand throb; he stared at it, trying to control his rage, trying to flex his fingers. He had made the decision. "No," he said softly. "No, you are the fool."

The Galdràgon's reply froze in her mouth when she caught sight of his face. As the white Àrd-dràgon stepped forward, she tried to cast a spell of warding, but it ended up in just a wild flailing of her hands; then, as he raised his sword, she spat a curse at him and turned to flee.

Blocking her escape stood the massive form of Morghath Bres. "You are not the only one who can skulk in shadows, Witch." The Fomóire seized her by the throat and hauled her up to his face. "Where go you? Running from or running to?" He tightened his grip until her face turned bright red. Cursing wildly, she raised her right hand, encased in blue fire, and struck at him a blow that would cleave stone or render a great oak to ashes.

Mathan-Bàn watched in cold interest as the cobalt lightning rocked the Fomóire, but his grasp on the old hag's neck never loosened. "D'anam don diabhal. Bitseach!" Morghath Bres growled.

The Galdràgon, fighting rising panic and incomprehension, summoned all her power and slammed her burning hands into Morghath's face. This time the Fomóire cried out and staggered, but still, his stranglehold never faltered. All the Galdràgon's diminishing senses could make out was that she was looking into the eyes of some terrible leviathan that had caught her, and it was about to devour her.

"Why are you fighting, Bitch?" he sneered at her through his ruined face. "There is nowhere left for you to go."

For the first and last time in her life, Sheela felt powerless; she clawed at the Fomóire, kicked, and tried to bite him. Chunks of burnt flesh came off in her hands, but it was of no use; he was far too big and far too strong. In her last act, she focused her mind enough to curse him and weakly spat into his face.

Mathan-Bàn grimaced as he heard the bones in the Galdràgon's neck shatter; her body automatically convulsed and voided itself one last time before she slumped lifeless in the Fomóire's grip. Morghath Bres looked disgustedly at the mess dripping from the corpse and promptly dropped it. His horrific smouldering mess of a face turned and grinned at Mathan-Bàn. "She will not be spreading any alarm, telling any tales, anymore." He stepped forward and stamped down upon her head, smashing it into a bloody pulp. Brains and blood splattered across the floor and onto the Àrd-dràgon's boot.

Mathan-Bàn sheathed his sword and shook the gore from his

toecap. "You have a plan then?"

"A plan." Morghath Bres bent to pick up the circlet that had fallen from his head. "Yes, a plan, of course."

"Tell me."

Morghath' ruined face twisted into an obscene grin.

Corvus noticed that the Isheen's leader physically cringed at the mention of this woman called Annis, as if her very name was painful to him. That interested Corvus even more; whoever this 'Annis' was, she was someone they all feared, Alban and Isheen alike. She had been only described to him as; The Witch that the King of the Alban's had sent to aid the MacRoths. He had put the story of how she had rained havoc upon the Isheen and Fomóiri down to the usual Alban exaggeration, and so he had not expected to see such alarm in the faces of these creatures; they were terrified of this woman.

The reaction told him a great deal about the Isheen; they had not caught her, she was still at large, and they doubted themselves against her, which meant they knew fear, and that could be used against them.

"Well?" he demanded of the Isheen's leader.

Faylinn shook his head slightly. "We do not have Annis Nic an Neamhain. She escaped into these tunnels," he smiled wearily. "In fact, I think she has just made good her escape from both of us."

"What?"

"The drumming. I think she has used her powers to take her out of this place, her or MacLeech."

"MacLeech is with her?"

"We believe so." Faylinn caught the intonation in Corvus' voice. "You seek MacLeech also?"

Corvus thought for a moment on how best to put this. "It would seem that my enemies and yours are the same."

Faylinn sensed the Daonna was playing games. "Why do you seek them?"

Corvus relaxed his position and made a clear visual point of sheathing his sword. "To kill MacLeech, something I should have done long ago, as for this 'Annis' she is part of a debt I have to repay."

Faylinn tried to hide his instinctive curiosity. "To her?"

"To another."

"And your business with her?"

"I have come to take her; that's all you need to know."

"Protect her?"

"No, her head alone would be enough for my purposes."

Faylinn raised his hand and waved back his warriors. The act gave him time to think of how to handle this. If this warrior was as powerful as Rànd claimed, then he might be well within their interests to send him after the Witch and MacLeech. However, this was not a decision that he could make. Only Mathan-Bàn could make such decisions, which meant taking this Corvus to an audience with the Àrd-dràgon. He looked into Rànd's eyes again, she obviously could read his thoughts, and there was terror in her eyes. What else can I do? Sweet sister, my love, what else?

"Corvus, if you wish to leave, release my sister, and you may go. Under my oath, you will have safe passage from this place for you and your warriors. But of your other request, I am powerless to oblige, though my master may well be willing to aid you. If you will allow me to take you to him."

Finally, thought Corvus. It was what he had gambled upon, a chance to speak to someone more than just a pawn in this game. He pretended to consider it for a while and then said, "I have to speak with my men first."

Faylinn gave a curt nod and stepped back.

Wal released the Isheen warrior into the hands of Taran MacReul and stepped up to Corvus. "Are you completely insane, man?"

Tàmh appeared from behind Wal's shoulder. "You cannot be seriously thinking of killing the Witch, Annis? She's more powerful than you could imagine. That's why they're all terrified of her."

"Damn the Witch," Wal shot the Bard a savage look. "An' what of the rest of my lads? Where's my Laird? We cannot leave without him."

Svein pushed forward and added, "Why don't we all just get out of here before these bastard Alfar grow bored and kill us all?"

Corvus ushered them farther back. "Listen to me. These people are scared for some reason. I will speak with their leader; if I can find out what is frightening them, then maybe I can strike a deal with them. A trade possibly."

"And her?" Wal nodded towards Rànd.

"She's one of our bargaining pieces."

"I'm coming with you," Wal said flatly.

Svein sheathed his sword. "And me."

"If you wish, but you, Bard," Corvus grabbed Tàmh's sleeve. "You're definitely coming with me."

Tàmh swallowed hard. "If it is who I think it is, then I would rather not."

The small group of Dhaoine and Isheen wound their way through the warren of tunnels and winding stairs to the upper chambers of the Craig.

Corvus watched with great interest as the Isheen's demeanour changed from the wariness of warriors at war to a deeper anxiety; they grew increasingly uneasy as the air grew fresher and the odd chink of daylight penetrated into the gloom. At the first signs of daylight, they drew scarves across their faces and pulled down their helmets. They indeed could not bear the light. Corvus had noticed it with the woman, but part of his mind had dismissed it as affected, an act to reinforce old superstitions, accentuate her difference, and help those watching to re-call old stories and fears. Nevertheless, these warriors were playing no mind games; they shunned the daylight with habitual efficiency.

The windows of the castle chambers had been covered with anything to hand, tapestries, banners, blankets, rugs and even cloaks still soaked in blood, anything to keep the weak, grey light out. Corvus understood that these people did not hate the daylight, they detested it, and he knew there had to be a genuine reason for that kind of loathing, though they seemed to have no problem with the fire's glow from the torches they carried. Maybe the Bard was right; they are cave dwellers. He began to look closely at them for the first time. The big eyes and the pallor of their hair and skins, it would make sense. A race of people that live predominantly underground. He tried desperately to re-call the tales his Mu'adib, Nebti Alem, used to tell of such people. Valentia, the nameless city of the Ancients, where people lived like rats in the catacombs below the ruins of the city. Only Nebti's stories told of hairy, half men, monstrous troglodytes, twisted and no longer human, not creatures like these.

They were uniformly tall, a head taller than even Wal, and rakishly thin though muscular, and they moved with an elegance and suppleness that clearly displayed their physical strength. Their faces were long and angular, with square jaws, shortish blunt noses, with large, widely spaced eyes which reflected green in the torch light. All the males were clean-shaven. However, Corvus reconsidered that observation as none showed any sign of facial hair below their sharply arched eyebrows, and it was difficult to define the males from the females at a glance. Their ears were their oddest feature, peculiarly prominent and pointed like those of a fox or bat. All were pale-skinned with paler hair, grown long and tied back. They were, Corvus conceded to himself, quite magnificent creatures, not skulking troglodytes. Only their formidable teeth gave away a sense of something primal about them, animalistic almost. If these people live underground, what places must they live in? He wondered.

Their armours were archaic-looking, ornate but old, and made of light materials, leather, padded cloth and chain, the metal being mainly bronze; they didn't seem to wear steel where it could contact their skin. Though they carried steel weapons, they all wore fine gloves of leather or linen, as if trying to avoid any contact with the metal. After his brief struggle with them at the tunnel mouth, it had amazed him how he had survived; they were so fast it had been like hacking at smoke phantoms. These were fearsome warriors of a race to be reckoned with, but his blows had struck home, and they had proven to be as vulnerable as any other to the keen edge of cold steel.

Their progress was unnecessarily long and convoluted as the Isheen avoided stepping out into the daylight to cross between buildings. In some places, they had already breached walls to allow them to pass from one place to another, and in others, they had hastily thrown up hoardings to give cover from the day light.

At one such breach between corridors, Corvus noticed that they had removed an enormous bronze mirror and placed it carefully against the wall where it reflected back the wooden vaulting of the ceiling and the heads and shoulders of those passing. Some part of a memory of something once told to him as a child came back, a fairy story, of spirits called 'Meliae' that haunted the ash forests and cast no reflection because they were not really there. Amused, he watched as his little group and its guards filed past the mirror and through the gap, all reflected clearly in the torchlight.

Well, at least they are real enough, he thought, taking an instant to look at his own reflection.

There was no reflection in the shiny concave surface of the metal, only darkness, a shadow, where he should have been.

Momentarily confused, he looked again, checking that it was not a trick of the mirror's angle or the light, but there was no reflection, no image rebounded in the bronze, just a shade, a sinister echo.

With awful clarity, Nebti's voice rang in his head, "The Meliae are ghosts, Andreas, and ghosts cast no reflections."

Is that what it is? Am I? His mind reeled, is that it? Instinctively his hand went to his mouth to stifle the dreadful noise that tried to escape from his throat. In rebellion, his throat seized, and he choked violently.

"Corvus?" Svein stepped back through the breach and reached out to help him.

Corvus brushed the hand away and gulped air into his lungs. His eyes streamed, and his head pounded savagely, but his mind cleared faster. More trickery, an illusion, the work of the Magician Finnvarra. Corvus tried to laugh and cough at the same time, and if not? Well then, what have I to fear? What is left for me to fear if what he said is true? "Men do not hallucinate their own deaths." He shook his head as if to clear the thoughts from it, hawked and spat into the mirror's strange reflection.

"Corvus?" Wal was looking at him as if he had gone insane.

With a slight dismissive wave, Corvus turned and followed the others through the gap in the wall.

As they helped him through the hole, his mind raced ahead, planning, evaluating, calculating. He had to get a grip of the situation and of himself. So far, he had worked on animal instinct, simply going with the events to see how they played out, chess moves on a board in darkness made only to see how the other player would react, but now it was time to think, to bring to bear the raven sharp faculties he had once been so feared for. He was being manipulated, played like a game piece, in a game of which he had no idea what the rules were, let alone the aim. However, one player had shown his hand, the one player he had focused upon, Finnvarra. Whoever 'Finnvarra' was. His manipulations and accusations burnt into Corvus' psyche, goading him profoundly, touching raw nerves, strands of pain that ran deep into his soul. He would cut the Magician's lying tongue out and choke him with it, and all the glamour, spells and illusions in this world would not save him. If I

287

am dead, Magician, so are you.

Whoever this Finnvarra was, Corvus was sure he was one of these creatures that surrounded him, but he was different, physically and in action. Corvus doubted that Finnvarra's demands and the aims of these 'Isheen' were the same. They seemed terrified of the Witch, yet Finnvarra sought her, believing Corvus could bring her to him. *Maybe it is she who is the key to this whole thing after all. The aim of all this is like some strange chess game; the objective is not to catch a King but a Queen.* Corvus stopped. *But whose Queen is she?*

"Are you well, my Lord?" asked Tàmh.

Corvus turned on him sharply, about to warn him again not to use that term of address but bit it back. Instead, he drew the Bard near. "Are these the ones that held you?"

Tàmh shook his head and whispered back, "No, the same people but not the same rath."

"Rath?" Corvus walked on, speaking low.

"City, tribal city." Tàmh kept close to him.

"Underground?"

"Yes."

"How many are there?"

"Raths? I have no idea. Hundreds maybe."

"How many were warriors?"

"What?"

"How many warriors can each 'rath' put into the battlefield?"

"From the rath I was held in? Thousands, maybe more, their men and woman fight," he nodded towards Rànd. "As you see."

Corvus thought on that; *say three to five thousand warriors from each rath and possibly any number of raths?* He grasped the Bard's shoulder tightly. "Hundreds of raths? How many? One? Two? Three?"

Tàmh shrugged weakly. "I really have no idea. Lots."

"Think," hissed Corvus.

Tàmh thought carefully, *why did Corvus want to know this and why now? The old Raven was up to something, plotting already.* "I was told once that there are four score north of the Aveeń river alone, not counting those in the far West and the South, but they are not Isheen."

"Others?"

"There are many tribes of the Daoine-Síth, these are the Isheen, who, the tales, say came to the North from the West after the fall of the Àrsaidh, the 'Ancients' as you call them. There are many others, the Daoine Faoi Cheilt, the Unseen, and the Sídhe in the far West, the Ælfen in the South, the Alfar and the Huldufolk in the lands of the Gothads, probably there are others."

"It is said that the Alfar hold the entire Mørk forest on the borders of Sæterlande," added Svein. "Their Gods alone know how many there are beyond that."

Corvus chuckled softly and shook his head. "Where were they when we marched through these lands? Hiding?"

"Maybe you should ask them," replied Svein.

"Maybe I will."

"They seldom take an interest in the affairs of other races," Tàmh added before turning away.

"They appear to be doing so now."

The Isheen had led them into a long corridor that ran into some kind of gallery. "The Great Hall. We're almost there." Tàmh pointed at the far doors.

Corvus stepped in close to him again. "Do you know who this 'Àrd-dràgon' is?"

"Yes. He is Mathan-Bàn, the "White Bear." Warlord of all the Isheen, ruler of Dùn nan Làidir, the Fortress of the Strong, it's said to be the greatest rath in the North. His line is royal blood, so one day his sister will be Bànrigh, Queen of the Isheen."

"Sister?" asked Svein. "What about him?"

Tàmh smiled knowingly. "Their crown passes from Queen to Queen, only the women may rule unless there is no girl child to inherit. She is the granddaughter of the old Bànrigh. It is their way."

Svein snorted his disgust at the idea. "No wonder they ended up living underground!"

"They've been under..."

Corvus stopped him. "This White Bear, what do you know of him? Have you ever met him?"

"Met him? No. They told tales of him."

"They said?"

"He is a great leader, wise and just, to his people, but he detests Dhaoine, our kind. He is the one they turn to first when they are in peril because he is a real warrior. He dominates their Council of Riaghladairs."

"Why?"

To Svein, it seemed obvious. "Because he is a Prince, of course."

The Isheen came to a stop in front of two massive doors.

"They have no 'Princes', no male Athelings, only the women may rule the Isheen. Though his family are of royal blood and they are hereditary rulers of the largest rath in the North. He was elected to the position of ruler of Dùn nan Làidir and then acclaimed 'Àrd-dràgon' due to his wisdom and victories in battle. He has the largest army at his call, and those that oppose him often meet unfortunate ends."

"Sagacity," repeated Svein.

"Clever," said Corvus, "and cunning."

Faylinn stepped forward and spoke to Corvus, but his eyes never left his sister's face, "You will wait here whilst I speak to my Lord."

Corvus looked around at the faces of Tàmh, Wal, Svein, and their prisoner Rànd and to the faces of the two dozen Isheen surrounding them. "I think we have little choice."

Faylinn turned swiftly and stepped through the doorway.

Tàmh quickly turned to Corvus, "If it is Mathan-Bàn, then this could be because their old Bànrigh has died and his sister, Fearchara, has ascended to the throne. Which cannot be good."

"Why?" Svein asked.

"When I was…in their company, so to speak, there were rumours amongst them that the Princess Fearchara Nic Darach was as mad as a bat. Some were frightened of her ever becoming Bànrigh."

"So, they've put a mad woman on their throne and started a war? They don't sound any different from the Gärians." Corvus chuckled.

"There is one other thing, though…if you'd take my advice,

that is?"

"What?"

"Their obsession with titles."

"Yes, what about it?"

"It's an honoured practice, a custom, to state exactly who they are and what titles they hold; some may even tell you the names of their ancestors. It's a way of ensuring proper deference to their status."

"Does it matter?"

"It's more than mere politeness. It's a formal ritual and a way they use to avoid misinterpreting each other's eminence."

"I have never needed to explain to any man who I am."

Tàmh smiled meekly, "Corvus, be careful not to insult them unwittingly. To refuse to give your name or title is to suggest that they are so inferior to you that they do not matter."

"Our Kings and Jarls never need to introduce themselves," added Svein.

Tàmh cast a disdainful glance at the young Gothad. "Your Kings dwell in a world of men, the Isheen dwell in a world of Gods and monsters; it pays to be clear about exactly who you befriend or offend in such a world. Believe me, I know, I was their 'guest' remember."

Wal laughed, "Aye, we should be glad they're not a bunch of nipple suckers like the Kerns!"

Turning back to the Bard, Corvus asked, "So who were you held by then?"

"By Moireach-Bàn of Cnoc a' Chapaill, the Hill of the Horse, she tricked me and kept me there for a year and a day."

"Why?" asked Svein.

Tàmh looked him in the eyes and answered, "Why do you think?"

Chapter 25

"The best laid schemes o' mice and men,
Gang aft agley,
An' lea'e us nought but grief an' pain,
For promis'd joy!"

To a Mouse
Robert Burns

The Àrd-dràgon Mathan-Bàn listened carefully as Morghath
Bres laid out his plan. As he expected, it did not take long, and it was
as simple as it was brutal and ill-conceived. It lacked any real
thought, though, with Morghath's enthusiasm and force of will,
Mathan-Bàn was quite sure the Fomóire could probably kill Balor.
What impressed him most was Morghath's passionate hatred of his
own kind; he did not mean just to kill the Fomóire's God-King, but
to abandon them all to their fate in return for power amongst the
tribes of the Sìth. It was amazing that this creature was intent on
destroying not only his father but his realm too. Morghath Bres
knew that without a successor to step into Balor's place, the Fomóiri
would tear their Kingdom apart in a bloody civil war, and all he
wanted to do was to watch his own kind destroy themselves.

Mathan-Bàn could hardly contain himself; this betrayer, this
malcontent, was going to hand him a way to shatter the power of
these ageless monsters. It would be the greatest victory imaginable
for the Isheen. Others had tried, in endless wars stretching back
through time, but none had succeeded. If he, Mathan-Bàn, could
throw them into civil war before launching his own attack, it would
be a masterstroke. A culling blow. The chance to expunge the stain
of the Fomóiri from the history of the Daoine-Sìth, to remove them
from the history of all the Fey, once and for all.

He could taste real battle already, and it tasted better than
this escapade of butchery. This had been no war for his kind, no
proud battle or noble cause; this was nothing more than a ridiculous
adventure at the behest of a demented child. A child Bànrigh,

deluded by those who would use her for their own ends. Her mind filled with fantasies of conquest and the sanctity of blood. They had connived to convince her of the destiny of the Isheen, the failures of the old Bànrigh, the need to restore the archaic rites and long-abandoned ways of worship, and how they would together restore the power of the Sìth, in glory and fear.

He had fought it at first, but Fearchara was in no mood to reason, drunk with power she had commanded him, screamed at him as if he were a cowering servant, to do her bidding. To go to war upon the Dhaoine, to burn and pillage and enslave, to recreate the golden age of the Daoine-Sìth out of the mire of burning ash and blood. An age that had never truly existed except in the fantasies the Galdràgon had put into her head. He had done his best to turn her hare-brained commands into a campaign that would bring about something more than pyrrhic victories and prisoner taking, a campaign that would put the Isheen, would put him, into a position of tactical strength. He had come to the Creag an Eagail because this, of all the Daonna fortresses of the North, was the one that would give him the strength to defy even his sister's will. There was power to harness here, not in the defences but in the very fabric of the living rock. Here was the Gate of the Dorsair, the thing the Dhaoine called 'the Heart of the Craig.' A power beyond the cantrips of the Galdràgon and her whores. However, everything he planned the Galdràgon had tried to undermine, subverting his actions for her own ends, bringing these monsters to the Craig had been her way of trying to thwart him, to stop him. He glanced down at the broken mess that had once been the High Priestess of the Isheen. Instead of thwarting him, she had delivered to him a much greater prize; he now held the Craig and the key to a war against an enemy worthy of the title.

If Fearchara wants blood, then she will have it, an ocean full of it.

In fact, it did not matter whether Balor or Morghath Bres lived or died; it would be enough that the attack upon the person of the Fomóire's God-King came from his own son, a Prince of the Blood. Ichor, Mathan-Bàn corrected himself, venom. The fruit of a poison tree is, by its very nature, poison. He looked carefully into the ruined face of the Fomóire. Those reptilian eyes held a level of insanity that must have been festering inside him for centuries, growing like a canker, an abscess ready to explode and unleash devastation upon his own kind.

Mathan-Bàn re-called the words of a long-dead Philosopher, his father used to quote, "… and traitors shall find no welcome at the hearth of noble Lords, for they seal their own fate with that of those they betray." He smiled at Morghath Bres when he finished speaking and nodded his agreement to the Fomóire's requests conspiratorially. He would provide the help Morghath Bres needed, and he would aid him to escape from the grasp of the vengeful. Mathan-Bàn made the statements with all the solemnity he could muster so as not to provoke the monster into demanding his oath upon it, but Morghath Bres wanted more.

"Your oath, your word on it. To seal this thing of ours, this bargain, this pact." He stepped forward and held out his hand in the manner of the Gothads.

Mathan-Bàn grasped his wrist tightly and answered, "You have my word upon it." Words are meaningless, hot air expelled from the lungs. You may have my word, betrayer, but not my oath.

As soon as Morghath Bres left, Mathan-Bàn summoned Cathadh to him. As emotionless as always, she greeted the sight of the Galdràgon's shattered corpse with a raised eyebrow and the scar at the side of her mouth tightened a little.

"What?" The Àrd-dràgon felt like a chastised child in her gaze. "If you have something to say, Cathadh, then say it."

"Nothing truly, Morair." That knowing smile crept into her eyes again. "I just wondered why you had not done this long ago?" she gestured towards the corpse.

Anger flared up inside him. If it had been any other who had dared to mock him like that, he would have killed them where they stood, but it was Cathadh, and all he could do was bite back his anger and huff loudly. "Remove it. Have it hacked up, incinerate the head and heart and have the rest thrown from the ramparts; let the eagles feed on her flesh."

Cathadh nodded solemnly. "Very good, Morair. I shall have the floor cleared immediately. There is one other thing, Morair."

"Yes?"

"The drumming has stopped, and we have word from Faylinn. He is bringing a Daonna, one of their leaders, to you."

"A prisoner? Who?"

"No, not a prisoner, Morair, a Daonna under an oath of safe conduct. A warrior, I do not know whom."

It was Mathan-Bàn's turn to raise his eyebrows. "Then, if Faylinn wishes for me to see this Daonna, who am I to refuse him?"

"Gun dàil, Morair." This time she smiled widely. "I shall make the proper arrangements."

"Do so."

Wal found the waiting gruelling. He still held the leather reins tied around Rànd's wrists and neck, but it was he who felt powerless. She stood now with her beautiful head held proudly, almost arrogantly high, deigning only to cast the occasional glance at him with a look similar to the way another would look at an insect crawling on the droppings of a horse. Her own kind stood about them like sentinels, unmoving save for their eyes, and Wal felt most of their eyes were on him. He found himself pulling her tighter, not for defence but, almost, for comfort. There was reassurance in her smell and the warmth of her body close to him. Rànd glared at him once again, but she did not struggle, as aware as much as he that she was in truth already free save for the act of cutting her bindings.

Corvus pulled his cloak tight around his shoulders to ward off the cold that seemed to emanate from the very walls of the castle. His mind was elsewhere, patiently running over the Bard's answers for some pointer as to how to react, but there were just too many unknown factors. These creatures were real, flesh and blood, and dangerous. Their Àrd-dràgon, no doubt, was no fool either, but so far, there was no explanation as to why they had attacked this place had emerged. They had to have a reason, a motive. It was that piece of information that Corvus needed. He knew he had to plan what he was going to say in front of this Àrd-dràgon. He required a bargain to strike, or all would be lost, but there was so much he still did not know, or, at least, trust that he knew. After the monsters he had met today, and what he had seen in the mirror, it would not surprise him to find that this 'Mathan-Bàn' and 'Finnvarra' were one and the same, nor would he be surprised to find MacLeech awaiting him the other side of those doors.

Faylinn led Corvus and the others into the darkened hall. The high arched windows had been covered here too, and the only light came from a few torches ensconced in the walls and from the fire blazing in the huge, raised hearth at the far end. The floor of the great room was empty, and long tables and other furniture were piled against the walls as if deliberately yet hastily cleared. As Corvus walked further into the hall, he cast about carefully; there were warriors in the dark recesses, and above, standing back in the shadows of the minstrel's gallery. Glimmering eyes and glinting armour, patient watchmen guarding their Lord.

A man stood upon the raised hearth, his back casually turned to them, theatrically warming his hands before the roaring fire. Giving his back to them was, as Corvus knew, a clear display of his belief in his own power, a demonstration of his lack of fear. Before the hearth stood a single white-haired Isheen warrior resting almost casually upon the quillons of a claymore. Its style much like that of the Albans, but more embellished, engraved and exaggerated. Corvus supposed this would be the Isheen Lord's champion and executioner, a steely-eyed warrior, to intimidate the nervous supplicants. It was all a strategy that Corvus understood, a dramatic act, to convey the message of the Isheen Lord's power over life and death.

Faylinn halted them before the Isheen champion, spoke a few words and then stepped up to speak to the figure warming himself at the fire.

"They're everywhere," murmured Svein.

"Aye an' there's been killing here," Wal growled softly back and nodded at the bloody mess upon the flagstones that was now soaking back through the hurriedly strewn fresh straw.

"I can smell that," Corvus answered softly. His eyes, though, were on the Isheen's Lord as he turned to them. He was taller than Faylinn, physically larger, and had the bearing Corvus expected to see; upright and proud. His white hair was tied up in a high knot at the back of his head and hung down in a swathe over his left shoulder. He was most definitely Isheen; their strange traits were exemplified in him. No facial hair, save for the arched eyebrows, his face was clean-lined and hard, showing little of the age that Corvus had assumed, but his eyes, with their hollow gleam, could have been a thousand years old.

He wore no visible armour, only a plain white robe with a mantle of darkest green. Upon the left breast was a simple motif of a white bear rampant. The same symbol, wrought in silver, decorated the heavy buckle of the sword belt at his waist; the sword, though was lost in the voluminous folds of the green mantle. At his throat, something glistened in the firelight, an amulet or talisman, some silver symbol of status, Corvus supposed.

Faylinn stepped down and stood beside the champion, his face impassive but his demeanour tense. One hand had strayed to his weapon's hilt, and his face was full of rage. Corvus wondered what his Lord had whispered back to him in front of the fireplace.

Mathan-Bàn looked for a long moment at Rànd and then over the faces of the gathered Dhaoine with an expression of disgust. Finally, pointing a finely gloved hand directly at Corvus, he said. "Who are you to dare to hold one of my own kin in my presence?" His voice rumbled around the great hall.

Before Corvus could speak, the Bard declared, "I am Tàmhasg MacKeelta, Bard to the MacRoth, Laird of Crìoch and Eagle's Craig. This is Andreas Corvidious, Corvus of Val Gär. Imperial Consul, High Questor and Governor of the Northwest Provinces, Commander of the northern armies, the conqueror of the Southrons, the conqueror of the Vanda, the destroyer of Mùr Ollamhan, victor of Sruth Fuil. Known to the Gothads as Valravn, the Raven of Gardariki. It is he who dares."

Corvus glared at the Bard and barked, "Shut up!"

Mathan-Bàn raised his eyebrows, unsure how to react to the young Daonna's outburst, part of him felt anger, part of him wanted to laugh, but something stopped him. "You presume to speak as a Filidh, though you are little more than a court minstrel masquerading as a Bàrd. If you value your wagging tongue, dare not to speak unbidden in my presence again." He laid his gaze on the young man for a moment to emphasize his words.

Tàmh nodded curtly and stepped back.

Addressing the whole hall, Mathan-Bàn continued, "Daonna lives are but short, and the Gärian General Corvus would be long

298

dead." With an unspoken word, he silenced the protests in his mind's ear from Faylinn and Rànd. "This man is not he."

Corvus found that too much of a slight to let pass unchallenged, though he had come here to appear to be 'reasonable,' or at least be seen to be, he was in no mood to be dismissed as a fraud by this dog-toothed troglodyte. He stepped forward challengingly, "If you are so mighty, look closely and see who I am." Corvus guessed if what he had seen in the mirror was true, this creature would be able to see something of it. It was a little bluff, but it could possibly work in his favour. "Or do you fear to do so?"

Rànd's warning rang clear in Mathan-Bàn's head. He glared at her and slammed her silent. Had she forgotten her place or gone mad with her newfound abilities? Faylinn attempted to speak too, but with a warning, Mathan-Bàn shut him out too. This Daonna cannot be who he claims to be; Corvus would be an ancient old man; this man is old by their standards but still vital, still a warrior. "Step forward, let me see you then."

Corvus stepped forward but was halted by Faylinn, "There is enough." Corvus glared savagely back at him, and for a moment, Faylinn felt a tinge of fear. This was all very wrong. "Your sword," demanded Faylinn, "Give me your weapons."

Corvus obliged, handing over his short sword and knife. "Little use here anyway with all your archers in the shadows."

Faylinn ignored him and tried again to get Mathan-Bàn to acknowledge his unspoken warnings, but the Àrd-dràgon would see for himself.

Mathan-Bàn studied the stranger carefully, though he had never been strong enough, or even interested enough, to take up the role of Fiosaiche, a man of knowledge, to his people, like all of his kind his tàlann had grown stronger as he had aged. His own abilities had turned towards the unspoken and clear sight rather than prophecy or the conjuring tricks of the Magicians and Priestesses. Concentrating upon the man before him, he drew on the wellspring of tàlann deep within himself, his ability to see things for what they truly were, to see through glamours and fith-faths and illusions, the deceits set to fool the eye, mind, or heart. It took him great effort, but as the clarity grew, he began to see what stood before him.

Upon the man's left shoulder sat a great black carrion bird, a raven, whose eyes gleamed back at Mathan-Bàn with the malice of an evil aeons old. The Daonna's face, truly seen, was ancient, the parchment-like skin drawn tight over the bone in a deathly grin, the silvery hair grey against the raven's breast, his eyes were bottomless pits devoid of life or emotion.

The Àrd-dràgon chanced to recoil but stayed himself and focused harder upon the abomination. Something was wrong with it, an illusion within an illusion, as the nightmarish image faded away, Mathan-Bàn could perceive the man beneath, a man he recognised, the man he had seen leading the Gärian Hastions at Steidh-Dòchais long ago; Corvus of Val Gär. The illusion broken he could now see that at Corvus' right shoulder stood a figure he did not recognise, an ancient old man dressed in a simple dwale coloured gown, straight standing and clean-shaven like a Gärian, his face was as remote and his eyes as cold as the stars.

Mathan-Bàn spoke to the apparition, who are you?

The spectre sneered, I am the spirit of Empire, the God of Misrule, the iron sword in every sheath, the nails in a hundred thousand boots, I am the Flamen Martialis. I am the spirit of Val Gär.

Mathan-Bàn thought on that for a moment. I do not believe you, phantom; you are nothing but a disguise. I command you; show yourself for what you are.

The phantom clouded over and seemed to withdraw like a shadow from torchlight, revealing another figure, a tall woman dressed as Death herself with ashes on her brow. One claw-like hand grasped Corvus' right shoulder, and in the other, she held a javelin; beneath her shroud, she wore a warrior's armour. Her face was that of one of his own, but terrible eyes burned with a ferocious passion beneath the tangled mass of jet-black hair.

The huge ethereal raven on Corvus' left shoulder cocked its head and cawed.

The phantom woman lifted her head and glowered condescendingly back at Mathan-Bàn.

Then look upon me.

If thou dare.

In a far-off place, separated from the worlds of man, the High King, Finnvarra, roared with anger as every piece on his gaming board other than the White Queen suddenly turned into a Black Raven. He smashed his silver goblet down upon the game board and threw the table aside in his rage. As attendants fled in terror, their King cast about for things to tear down and destroy. Seizing a sword, he struck one cowering slave dead and threw the corpse across the chamber before turning to hack and slash his way through the furniture. He screamed his curses upon her, the meddling bitch! He cursed her with every ounce of his being, curses with all the skills and power at his command, curses that could have damned nations and untold generations to the end of time.

Then unexpectedly, at the height of his rage, he calmed at the sight of the girl still sitting by the upturned table, her beautiful face still in passive repose. As the King watched, the young warrior righted the table and began patiently to replace all the pieces upon the board.

Taken by the absurdity of it all, Finnvarra began to laugh.

The first few flakes of snow, as big as copper pennies, drifted lazily down out of the slate grey sky and settled on the grass at Ker's feet. One large feather-like flake settled on his nose, but he angrily brushed it off. They were now less than a day from the crannog. Although the going was necessarily slow because of the wounded having to rest every few miles, they were still moving far too fast for Ker's liking. As his wits had returned to him, and so had the realisation that when they got back to the crannog, Meg would tend their wounds. Meg was the best healer any of the men had ever known. Undoubtedly, she would minister to Gabhran and the warriors first, but then she would tend to Ned, and then he would wake up properly and...Ker dreaded the idea of it. Once Ned was awake, he would instantly tell everyone what had happened to him, and then the questions would start; what were they doing out of the camp? And Ned, stupid Ned, would tell everything.

It wouldn't take the others long to work out what he had been up to; oh sure, he could lie, but that was the problem; he knew he could lie his way out of most things, but this was different. His lies would end him up in front of her, and he knew that bloated

Gothad whore would smell the lies on him like a fly can smell shit. Everyone feared her, even the warriors, they said she was some kind of Witch, not like the one the others were talking about, but she could see through men like glass.

Ker knew if he stood before Jorunn MacRoth, he would be damned. The bitch would look at him with those pale eyes of hers and see every lie he'd ever told, every vicious little act he'd ever done. All the things he had stolen from the others, how he'd bullied Ned and Ag, how he'd poisoned the puppy the Laird had given Meg just to see it die, and the trouble he had caused between Big Wal and Hamish MacReul over the stolen jewel from Wal's dirk.

Ker realised he was trembling, not from the cold but from fear. He was terrified. If Lady MacRoth didn't have him hung, the MacReuls would cut his hands off and brand him for the thief.

Ned would tell, Ker was sure of it, as soon as he awoke, he'd tell, he'd whine and bleat like a goat, and, if he were lucky, Ker would swing for it.

He spat on the ground beside him, bloody Ned, how he wished that creature had killed him, stove his skull in and dragged his soul down to whatever hole it crawled out of. If Ned had died, it would have been so much easier to make up some reason to cover up what he'd been doing out of camp. So much simpler to place the blame on Ned; after all, he was a halfwit, an amadan, wasn't he? He wandered off, of course, because he's stupid, so I went looking for him in case he had gotten lost. After all, I look after him, don't I? I have to look after him because you always stick me with the idiot, don't you? Yes, there was the germ of the tale, the believable lie. It was what he'd already kind of told Wal. Well, of course, he had left out the stuff about Ned being an idiot. It seemed to satisfy Wal for now, but when Kemble had heard the tale, he had questioned him on it. Ned was the Laird's own blood, and Kemble wanted to know exactly what had happened to him. The old man was sharp, but he had been called away to tend Gabhran before his questions could lead to any immediate conclusions. Ker had managed to keep out of his way since, but it fore warned him of things to come.

Less than a day to Crannag-mòr and he had to do something about Ned fast. If Ned wasn't going to die, then maybe he would just have to help him on his way.

Later they stopped by a small stream to fill canteens and water the horses. Most of the men were eating, drinking, pissing, or trying to stamp the feeling back into frozen limbs and feet. All too busy to take any notice of Ker. Kemble and a knot of the others were around Gabhran, either watching him die or taking orders. Ker didn't care which, leaving only one of the walking wounded to watch over Ned. Ned was on the ground, wrapped tightly in a blanket and tied to a litter made from sticks and saplings. A light covering of snow was already forming over him. Ned's watcher, Uilleam, was nursing a broken arm and a few grazes of his own, though mostly it was his pride that had been hurt as everyone knew he had gotten his injuries falling off his horse when the Trows attacked without even drawing his sword. So now, Uilleam sat sullenly beside the comatose boy fiddling with the strapping on his broken arm and wishing he had broken his neck instead.

Ker wandered over to them through the crunching frozen grass. "If you want Uilleam, I'll look after him for a while." Ker felt emboldened enough to talk to the young Clansman with such familiarity because he knew how despondent Uilleam felt.

Uilleam looked up at him blankly. "Hu?"

"Go on, it's cold, get some food. I'll sit with him." Ker gave him a quickly timed knowing smile, "It'll be fine."

For a dreadful moment, Ker thought the young clansman was going to come on all haughty and try to put him in his place, but, at last, he just shrugged, climbed to his feet, and walked off towards where a group of his cousins and friends were huddled together sharing food.

Ker watched him go with a mix of relief and savoured delight. Uilleam had made a fool out of himself and had been taunted by the older men when they found out what had happened to him; then, to add to Uilleam's embarrassment, Wal had set him to nurse Ned. Ker delighted in seeing one of the arrogant bastards brought down to size, finally getting a little taste of the humiliation he had to go through every day of his life.

Ker allowed himself a half-choked off giggle as he settled beside the still form of Ned. "Well, how are we, Neddy, er?" He brushed the snowflakes from Ned's brow and tugged the blanket up around him.

"Having pleasant dreams, I hope?"

Ned stirred slightly but grew quiet again.

"Good old, Neddy. You be quiet now." Ker looked around carefully. This time he made sure of what everyone was doing. Kemble was talking to the leader of the Kerns that had accompanied them since this morning. One of the slaves was tending Gabhran, and the rest of the men, warriors, stewards, and slaves were eating or resting. Some were bitching about the snow and wrapping themselves in more layers of plaid and fur. No one was taking the slightest notice of him or Ned. If there was a right moment this, was it, but suddenly Ker was at a loss as to what to do. He had never killed anyone in his life, well poisoning a wolfhound puppy, and tormenting a few rats didn't really count; how was he going to do this? He could stab Ned or cut his throat, he kept his knife keen, and it was a sturdy blade, but that would mean blood everywhere and not even a dullard like Uilleam would miss that. He could strangle Ned, but Ker had seen men strangled; their eyes bulged, and tongues turned black, and probably Ned would fight even in his sleep.

It occurred to Ker that he could beat Ned on the head with a rock, nothing big, just a good-sized one, right on the place where the Isheen woman had hit him, finish the job she'd started. That idea appealed to Ker, clean and straightforward, but he could see no good-sized rocks as he looked around. Everything was rapidly disappearing under a white blanket, and then it occurred to him that even if he found a rock, he would have to turn Ned over to get to the back of his head. In frustration, he grabbed one of the gloves that Uilleam had left on the ground beside the litter and slapped himself across the temple. Think! Damn you! An idea popped into his mind instantly, like a voice out of nowhere; people choke in their sleep.

He found himself staring at the reinforced leather gauntlet, at the bronze rings sown on the back and the coarse stitching along the sides. He slipped the glove on and clenched his fist.

"Oh Neddy, did I nea tell you to be more careful what ye

eat?"

He took one last look around to check no one's attention had strayed back to him before setting himself over Ned. He used his body to cover any view of what he was doing. It was so simple, really; he opened Ned's mouth and shoved the unconscious boy's tongue back down his throat with his gloved fingers.

Ned gasped, choked, and began to struggle as the gag reflex kicked in, but Ker was expecting it and rested his whole weight on Ned's chest. Instantly Ned retched and began to vomit, exactly as Ker had expected; he pulled out his fingers and slapped his hand over Ned's mouth and nose and held it there until Ned's struggles subsided.

It seemed like an age before the boy stopped moving, but Ker knew he had to wait to be sure he could not make a mistake. After a while, he lifted his hand. Ned was still now, his eyes open and his mouth and nose caked in vomit. Ned was dead, really dead; Ker was delighted. Quickly he pulled off the glove and threw it aside, grabbed Ned's shoulders and shouted, "Ned! Neddy!" But Ned didn't move. Ker jumped to his feet and screamed for help.

Chapter 26

"I met a Lady in the meads
Full beautiful – a faery's child,
Her hair was long, her foot was light,
And her eyes were wild."

La Belle Dame sans Merci
John Keats

Mathan-Bàn could feel her power permeating the hall, flooding into his reality as if some supernatural dam had burst. He wondered momentarily if they could all see her too, even the Dhaoine? He judged by their unease; they could at least sense it. It was as if a thunderhead was forming inside the hall, a vast massing of energy around the phantom.

Who do you say I am?

Mathan-Bàn answered without hesitation. You are the Great Queen of Battles, the sister-wife of the Dagda, mother of Gods; you are the Giver of Victories, the Bringer of Strife, the Voice of Destruction. You are the Great Queen. You are the Morrigan.

The Goddess smiled, it was not a pleasant sight, and inclined her head to acknowledge his exaltation.

Am I not also Maid and Mother?

The Purest One and the Giver of Life?

She who is spring, summer and winter?

Mathan-Bàn recoiled, Great Queen, have I offended you?

The Morrigan's expression grew distant.

This one is mine own.

You may not interfere. Let him go unhindered, and, though you stand here defiantly in the blood of my Priestess, I shall grant you the victory you wish for.

Mathan-Bàn bowed his head reverently.

Understand me, Mathan-Bàn.

Defy me, and I shall remove your name from the annals of time. As you shall wither, so shall your bloodline, your house, and your people.

Your name shall only be whispered in memory of my curse upon you.

Leave this one be.

Corvus watched as the face of the Isheen Àrd-dràgon grew distant and intense. For a moment, fear flickered across his face, and then he nodded as if in conversation with some spirit or power none other could see. By the faces of the other Isheen, Corvus gathered that they too could sense or see the thing their master was communicating with. The hall had grown noticeably colder as if all the heat from the hearth was being sucked out of it. Corvus watched as his own breath hung in the air before him. It was sorcery for sure; there was a dull metallic taste in the air and a sensation of heaviness, a charged feeling, like that of a thunderstorm gathering. Some presence was here now, something truly potent. He had only felt such power once when he had stormed into the cave temple of Hekate outside the city of Leucothea, in pursuit of the Ephor Politis who had sought sanctuary there, and the High Priestess, Mormo, had manifested the Goddess before him.

Suddenly Mathan-Bàn snapped out of his contemplation and spoke. "So, it is you, Corvus of Val Gär. I am Mathan-Bàn, Riaghladair of Dùn nan Làidir, Àrd-dràgon of the Isheen. I do not welcome you here, but here you are."

"It was not my own choice."

"What is your purpose?"

Corvus thought for a moment, whatever it was Mathan-Bàn had seen and spoken to had changed his whole attitude; maybe now was as good a time to show his own hand. "I want the Witch Annis Nic an Neamhain, and I want free passage to leave this place unharmed, both I and my men."

Wal grasped his arm. "We do not leave here without our Laird and all our kith and kin, alive or dead."

Corvus looked at the big Alban and then back at Mathan-Bàn. "Their Lord and any prisoners you have taken."

Mathan-Bàn took a deep breath. "What prisoners we have taken will be freed to you, but we do not hold either their Chieftain or the Witch. They escaped, with the aid of Mer Maqq Lighiche, into the tunnels and through the Dorsan, the stone they call 'the Heart of the Craig,' it is a portal to another place."

Corvus looked at Wal. "Is that possible?"

Wal looked dubious.

"Yes, it is possible." Tàmh whispered, "The Heart of the Craig is a stone buried deep in the bowls of the Craig. It has always been believed to be a gate, although it has never been opened to my knowledge. The Witch is mighty, and with MacLeech's aid, they may have opened it."

"A gate to where?"

Tàmh shrugged. "No one knows."

Mathan-Bàn stepped down from the raised hearth and spoke into Faylinn's ear, it only took a moment, but it was enough to convey his intentions.

"Why do you seek the Witch Annis Nic an Neamhain?" asked Faylinn.

"That is between her and me," replied Corvus.

"Do you mean her harm?"

Corvus was entirely stunned by the question. "I need to find her, that is all," he lied. "I have no intention of harming her. The reason is between her and me."

Mathan-Bàn looked closely at the Gärian; whether he was lying or not was hard to tell.

Faylinn continued, "She is powerful and guarded by a mighty giant and a shapeshifter, and she travels with Mer Maqq Lighiche the Taibhsear of the Kerns. You would be best advised to let her go."

Corvus looked to the towering Àrd-dràgon. "You forget who I am."

Mathan-Bàn ignored him and stepped back up to the hearth.

Faylinn spoke for his master, "The Àrd-dràgon will grant you your requests, the prisoners and your freedom, and he will aid you in your quest to find Annis Nic an Neamhain, but on condition."

Corvus ignored the words coming out of Faylinn's mouth and addressed his replies to the back of Mathan-Bàn. "I assumed there would be conditions. What is it you want from me?"

Faylinn hesitated and looked to his master.

Mathan-Bàn turned. "I want you to find the Riataiche and bring her here first, to me."

"Riataiche?"

Mathan-Bàn smiled knowingly. "Half-breed. She is a very rare thing, Corvus, both of your kind and of ours. To some of our kind, she is an abomination, looked upon as your kind would look upon the offspring of a man and a dog, though to others, she is more than either of us."

"You?"

"I want to know more of her before I hand her over to you."

Corvus laughed loudly. "You expect me to deliver her to you with no guarantee that you will not keep her. I am not that stupid."

Mathan-Bàn nodded. "You are mistaken, Corvus. If she comes with you, it will be on her own accord. I doubt if even I could detain her against her will."

Corvus thought for a moment; maybe it was time to try a different tactic. "I would speak to you alone first. You and I."

The hall had been cleared, even the archers in the shadows were gone, leaving Mathan-Bàn and Corvus alone save for the silent brooding figure of Cathadh, who had ignored her master's command to leave.

"Come," Mathan-Bàn waved Corvus forward.

"I said 'alone'."

Mathan-Bàn cast a glance at Cathadh. "She is my Banacheileadair and my bodyguard, and even if I dismiss her, she will not leave. If you are to speak, you may speak freely in front of her."

Corvus, who had not realised it was a woman under that harness, took a long look at her and then stepped up to join the Àrd-dràgon.

"You have something to say, Corvus. Then say it."

Corvus reached out his hands to the fire. "There is another who seeks this 'half-breed' woman. One who demands that I find her and bring her to him."

Mathan-Bàn raised an eyebrow quizzically. "Who?"

"He appeared to me at the Crannog of Lady MacRoth. He calls himself 'Finnvarra'." Corvus watched carefully, but the Àrd-dràgon didn't react. "He says he is some kind of Druid King."

"And why does this 'Druid King' say he seeks Annis Nic an Neamhain?" The Àrd-dràgon's face grew hard, and there was an apparent mordant tone in his voice.

Corvus looked up at Isheen thoughtfully for a moment. Either he was in league with Finnvarra or, as his tone suggested, unaware of his meddling and not happy to hear of it. Corvus had a natural sense for disunity, and if there was a chink to work on here, then maybe it could be exploited for his benefit. He decided it was time to make his gambit, play the honest fool card and see where the other cards fall. "Finnvarra says she is his granddaughter, a child forced upon his daughter by rape, and that it was I who fathered the child after the battle of Sroo Fool. He demands that I find her and bring her to him as penance for my wrongdoing."

"Sruth Fuil," Mathan-Bàn corrected him. "Finnbharra sent you here?"

"No, the wife of the Laird, someone I owe a debt of honour to, sent me here. But Finnvarra was first to tell me of the Witch."

"Did he tell you why he wants her?"

"I neither know nor cared to ask."

"Is she your blood?"

"No. I don't know. I am a man of honour. I do not rape women, prisoners or not."

"If she were his daughter, then you could not have taken her by any force you possessed. Unless she came to you willingly."

That had already occurred to Corvus. "Who is this 'Finnvarra'?"

"Finnbharra is the King of the Daoine Faoi Cheilt, the Unseen Ones. An ancient power in the West."

"More powerful than you?"

Mathan-Bàn paused as if weighing up the question. "No. He is an old meddler, a fool, more interested in games and riddles than reality. Once he ruled the most powerful tribe in the West, but now under his rule, his people, those who have stayed loyal to him, have grown debauched and soft, without aim or purpose. There is no mettle in them."

But there's mettle in you, isn't there? Corvus thought, and you have more enemies to test that mettle than just those things on the shore. "Then, if I find her and bring her back here, I have no guarantee that you will not take her prisoner and leave me to the mercies of Finnvarra."

"True enough, but you are not afraid of him or me, and as you say, you are a man of honour. But you are not honour bound to him, are you? So, you will do as you wish. Did he threaten you or try to coerce you? If he thought he could control you, he is undoubtedly a greater fool than I suspect him of being, and you have already seen this as an opportunity to repay him for his audacity.

"I know what kind of man you are and how your mind works; you are a warrior, a leader like me. We both have the same weakness, our pride, our uaill, and those who dare to affront that uaill will pay dearly for it. Though our prideful natures can often lead us to make decisions against our better judgement. You must be careful, Corvus of Val Gär, do not let your injured self-esteem lead you into a confrontation with forces you cannot counter. You no longer have an army at your back. As for myself, I can only offer you my word. If you will take my message to the Witch, then I will not hinder you. Neither will I betray you to Finnbharra, though I may not defend you from him either, I doubt if you need or want protection anyway."

Corvus was surprised by the Àrd-dràgon's candour. "And if I refuse?"

"Then you refuse. Take the prisoners and go on your way; they are not important. I have given you my word on it, and so it stands."

Corvus sensed the Àrd-dràgon was in a mood to speak his mind, so he pressed on. "What do you want with this woman?"

"Our people are at war." Mathan-Bàn turned towards the fire. "Not only with your kind and those out there, but with ourselves." He clasped his chest. "Inside. We are too long under those who rule through birth right, not through strength, our blood runs thin, and our future is as stale bread. Those who lead us think that bloodletting is the only way to revive our people and offset the stagnation, but that road only leads to madness. I want to end that madness, to make my people strong; slaughtering innocents on sacrificial stones will not make us strong." He sighed heavily, though there was much more blood to be shed. "This Riataiche, Annis, is powerful beyond expectation. I watched her sweep the Fomóiri from these walls like leaves before a breeze and with as much effort.

She wields true power, yet, so I am told, she also possesses the judgment to use it wisely; our people need that kind of strength."

"You need that kind of strength?"

Mathan-Bàn turned back to him. "Yes, Corvus, I need that kind of strength if I am to end these incessant wars and internal strife and restore the dignity and honour my people deserve."

Chapter 27

...for it is an olde sawe, he feghtith wele that fleith faste.

The Wolf and the Hare

Gesta Romanorum.

[LVII.] Addit. MS. 9066.

Allasa MacKeeask often climbed all the way up to the Bodaich Mhóra to pray, though she wasn't a great believer in Gods or spirits, in some way, just sitting beside the three great stone sentinels and telling them her hopes or fears always made her feel better. It was as if just talking were a way of putting things into perspective. She knew others from the village came up here to pray too, and sometimes they left little gifts for the spirits they thought inhabited the stones. Allasa didn't; she didn't even truly pray, just talked, like she used to talk to her grandmother when she was alive, about anything and everything. She loved it up here, overlooking the little bay, she could even see the turfed roof tops of her village if she climbed up onto the shoulders of the Bodach Mór himself, but she didn't like to; it felt wrong somehow, disrespectful. Though she had to occasionally if she thought someone was looking for her or had followed her.

Allasa was more careful these days, though because of Bothan, the village Priest did not hold with such things; to him, these stones were just stones, nothing more. If people wanted guidance from the ancestors or the Gods, they were to do so through him. He was to be the only intermediary; any requests for advice or guidance had to be put to him, and then, on the chosen day, he would go into the tomb of the ancestors and speak to them. He would allow no one else, not even his twin sons, to speak to the ancestors; no one could play any part in his appointed role in communicating with the other world. The sons of Bothan attended him during ceremonies for the Gods and during the festivals, but they were, like everyone else in the village, forbidden to enter the tomb. Allasa wasn't surprised that he kept the boys out of things as they were as dull as ditch water. "Daft, both o' them," as Mother Oighrig called them.

Allasa didn't believe in anything that Bothan said anyway, he was either a poor Seer or a liar, and he couldn't do real magic, not like her grandmother, who had been a real Fiosaiche. In fact, Allasa was sure Bothan was just a fraud. She didn't like thinking too much about her grandmother because it only made her realise how much she missed the old woman. She'd been strong but kind and gentle and had promised Allasa that one day she would be the village's Fiosaiche.

It was the thing that had filled Allasa's mind and dreams for years, but when her grandmother died, the Chieftain, Harailt, had sent Bothan and his sons over from Ardiar where they worship their crops. Allasa detested him on sight, he was a foreigner with strange ideas, and he showed no respect for the old ways of her grandmother and the traditions of the villagers. He had even forbidden people to sacrifice to the sea and had demanded that they stay away from the standing stones because, he said, they were evil. He had even forbidden the attendees from entering the tomb of the ancestors to tend the remains, saying it was his task alone. There was little she could do, even as the direct descendant of the old Seeress. She wasn't even a woman yet, not old enough to marry, so all that was left to her was her anger and the odd opportunity for petty revenge.

Most of the villagers despised Bothan, and recently their tolerance of him had been growing short, then things had almost come to blows on the day of the festival of Shoney O'Shean when he had tried to physically stop some of the fishermen from going down to the bay to cast votive offerings into the sea. The Elders did nothing, they just hummed and hawed and said that it was the Chieftain's responsibility to deal with him, but Harailt sat two days' journey away, at An Sailein.

In the chaos of the argument, Allasa had taken her opportunity to vent some of her spite at the Priest. She had thrown a lump of goat poo at him, but it was hard frozen in the middle and almost knocked him out. Murdo and Naill, his sons, had tried to beat her for it, but her uncle, Ceard, who was the village Smith and an Elder, stopped them. Bothan was furious and had demanded to have her punished by the Elders, but her uncle had refused, and when Bothan threatened curses upon her, her uncle, a massive block of a man, threatened him with more immediate harm in return.

The Priest, though, was not one to give up easily, and Allasa knew it. She also knew that he was out to get her back for the humiliation she had caused him. Murdo and Naill had tried only yesterday to catch her as she tried to sneak out of the village, but she easily outwitted and outran them and was back at her uncle's forge before anyone was the wiser. The boys had stomped and snorted around outside like angry bullocks but had not dared to face the wrath of the Smith.

Now the atmosphere in the village was becoming strained, and she seemed to have somehow put herself in the centre of it. Though few people of the village liked the Priest, some felt that what she did was so disrespectful that she should be punished. Others felt only glad that someone had finally stood up to the over-mighty foreigner, even if it was only a girl child of nine summers, and many cruel jokes involving Bothan, goats and frozen turds were being swapped openly.

Even Allasa had begun to fear that the whole thing was getting out of control and that she was in more and more danger. True, she hated Bothan, but she was only a child, and he was the village Priest. If he really used his authority or appealed to the Chieftain. she wasn't sure if her uncle Ceard could protect her. Then this morning, her aunt and uncle had a terrible argument, after which her aunt had turned on her, scolding her for bringing such trouble on her uncle's head, she had called her, "An ill-deedie, wickit wean!" Then chased her out of the house with the besom broom.

So Allasa had decided to climb up to the Bodaich Mhóra and pray, she would ask for help or maybe for the Gods to make the Priest go away, or strike him dumb or blind or something, anything so he would leave her alone.

She had climbed most of the way up the outcrop and stopped at the foot of the mound where the Bodaich Mhóra stood, the 'Big

Auld Men,' three towering chunks of stone, two slightly smaller and smoother than the third, the Bodach Mór himself, a monolith almost twice the size of the others. Old wives' tales told of three rampaging giants turned to stone by an eclipse or cursed by a Witch to a strange cold immortality, but Allasa didn't believe any of it. She turned, as she always did at this point, to look out across the bay. It was a perfect day, cold and clear.

The rugged landscape around her swept down to the little white sandy beach where the sunlight glittered upon the breaking waves. She could see the other children playing at the water's edge, chasing the surf in and out. Allasa loved her little island, and her little village huddled in the shelter of its stone revetments but, since her hopes of being the village Seeress had been taken away, something inside her yearned for more than this little place. She knew she didn't really fit in here, and as she grew towards adulthood, she felt it more deeply.

Most of the other children shunned her, some of the adults too. She was different, like her grandmother and her mother, and 'different' meant feared. Her grandmother and uncle had told her often that this was only a tiny place in a vast, wondrous world, and now she often dreamed of escaping into it, of sailing away to An Sailein and beyond to the mainland. She would go on such adventures and see and do such things that the villagers of Ebb Dwallion could only dream of, though one day, she knew she would return here. She would come back from her travelling and be welcome here, and she would be happy, so long as Bothan was gone.

Allasa sighed and climbed up to the stones. When the sun shone on them, they sparkled, and she could see all manner of strange colours on their surface. Running her hands lovingly over their surface, weathered smooth by the unimaginable passage of time. Allasa loved these stones as if they were her family. She had never known her mother or father, and now increasingly often she felt unbearably alone, but not here, not in the presence of her friends, these stone giants.

But something was wrong, the colours in the stones were wrong as if they were shifting...

"What are ye doin' here, hen?" Bothan stepped out from

behind the Bodach Mór.

Allasa wheeled around to run, but behind her had appeared Bothan's sons, like two identical ginger ox calves, as big and stupid-looking.

"A'm waitin' to know?" Bothan's big round ruddy face was full of delight.

Allasa panicked, stumbled over her own feet, and fell.

Bothan rested upon his staff and chuckled. "Ay, look at you. Nae so full o' yerself now. Do ye no have somethin' clever to say?" He sauntered towards her.

"Look, Daddy!" called Murdo, "A found this." He was waving a headless chicken about gleefully. "It's wan o Oighrig's birdies!"

Bothan bent over her, "Sae ye have been up here doin' worship to these damned stones, have ye no? I will have ye for a Wutch, ye know." He poked her shoulder painfully with the ferrule of his staff. "A'll see ye no pay richtly for ye ill-doing'."

Allasa wanted to scramble away, but she was too frightened to move. All she could do was stare up into his mad eyes. "Ay, we will learn what the Elders make o' you. A'll have to clean your mucket wee soul, ye wickit wean!"

"Ye'll no goin' to like eatin' ye own weight in goat shite," laughed Naill.

"Haud ye wheesht!" bellowed Bothan, his eyes bulging with rage, bits of white spittle were dribbling down his chin and sprayed in her face. "Up ye get, quick!" He snatched up a handful of her hair and hauled her to her feet.

Too terrified to struggle, she just burst into tears and began to plead for her grandmother, who had been dead now four winters and tried to beg Bothan not to hurt her. The Priest's sons just laughed and yelled more brutal things, but she was so frantic that she no longer heard them.

Allasa opened her mouth to scream, but the noise died in her throat. Behind the Priest and his sons stood the Bodach Mór, and at the centre of the stone had appeared a small pulsating light, and it was growing rapidly. Allasa was awestruck.

Bothan noticing the child's gaze looked around in time to see an immense flare of rainbow light erupt out of the centre of the stone. Staggered and half-blinded, he threw Allasa aside and shielded his eyes. As the light abated, he gathered his wits, thrust forward his staff, and demanded loudly, "What sorcery is this?"

Allasa watched, amazed as some writhing thing burst out of the stone and crashed to the ground only a few feet from them. A warrior's equipment scattered on the ground, and out from amidst leapt a massive grey wolf.

Murdo and Naill, who were already backing away, instantly screamed and fled, leaving their father to face the creature.

The grey wolf, bigger than a moorland pony and wearing a golden torc for a collar, snarled viciously at the Priest, shook itself nonchalantly and loped off down towards the bay.

Allasa turned to speak to Bothan, but his face was so white she would have thought him dead if his mouth had not been soundlessly repeating something. He held his staff before him like a weapon, but his hands were shaking so violently it looked as if he was trying to stir the air. Allasa, struck by the absurdity of it all, abruptly began laughing hysterically. Another flash made her turn back to the stone as out of it stepped a giant in armour, carrying a great boar spear; he was almost as tall as the monolith itself.

Allasa instantly reasoned; it was the Bodach Mór, the spirit in the stone; he had heard her pleas and had come to save her. Gleefully she dashed forward, but Bothan caught her by the scruff and dragged her back.

"Do na go near it!" He thrust her behind him. "Have ye no done enough trouble already? Run awa! Now!"

Allasa was suddenly confused. Bothan was terrified, physically shaking with fear, but he seemed to be trying to protect her. At that moment, she saw the Priest differently. She had spent so long despising him that she had never thought that he could care about her, or that he could one day be brave, but, as he lifted his staff and stepped forward to confront the Bodach Mór, for that moment, he was the most courageous and stupid man she'd ever seen.

"Get awa! Ye no welcome here!" The top of his staff suddenly burst into flame, and he thrust it towards the giant. "A command you to quit!"

The Bodach Mór did not quit; he loomed over Bothan, as

massive as the wall of a broch. Allasa could see him clearly now. He was an incredibly huge man, with a tremendous flaming red beard and wild hair; the face under the beard was grim and as hard as rock itself.

To her shock, Allasa realised that everything her hero was wearing, the strange armours and furs, were spattered with dried gore as if he had come fresh from some great battle. Bothan tried to shout something more, but it only came out as a terrified yelp, as the Bodach Mór swung his great boar spear and shattered the staff in his hands. Bothan cringed away, but the Bodach Mór knocked him sprawling to the ground.

Allasa cried out, more from surprise than fear.

The Bodach Mór looked at her with the palest blue eyes she had ever seen, and then he smiled. "Do not fear. I will not harm you. Who are you, child?" His voice was deep and authoritative, but she could hardly understand his accent.

"A'm Allasa MacKeeask, Laird."

Bothan tried to say something, but the Bodach Mór rested the ferrule of his spear on the Priest's chest, and he fell silent.

"Where are we, Allasa?"

"Clachan o Ebb Dwallion, Laird. The Isle of Na-Elan." Behind him, the strange rainbow light repeatedly flared as others, ordinary men all dressed as warriors, stepped out of the heart of the stone. "Are you no the Bodach Mór, Laird?" Allasa bravely asked.

"The 'Bodach Mór'?" The giant glanced back at the three huge monoliths. "Ah, the stones!" He laughed and shook his head, "No, child, I'm not."

Allasa summoned all her courage, "If ye no the Bodach Mór, who are ye, Laird?"

"I am Jacobis Arnflinsson of the Jötunn Vör."

At the sound of the alarm raised by the priest's sons, the village men gathered their tools and weapons and raced out of the gateway to meet the threat. The village acted as a single entity in moments like these. Anything that threatened one of them, even if it was their much-despised Priest, was a threat to them all. With Ceard, the village Smith, at their head, they marched up the track towards the standing stones.

Murdo and Neill stumbled along beside Ceard, blathering wildly about the huge wolf that had attacked their father and chased them back to the village, but everyone knew there hadn't been wolves on Na-Elan for a hundred years, well, no four-legged ones. Though it had been half a lifetime since any of them had seen battle against the wolf coated Gothad raiders that used to plunder these island settlements, memories were kept as keen as the harpoons, axes and spears they now carried.

As they climbed the rough track toward the tòrr, where the stone sentinels kept their watch, the keener eyed amongst them started to make out a group of strangers gathered around the monoliths. Ceard, his eyes dulled from too many years at the forge, strained to make out anything other than a blur in the distance, but his faith in the eyes of the village fishermen was unquestioning. "Murdo, awa down to the clachan, laddie. Tell them it is reavers. Run!"

Murdo did not require telling a second time. With Neill hot on his heels, he ran off back to the village.

Ceard gathered the men about him and spoke to them quietly and calmly. "If they are reavers, then we have to fight them, either here or at the clachan gate. Alan."

Alan, the village's finest seaman, stepped neatly forward.

"Take half the lads back to the clachan an' help to guard the gate. If we dinna come back, you will know it's a fight they seek."

Alan nodded sombrely and turned away.

"Breac?"

The big, ever-smiling, freckle covered face of Breac, the village's best and wiliest hunter, appeared out of the knot of men, though he wasn't smiling now. "Ay, Ceard?"

"Take a dozen lads an' follow the goat path up to where it

turns back on itself, we will meet ye there, dinna show yeself to them, we need to keep them unawares."

"That does nae leave ye with a lot o' hands."

Ceard nodded. "Ay, better they dinna know how many o' us there are." He addressed the others. "A show o' strength will only let them know how many we have got to rammie with them. Richt?"

Some mumbled agreement, others nodded, and some just continued to look as terrified as goats going to the slaughter.

Ceard led the remaining handful of villagers up the path to meet the raiders. He knew what would happen; they would meet the raiders, try to bargain, or buy them off, but it wouldn't be enough; it was never enough. Then they would fight. If they were just opportunist raiders, wild men with no real expertise, then maybe Ceard and the village men would have a chance, but if the raiders were real warriors, then Ceard knew he and most of his people would not see the sun rise tomorrow. None of his villagers were warriors, good men, stout and hardy, fishermen and shepherds, but not fighting men. Though he knew they'd all make a good account of themselves. "Better to die on ye feet than on ye knees." As Ceard's father used to say when he told his old stories of the days when wild-eyed Gothads used to attack once or twice every summer. Back in the days when all the village men had to be warriors. Then he used to take down his old battle-axe and recant the tale of every notch and chip on its bearded head. "Make them pay for their rapt with their blood." Ceard hefted the axe in his hands, a good weapon; his father would be proud of how he had looked after it.

About half a mile farther up the track rounded a small hillock, and they could now see clearly the raiders coming down the hillside to meet them. Ceard counted about two dozen of them, Alban warriors by their look, well-armed and led by a huge man. There were more of them about half a mile back still gathered at the feet of the Bodach Mór. The fishermen estimated another dozen or so. Ceard wondered where they had come from and how they had gotten this far inland? They must have come overland from Geuru Bàgh, he decided, but it wasn't important, they were here, and it was up to him to deal with them.

Ceard stopped and organised the villagers as well as he could by forming two rows across the track, putting himself out front. Breac, he prayed, would be in place by now, waiting to spring the ambush. Now, all he could do was wait in the cold, pale sunlight and watch as the raiders approached. Some of the villagers muttered about returning home. Some joked humourlessly about running away. Ceard stiffened their resolve with a few harsh words reminding them that they were the only things standing between these murderers and their own wives and children.

As the raiders drew near, Ceard realised just how tall the man leading them was; he had never seen a man as big, he stood half again as high as any of the others and built like one of the great bears that sometimes swam across from the mainland in search of seals and salmon. The others were a mix of Albans wrapped in swathes of plaid and Kern warriors from the mainland in their heavy orange shirts. Ceard wondered for a moment what they were doing banding together, but it wasn't significant; they were all strangers to him.

The giant stopped about five yards from Ceard and rested upon the great boar spear he carried. The raiders fanned out in an arch behind him, displaying their weapons and armour. Ceard knew it was a silent threat meant to intimidate the villagers, and it was working; a knot of fear had appeared in the pit of his own stomach. They were a motley crew of hard-looking men, bloodied and scarred; they seemed as if they were fresh from some battle. Abruptly a terrible thought came to him, had these raiders come along the coast from Wastle Inlat? Ceard had cousins at Wastle Inlat and a sister at clachan of Còsag. They could be all dead for all he knew. He gripped his father's battle-axe tightly and tried to let the anger rising in him smother the fear in his gut.

In a show of bravado and fearlessness, Ceard stepped forward and demanded, "A see ye big man. What are ye doin' here?"

Suddenly out from behind the big man burst Allasa. She ran across the gap between them and threw herself into Ceard's arms. The Smith struggled to juggle the child and not drop his weapon. "Allasa! What..?"

"Dinna fear, Eme! He's the Bodach Mór! He has come, it's the Bodach Mór, he's really come!"

Ceard put the child down and pushed her behind him.

An Alban, older than most of the others, stepped out from beside the giant. His dark ginger hair was tied back, his greying beard closely cropped, he looked strong, but his slate-grey eyes looked tired beyond imagining. "Are you Ceard?" he asked.

Taken aback by the use of his own name, it took Ceard a few seconds to answer, "Ay, A am."

"I am Angus MacRoth. I am Laird of Cree'uch and Eagle's Craig." Ceard looked carefully at the man; he had the air of a Laird and the fine gear, though it was tattered and blood stained now.

"Ye're a long way from there."

"My fortress was sacked, and we were forced to flee. We...."

"They came out o' the stones, Eme! They...." Ceard hushed her.

The big man spoke, "As the child said, we came through the stones."

"Wat?" Ceard demanded incredulously.

"It's true!" shouted Allasa, "He's the Bodach Mór!"

"Haud ye wheesht!" Ceard barked at her.

Allasa stamped her foot and glared back up at him, her face a mask of frustration.

"Listen to me, Ceard. My name is Jacobis Arnflinsson, I am of the Jötunn Vör. I'm not the 'Bodach Mór' as the child insists, but we have come through the stones; they were our only means of escape. We mean you no harm, you have my word, but we have wounded men with us, and we need shelter and food. We will trade for both, or if you take coin, I have silver enough for all." He paused long enough for his words to sink in, and then he addressed the assembled villagers as a whole. "Look upon us. If we were vargr, have we, not the numbers, to take anything we wished? Instead, we ask, and we offer silver or trade in exchange. We are not reavers, and we ask only for your hospitality."

Ceard ignored the murmurs from his fellow villagers. "We canna trust ye on ye word. You come with ye wild yarns an' blood on ye hands. A'm nae a daft wean. No man can travel through stone, Bodach Mór or no."

There was some commotion at the back of the raiders as an

old man pushed his way through. His wild hair streamed out behind him like a grubby halo in the wind. He was dressed as a Seer, in the dirty tatters of a yellow Kern shirt under a blood-splattered cloak of white ox hide. As he moved, his mantle rattled with an array of animal bones and charms. He set his deer skull-topped staff before Ceard, cocked his emaciated head to one side and fixed the Smith with a cold one-eyed stare. The old man's face was covered with a mess of ritual tattoos and scars, like a battered leather mask, and his breath was as fetid as rotting fish. He reached out and poked Ceard in the chest with the long dirty nail of a bony finger.

"Who are you Smith to say what canna be? Has this place been so long without a real Priest that they look to a Burnewin like you to guide them on the ways o' Warlocks?" Something deep in the white orb, where his left eye should have been, glowed menacingly. "Or mabbe you think yeself wiser than A?"

Ceard had only ever seen the Tysher once when he was a small child, but he recognised everything about the old man, from his garb to the lightning inflicted blindness. The wizened old man's face crinkled into a strange toothless grin, "Ay, Ceard, son o' Ilisa Mhòr nan Òran, A remember ye to. Is ye mother well?"

Ceard swallowed hard. "She is nae. She's dead these past four winters now."

The old man looked sad for a moment. "A pity that. She was a good woman. Och well, man, has her hoose no welcome left for me?"

Ceard wasn't about to trust these warriors or the big man with his clever words and promises of silver, but there was no possible way he could refuse the Tysher. He turned to the other villagers and said, "A know this man, he's Mer MacLeech, the Tysher o' Lya'ud. A will provide him with the hospitality o' my house."

"Ay, ye can have him," yelled one of the village men from the back. "A'll have the big yin with all the silver!"

Chapter 28

"Bheirinn cuid-oidhche dha
ged a bhiodh ceann fir fo 'achlais!"

"I would give him food and lodging for the night
even if he had a man's head under his arm!"

Gaelic Proverb

The people of Ebb Dwallion did their best to entertain their unexpected guests with what little they had to give. They tended the wounded, fed the hungry and found somewhere dry and mostly comfortable for everyone. It was strange for the villagers to find both mainland Kern warriors and Alban clansmen sitting together at their hearths, even more bizarre to find a Gothad and a Vörish giant, but they accepted them with cheerful hospitality. Mouth music and singing filled the smoky houses. What little wine they had was shared, and gifts were swapped. As the visitors relaxed, they began to talk of what had brought them there. They spoke of the desperate battle they had fought against creatures from another realm and how they had escaped. The villagers listened, enthralled, but some quietly began to wonder precisely what they had brought into their midst.

Talk of sorcery and of the Witch called Annis Nic Neamhain concerned them, a few had heard the name before in dark tales, and others grew apprehensive, some even openly stating their fears. Giving shelter to warriors, even Albans, and the Tysher was one thing, but accepting a powerful ban-draoidh into their village was another. Some whispered their concern that maybe Bothan, the Priest, had been right when he had tried to stop them from entering the village. They should never have allowed them in.

The villagers, as ever, looked to their Elders for guidance. The Elders, four old men and one woman, the most respected and wisest minds of the village, gathered at the house of Ceard the Smith and sat down around Ceard's hearth with the apparent leaders of their honoured guests. Coinneach, a wily old man who resembled a sea eagle with his long lank grey hair, sharp eyes, and prominent nose, was their spokesman. Firstly, he greeted the newcomers formally and introduced the Elders one by one, being careful to maintain a pleasant formality and pointing out that though Ceard was an Elder, he could not speak for them all. The newcomers, in turn, were careful to show polite respect as Angus introduced them one by one, except for MacLeech, who placed himself at a distance and seemed to be above it all.

Once the formalities were over, Coinneach began to put forward the questions they needed to ask; how did you come here and why? Why were you at war with the Sith? What of these, Isheen? Could they follow you? Who is this woman that you talk of? Is she a powerful Sorceress, as some say? How do we know we are safe? From her? From you? And where is the wolf that Bothan and his sons saw?

At first, Angus tried to answer each point in turn while avoiding the most awkward questions, though his carefully crafted explanations only led to more questions, and soon issues were lost in meaningless details. Angus silently wished he'd not sent Kemble back with Gabhran; the Grieve would have been in his element in this situation. Jacobis tried desperately to help the Elders make sense of it all, but as time drew on, people on both sides became frustrated at having to repeat themselves, explain minutiae, and draw everyday analogies with concepts they could use barely grasp themselves. If it had not been for Coinneach's astuteness, Ceard's patience, and Jacobis' unfailing good humour, it could have all ended badly.

Even after three hours and much wine, the Elder's seemed to still be unsure of most of what the newcomers were telling them. Finally, out of frustration, Angus turned to MacLeech, who sat a little further back, apparently dozing, and demanded angrily, "These are your people MacLeech, you're their Tysher; You explain it to them!"

MacLeech opened his one good eye and smiled back at the Laird. "Och, an ye were doin' so well, A did nae think ye were needin' my help."

Jacobis patted Angus' shoulder firmly, a reminder of where he was and in front of whom he was speaking. Angus gritted his teeth and sighed. "Aye, well, we do need your help," he admitted.

MacLeech's smile turned into a broad toothless grin. "Ay, lad, ye did nae but have to ask!"

Here we find ourselves.

Fugitives, seeking comfort from the mercies of the poorest people.

Of what little they have, they give freely.

Such generosity.

And I, like an unseen guest.

Availing myself of their hospitality.

Though they pretend as if they do not even see me.

Maybe they cannot.

I sit by their hearth, trying not to look into the fire.

Trying not to see our future played out before me in the dancing flames.

The Elders sit with us in the house of the village Smith.

A good man.

They are all good people.

Kind people.

Now they listen with reverence as their Tysher speaks to them.

Their minds full of confusion.

They have welcomed us, but they fear us.

They fear offending the Tysher.

They fear the warriors.

But they fear me more.

Their eyes fleetingly turn to me and away as if they dare not even look upon my face.

Am I that terrible to look upon? That horrific?

What do they see? I wonder.

I could see through their eyes if I wished...

I do not.

Maybe I fear that too.

To see the creature they see,

To see the Cailleach Dubh.

The monster I have become.

Can they see the blood on my hands that no water can wash away?

So much blood.

I sit here, in this little house of stone and turf and wait.

For what?

They should cast me out, drive me away.

I know that some want to.

I would not fight them,

But it is fear that holds them back.

Finally, MacLeech finishes his tale, and they ask their questions, their wise questions.

He patiently answers each. He assures them that no one and nothing can follow us through the stones and that the Isheen do not know where we have come.

He promises them that their village is safe.

He promises them that they have nothing to fear from me.

His promises are shallow.

They accept his word with the faith of children, his authority unquestioned.

Still, they dare not look upon me.

The smoke in here stifles my breathing.

And I cannot endure the wraithlike figures that take smoky form amongst the rafters.

They mock me.

I stand, which alarms them and hurry from the darkness into the light of the sunset and the fresh air.

Fyn follows, my constant guard.

Follows me outside into the night.

He chooses to keep his distance.

He, too, has a need to be alone.

To struggle with what lies within.

The little village is strangely quiet.

Though many tales are being told, it is in hushed voices and soft ballads.

Fearful of the things that walk abroad this evening.

They are careful to keep their voices low.

They have hidden all their children from me.

Mothers and fathers secreting their precious young away from the creature that now walks in their midst.

They whisper a name in the darkness.

Black Annis is here.

I know the Priest is playing upon their fears.

He is exercising the last vestiges of his power over them.

Somewhere in the shadows, he is watching me even now.

He is so full of bitter resentment.

Their obedience to the Tysher angers him.

They have so readily cast him off.

Returned to their old ways.

Ways that he despises.

He despises many things.

I recognise that bloody black rage inside of him; I have seen it before.

In the eyes of another Priest.

Long ago.

I could reach out to him.

I could smooth his mind, or I could end his thoughts forever.

I draw the cold clear air into my lungs and taste the sea on my lips and push away the dark thoughts that abound in me.

Oh, my mother, what gifts you gave me.

What curse.

The creature within me rages.

Louder than ever.

Now it has fed on blood, violence, and the life force in the Stone.

So strong.

I will not.

I must not.

Ever.

Give in.

I am flesh and blood now.

A mortal woman.

I love, and I am loved.

I will not be a monster.

Chapter 29

"Óðinn tók höfuðið
og smurði urtum þeim er eigi mátti fúna
og kvað þar yfir galdra
og magnaði svo að það mælti við hann
og sagði honum marga leynda hluti."

"Odin took the head,
and smeared it with such herbs that it would not rot,
and sang words of magic over it,
and gave it such might that it spoke to him
and told him many hidden matters."

The Ynglinga Saga
Snorri Sturluson

Allasa had been intently watching the strange woman from the moment she stepped out of the rainbow light in the stones. She knew the woman was different from the rest of them, even from the Bodach Mór himself, because of the way the geasan light still clung to her, a shimmering aura of shifting nameless colours. Allasa had always been able to see something of the 'richt colour o folks', as her grandmother called it. She had inherited the ability from her mother, or so her grandmother had told her, but she had never seen colours like these. Seeing the colours was easy for Allasa. All she had to do was concentrate on them a little until her vision blurred, and then the colours would just be there, around them. Most of the colours were simple, translucent blues, yellows, and greens; sometimes, they even seemed to change with their moods, stronger when they were happy or darker when they were angry or sad. Bothan's colours were often muted, dull browns and earthy reds, while Ceard's were often orange and golden yellows, but the strange woman's colours were unique. There were hues and shades Allasa had no names for, and they changed and constantly flowed with an intensity that made it impossible for Allasa not to see them. She was fascinated. Not even her grandmother's colours had been as strong or as vibrant.

Since the morning, she had spent some time deliberately watching all the other newcomers, scrutinizing each one to see if they too had strange colours. Most were little different than the villagers, which disappointed her somewhat, even the Bodach Mór's pale blue aura and the Tysher's silver were unremarkable, only the Gothad that turned up late in the afternoon was strange for he had two auras, one sea blue and the other, that hung over him like a shadow, was slate-grey tinged with crimson, so dark it looked to Allasa as if his spirit was bleeding. Allasa knew that there could not be anything good about that shade and so had done her best to avoid him, but her interest in the woman drew her.

She had learnt that her name was Annis and that she was a Witch, which didn't concern Allasa. Her grandmother had often been called a Witch, though never to her face, and it was probably true that her mother had been one too, though her grandmother detested the term.

"Wutch! Stupid men, they give themselves grand titles but miscall us 'Wutches'! There's no one o' them could birth a wean or cure a fever! My father was a Tysher an' my grandfather was a Druid an' his father afore him, an A'll no be called a Wutch!"

Allasa didn't even really know what a 'Witch' was; many people, mainly the men, called other people, mainly the women Witch. However, Allasa wasn't sure she knew what it meant until now, and not until she had laid eyes upon the Witch Annis.

Taller and thinner than the village women, she was fine-boned and delicate looking with strange dark skin and huge eyes that glittered in the dying light. Her hair, so long that it hung down to the middle of her back, was so black it looked almost blue. She wore the simple clothes of a Gothad woman with a pale fur wrapped around her narrow shoulders, but she stood with her head up with all the courage of a princess.

Allasa thought Annis must be the most beautiful woman in the whole world. She was so different from everyone else she might well have been of another race; maybe she was a Sìthiche woman from the wistful ballads that Sèist MacWhorter sang. The idea thrilled Allasa even more. She had to get closer to her, to speak to her, maybe even to touch her. Summoning all her courage, Allasa seized her moment. Stepping out from behind the forge door, she walked purposefully towards Annis. She could sense the Gothad skulking in the shadows and heard the strange guttural snarl he made, but she ignored him and walked on past.

She stopped in front of the Witch and announced, "A'm Allasa MacKeeask, A am. They say that you're a Wutch." She knew it wasn't the best way to begin. Though she had practised most of the afternoon, she didn't know any other way to start, and now the words just tumbled out. "My granny an' my mother were Wutches an all, an A should be one, but there's nae one to teach me richt. Eme wants me to be like the other lassies, but A canna! A'm no like them!" Allasa's nerve started to slip, the words were coming too fast now, and her eyes were beginning to burn. "Do ye no see? A'm not like them. Ye see A'm no!"

The Witch smiled faintly but her huge sad eyes, as green as the northern sea and as fathomless, searched Allasa's face as if looking for something.

Allasa bit back the tears that were about to cascade down her cheeks and said firmly, "A'm no like them, A'm like you." Immediately the tears came, and it was all she could do to choke out the last words before throwing herself at the Witch. "A want to be like you!"

The familiar sound of Timmon's voice woke Ag. The Cook was talking to someone in hushed tones, trying to answer questions, trying to explain something. A cool hand lay upon Ag's brow, and someone was dripping water steadily onto his lips, it tasted good, but as his conscious mind took over, he tried to swallow and breathe at the same time and choked.

Voices, women's voices, unfamiliar yet comforting fussed around him, firm hands lifted him, and a lantern was brought to light the little nook where he was laying.

"Ay, there you are Aggy, how do you feel?" Timmon's big hairy face swam into Ag's vision. "Have ye still got your senses, laddie?"

The women's voices tittered and scoffed at the Cook's manner. A gentle hand stroked his head, and another lifted the water bowl up to his lips again.

Ag sipped and tried to make out the world beyond the lamplight and Timmon's bulky presence. He was in a building, a round house probably, with dry stone walls made of flat grey slates and a high beamed ceiling, smoke hung halfway up to the top of the roof, reflecting the fire light like an evening cloud reflects the sunset. It was warm and full of comforting smells and soft murmuring voices. The place seemed full of people.

"Can ye no talk to me, lad?"

"A.." He didn't realise how difficult it would be to speak; his throat felt like it was full of dry sand. "Aye."

"Good lad," Timmon laid a big podgy hand on his arm and smiled. "I'm sure glad to see ye still with us. Now rest a while. A'll awa' an' get some broth for ye as soon as A can."

Ag tried to prop himself up on one elbow, but the woman's hands behind him took over and propped him up with a bundle of something soft and firm. She then straightened the blanket around him and wiped his chin. She was a middle-aged woman, with a round face, whether beaten but still kind, and with strong arms and hands. She smiled reassuringly down at Ag and spoke. "Lay back a wee while ye safe here."

At that, a jumble of memories flashed into Ag's head, something flapping at his face, the torn table. Rolf's hand around his throat. Rolf's face…He could remember Rolf's face, but it wasn't Rolf's face. It had become something other, something inhuman as if the mask had slipped, and behind it was a grinning monster. Fear gripped him, and he began to shake. He could see the thing Rolf had become leering over him, prodding him in the belly with a butcher's knife, chuckling to itself. This time though, his mouth was free to scream, and so he did, with all his might.

It took several minutes for Timmon and the woman to calm the boy down again, reassuring him that Rolf was gone forever and that they were no longer in Eagle's Craig. Timmon explained to Ag what Kemble had told him. The Witch had discovered Rolf, or the thing pretending to be Rolf, and had destroyed it, and that the Vör and the others had rescued him. Ag couldn't remember any of it, but for some reason, he could see the Witch's eyes and hear her calm voice inside his head, but he knew that was daft because the Witch never spoke.

Later Timmon sat on the side of the bed, fed Ag some fish broth, and told him tales of witchcraft and shapeshifters and the battle they had fought against the Isheen and the Fomóiri. How he had had to run for his life through the tunnels carrying Ag on his back and how they had escaped through the Heart of the Craig to this little Kern village on an outlying island he had never heard of.

Tears welled up in the boy's eyes, and he asked, in a quiet voice, the names of those dead and those missing. Timmon told him, listing names the boy had known all his life, friends and relatives, masters, and slaves. Wrad, Ag's older brother, who had died fighting on the shores below the Craig and Gabhran MacRoth who had been struck down while trying to drag a wounded man into the safety of the fortress, and dozens of others, some Timmon could only remember as so and so's cousin or brother, or someone's son. Of the Kerns, once his own people, he knew no names but did his best to recount their deeds and losses too.

The Cook stopped speaking as Ag slid down into the bed and turned his face to the rough slate wall. He was sobbing silently, dreadfully, one hand clasped to his face and the other plucking at the stones. Timmon rested a hand upon the boy's back and desperately tried not to be seen to be crying too.

As he watched the village girl throw herself into Annis' arms, Fyngard felt an odd pang of resentment mixed with something else, something darker. He stifled the emotion immediately and straightened himself, physically shrugging off the animal instincts that still lingered in him. Sometimes the division between the nature of the beast and the nature of the man blurred too much, and he found it difficult to assert himself. He knew that it was a price to be paid. He had been warned exhaustively back before the initiation ceremonies, one day, he would have to make a choice, no more half-life, no more duality. A simple option of either one thing or another; to give in or give up.

He didn't think about it often though, he was still strong in spirit and stature, and he was confident that his will could keep control at all times. There was no need to worry about something so far in the future, but that had been before the battle on the strand and the journey through the stones. He knew he had lost control entirely during the battle, more completely than ever before. When he had hit the Southron's shield wall, there was little of Fyngard Kvällulf, the Ulvhinna warrior, left, just a frenzied beast bent upon the destruction of everything in its path. Drunk on the power and blood lust, like a wolf let loose amidst a penned flock, he had ripped into the Southron's lines, their Mänsklig reactions were pitifully slow, and their weapons had been useless against him. He had toyed with them, leaping amongst them, rending, and tearing, slaughtering them with impunity. It had felt wonderful.

But when that feeling slipped away, he had been left with a terrible sense of dread, greater than anything before; the Wodfreca was stronger than he had ever imagined. It had wrought physical changes upon him before, but nothing like that, nothing so awful, nothing so complete. Then he had passed through the light in the Heart of the Craig, and it had been like no other experience in his life, not even his first joining with the Wodfreca during the Ändring. All his conscious control over the beast had fled, and the change had been so utterly complete that he had awoken at the water's edge totally naked, afraid, and confused. He had had no idea how he got there or where he was, and, even now, the Wodfreca had still not left him.

Every bone and every joint in him hurt, and he was unbearably tired, yet he dared not sleep until the spirit was utterly gone. Muffling a yawn, he was careful to cover his mouth from prying eyes. His teeth were still too long and too sharp to let any man see, and his entire back itched furiously from the thick grey hairs that still covered it.

Controlling himself, he tried to focus his mind on Annis and the child. They stood in the middle of the little courtyard embraced in the glow of the sunset, almost unmoving. Annis hesitantly, as if the girl were made of Aelathian glass that might break, began to soothe the sobbing child. Her long delicate hands gently stroked the dark hair from the child's face, wiping away her tears. Fyn could see the eagerness in the girl's eyes as she gazed up at Annis; there was wonderment there, enthrallment.

An unintentional spell was being cast, a spell more potent than any simple enchantment or binding, a spell that would weave the two of them together for a lifetime. Fyn knew how powerful that spell was and how difficult it was to live with, though he too had once gladly fallen under its influence, under her influence. Sometimes the weight of that spell bore down on him like a mountain of rocks upon his back. He knew what the emotion he had felt was; jealousy. He had felt jealous of a crying child, jealous because she had been able to reach out and grasp the very meaning of his existence, the focus of the spell, the woman he loved, jealous because he could not even put it into words inside his own head for fear that she might hear them.

Forcing his own feelings away, he watched over them both; the Völva and her new acolyte. Damn fool, jealous of a child. He rubbed agitatedly at his face and shook off the last vestiges of the spirit that still haunted him. If you are a man, Fyngard Kvällulf, then act like one, not a whining puppy! Wallowing in these emotions was tantamount to betrayal of everything he believed in. He had taken an oath, and this was one he must always keep. Annis was his charge, Jacobis was his friend, and this was his chosen path.

Fyn was still trying to regain his composure when he noticed a shadow detach itself from the side of one of the stone roundhouses and approach Annis. Drawing his dagger, Fyn fell into a crouch instinctively and had to catch himself before the spirit flooded back. Control, he knew, was what was required, not the ravening beast. His senses, still heightened by the Wodfreca, instantly recognising the smell of the village Priest before his eyes picked him out of the shadows.

The Priest had been shunned and ignored by the villagers from the moment MacLeech had arrived. Earlier, he had tried to make some sort of pronouncement outside the gate, but few bothered to acknowledge his existence, let alone his words. He had then seized a harpoon off a villager and confronted MacLeech, but he was knocked down and disarmed by his own people before any of the warriors could get to him. Several men then hustled the hysterical man away to one of the far houses, more to protect him than to protect MacLeech.

The Tysher had seemed to find it amusing; he laughed loudly and shouted over the protests of the struggling Priest. "Dinna worry aboot a quarrelsome Priest! He does nae have any real power. Yon man is soft an' his religion weak. Keep him, or cast him out, but dinna bother your heads to heed him!"

It had been a carefully thought-out condemnation. No sentence of social banishment could have been better put; in those few words, MacLeech had stripped the Priest of what little authority he had held over the village and, by the howl of abhorrence from the Priest, he had known it too.

Now, as the Priest stalked towards where Annis still embraced the child, Fyn could tell that he was well fortified by wine, though he didn't have the gait of a drunk. Fyn could almost taste the heady mix of fear, sweat and hot blood that emanated from him.

To Fyn's alarm, Annis, distracted by the child, seemed not to have noticed the approaching man. He drew himself further back into the shadows and down, one hand touching the cold earth, like an animal, taut and ready to strike. He choked back a guttural growl as he fought to maintain control over the power rising inside him again.

"Wutch! Sìthean half-breed whore! A know ye! So ye came to claim one o' your own true kin, have ye?" The Priest stopped only a few paces from them.

Annis did not react, her head stayed bowed slightly as she continued to caress the child, but the child whimpered and tried to shy away from the ranting man.

"A monster's get the pair o' ye. Get ye gone from this place! There are good folk here, and ye no welcome! Get!" Emboldened by alcohol or by Annis' lack of reaction, he took a step forward, flinging his arms about wildly. "Get ye gone! Back to the hole, ye crawled out o'. Go on, awa with ye!"

Annis merely turned away from him slightly to shield the child.

The scene was now developing an audience. Villagers and newcomers spilt out of the houses to see what the shouting was about.

The Priest seemed to revel in having his spectators once more and turned to address them. "See, they brought this thing into our village! A Sìthean monster! The cailleach dhubh nam bean! Look, in the name of God, open your eyes! Do ye no see!" he pointed at Annis. "Do ya no see who she is? Black Annis, it is! They've brought the Hag o' the Hill into our homes to steal our weans an' murder us in our beds!"

A murmur of disquiet amidst the crowd was silenced as Jac burst out of a doorway, roaring like a bear, closely followed by the village Elders and MacLeech.

Upon seeing the giant and the Tysher, the Priest turned and snatched at the child clinging to Annis.

Fyn moved, but it was all too late.

Annis' head came up, her eyes blazing like coals, and her hand shot out, open-palmed and splayed. There was a sound, strange even to Jac and Fyn, like a heavy sail that had snapped in the wind and everything and everyone stopped.

I silence the Priest.

The words in his mouth and the thoughts in his head die swiftly.

I need not hear them.

I know them well.

I silence them all.

A moment snatched into the palm of my hand.

A glistening pebble seized from the bed of the river of time.

A glittering fragment of a universal.

Stopped.

Some try instinctively to assert themselves against my will.

I will not allow that.

Against the onrushing tide of time.

I prevail.

The Priest's eyes are still wide open in shock.

I have left only him aware.

I reach out to him.

Run my fingers down the side of his face.

His sweaty skin is cold to the touch.

Hear me now.

Do I destroy you?

Should I?

I know what you are.

I have met your kind before.

You will not have this child.

My child.

If I were the monster you fear.

It would be so easy.

To shatter your spirit into a thousand pieces before the wind's twelve quarters.

To leave you as nothing but a burned husk.

And how I want to.

And how I desire to.

But I will not.

You shall taste the mercy of the Cailleach Dubh.

Of Black Annis of the Hills.

I send you from this place, Priest.
Never to return.
You shall run before the dying of the light.
Before the edge of the darkness.
Never to rest.
Unto death.
And a thousand years beyond.

Go.

Go now!

The man who had once been the Priest called Bothan collapsed to the ground before the woman and child. As he scrambled back to his feet, he realised he was surrounded by a mob of people. Some looked on concerned while others looked hostile, but he recognised none of their faces. The tall woman in front of him turned her head away, and instantly he felt nothing but utter terror and revulsion. Choking back a cry, he staggered away from her but found his way barred by the crowd.

"Stand aside!" A huge man amid the crowd bellowed, "Let him go!"

The crowd parted silently, and the man whose name had once been Bothan, who had once been a Priest, fled.

As he ran away from the tiny hamlet on the seashore, he heard voices shouting after him and cursing him by a name he didn't recognise. Some laughed, some threw things, and others tried to chase him, calling him "Daddy," but he outran them all.

It was the beginning of an endless flight before nightfall that would drive him across the face of the known world and beyond. Unable to outrace the darkness. Each night would bring no rest, and each day would be spent trying to outrun the passing of the light.

The events of the day weighed heavily on everyone, villagers and warriors alike. Some stayed up almost until dawn talking and drinking, others tried to rest and get a few short hours of sleep, but few slept well.

Outside the Smith's house, Ceard took the opportunity to speak freely to the Elders as they departed. He was uneasy about how his niece had attached herself to the Witch and was worried that Allasa might want to follow her when she left the village. Ceard tried to explain how he could not allow that. She was his sister's daughter, and it was his responsibility to look after her, but Coinneach had told him to think on it.

"That lassie's got a lot o' her mother and grandmother in her, she does nae fit in now, an' when she's a grown woman, she'll be nothin' but trouble to us all. A know what trouble her grandmother caused growing up, an' do ye no know the trouble we had with your sister? Do you no think on what kind o' life she'll have here? Aboot half the clachan women are scared o' her already an' some o' the men. ye think on it, laddie, there's nae one here to teach her proper ways, she'll be like a wild pony, strong, proud and untameable."

"More like a Kelpie!" Ceard's wife had added venomously.

"Ye no saying A should let her go with…them?" Ceard replied incredulously.

Coinneach nodded, "Ay laddie, ay, the Wutch is her own kind. Maybe let her run with them." The old man bade them goodnight. As he turned to leave, he paused. "We have to hav' them gone. They canna stay here a moment longer than must. Bothan was richt aboot that; they bring danger."

Ceard and his wife returned to their home and picked their way over the strangers and their gear to the little spot they had reserved for themselves to rest. Ceard wondered how, after such events, these men slept. He knew that tonight, no matter how tired he was, he would not sleep at all.

As they climbed into the small space they had for a bed together, Ceard's wife said softly, "He's richt, Ceard; she's better off with them."

The Smith, a man who had never felt failure in his life, felt as if he had somehow to reconcile himself to failure now. He looked over to the far side of the big room to where the woman Annis and Allasa, his niece, were huddled together seemingly asleep and sighed, "Ay, hen, A know."

As he lay back, he prepared himself for a night of restlessness, resigned in the knowledge that the turmoil in his mind would undoubtedly keep him awake all night. But sleep overtook him quickly, drawing him down into a troubled dreamworld where both he and Allasa were children fleeing from phantoms in the mist.

Something touches me.

In the darkness of my dreamless sleep.

Brushing at the edges of my awareness.

Like the diaphanous wings of a moth.

And I am awake.

I listen for it to come again.

I can sense the restless dreams of the child in my arms and the men that surround me.

Was it someone's dream that awoke me?

A phantom that escaped a sleeping mind to wander.

No.

There it is again.

I can hear it.

As clear as a ringing bell.

A voice inside my head.

Calling me.

I rise carefully and follow the voice.

Out into the darkness of the courtyard.

Who are you?

The voice that is not a voice calls me by a thousand different names.

Somewhere out in the darkness, it awaits.

The village gate stands open.

Though its warden sleeps.

Should I fear this voice that calls to me?

I who have chosen to fear nothing in life.

I wrap my shawl around my shoulders and enter into the moonlit realm of land and sea.

Cloaked in a mantle of sea mist.

Beyond the safety of the stone walls, the voice is stronger.

Calling, commanding.

A compelling desire to pursue.

Am I being summoned like a wraith to the presence of some master?

I could refuse.

But the curiosity in me wins out.

Beyond the sand dunes, the gentle slopes are covered in coarse grasses.

I climb up and away.

Ignoring the things swirling in the vapours about my feet.

I can hear you.

Where are you?

Here, upon a high place, I cast about.

I look to the Bodach Mòr and his brothers, but they are silent.

Eternal sentinels watching the horizon.

Appearing to be floating above the mist.

Their ancient faces forever enduring.

Suffused in the silver glow of the moon.

I look out to the sea.

But its song does not involve me.

Shedding its misty tears upon the shore.

As it sings to its sweetheart.

The moon.

I look to the land.

Far beyond the haze.

To a distant hill.

A massive brooding presence in the landscape.

A hill that is not a hill.

From there the voice calls once more.

The path down to it is overgrown.

For long years it has remained untrodden.

But I find my way.

The mist parting before me.

Down into the little valley of the tùnga.

The voice is quiet now.

But I can still feel the desire.

Like a lodestone, it draws me on.

The mound is immense.

Shrouded by the mist.

The great tumulus awaits me.

Ahead the tùnga's entrance has been unbarred.

And a light burns within this house of the dead.

Beyond the narrow passageway.

A corposant glow, as blue as lightning, throws strange flickering shades about the crypt.

Shadows caper and dance across the vaulted ceiling and the dark slate walls.

It has been too long since anyone has entered this place with reverence.

To succour the dead.

To beat the bodhran drum and to sing.

In this place, where the ancient dead hold court.

To consult their wisdom through augury and prayer.

They once were the Luchd-dìon nan Daoine.

The Guardians of the People.

Ancestors so old that few in living memory knew the names they bore in life.

For in death, what consequence have names?

And to the spirit-born and reborn again.

The language of men has no meaning.

Air blown from the mouth.

Its sense lost to the winds.

In the flickering glow, eyeless sockets regard me.

Their parchment-thin skin, blackened over aeons, has flaked and split.

Yellowed bone skulls glare at me from behind rotting faces.

But I do not fear them.

These five Ancient Elders.

Preserved, wrapped and bound.

Guardians of a people's past.

Arbitrators of their present.

And augurs of their future.

Yet, they have grown angry at their abandonment.

The dead of ages have not been tended.

The Guardians ignored.

The bones of past Elders lay scattered about the floors of the chambers.

Discarded and gnawed by the beasts that have been allowed to ravage this sacred place.

Even the Guardians have not remained unassailed.

Yet, they have endured and endure still.

This desecration is at an end.

You will be ignored no longer.

They know my sincerity.

They understand my purpose.

They speak to me.

I listen to them carefully.

And take counsel.

From the Dead.

Urra is the oldest.

His presence saturates the tomb.

Once a mighty warrior King to his people millennia ago.

A Taibhsear of great renown.

He is inside my mind.

His thoughts touch mine.

With the cold clarity of the Dead.

I do not fear him.

He fears for heredity.

The legacy of the Dead to the future.

Their ancient blood runs thin.

Embodied within one fragile child.

The last of his line.

I understand.

I promise I shall guard her.

And lend her my strength.

She shall become stronger than us both.

Urra is pleased.

They are contented.

But the Dead cannot be indebted to me.

Such an obligation is dangerous.

For us all.

I insist on my recompense.

My payment for my oath.

Tell me, Urra, the things that lie beyond my knowledge.

Raise the obscuring veil.

On secrets lost in time.

Tell me of my mother.

Tell me of my past.

Who am I, Urra?

Tell me that.

Urra tells of the mother I never knew.
Of the fate that befell her.
The punishment laid upon her.
For an act of love.
Urra, tell me what I must do?

Although asleep, Jorunn Kolinka found that the awareness of her body's discomfort followed her even into her dreams. Although Meg and the other women regularly assured her that all was going well with her pregnancy, Jorunn's private fears grew along with her soreness and irritability. She could not stand for long before her legs hurt and her knees trembled, the walk from her quarters across the bridge to the land was enough to exhaust her for a whole day, and her back hurt incessantly. She was constantly bad-tempered, short of breath and pissing all the time, all of which she could manage and was to be expected, but worse of all, she could not sleep. No matter how she tried, she could not find a way to lie that allowed her enough comfort to relax and, as if to add to her woes, the child she carried was often at its most restless at night.

Nights like tonight had become the norm, unable to lay down on either her side or back, she sat half propped up on furs and cushions, dozing between the sharp twinges of her body and the rough movements of her unborn child.

Tonight, Meg had given in to her pleas for something to help her rest. It was a strange foul-tasting dram of jollop that almost made her gag, but at least it helped her get some sleep, but it was not a restful one. Jorunn seldom dreamt. She understood that when you dream, too many unwanted memories can creep back into your head, memories that you may have spent a long time driving out of your waking mind. She had learnt how, by force of will, not to dream. It was a skill her mother had taught her, one of the many forms of self-discipline and emotional control she had imparted to her daughter. "Ways to survive," she had called them. Valuable lessons that had helped keep Jorunn alive and sane.

These nights she relied upon it to stop her mind from chasing around and around after the dark thoughts and terrible worries that filled her waking hours. To put aside the dreadful fears as to what might happen to her and her unborn son if Angus never returned from Eagle's Craig.

This night, the mix of her own discomfort, her anxieties and Meg's jollop was more potent than her mental defences. Her fitful drug-induced sleep was full of strange dreams.

She was a child again. Laughing and playing in the sun-drenched palace courtyards of Leucothea. Splashing in the fountains with the other children. The shades of her brothers. Shadows in silhouette. Nothing else was real except the man standing watching her. A terrible man with hollow eyes. His hands covered in blood. Dressed in a tuigen mantle of black feathers. He spreads his wings and flies away.

In a dark place. Now running for her life. Chased through darkness. Through endless tunnels. Walls made of bones and flesh. Running towards the sound of a beating heart.

Was it her own?

There are others with her. Men she knew but could not recollect their names. Fear in their faces. Something terrible is coming. The sound of the beating heart is terrifying.

Angus. Angus was there. And a woman. A strange woman with sad eyes. Huge sad eyes like deep wells of water. Standing before a great black stone. But the woman is not a woman. She is a Valkyrie. And the stone is not a stone; it is a beating heart. The heart of an unborn child.

A voice. A familiar voice. What was it saying? "The blood of the MacRoth's is in these stones, Jorunn." Angus? "All the Chieftains of the MacRoths have been born here."

No. No, that Is not true.

The Craig. She was flying above it in the cold clear blue sky, on the mighty wings of an eagle. Below her was the Craig. The fortress sitting upon the rock, but it is no rock. It is the back of a vast beast.

A huge watching Dragon.

Now back in the great hall of Eagle's Craig. Where a man, who is not a man, stands warming himself at the fire. A tall man with white hair and no eyes. He is a Nihtgengan!

"The blood of the MacRoths is in these stones, Jorunn." Angus' voice again.

"Don't come here, Lady. Don't bring your child to this place." The white-haired Døkkálfr smiles.

The ground is rocking. Another voice.

Soft.

"Ma Leddy, ma Leddy…. wake up!"

A vicious jolt of pain from her back finally snapped Jorunn awake.

Nissien's face is a mask of worry as he clasps her hand to his chest.

Meg's kind, wrinkled face floated over her, "A'm so sorry I had to…."

"What?" Jorunn blinked off the last vestiges of her sleep and tried to push away the weird images. "What is it? What's wrong? Is it the Dragon?"

Nissien smiled and shook his head.

"What?"

Meg looked confused, "It's the King, ma Leddy! The King is here!"

Chapter 30

"All spirits are enslaved that serve things evil."

Mary Wollstonecraft Shelley.
Prometheus Unbound.
II. iv.110.

Morghath Bres stood on the burnt remains of the bulwarks thrown up by the Albans to defend the strand. The revetments had been very well designed and stoutly built. They reminded him of the kind of defences the Jötunn Vör used to protect their villages and encampments. Someone had told him that the Witch had such a creature in her service and that it was he that killed Starmer, the spy that Ruadan Ōg had placed in the household of the Alban Chieftain. Morghath Bres patted the charred timbers. They were still solid. Good work. He would have liked to have met this Vör.

Morghath Bres had spent most of the day prowling the strand, trying to avoid returning to his father's warship. His excuse, given only to those whom he knew might question his actions, was that he needed to keep a close watch on the Isheen's activities. Which, in part at least, was true. Truer still was that he had other work to do and that work could not be done in the presence of the Fomóire's God-King. As he had anticipated, the summons to attend upon his father came at midnight.

Balor had been exhausted by the ordeal of meeting with the Isheen's Àrd-dràgon and had slept since he had returned to Roth Ramach, his great dragonship, and whilst he slept, his son, of whom he was so proud, had been putting into place the plot to murder him.

Contrary to what most outsiders thought, the Fomóiri were not one race; there were at least a dozen different peoples amongst them, including all the renegades and outcasts. The Fomóiri were a strange confederation of tribes, each incredibly powerful in one way or another though weak in the very things their traditional enemies had in abundance; numbers and technology. Few true Fomóiri had ever really grasped the magic of metalworking, shipbuilding or construction. The trouble could be identified in the Fomóire fortresses; they were impressive in size and awesome in grandeur but often poor in military effectiveness. Over time, through political necessity, the depredation and deprivations of war and intermarriage, the Fomóiri had become a mongrel people. It was a dilemma that the true Fomóiri had identified millennia ago, after their terrible wars against the Sidhe and the children of the Aois Dàna. They had aimed to solve the problem by openly accepting anyone, tribe or individual, who wished to join them, so long as they accepted the rule of the Fomóire's royal houses.

Morghath's mother, of whom he was surprised to find himself thinking off, was a Duine hostage, the daughter of the Gothad Jarl Thorkel Bear-legs who had fled his homeland to join the Fomóiri. Dhaoine of all sorts made up a substantial number of the Fomóire people. They brought with them skills, cunning, and a knowledge of one of the Fomóire's greatest enemies; the Duine kingdoms of the North. Pure Duine warriors were seldom seen among the Fomóire's battle host, the T-uafás Mór, because of their value as spies and agents of sabotage and provocation. The actual fighting was left to the strong old races like the Korrigans and Nains, driven from the coasts of Armor, Urisks persecuted from their highlands by the Isheen, the Trow and Sea Trolls hounded from their traditional watery hunting grounds and so many others. As a child, Morghath had seen Nykir, Cyning of the Niceras, the mighty water-etins, driven from their hunting grounds amidst the coves and bays of the coast of Èathel, by the Dhaoine they call 'Southrons.' He had seen Hilditönn Thrymsson, Vortigern of the Thurse, forced to do homage to Balor in return for sanctuary for his kind in the newly conquered Eas-Ruaidh.

These primaeval races had reason to fight and love for battle. Few, save the Urisks and the Korrigans, had any real society other than rule by the strongest. Those races, at least the Fomóiri, most ancient of them all, gave one great legacy; their social order and culture.

The Fomóire's real strength resided in their closeness to the primordial powers and their abilities to use such forces. The true

Fomóire were birthed not from the sea but of the sea. Their ancestors were virtual elementals, able to control the sea and the winds at will. The first Fomóire Kings had been Gods. Morghath often thought of those long-lost aeons when his race was the most feared of all; how had they come so low? What had brought them to this? He reached up and absent-mindedly picked a piece of burnt flesh off his face.

Some amongst the Fomóiri blamed the policy of adopting others into their tribes as the root of their decline, some blamed the Sidhe and their kind, some blamed the Dhaoine and their insatiable greed. Morghath Bres knew it was all of those things, and yet none of them as much as it was the weakness of Balor himself. Balor MacCenchos, the so-called God-King of the Fomóiri, was dying. Or at least his powers were; he was growing weak, forgetful, his mind wandered, and all he seemed to wish to do was sleep. Even his control over the enthralled shades that made up the Maccaib Bais, the Band of the Sons of Death, was waning. Morghath Bres could tell it in their eyes, and he had heard them whispering to each other in the darkness below the decks of Roth Ramach; they were becoming far too aware. Balor had also failed to summon and bind the souls of the Fomóire warriors they had lost last night. He had let the Witch send them on to the Gods or oblivion; either way, their chance for immortality had been lost.

The murmurings of descent had been growing for a decade or more since the last time the Horde had sallied forth against the armies of the Fée's sorceress, Grac'hed Coz, in aid of the Korrigan King. When the battle on the beach of Juno had turned disastrously against them, Balor fled, leaving half the Horde to be slaughtered in the surf. The Korrigan's King, Yann-An-Ôd, though he bent his knee and paid homage to Balor, had never forgiven that act of betrayal, and few others had forgotten it. Morghath had never forgotten it either; he had been left fighting on the shore when Balor turned his great dragonship about and sailed away. Morghath and Yann had made a promise to each other as they stood upon that windswept beach watching Balor sail away. One day they would take their revenge upon the ageing monster, that they would, one day, aid each other in destroying Balor.

Morghath had spent the day preparing for Balor's summons when it came. He had sent a messenger to Yann-An-Ôd and to Nykir of the Niceras, telling them to prepare to act upon their best-laid plans. To his allies and sympathisers amongst the other Fomóire races, he sent other words, warnings, or alarms depending on what role they were to play in his murderous scheme.

He summoned Ruadan Ōg, commander of the Saighdiúirí den Fomór Dubh, the corps of the best and bravest of the pure Fomóiri, and Morghath's closest ally. The one true Fomóire close enough to Balor to be of any aid to Morghath. Ruadan was the only one who hated the God-King even more than he did, and Ruadan's loathing ran as deep and cold as the Abyss. Ruadan's true loyalty lay with the bones of Tethra, the last King of Eas-Ruaidh, the Red Cataract, whom Balor MacCenchos had murdered to clear his path to the throne of Tir fo Thuinn. Balor had never suspected such deceit because it was born out of something alien to most true Fomóiri; fidelity. If Ruadan's treachery had been born of simple greed, avarice or lust for power, Balor would have smelt it on him as a dog smells fear, but fealty to a murdered King was beyond Balor's comprehension.

Ruadan's secret was Morghath's one true steppingstone to freedom. He had discovered it several decades ago when he had stumbled upon Ruadan sacrificing to the spirit of the old King, and he had been wise enough to understand what power it gave him over the champion. Only recently had he revealed his knowledge to Ruadan along with his own desire to be free from Balor's domination, and Ruadan had offered his own blood to seal their contract.

Ruadan Ōg was a true Fomóire of archaic lineage; his bloodline stretched back to the wars in the western islands against the Sabre, the fathers of the Sidhe. He was a massive creature, vaguely human in shape, but more akin to the tremendous red-crested salamanders that live in the rivers in the Burning Lands far to the East. Huge and awesomely powerful, his weapons were his teeth, claws, and great armoured tail. His battle armour was his own plated and gnarled skin. Few had survived his onslaught in battle, and none had ever survived single combat against him.

Morghath Bres knew that, for all his terrible countenance, Ruadan Ōg was one of the most intelligent and capable of all the Fomóire warriors. He knew battle magics, spells and illusions, and could cast the cnámha to foretell the future; he was also one of the wisest of them all.

He sat with Morghath Bres for a time, his eyes closed in contemplation, listening to the tale of what had happened in the great hall of the keep, the death of the Galdràgon and the pact Morghath Bres had struck with Mathan-Bàn. When Morghath had finished, Ruadan lifted his massive saurian head, opened his slitted orange eyes, and glanced up at the waning moon as it made a brief appearance through the cloud cover. After a few moments, he spoke, his sibilant voice like steam escaping from a sealed pot. "If the time is to come, let it be now. Balor grows weak, and you are strong, in arm and mind. Blood for blood."

Morghath Bres didn't know whether to feel elated or terrified by Ruadan's reaction. "Then it is so, what must be done shall be done. Blood for blood."

"So be it."

Ruadan Ōg left to prepare the way for the assassination of Balor with all the cold, methodical proficiency he had served him with for aeons. He would stand down the Blackguard that protected the God-King and use his sorcery to dull the minds of the Marbh Feargach, those spirits bound to eternal servitude at the oars of Roth Ramach. Tonight, he alone would attend Balor, son of Cenchos Mac Octriallach of the Stones, and tonight he would send the old monster to oblivion.

The messenger brought the summons to Morghath Bres at the very turn of midnight. Morghath listened solemnly before sending the messenger away. Climbing up on top of the barricade, Morghath Bres, son of Balor, faced the pallid moon and prayed.

"Gealach, oh mother Domnu, the time has come; the appointed time falls. All that passes before shall be altered, and all that is to come shall be changed. Give me your strength and your blessing. Blood for blood."

Something was dancing in a shaft of light before him. A sprite that had intruded into the dreams of Balor, God King of the Fomóiri. Irritated by the intrusion, Balor roused from his stupor and prepared to swot the sprite like an irritating fly.

Suddenly the wisp cried out in a voice so powerful that it stayed Balor's wrath. Instead, he concentrated, focusing upon the sprite.

The wisp coalesced into the form of a proud young woman, a Sidhe, radiant and beautiful.

Who dares to disturb me? Demanded Balor.

The Sidhe defiantly stepped forward. I do.

Curious now and a little amused by the Sidhe's audacity, Balor asked; So, phantom, who are you? Have you a name?

In life? I was the mistress of Dùn nan Eilean. My name was Sheela na Cìoch; I was the Galdràgon of the Isheen.

Morghath Bres climbed aboard the colossal ship. All was quiet, almost unnervingly so, but Morghath was expecting it to be. If Ruadan had kept his part of the bargain, then most of the Fomóiri had been sent away and the shades of the dead that served at the oars of the ship would be subdued. Morghath looked down along the benches where the Marbh Feargach sat. The eyes of the enthralled spirits turned to him. They usually burned with all the ferocity of the damned's hatred for the living, but they were pale now, duller, as if the evil in them had been almost extinguished, leaving only the baleful embers.

Morghath pulled the hood of his feathered cloak lower, patted his sword hilt for reassurance, and strode purposefully towards the doors of the Àrus Mòr, the huge edifice built at the stern of the dragonship, where Balor held court. The Àrus Mòr was constructed of high vaulted timbers in a style older than the Gothad's halls and sat on the ship's back like some massive shingle backed parasite. Duine hands had built the fabric of it a thousand years ago, though it was only Balor's will that allowed for it to prowl the seas without capsizing or sinking under its own weight. The great hall of Balor, though, was much more than just a physical building. The Àrus Mòr existed in two places simultaneously, one upon the back of Roth Ramach and one at the heart of Tir fo Thuinn. From behind these great doors, Balor's armies could pour into the world of the Sidhe and the Dhaoine. Morghath Bres hesitated as his hand came to rest upon one of the enormous bronze doorknobs. To enter the hall was to step back into the heart of the kingdom of the Fomóiri.

Morghath Bres pushed open the door and stepped through into the gloomy hall with an affected air of confidence. He had expected the darkened hall to be empty save for Balor and Ruadan, but another stood at the foot of the dais on which the God King's throne rested. The shaggy goat-headed form of the Seanghal, Gormul, of the Urisks. Morghath was alarmed when the Seanghal did not bow or show any sign of respect as he approached. She just lent on her staff and growled something incomprehensible. Morghath immediately realised that something was very wrong. Not only was the vile Urisk Seanghal in the hall, but Ruadan's rightful place beside the throne was empty.

Morghath, ignoring the Urisk's impertinence, bowed reverently to his father's massive, slumped form. Balor's one remaining eye was half closed and his breathing heavy. The God-King seemed to be dozing again. Unnerving as it was, he knew there was no other course of action than to feign innocence and try to bluff his way out of any immediate danger. Balor's fury was terrifying, but he was malleable, and his own son's word would carry more weight than most.

"Ardrigh, m'athair, you summoned I?"

Balor's monstrous head raised a little, and his eye opened slightly. "I summoned you, flesh of my flesh. To see what lies in your heart." The tone was flat and coldly unemotional.

Morghath Bres immediately slipped into the act of a confused son, unjustly accused. "M'athair, what have I done? How have I offended you? My heart is yours; take it if you wish, but do not doubt it. I am Morghath Bres, your loyal son."

Gormul mumbled something under her breath and turned away.

Morghath seized upon it. "Is this my accuser? This wretch, this cac ar oineach? Who is this thing to accuse such as me?"

Balor ignored the outburst. "A spirit came to me, telling tales and crying for revenge. The Galdràgon of the Isheen is no more; she is dead."

Morghath Bres knew he had a simple choice, brave it out or lie. "This is true. By my own hand, she died. I killed her." To emphasize his words, he tossed back the cowl of his cloak so that Balor could see his ruined face.

Balor's eye opened wide in shock.

"She did this." He turned the left side of his face so that his father could clearly see the extent of the damage. "I killed her, extinguished her life, to end her scheming. She tricked us into coming here, knowing the trap that awaited us, in hopes that we would shatter upon this place like waves upon the rocks. While our warriors died, she celebrated and set plans to do murder unto you. Ardrigh, she plotted to betray you! To destroy you. Thus, I consigned her to oblivion, to that place beyond life, but it would seem she will not stay there; she will not be gone. A liar and schemer in life remain a liar and a schemer in death." Morghath was delighted with how the lies formed in his mouth and were said before he even had a chance to think them properly.

Balor shifted uncomfortably. "She told that you struck an accord with Mathan-Bàn, a pact of betrayal, to do murder unto me." The words were hard, but the tone was less sure than before, less resolute.

Morghath snorted and shook his head dramatically. "If the Ardrigh believes this, then my life is yours to take, I give it freely, but I swear this is not true." He stepped forward and knelt at the foot of the dais. "Lies, m'athair! These are the lies of a demented wight, sick with the desire for revenge, poisoned by her own craving for retribution. She no longer knows truth from lie or lies from truth." He looked up with his best pleading expression, a little ruined now, but still, he hoped, effective. "She aims to twist your heart, my father. To turn you against I. To satisfy her revenge and to destroy us all."

"Of Mathan-Bàn?"

"Lies!" He sprang indignantly to his feet, "I have made no pact with the Sithean, done no deal. I am my father's son, and I do no treaty with the children of Danu."

Balor caught onto something in his son's tone. He stiffened, gurgled throatily, and clacked his kyped jaws together. Morghath could feel the fury building up in the monster but was unaware of its focus. If he were the object of Balor's rage, then he was dead already; if not, then he had survived this inquisition by the skin of his teeth. All he could do now was stand and await the judgement.

"Gormul!" roared Balor.

The Urisk's name startled Morghath, as he had forgotten about the creature's presence in the midst of his denial.

The Urisk lifted her great horned head. "Ardrigh?" Her demeanour was low, and her voice nervous.

There was a sickly yellowish light growing in the eye of Balor, the inherited power of the God-Kings of the Fomóiri, the basilisk power to kill with a look. "Speak the truth unto me, Seanghal."

"Always, Ardrigh," replied Gormul. Morghath noticed how

the thick hair on the back and shoulders of the Urisk was standing out like the fur on a frightened cat.

"My son, flesh of my flesh, stands accused. What say you?"

So, this is what she's here for, the purpose of her presence, thought Morghath. To put me to the test, the scrutiny of a Truthseer. The Seanghal of the Urisks straightened up and locked her gaze with Morghath's. The Seanghal's caprine eyes were the colour of fresh grapes, and they burnt as painfully as the Galdràgon's magic. He fought to bury his feelings from her terrible stare, but every veil he hastily threw up was torn away as she probed deeper into his thoughts and desires, seeing everything, exposing everything. Morghath realised his hand was creeping towards his sword hilt, but he knew it would be futile and let it drop. What use to fight? He thought. Better to die than to serve as a slave to this monster. Do you hear that, Gormul?

Yes.

Gormul dropped her gaze and stepped back from Morghath's reach. With one hand, she flicked away the long hair that had fallen across her face and smoothed down the thick fur below her mouth. She then gave a tired sigh and answered Balor's question. "Aye, Ardrigh, I see."

Fear had crawled up Morghath's legs to take residence in his gut. The back of his legs were weakening, and he felt sick.

"It's a lie, my Lord. The Isheen Witch's words are lies. I see no deceit in the Prindsa Morghath's heart. The Isheen plot against each other and against you, my Lord." Gormul gave Morghath Bres a deliberately expressive look. "What the Prindsa Morghath Bres says is true."

Morghath almost laughed with relief.

Balor thrashed about wildly on his thrown, croaked loudly and then roared, "Ruadan! Ruadan!"

Ruadan appeared like a spectre out of the gloom. "Ardrigh?"

"Ruadan, the treacheries of the hole dwellers offend us! Bring me my chariot and gather the Horde. They have no Witches to aid them now, no Sorcerers. We shall soak this place in their blood!"

Mathan-Bàn could not sleep; in fact, he seldom slept even when he was in the safety of his own palace at Dùn nan Làidir. Instead, he sought rest through meòrachadh, seeking his own anam. For him, it was never as simple as it was for his warriors; too often, in the comfort of his own quarters, he had taken the route of oblivion through strong wine instead. However, this was no place for him to find refuge in his cups, and so he was trying unsuccessfully to meòraich in the small chamber Faylinn had found for him to rest in.

He sat quietly and tried to let the events of the day slip from his mind, but they would not go. They hung around like dark shadows in the corners of his consciousness and sallied forth as soon as he caught sight of them. Corvus, a Daonna who should be long dead, whose destiny seems to be pulled between the forces of the most powerful Sidhe King in the West, Finn Varra and the most feared of the Goddesses, the Queen of Battles, the Morrigan. What purpose did she have for Corvus, and why bring him here? She had forbidden Mathan-Bàn to raise a hand against the Daonna, yet she had brought him into the very heart of this war.

Finn Varra also loomed darkly in Mathan-Ban's thoughts. The most dangerous of all the Sidhe, the one that Mathan-Bàn knew someday he would have to destroy if he were ever to truly liberate his people from the degenerate mire they were sinking into. As Ardrigh of the western kingdoms, Finn Varra still held titular overlordship of all the Sìthean races. Mathan-Bàn had never personally paid homage to Finn Varra, and he knew that whatever happened, Fearchara never would. As Àrd-dràgon, one day, if he were to free his people from this stinking mire of inertia and decadence, he was destined to march the armies of the Isheen against the power of the Ardrigh of the Daoine Faoi Cheilt; against Finn Varra. The Morrigan had promised him victory over his enemies if he obeyed her and did not harm or obstruct Corvus, but what use was such a promise from the Queen of Battles? A Goddess of death? Legend told of her promises; they were like a viper, as fleet as quicksilver and as poisonous, even if she honoured her vow, he doubted it would bring him anything but disaster.

And then there was Morghath Bres and his insane plan to

murder Balor. Mathan-Bàn was unsure as to what he should do with Morghath, he could simply let him carry out his plan and, whatever the result, successful or not, let it plunge the Fomóire's into civil war, or he could warn Balor of his son's betrayal and thus preoccupy the old monster. Maybe long enough to set his own plans into motion and outmanoeuvre the Fomóiri completely. The idea of the Fomóiri at civil war truly appealed to Mathan-Bàn, but he did not regard Morghath's chances very highly. Balor was, after all, almost a God, and Mathan-Bàn did not believe that Morghath Bres had the strength or the wit to destroy him.

In truth, the situation was lurching towards disaster, and Mathan-Bàn knew there was little he could actively do about it apart from helping it on its way. The only positive thing that had happened since they had seized the Craig was the death of the harridan Galdràgon, something, he admitted to himself, he had enjoyed immensely. Watching the old hag thrashing about as the Fomóire crushed the stinking life out of her had been marvellously satisfying. He had almost applauded when the bones in her neck shattered so loudly that they could have been heard outside the hall.

Mathan-Bàn was an Isheen warrior and knew that no real warrior ever flinched or felt any pang of conscience at witnessing the death of his enemy. Still, now in the quiet of his room, he wondered if it had been the right thing to allow to happen. He asked himself whether the old hag could have been right all along. Maybe he was weak and lacking in vision, perhaps…

There was a faint noise from the bed behind him, and he looked back to see Cathadh turning in her sleep, restless as always, one arm was tucked under her head, the other, lithe and muscular, flung out of the bed, her upturned hand wide open as if reaching desperately for some invisible thing. She had slipped unwittingly into sleep due to exhaustion, and so he had let her rest. Her strong, proud, scarred face was softened by slumber into the face of another woman, beautiful beyond words, a woman he loved dearly. My only true friend, as pure as the drifting snow and as strong as the glaciers of Jötunheimar. You should be my Bànrigh.

A Queen, the thought struck him almost physically. What purpose is there for all this bloodshed but to satisfy the lust of a mad child playing at being the Bànrigh? Fearchara was the problem he had been avoiding thinking of. He could do little about the others, but she was the one thing he could act upon, especially now that the Galdràgon was dead. There would have to be a new Galdràgon drawn from her acolytes, and he had the best of them here in this place, this tomb, under his protection.

"Leannan, I have experienced many places and travelled far in your service, but I have never known such a place as this." Cathadh had said to him after they had made love. "The citadel seems to be alive as if the very rock is aware of us." She hushed him before he could speak, "I have seen those strange places where spirits inhabit the ancient stones, the trees and the water, and those places where the Gods manifest themselves, but they are not like this. This place is aware; it has a will, in the way the Drùidh mean it, a power of its own. Not a presence that resides here but as if we are in the belly of the beast and it is scrutinizing us, deciding whether to digest us or spew us out again."

He had smiled and raised an eyebrow, "Evil?"

She turned to him with the most earnest expression he had ever seen on her face. "No, more than that. Did you not feel the change when the Witch escaped? The very rock sighed, and that beating, it was as if we could hear the heartbeat of an Talamh herself. Leannan, this place is not evil; that is too simplistic. I feel this place is judging us."

"Judging?" He had asked sceptically.

"Yes, judging. And if we are found wanting, I truly dread what will happen." She was whispering now. "This...place, this thing, has the power to turn us against each other, to seal our fate here, entomb us. Did you not see the insanity in the Fomóire Prince's eyes?"

"I thought you were there somewhere."

"I am never far from you, Leannan." She smiled slyly, almost shyly. "But did you not see the madness? It will turn the Fomóiri against each other until they are consumed by their own lunacy. I fear that if we linger here, and it finds us wanting, it will turn us on each other too. The Ancients called this place the Rock of Fear, and I know why; this place breeds discord and madness."

Cathadh had been absolutely right, and he knew it. There was a presence in the Creag, something truly powerful, he had felt from the minute he had set eyes upon the citadel that it was watching him too, and like all the others of his kind had felt the very rock heave a sigh when the Witch Annis had escaped. A pensive sigh, like that of a lover, or a mother, bidding a loved one farewell.

Annis Nic an Neamhain, daughter of the Battle Fury, in the Western tongue, the language of the Sidhe, but in the language of the Dhaoine, it meant something different, a jewel, a pearl, a wondrous thing to be cherished, but a thing born out of misery.

And he, the dark Lord of the Gärians, her father? If Corvus was correct, then this riataiche was the granddaughter of Finn Varra himself. It would help explain Finn Varra's interest in her and why Balor wanted her so much. If she were Finn Varra's granddaughter, she would make an ideal hostage for the Fomóiri to use to dictate the terms they wanted out of the Ardrigh of the Sidhe. Blood kin is blood kin, and there is no possible way that Finn Varra could be seen to turn his back upon his own blood without seriously damaging the respect that he needed to maintain his position.

She would be an ideal bargaining piece, but as Mathan-Bàn's grandfather had often warned, sometimes the cost of removing the other player's best pieces from the board can be ruinous. Maybe he would let Morghath Bres know to where the Witch had escaped and allow the Fomóiri to try to take her hostage. No doubt the cost to them, based upon what he had witnessed on the battlements last night, would be more than ruinous; it would be disastrous.

No, he decided. Annis will be of far more use to me than as just a bargaining counter. She is half Sidhe blood, and for some reason, possibly to do with her father's bloodline, she is far more potent than either the Galdràgon or I, ever thought possible.

Could he come to an arrangement with her? A pact? After all, he needed a strong ally, but that also meant trying to keep her from whatever ends Corvus had in mind.

Corvus wanted some kind of revenge upon Finn Varra, but would he go as far as harming his own child? If indeed she was his child. The Àrd-dràgon shuddered as he remembered observing the tactics of the Gärian Generals as they campaigned in the North; their utter ruthlessness and cold efficiency had even frightened him. At Steidh-Dòchais, Mathan-Bàn had watched the Gärian General brutally destroy the last hope of the Kern tribes of the North with such carefully controlled savagery it had made his own blood run cold.

Would such a man harm his own flesh and blood?

Undoubtedly. The thing that resides inside that man is more monstrous than any Fomóire, and he is protected. To openly go against the will of the Queen of Battles would be an act of inconceivable stupidity. I cannot be seen to raise a hand against him, but I cannot allow him to squander the life of the Witch Annis either.

And Finn Varra? Mathan-Bàn shook his head. Finn Varra was a problem that would have to be dealt with someday, but it was nothing he could concern himself with in the present. If the Ardrigh of the Daoine Faoi Cheilt wishes to hinder the plans of the Àrd-dràgon and Riaghladair of Dùn nan Làidir, then he will have to come out from behind his smoke and mirrors and stand his ground. He chuckled softly to himself. And I doubt he'll ever do that willingly.

At these times, patience was a great virtue, and he had an endless reserve of it. For now, Mathan-Bàn would wait and allow events to take their course. Until that is, he saw a clear opportunity for decisive action. All he could hope for was that his hand would not be forced by circumstances first.

Let all these lunatics dance upon the head of a pin; I will simply await the right moment to knock it from under their feet.

The sound of hurried footsteps alerted him long before they reached the door of his chamber. He knew the stride, the step, it was Faylinn, and he could sense the urgency. He quietly awoke Cathadh with a gentle kiss and whispered a few orders to her. She nodded and was swiftly up and away, leaving him alone to dress as fast as he could.

Before, Dorrell, his bed-chamber guard, a warrior chosen for his discretion and pragmatism, could challenge the intruders Mathan-Bàn had flung open the door.

"What is it, Faylinn?"

Faylinn gave a curt nod, "Morair, there is a messenger from

the Fomóiri. She demands to speak to you immediately."

"Demands?" Mathan-Bàn fastened his sword belt. "Who is she who demands?"

Faylinn ignored the sharpness of his Lord's tone. "Morair, she is most insistent and claims a message for you only." Faylinn seemed anxious.

"Well then, let us not keep her waiting." Mathan-Bàn closed the door firmly behind him. "Take me to her."

"She awaits you in the great hall."

The Àrd-dràgon waved Faylinn onward and began to follow him. "And who is this messenger, Faylinn, whose message cannot wait?" A host of concerns ran through Mathan-Bàn's mind, was Balor dead yet? Had Morghath Bres failed? Or was he betrayed? Maybe Morghath's whole act had been just a ruse to provide the sea monsters with an excuse for war.

"It's an Urisk, Morair."

"An Urisk!" Mathan-Bàn laughed. "Why would they let one of those cave dwellers off the leash, let alone to carry urgent messages? Can it even speak properly?"

Faylinn began to descend the spiral stair that would take them down to the level of the great hall. "Yes, Morair, it can speak quite well. It claims to be one of their Seanghal."

"Seanghal! Little more than bone waving Hedge Witches." Mathan-Bàn's hatred of the Urisks ran deep. To him, they were nothing more than a degenerate race of goat-headed creatures with no culture or society, a race of horned monsters whose bodies were covered in thick matted hair, disgusting in both appearance and smell. They were less than animals. Urisks considered anything that fell into their claws as food, especially the dead of other races. The Urisk did not eat the dead for ritual, veneration, or power. They ate the dead for food, sometimes even their own. Mathan-Bàn's father's brother, Scrymgeour, had been one of those unfortunate enough to be taken in battle by the Urisks two centuries ago. His grandfather, Shardik, had exterminated the Urisks clan responsible, the Nealcail, in revenge. Though for all that, all that was left to cremate of his uncle was his half-eaten corpse.

Mathan-Bàn stopped Faylinn at the bottom of the staircase.

"Tell me, who of ours has the strongest tàlann?"

"You, Morair, you are the strongest of us all. The Galdràgon forbade us from bringing any of our Drùidhean or Fiosaichean."

"I am aware of that, Faylinn," Mathan-Bàn smiled knowingly, "So who did you bring?"

Faylinn looked up into his master's eyes. "Luthias, and Aeneas MacErvin, the young Battle Priest, there is also the Galdràgon's acolytes, Kyla is dead, but Eirica is very strong."

Instinctively reading Faylinn's surface thoughts, he knew there was more to be said. "What is it, Faylinn, who else?"

Faylinn shifted uncomfortably. "Rànd."

"Rànd? Your sister is without the tàlann, she is a great warrior, but she has never...of course! She spoke to me."

"She has now. Something has awoken in her. Unfocused and untrained, but much stronger than I."

Mathan-Bàn shook his head in amazement. Rànd had always been one of his favourites. However, her lack of tàlann had always been a point of some amusement and embarrassment for her own family.

"Summon them all."

"Morair?"

"If I am to meet this Urisk thing, I will have them all with us."

"Immediately."

"And Faylinn, muster the Gaisgich an taighe."

"And Cathadh?"

Mathan-Bàn allowed himself a soft chuckle. "She already knows."

Gormul of the Urisks stood in the centre of the great hall and shivered. She hated the works of Dhaoine, their peculiar ways of hacking up the living rock and then piling the dead material into these strange constructions. Mostly she found such places unnatural and nauseating. However, this one was more; there was a sensation of brooding menace here, maybe because the place was still half living rock. She shifted from one cloven-hoofed foot to the other and back quickly, a little dance and a few words of warding under her breath to keep away the attentions of the presence that inhabited the Craig. Balor was powerful, but Gormul felt that whatever resided here was as strong as the earth and ancient as time itself. Gormul's people called it "Foighidinn nan Dràgon," Draigon Patience, their legends told that a Draigon could rest for thousands of years until all had forgotten and saw it only as a sweep of hills or a range of mountains until forests blanketed its flanks and lochs pooled in its hollows. Nonetheless, all that time, it can remain patiently aware, watching, and waiting, endurance beyond the comprehension of the Gods. Under the pretext of wiping her nose so that none of his Isheen guards around the walls would notice, she made a quick warding sign and wondered if such a beast lay at the heart of Eagle's Craig.

Gormul sniffed back the mucus that had started to run from her highly sensitive sinuses and almost gagged on the bitter taste. The stench of the Dhaoine and Sìtheans was beginning to make her lightheaded. The question of how much more of this she could take without throwing up was becoming a critical one. They had left her to wait in this 'hall' as they called it. To her, it seemed more like a vast cavern made out of the rotting dead bones of the earth, almost an entire candle's height ago.

She had paced the 'hall' methodically, inspecting every inch of it thoroughly. Blood had been spilt here very recently, hot blood, shed in violence, that still remained on the flagstones beneath the rushes and hung in the air. She counted the guards, worked out the possible entrances and exits, warmed herself at the huge fireplace, scrutinized the tapestries, of which she had no idea what possible use they could have, and appraised the banners and shields covered with smoke dust and hung too far out of reach to be any use. She admired the craftsmanship of the wooden vaulted ceiling but shuddered at the cost to the living forests and paced the floor in its entirety once again.

She was just about to run through what she was to say to the Isheen's leader for the fifth time when the doors at the far end of the 'hall' were theatrically thrown open.

The Sìthean filed through the doorway with deliberate solemnity and practised grace. An armed vanguard first, followed by their Àrd-dràgon himself, closely escorted by two young attendants. Behind him came a group of adolescent girls dressed in sacramental robes accompanied by two more warriors. Their arrogance, their cold haughtiness, and their belief in their own superiority radiated from them. Gormul admitted to herself that they were impressive, even as she quelled the compulsion to attack them on sight. This was Mathan-Bàn, the great White Bear of the Isheen, grandson of Shardik an Mathan, the butcher of the Nealcail. Gormul straightened and lifted her magnificent head with all the arrogance she could muster and proclaimed loudly. "I am Gormul, Seanghal of the Urisks, last of the Baobh of the Nealcail clan." The look on Mathan-Bàn's face was worth every second of the time she had wasted waiting for him. "I bring you a message Mathan-Bàn, but one for your ears alone."

Mathan-Bàn looked furious. "Speak as you will, creature. I have no time for your games." The Àrd-dràgon's retinue fanned out around him, all tall, pale, and imposing. Their smell was disgusting.

Gormul stopped herself from snarling back in answer. "I bring word from the Prindsa Morghath. His words are for you only."

Mathan-Bàn seemed to consider Gormul's insistence for a moment then replied. "Creature, you may speak freely."

Gormul growled deeply. "I am Gormul of the Urisks. You will address me as such."

The young Isheen, Faylinn, who had left her waiting in the hall, stepped forward and spoke softly. "Gormul of the Nealcail clan, my Lord, Mathan-Bàn, awaits your message. Speak it now."

The Seanghal deliberately took time to meet the gaze of every one of the assembled Isheen in front of her before meeting the ice-cold stare of Mathan-Bàn. His glare was as intimidating and as unwavering as the great snow bear he was named after. Gormul could feel their power; at least half of them were gifted in some way or another. He had brought forth an assembly of Isheen sorcerers to confront her; she was flattered.

Mathan-Bàn cleared his throat and spoke, "I am the Àrd-dràgon Mathan-Bàn, Riaghladair of Dùn nan Làidir, if you have anything to say then speak now." From beneath the thick mane of brown hair, Gormul's eyes returned the Àrd-dràgon's cold stare; the creature was obviously revelling in this confrontation. Mathan-Bàn had always thought that the Galdràgon was the vilest thing he had ever encountered, but this tattered thing was far worse. Its massive, dun-coloured head was heavily battle-scarred, crowned with great curved horns, and decorated with a bizarre headdress of feathers, bones, and cowry shells. The animal hide it wore for a cloak over its rags was uncured and so caked with dried gore that it was impossible to say what it had once been. It offended Mathan-Bàn's sensibilities to know this thing was alive, let alone to be in the same room as it.

Gormul sneered, showing an array of strong yellow teeth. "The spirit of the Witch, Sheela na Cìoch, has betrayed you to Balor." She let that hang in the air for a long breath. "He is enraged, thinking that you alone are plotting against him. The Prindsa Morghath Bres sends you warning that Balor has summoned the Great Horde of the Fomóiri and will attack you at the break of dawn. The time he believes you to be at your weakest."

Mathan-Bàn's gaze never wavered. "And Morghath? What of him?"

Gormul paused to scratch behind her left ear. "Ah...I stood assurance to Balor that the Witch's ghost was lying, trying to turn him against his beloved son."

"Why?"

Gormul paused for a moment to organise the words first in her head. "My people and yours have warred for as long as our histories record. For all time, your kind has persecuted us. Your own blood kin almost succeeded in extinguishing my own tribe. Now, only a handful of us is left. My people, my tribe, were forced to accept sanctuary under the protection of Balor MacCenchos, and his rule to stay alive, but the protection of Balor is slavery in any other words."

Mathan-Bàn's face had grown as dark as a thundercloud. "We have a blood feud, you and I, a dìoghaltas, your people, your tribe, and my family." He pointed a long, elegant finger at the Urisk, "Fuath is folachd, that is still not settled."

"Then this is the time; we must settle it here and now. Too much blood has been spilt, my tribe has almost vanished, our homelands lost, and my people forced to seek sanctuary in enslavement. Have you not had enough? I speak for my tribe and all those of the Urisks who suffer under Balor's hand. We forgo our revenge upon you and yours. We forgo the weighing of the balance. It is the will of my people to petition for peace between our peoples. We want our freedom and to return to our homes in the Highlands. Give us that, end this, and we will not raise our hands to aid Balor against you. You who is said to be the wisest of all the Isheen, the great Mathan-Bàn, show your wisdom now. Give us your words of peace, and I will give you victory over the Fomóiri ."

Mathan-Bàn raised an eyebrow, "How?"

"I know many of the Fomóire's secrets, and I know where their weaknesses lie. Mighty Balor is not invulnerable and not all-knowing."

"And of Morghath?"

"I serve no one, only my people, but Morghath's aims serve ours too. I aided him and will continue to aid him against his father. He is a viper clutched to his father's bosom, and Balor is clutching tightly. When he strikes, if I have your oath, I will aid him."

To Gormul's utter astonishment, Mathan-Bàn began laughing.

Far below the place where Mathan-Bàn and Gormul stood, down upon the little stony beach, the Great Horde had begun to spill on to the shingle. The first to clamber onto the shore was the Nains and Urisks. They crept along the water's edge, silently killing the Gothads and Southrons that had been set to guard the longships. In the pre-dawn darkness, a dozen lives were extinguished before the victims could realise their fate.

After the first creeping assault, out of the ice-cold waters came the Sea Trows and Thurse; giant hulking creatures, heavily armed and armoured. Behind them came the warbands of pure Fomóiri. As quietly as they could, they moved to secure the strand for the next wave of the Horde. Though Ruadan was capable of far more complex tactics, he knew that few of his warriors could count beyond the sum of their fingers, let alone understand anything other than the most straightforward of orders. The plan of attack had to be simple and easily carried out. Silence the guards on the shore and the boats, gain control of the strand as quietly and quickly as possible and then allow the Horde's numbers to swell. The Horde had to gather its strength before launching the assault upon the Craig, but during that time, as Ruadan knew, they would be at their most vulnerable to a counterattack. Though the first skirmishers, the Dhaoine, Urisks and Niägriusar, were already halfway up the paths leading up from the strand, the others had to prepare to defend their brothers as they swarmed off of Roth Ramach and out of the water. Battle standards were raised; war bands grouped together, racial, tribal, and personal affiliations were demonstrated and displayed. The various warriors quickly began to get restless and excited; they were proud and sure of victory; some could already taste the blood of their enemies. And the idea that it would be Sithean blood was driving some of them almost wild with anticipation.

Ruadan went down into the madding mass of the Horde and tried to silence them, but it was useless. This wasn't an army to be disciplined or controlled; this was the host of the Fomóiri, the Horde. They were here to do only one thing, and most understood only that one thing; to destroy the enemies of Balor. They clambered to get near to Ruadan, to touch him as if he were their totem, their inspiration. Ruadan physically reached out to them, allowing them to touch his body; their eagerness was spine-tingling, even to an ancient creature like him.

Suddenly an awful sense of sadness overtook him. Here he was, their beloved Warlord, and he was sending them into a trap, a trap he had helped create.

"Go!" he hissed softly. "Téigh, maraigh iad go léir!"

A huge roar went up. The Horde began the assault, a thousand or more creatures of all shapes and sizes charged up the strand towards the brooding black citadel that towered above them. Some clambered up the paths while some simply scaled the rocks, climbing like spiders up the almost sheer cliff face.

A cry of warning went up from along the beach as a few surviving Gothad crewmen had managed to launch two of their longships unnoticed and were rowing frantically out to deeper water. In their frustration, some of the Horde ran back into the loch after them only to be met by a volley of arrows and spears.

Ruadan watched with admiration as the Gothads made their desperate bid for freedom, but he could not allow them to go. With a simple nod of his great saurian head, he sent the signal to the Afanc Trows that still waited in the deep water. On land, their hulking bodies made them into little more than lumbering monstrosities, but in the water, they were as sleek as the Orcas and every bit as fast. Each as large as a bear and 9estronger than ten Duine men, they leapt clear out of the water and over the low sides of the longships with terrifying grace.

The Gothad's attempt to flee was ended in a few seconds of horrific slaughter before the victorious Fomóiri dragged the two ships down to their watery graves.

As Ruadan turned back to watch the Horde struggling upwards towards the waiting fortress, he spoke openly. "For you, my beloved Lord, for you." But he did not mean Balor.

Out of the milling mass of warriors shoving eagerly forward burst a mighty Thurse warrior struggling back to Ruadan. Almost as tall as Ruadan himself, the Thurse, one of King Thrymsson's champions, strode towards where the Warlord stood.

Though there was boldness in the Thurse's eyes, caution won out. He stopped and knelt at Ruadan's feet.

"Speak."

"Lord. The enemies have fled."

"What? Stand up, Giolla. Explain yourself," hissed Ruadan.

The Thurse lifted himself up carefully. "My Lord! The camp the Isheen's mercenaries set up outside the gate of the fortress is empty, and the drawbridge has been raised."

Ruadan Ōg gazed at the Thurse, his leather-like black skin and high, sloping brow now glistened with perspiration, and his eyes flitted about, not daring to meet the Warlord's gaze.

"They were expec...."

"Silence." A swipe of Ruadan's claws ripped the words out of the Thurse's throat before he could finish speaking them.

The warrior staggered forward, one hand clutching the gaping wound in his neck while the other seized hold of Ruadan's arm. The Warlord pulled him forward and held him. The Thurse warrior struggled failingly but managed to pound his fist helplessly upon Ruadan's chest before the last of his lifeblood spilt out of him.

"I know," Ruadan whispered to him. "I know."

Chapter 31

"Hear me, you who can hear,
and learn my words. You who know me.
I am the voice that is heard by all,
I am the sound that cannot be grasped."

"I am the silence beyond comprehension,
and the idea never forgot."

The Thunder, Perfect Mind
Gnostic Tractate
Nag Hammadi Library
Loose translation by Mat McCall
Based on G. W. MacRae

Where am I?
Why have you brought me here?
Who am I?
I ask the reflection in the water.
My name is Annis.
The name Mother gave me.
My age?
In the mirror of others' eyes, this shell seems young, but I could be as old as time.
Or more.
I don't know.
The Nàdur inside me is ancient.
And knows its own way.
An Alchemist, a Truth-seeker, once told me that we are all made of the dust of stars.
And that the stars are as old as time.
But the Nàdur inside me remembers a time without stars.
I was born.
This shell was born.

Not so long ago.
Orphaned at the moment of naissance.
Aware.
Of Death's cold hand upon my Mother's brow.
Even in her womb.
I was born into bereavement.
][]The first eyes I saw were my Mother's.
Born into sorrow and fear.
The first hand I touched was Death's.
Born into a dark inheritance.
I screamed.
As a newborn cries.
And the Earth shook.
I should have died.
Suckling at my dead Mother's breast.
In the Great Forest.
Alone.
I should have died.
Yet, my Mother's last wish brought rescue for me.
It would have been better to have died.
Foundlings are never accepted.
No matter how much those that foster them try to love them.
Most strive to be accepted.
To live down the taint of their past.
How could I?
How could they let me?
As I grew, the Nàdur inside me grew stronger.
It raged at its confinement.
Its power almost destroyed me.
It destroyed others.
Especially those that loved me.
And those I loved.
Until I understood the things my Mother had tried to
teach me.
No matter what happens.
No matter what is done to me, to this shell.
No matter the beatings.

And the wounds I will always carry.

Though they scar my flesh, my heart, and my soul.

I will not give voice to the Nàdur.

No matter what.

Those that will not strike back.

Are prey for those far weaker than themselves.

Jackals in the form of men.

Craven cowards and weaklings, driven mindlessly by their base fears and desires.

I was driven out, again and again.

From village after village.

With fire and stones.

From coppice and wood store, from haystack and sty.

No shelter for the Sorceress.

No succour for Black Annis.

Until I came to rest in the Great Forest that had been my crib.

And found some little peace.

Far from the abode of men.

How things change when those that hate you need you.

When Tiesis' hand passed over bed and cot.

The White Plague from the East.

Consuming all save the strongest.

When their potions didn't work.

When their prayers fell on silent ears.

When even their Healers died.

When all else failed.

Then they came to me.

Mother's cradling dead babies.

Father's burying sons.

A dying infant was thrust into my arms.

Men begged at my feet.

How could I turn them away?

The power to destroy is only the dark side of the ability to heal.

Hate is only the dark side of love.

I breathed life back into the cold blue lips of children.

I called the souls of husbands and wives back from their final journey into the never-ending light.

I drove Tiesis' cold shadow from the villages of the Great Forest.

And spared the lives of thousands.

I became their Witch.

But never to live amongst them.

For I can see the future.

Written in the sands of time and the hearts of men.

There would come another plague from the East.

A Narbonensian Priest.

To bring strange Gods and a new religion unto the edges of the Great Forest.

A Missionary to spread the word of the Gärian's cruel Gods.

At the point of a sword.

A Sorcerer, trickster and charlatan.

With a congregation of liars and thieves.

All hungry and immoral.

More jackals to hound me.

But I would not fight.

And I would not yield.

And evil cannot stand defiance.

It hurt them more than any lash could hurt me.

That one woman would stand silently against them.

That winter, their Priest came to me.

With offers and threats.

Soft words and rough hands.

With a fire in his heart and madness in his eyes.

Demanding, threatening, menacing.

Proud and confident in front of his jeering mob.

When bribes and offers and soft words failed.

When I smiled at his threats and posturing.

When I gave him nothing.

He took the only thing he could.

And then threw me to his congregation of jackals.

When they had had their fill, they burnt my home and set the baying mob upon me.

Those whose lives I had saved.

Whose children I had restored to them.

Driving me into the winter's night with staves and rocks.

With burning brands and hunting dogs, they pursued me.

Into the frozen wastes beyond the realms of men.

And inside me, the Nàdur roared.

To stand and fight.

But I would not give it voice.

I would not open my mouth to give form to the words of destruction.

For if I had screamed that night.

I could not have lived in the silence that would have followed.

I am Annis Nic Na Neamhain,

Daughter of Anann, the Seventh Child.

And I will not be a monster.

Now tell me, Urra,

Why did you bring me here?

Fyn shook Jacobis roughly. "Wake up! Damn you, Jac. Not only do you smell like a bear, you sleep like one. Wake up!" He punched the sleeping giant on the shoulder brutally, "Jac!"

Jacobis stirred, moaned, and tried to roll away.

Fyn punched him again, but the giant only answered with a grunt. Fyn shouted in his ear, "Wake up!"

"It's nae use, the big man's well under." MacLeech jabbed Jacobis in the back with the pointed end of his staff. "There's no way to get him outta that stupor."

"We'll see." Fyn fetched the nearest water container and poured the contents over Jacobis.

Both men leapt back as the giant came up off the floor faster than expected. Fists bawled and his face set in a battle scowl, he looked ready for the fight, but as he leapt to his feet, he struck his head on a rafter hard enough to loosen a shower of dust and dirt and swore savagely. After a quick look around, he relaxed a fraction.

"Hva??"

Fyn stepped forward. "Annis is missing."

The giant looked at him uncomprehendingly, "What?"

"Annis is gone."

"How?"

"We've been under some kind of spell; I couldn't wake you. The others are still sleeping. She's gone."

Jac tried to shake himself awake. "How long?"

"I don't know. I fell asleep by the fire; I think I was the last."

"It nae could have been long. It's no dawn yet." MacLeech pointed out.

Jac's senses were almost clear now. "So how is it you're awake then?"

"A didnae need any spell to put me to sleep, ae good meal an' ae warm bed was enough. Anyhow, if she'd tried, A'd have known it."

"She?"

"Aye, big yin. It was ye lassie's work no mine."

"I think so." Fyn agreed. "I woke him up while I was trying to wake you."

Jacobis swallowed hard as his heart skipped a beat. "Which

way did she go?"

"Out of the compound, off towards the hinterland, I think. I had to decide whether to follow or to try to wake you."

"You did right, old friend." The giant patted him firmly on the shoulder. "Magiker, if you've any real skill's then wake this lot up. We're going after her. If we're not back by midday, then get the Laird on his way to the mainland." He reached for his armour and weapons.

MacLeech looked at him quizzically. "Aye, alright."

"What?"

"A canna make promises. They'll probably want to come scouring about after ye."

Jacobis shrugged his bear hide cloak over his shoulders. "Alright, if they want to, but have them ready to move out by midday whether we come back or not."

The Tysher mumbled an agreement.

"Have you any idea where she's gone?" asked Fyn.

MacLeech thought for a moment and lied. "No." He, too, had heard the calling of the Tàcharan and had watched her go out into the night, but he knew the power of the callers, the ghosts of the ancestors, and he had no intention of following her. Where the call of the Tàcharan had led her, he could guess, but that was for them to find out. These island people's ancestral spirits were older than the race of the Kerns they now saw themselves as part of. In places as remote as this, language and customs change, but the blood and bones of the people are in the soil that has nursed them for a thousand generations. MacLeech knew many powers that walked the worlds and those places in between, and he had learnt early in life that, as a rule, the older these powers, the more potent they were. If they wanted the Witch, he was not going to interfere. She was like a candle flame to a moth. Things, mighty and powerful, were drawn to her, but they did not realise that she was not a candle flame flickering in the wind but a roaring balefire, capable of consuming everything. Let the Tàcharan summon her; they have no idea of what they are dealing with. He wondered if the Vör and his shape-shifting friend had any proper understanding of her either or were they both so blinded by love and infatuation that they too were merely moths to her flame.

He watched them step out into the cold grey mist of the dawn, desperate in their desires, though confident in their abilities. The watery light threw their shadows onto the misty vapour creating monstrous forms, a giant as tall as an ash tree and a beast bigger than a bear.

A deep sense of foreboding clutched at Mer's heart. A time was rapidly approaching when he would have to make the choice he had been avoiding since his arrival at Eagle's Craig; throw his lot in with the Witch and her brood or honour his pledge to Finn Varra. He reached over one of the sleeping men, picked up a half-full mazer, and took a long swig. Honour? That's no somethin' Finn Varra knows much about. Finn Varra had never given him any idea of who or what this Witch, this Fees'sacher, was or what she was capable of doing. MacLeech had seen power used before, raw force, he had seen the work of the mighty Magicians of the Gärians and the Alban Druids, he had seen the illusions of the Sìthean, and the battle magic of the Gothads, let alone the powers of the Gods called down upon men's heads by Priests of a dozen different deities, but he had never seen one so mighty as this fragile young woman. She had swept the Fomóiri off the battlements of Eagle's Craig like autumn leaves before a storm, she had opened the portal in the Heart of the Craig that he believed had been sealed by the Ancients a thousand years ago, she had guided them unerringly through the Conurd Mòr, and last night he had seen her stop the passing of time itself. The dreadful realisation had come to him; that kind of capability could only come firsthand from the Gods.

What exactly are you, lassie? He swilled the ale in the wooden cup and swallowed the contents in one gulp.

Fyn and Jacobis climbed up the little goat path towards the standing stones, one of the highest points on the tiny island, to better understand the lay of the land. At the Bodaich Mhóra stones, they stopped and spent a few moments debating the merits of the features in the landscape. Fyn found it ominous that he could not sense her. Since the very first time he had met her, he had felt her presence almost constantly, even when separated from her by miles; he had known she was there somewhere, but now the feeling was gone, and it terrified him.

Jacobis seemed as calm as ever, hiding his apprehension and fears behind his well-worn facade of pragmatism and reason, seldom appearing to grow angry or despondent. He scanned the distance carefully with the eyes of a practised hunter of beasts and men.
"Not a sign. No tracks, no nothing."

"I can't even sense her." Fyn began to climb up onto the largest monolith, the one they had stepped through yesterday. "Maybe she's left the island."

"No, I don't think so."

Fyn checked his footing and stood up on top of the stone. "Why?"

"Because she would not have abandoned us without word or reason. She's still here somewhere. I can feel her still."

It stung Fyn to be reminded of the strength of the bond between Jacobis and Annis. He was her lover, and there was something deeper there too, linked to the manner in which they had met and the lives they had led long before she had walked into the hall of Jarl Turfeinar and into his life. Why had he followed her ever since? Abandoned his Ulvhinna kin and broken his Högtidligt Löfte oath, for what? To chase after a Völva, a Witch woman, who he could never...

"There!" he pointed.

"What?" Jacobis strained to see what Fyn was pointing to.

"You won't be able to see it. Over that way, beyond the woodland, there's a hill of some sort. Man-made by the look of it."

Jacobis looked up at him concernedly. "A rath?"

Fyn caught his breath; the idea had not occurred to him. "No," he said hurriedly, more out of wishful thinking. "Looks like a

387

burial mound."

"A barrow?"

Fyn jumped down. "Bigger."

"How far?"

"Four or five miles."

"If you can get there before me, then you'd better go."

Fyn nodded gravely and took off his weapon belt.

Mer MacLeech, the Tysher of the Kerns of Lya'ud, stood in the centre of the roundhouse amidst the spellbound sleepers, sipping from a wooden cup full of fion. He guessed the wine was probably Aelathian traded over vast distances for Kernach gold, sealskins, and ivory. It was old and a little fusty, but MacLeech had long ago developed a taste for it.

He looked at the faces of the men, women, and children around him. Kerns, his own people who looked to him for leadership and guidance, and Albans, their age-old rivals. Enemies, often on the mainland, so closely related that it was hard to tell them apart, but not here. Here the differences were striking. The bodies and limbs of the islanders were longer and more delicate than the Albans, their skin and hair paler, no ruddy complexions or reddish-brown or copper heads amongst them.

Two peoples so different yet so close. His eyes alighted upon a small child wrapped in the tattered remains of a saffron léine, cradled in its sleeping mother's arms; someone had blanketed them both in a swathe of Alban plaid. That someone slept peaceably only a few feet from them; Angus MacRoth, the Chieftain of the MacRoth Clan and Laird of Eagle's Craig.

"An interesting sight."

Mer spun about to find the towering figure of Finn Varra, the Lord of Tir Eile, standing behind him.

"Ardrigh."

"Yes, Maqq Lighiche." Finn Varra stepped towards the Tysher. "A storm gathers, Maqq Lighiche, over the land and the sea. I see blood and fire in the water."

"Aye, there's been strife as you forespoke."

"Well, where is the Witch?"

"She's here. On the island."

"How did she get here, Maqq Lighiche? With you and these others? Did you fly?" Finn Varra appeared to be growing angry.

MacLeech knew where answering that question would lead, and so he avoided it, "What is it ye wantin' with her?"

"I do not answer to you, Taibhsear. It was you that came to me, beseeched me, to aid you against the Isheen. It was you that pledged your word to me. I have helped you. You know what they want and how to stop them. You have made your alliance with the Albans that will bring you the peace you seek. Now fulfil your part of the bargain and give me the Witch."

For a split second, MacLeech saw something in the High King's eyes, was it fear? Emboldened, MacLeech smiled knowingly up at Finn Varra. "No."

Finn Varra's face grew dark. "Would you defy me, Maqq Lighiche? Think on, little man. No mortal has ever done so and prospered."

MacLeech nodded in acknowledgement. "Ay, that A know, but A dinna have the Wutch to hand over to you. And if she was here, A do nea have the strength to make her do anythin'. She's beyond my simple skills. Ay, but ye know that already, don't ye?" He reached for the ewer that stood on the floor and refilled his cup. "She's no ye grandchild, is she, Old One? An', even if she is, you're more frightened o' her than A am o' you. A have seen the things she can do. If you want her, Ardrigh, go an' get her yeself." He paused, savouring the advantage for a moment. "If ye dare."

Finn Varra's face was a mask of rage now. "You are nothing!"

MacLeech ignored the insult, "Last night A heard the Tàcharan of these wee people callin' to her, she went out to them, but she has nae come back. Her men are out there searchin' for her now. If they find her, if they come back themselves, that is, then you can have her. If ye the stomach to try. But A warn you Old One, they will nae let her go without a fight an' she is more powerful than you ever imagined. She's nae one to be easily added to your collection of veiled lassies."

Finn Varra shook his head slowly.

"Who is this Wutch? What is it she means to you, Old One?"

"Revel, little man, in this time for you shall not see its like again." Finn Varra drew himself up and boomed, "This place you look upon so fondly shall suffer for your arrogance, here the sky shall darken as night and the black rain shall fall, everything that lives upon the land or in the water shall die. The harvest of the earth and the sea shall turn to ashes in the mouths of the starving. This place shall wither and die."

MacLeech spat to his left and quickly cast a warding sign.

Finn Varra raised a hand defensively. "Your cantrips have no power against me, Maqq Lighiche. You knew the cost of your dishonour. You have broken your word, now see those you care for suffer for it."

"Ah, go back to your games, ye po-faced pointy-eared old bastart!" MacLeech managed to get the last words in before Finn Varra smiled condescendingly and vanished.

"Cack!" He threw the dregs from his cup at the place where the Sìthean had stood, "Do ye no see Old One? It's you whose time is comin'."

Fyn found Annis lying motionless on the gravel beside the door-stone that sealed the entrance of a great tomb. Her tattered clothes were covered in filth and wet from the mist, her eyes, though open, were rolled far back into her head, and her tightly clenched teeth were bared in a horrible deathlike scowl. Fyn anxiously checked her breathing, her skin was as cold as ice, but she was alive. He cradled her head in his lap, brushed her wet hair off of her brow, closed her eyes and gently smoothed her features.

His fingers lingered a moment longer on her face, tracing the contour of her cheek along the edge of her mouth and down the line of her jaw. A yearning that he refused to give shape to welled up inside his breast. A painful desire he could not allow to take true form, though it tore at his heart, he could not give in. He would not allow it to betray everything he believed in and everyone he loved. Gently he rocked her and whispered softly in her ear, "Käresta, väcka, väcka." He hugged her closer and kissed her softly on the forehead. "Wake up, wake up. My love, you can't leave me here alone."

Chapter 32

"The woods are lovely, dark, and deep,
but I have promises to keep,
and miles to go before I sleep,
and miles to go before I sleep."

Stopping by the woods on a snowy evening
Robert Frost
1874-1963

I am awake.
      Conscious.
Was I ever asleep?
      Dreaming?
            In the Land of the Dead, who is there to dream?
I have seen the Black Land beyond the Great Plain of Tir Eile and the River of Suileath.
      I have supped ashes with the Dead.
            They have told me their secrets, and they have told me mine.
      Oh, my Mother, such secrets!
            That which you kept from me.
                  Memories only the Dead would keep.
Secrets only they know.
      Now I am awake.
            In this safe little place.
     The house of Coinneach, the village Elder.
They fuss about me, their faces full of concern, their minds full of fear.
      Jacobis stands by the door.
His appearance is passive, but his mind is reaching out to me.
      Calling me back.
            Willing me back.
               I am awake.
                  I answer him.

Tell him where I have been.

Explain to him what I must do.

His mood grows darker, and there is anger there. But he has grown adept at hiding the rage from me, so I can see only flashes, but I know it is there.

I feel it.

They feel it too, and that is why they nervously skirt around him.

He who once served a Storm God.

Man, warrior, and Priest.

I open my eyes.

They brought my child to me, my Allasa.
　　　Now it is she who speaks for me.
　　　　　I do not speak through her.
　　　　　　　She speaks for me.
My thoughts expressed into sounds.
　　　How strange?
　　　　　Opening her mouth to form thoughts into words.
　　　Allasa's mind is so keen.
　　　　　She has great skills.
Together.
　　　We tell them.
　　　　　We explain.
　　　　　　　I watch their faces.
It is strange how the thoughts are written on a man's face.
MacLeech is careful to submerge his doubts, but even his face betrays him.
　　　Mostly I read fear.
　　　　　Have I gone insane, they ask?
　　　Have I?
No.
　　　We tell them of the warning I bring from the Ancient Elders.
　　　　　Of the places I have travelled to.
　　　　　　　The future I have seen.
The danger.
　　　I watch their faces.
　　　　　I must go back.
　　　　　　　I must return.
　　　To the Eagle's Craig.

MacLeech sat by the Smith's hearth, slowly beating out a rhythm on his drum. The bone drumstick flickered back and forth between his fingers, hardly touching the surface of the bodhran. The drum was old. It had been his grandfather's, but the skin was fresh. He had cured and stretched it himself, preparing the hide carefully from the flayed back of an Alban Druid of no little power. His name? The Tysher could not remember, but the skin from his back had made a good drum skin. MacLeech smiled knowingly to himself and twisted the clavicle in his hand; it also was a trophy, he had taken it from the skeleton of a Vör, from an ancient grave he had found. It was longer than his hand and now carved with symbols of power, a written language long dead and almost forgotten by all, except Mer MacLeech. He caressed the skin of the drum allowing his fingers to trace the faded tattoos that had once adorned the Druid's back, and then went back to softly beating out the rhythm.

"Well?" Angus' face was rigid with anger. "Are you just going to sit and bang on that thing?"

The Tysher did not answer.

"Answer me, man!" Angus made a grab for the drum, but Fyn stayed his hand.

"Talk, Magiker. Damn you." scowled Fyn.

MacLeech closed his good eye and began. "She has spoken. If she wills to go back, then she will. There's nothin' A can do to stop her. She has spoken to the Tàcharan, the spirits o' the Mighty Dead; they have told her things."

"What 'things'?" demanded Angus.

"A don't know, A canna see."

"Why not? Are you not a Tysher, a vision Seer? Can you not see?"

"Aye, A am, but ae man canna see the sun if a cloud passes over it. A canna see. She blocks my vision."

Sensing something perturbing, Angus asked, "Deliberately?"

"No, A no think so. It's like holding a candle up to the bright sun; how can ye hope to see the flame?"

Angus huffed loudly, stood up and paced to the door thrusting his head outside. The air was crisp and cold, a bright clear morning light, but it did nothing to lift his spirits. He had not really considered when or how he would return to Eagle's Craig. In truth, he would be relieved if he never saw the place again, but it was a matter of course that he would one day, someday, go back to reclaim his castle. He had put it to the back of his mind to be dealt with in the future, knowing that King Cathail an Ain-diadhaidh would not be able to raise the army, the Feachd, before mid-spring at the earliest, so there would be time to plan and to prepare. Angus had expected that he would return to Eagle's Craig in the late spring with the King and with an army of thousands, siege engines and Druids, behind him. Not with just a handful of bloodied men, some of which were too exhausted to stand, let alone fight.

Returning to Eagle's Craig now would be suicide. But if she goes back, I go back. I cannot lose face in front of my own people.

"Aye, man, you'll have to go with her, whatever," MacLeech called to him.

"And you?" Angus rounded on him. "Are you going back?"

The Tysher opened his eye. "Aye lad, A'm game for it."

Angus turned to Fyn, "And you?"

Fyn stood up, "Where she leads, I go."

Bloody Sorcerers! Thought Angus.

He has such a kind face. Strong.

A patient face.

I try to explain.

To tell him what I must do.

Though he does well to hide his feelings.

His face betrays his thoughts.

I tell him of them.

The Ancient Dead.

The Tàcharan, the Guardians of these people.

I told him about the things they showed me.

Secrets of the future and the past.

He listens.

His face is composed.

Although his feelings are intense.

His love for me burns inside of him.

It feeds his anger and frustration.

He who fears nothing fears for me.

I must return.

Alone.

"Alone?"

Jacobis nodded solemnly.

Fyn shook his head. "She can't go back alone. We can't let her."

"We cannot stop her."

"Where is she now?" asked Angus.

"She is resting and preparing herself. Allasa is with her."

"Fyn is right. We can't let her go alone."

Jacobis sighed and rubbed his face with both hands. "She forbids it." He looked into Fyn's disbelieving face. "You know what she is like; once she gets an idea into her head, she can't be argued with."

"Why alone?" asked MacLeech.

"She refuses to say." Jacobis lied.

MacLeech looked back at him in a way that left Jacobis in no doubt that he did not believe him, but he did not argue the point; instead, he just went back to beating out a rhythm on the bodhran.

Angus sat down opposite Jacobis and asked. "Are you truly prepared to let her return on her own? After what you told me? Are you really willing to let her go alone?"

Jacobis looked thoughtful for a moment, but in truth, his mind was already made up. "No. No, I'm not."

"Me neither," added Fyn.

I stroke fine hair from her face.

And brush away a pearl-like tear.

My child.

My Allasa.

I must go soon.

"Why?"

I must go to meet a man.

A man whose fate is inexorably linked to mine.

"A don't understand."

Of course, you don't.

Though one day you may.

I, like you, have never known the man who was my father.

But now I have been told the secret that my Mother kept from me.

The secret she took to her grave.

I am going to meet my father.

And I must go alone.

"No! A won't let you!"

Hush child, you cannot come with me.

No one can.

You must stay here with my men.

They will take care of you.

And if I do not return.

The tears in her eyes are almost beyond my bearing.

And if I do not return.

If I die.

Her tears flow freely now.

From the bottomless well of a child's loneliness.

I who have found her must abandon her again.

I know her anguish well.

I carry such a dark place inside of me still.

You must be strong.

For me.

Look to Jacobis, for he will guide you and teach you.

And Fyn will protect you.

You will grow to love them and they you.

I take off my shawl and drape it over her little head and shoulders.

My shawl.

My mother's mantle.

You must continue for me.

You must learn to become.

There is great power in you.

From your mother and her mother and hers and hers.

In the blood.

Down to you.

"Am A like you?"

No one is like me.

Yes.

You shall be my daughter.

My inheritor.

I kiss her face and the palms of her tiny hands.

Sealing our pact.

And hold her tightly against my breast.

One thing I must tell you.

One warning you must heed.

Urra's warning.

Beware the Raven.

And the man I go to meet.

Allasa could not remember the first time she had stepped through her uncle's doorway or how many times she had done so since that day, but this time it was different. When she entered, all the men stopped speaking and looked at her, strange looks, as if she was different somehow, changed. The house was packed with men, villagers and foreign warriors, more men than she had ever seen. She stood in the doorway, unsure of what exactly to do, unable to read their expressions but able to feel their thoughts. Confusion. Hers or theirs? She was uncertain; Annis had told her that it would become easier to understand as she grew. For now, she was to focus only on one person at a time and not to concentrate too hard.

"Yes, child?" The Alban's leader asked, his voice soft and unthreatening.

Allasa tried to reach out to his mind, but it was no use; instead, she spoke. "Annis has…" her voice nearly gave out on her. "Annis is nae here anymore."

In the sudden general uproar, Angus leapt to his feet.

"Calm down!" shouted Jacobis.

Angus rounded on him. "If she's gone, how are we…?"

Suddenly the Vör stood up. Inside the house, he really appeared like a giant, his head only inches from the apex of the ceiling rafters. His demeanour alone was enough to silence the assembled men. "She has gone, and we shall follow, but if we rush after her, she will turn us back. We will bide here a little while until it is time. Men, go arm yourselves, prepare, then we shall gather and share one last drink with our hosts before we leave."

Angus waited until the warriors had disbursed before he finished the question he had started. "If she has gone, how are we going to follow her? We came here…." The whole experience was too unbelievable to put into words. "We came here by…sorcery. How can we get back? I'm no Magician, and I don't know any spells for walking through stones. Do you?"

"A do," MacLeech said softly.

"Oh aye, I saw you before. It almost killed you, you old fool."

MacLeech put down the bodhran and calmly got to his feet. "Ay, ye right enough there, but that was comin' here, goin' backs different, like retracing ye steps. An' that stone will be still full o' power from when she passed through it. A can get us back."

"What about the others? The wounded, Ag, and the Cook? We'll have to leave them behind."

Jacobis nodded. "We cannot take them with us."

Angus turned back to MacLeech. "I want your word."

"For what?"

Angus stepped nearer. "Their safety. Your word they'll be safe here."

MacLeech chuckled. "Ay, Laird. They'll be safe here."

"Ye can have my word on it too," Coinneach, the village Elder interjected. "They're welcome to stay here for as long as it takes ye to com' back for them."

"If we come back," remarked Fyn sombrely.

Coinneach smiled, "Then they'll hav' to learn how to fish."

Allasa didn't like that aside. "Annis will com' back for us, she promised!"

Jacobis reached out and pulled the child to him gently. "Well, we can't argue with that, can we?"

Timmon the Cook had heard the word that the men were going to return to Eagle's Craig and had decided that he would not be left behind.

He had spoken carefully to Diorbhail, the kindly old woman that had taken over nursing Ag, and she promised to continue to take care of the boy for him. He had then borrowed an old billhook from Diorbhail's husband and prepared to join the warriors. He knew they would try to turn him back, but this was important to him, he was a man, not a joke, and this was as much his fight as it was theirs; in fact, it was more personal. Those monsters had murdered Rolf, and, although he had never liked him much, Rolf had been one of his charges, and then that creature had tricked him for weeks, lurking about in his kitchens and storerooms, and finally, the beast had tried to kill Ag. Ag was Timmon's favourite, a good boy, unassuming and honest, a sensitive child, that the Cook had come to think of as almost his own. Also, he felt he had a personal count to settle with the monsters that had driven him from the only place he had known as home for the last forty years.

He stroked the sleeping boy's head, whispered his goodbyes, and promises into his ear, and then set off to join the warriors gathering outside the village walls.

As he was about to leave the village, Timmon noticed that the warriors had set aside some of the equipment they had arrived with, damaged and broken things, equipment that would be more of a hindrance than a help in the fight ahead, on top of the pile lay a carynx, a Kern war horn. One of MacLeech's warriors must have carried it all the way here only to discard it now, but to Timmon, it seemed such a terribly sad thing to have done with a sacred object. He picked it up and inspected it, it seemed like a lifetime since he had last touched one, but it felt good to hold. The mouthpiece was split, but he could quickly fix that. For a moment, he thought about it; maybe he, the one the warriors saw as only the fat old cook, and this broken and discarded instrument, could be of some use after all.

Fyn inspected the men gathered outside the gate of the little village. They were fed and rested and looked ready for the fray, their weapons and equipment all cleaned and prepared, their eyes clear, and their heads up and proud. Kerns and Albans stood shoulder to shoulder in the morning light. They were good solid men, but there wasn't enough of them. Fyn did a quick headcount, eighteen fighting men in all, not counting the boy with the enormous ears called Calum and the fat old Cook; eighteen and a half if you did. Barely enough to form a raiding party, not enough to even to half-man a good-sized longship, and certainly not enough to make any difference in the tunnels of Eagle's Craig against the Isheen and the Sea Trolls they had brought with them.

Nevertheless, they looked as brave as he knew they were, and that at least meant they would fight and die with honour, as men, on their feet. He could see it in all their eyes. They knew that there would be no chance of victory. Their only real hope was for a glorious death and to take as many of their enemies down with them. Whatever a 'glorious' death was. Fyn was sure that he had once believed in that concept. In fact, he had lived for it, the ideal of a heroic saga worthy death, but somehow it had slipped away and become meaningless to him. There was no glory in death, no laudable valiant final achievement to catch the eye of the Grim One, nothing. Only pain and suffering and the pointless muttering of the Skalds.

Yes, he would go back with them, but not for victory or revenge, but because his life was as linked to Annis as much as Jacobis. He would go back because he had to, because…

Jacobis strode out of the village gateway and stopped beside him. "They're ready?"

"Yes."

"Where's the Magiker?"

Fyn shrugged, "I thought he was with you."

Jacobis was about to shout for the Tysher when he appeared out of the gateway with a dozen village men led by Ceard the Smith. They were all armed as best as possible and dressed in a few tattered remnants of armour. A few sported yellow léine shirts, dirty and faded with age but still serviceable, a couple even had tall, crested helmets, battered and aged, but worn with self-conscious determination. A ragtag Warband of fishermen and villagers, most of whom had never fought anything meaner than a bull seal.

When they reached where the others were gathered,

MacLeech stopped and rested upon his staff. "A brought som' help, A thought we'd need it."

Angus ignored MacLeech and stepped forward to address the villagers. "It is good of you, but this is not your fight. Go home to your wives and children."

Ceard shook his head slowly. "It is our fight if it's yours. Ye honoured us by accepting our hospitality, an' now we must see you safely home again."

"You wouldnae insult them by refusing their help," added MacLeech. "An' we need their help."

Fyn agreed, "We need every man we can get."

Angus knew they were right, but it wasn't easy for him to look at these people, simple fishermen and farmers, and ask them to face what awaited them at Eagle's Craig.

Ceard seemed to understand Angus' hesitation. "The lady you call Annis has fostered Allasa, my niece, and given me her word as bond on it. A have an obligation to her as well." This was greeted with a general murmur of approval from the other villagers.

"What say ye, big yin?"

Jacobis nodded. "We need all the men we can get. If they're willing to fight, then I'm grateful to them, but the creatures...."

"Och, we heard all the tales last nicht aboot monsters an' beasties, an' all." Ceard seemed amused by the idea, "A have this." He thrust the head of his old battle-axe into the earth, "An' A have these." Out of his pouch, he drew two tightly wrapped bundles and handed them to Angus. "Woad an' seal's fat, to hide us from them, an' red ochre for maskin' our scent."

Angus took them and looked quizzically at MacLeech. "Do they work?"

MacLeech winked back at him. "Who knows?"

When they reached them, the stones still audibly hummed with the residue of the power unleashed by Annis' passing. MacLeech touched the surface of the Bodach Mór itself and began to draw the energy into him. It was heady, intoxicating; the essence of the Witch's energy flooded into him like drugged wine. The Tysher almost panicked. He felt like a swimmer caught in the backwash of some mighty leviathan. He struggled to gain control by force of will over the sudden overwhelming of his senses. Slowly he brought his own abilities to bear and began to focus the energy through himself and back into the megalith.

Jacobis, Angus and Fyn organised the men as the old Tysher struggled to re-open the portal. They hurriedly tried to suggest some kind of plan of action, a battle plan, rather than just throw themselves at the first enemy they would see. As Angus explained to them, the goal was to hit whoever got in the way as hard and as fast as possible, to keep moving forward and to find Annis. Once they found her? Well then…he honestly had no idea.

Jacobis took over, telling the men that their aim was to find Annis and, if possible, rescue anyone still trapped in the Craig or taken prisoner, and then to escape. As for a 'battle plan', it was to be simple; "Follow Fyn and me, whatever happens, stay as close behind us as you can. There is a good chance of us being outflanked or ambushed in the tunnels, but the Isheen do not know the tunnels, as well as Angus and some of you do. We need your ears and eyes to watch our backs."

Angus took over, "Don't get lured off into chasing fleeing enemies, and don't think you can make much of an effect on your own; this is no time for heroes. We have to fight together, as we did on the strand and in the halls, we hold together. If we hold together, we will win. They are not immortal, they are not Gods or Demons, and they have no magic that will save them from a spear thrust into their bellies. Hate them, but do not fear them," he drew his sword. "They have taken what is mine by birthright, the place that my family were entrusted with keeping and guarding for the safety of our people. I cannot allow that to pass unavenged, or I should die trying."

The Albans amongst them cheered their approval, and

Timmon gave a quick tentative blast on the carynx that seemed to delight most of the Kerns.

"That's cheered them up," Fyn remarked just loudly enough for Jacobis to hear.

Timmon let off another faltering blast from the war horn. The sound split the air like a knife, causing some of the men to cringe away from the noise while others laughed merrily and encouraged him on.

"I told you once that when they had met their enemy, you'd see they are as brave as lions."

"Are we taking our musical friend and the one with the ears with us?" Fyn pointed out Calum, who was pleading desperately with Timmon not to repeat the performance.

"Aye," replied Angus. "They've earned their place. Calum killed at least three Southrons with that crossbow of his, and Timmon demanded to come."

Fyn looked at the Laird sceptically. He could still see three men trying to push the Cooks fat arse through a tiny storeroom doorway. "If he can't keep up, we will have to leave him behind."

"Aye, and if you can't keep up, we'll leave you behind too," Angus replied.

Sensing the tension, Jacobis interceded. "No one is going to be left behind. We need every able-bodied man or lad we can get our hands on. Anyway, with a Cook with us, no matter what awaits us, at least, we know we'll not starve even if we have to eat the Fomóiri ."

Angus laughed.

Fyn grinned humourlessly. "I'd rather eat the Cook."

For the gathered warriors standing in the freezing wind, it seemed to take an age before MacLeech was able to open the portal in the stone.

Ceard watched the Tysher's every move and gesture keenly, as he always had watched his mother when he was a child. Sorcery, or whatever it was, had always fascinated him, though he had not inherited a smidgen of the art himself. It was true that some in his community felt his work at the forge was some form of sorcery. How he could feed common dirt and stone into the heart of the fire and bring forth metals, but Ceard knew all too well the mysteries of his craft could be learnt from a master and explored through experimentation. There was no magic about it. What MacLeech was doing was true sorcery.

Suddenly everyone about him gasped as the centre of the Bodach Mór appeared to become liquid. It was as if it had transformed into a pool of still water possessed of a strange luminescence. In moments, the whole of the gneiss megalith had changed into a tower of shimmering water.

Opening the portal took a heavy physical toll on the old Tysher. He staggered as if under a terrible weight, cursing loudly, but he managed to hold it open long enough for the warriors to step back into the land of Tir Eile.

Ceard, knowing that the other village men would all be watching him and taking their prompt from his actions, did not hesitate. He boldly strode through the shimmering pool into another world.

Allasa sat with her arms wrapped around her knees, chewing on a yarrow stalk while she watched the men walk into the glimmering light. As she watched, she found herself repeating an ancient prayer her grandmother had taught her. "Kin ah be an island in th' sea, kin ah be a hill oan th' land, kin ah be a brammer whin th' moon wanes, kin ah be a warkers tae th' wappit ones." She climbed to her feet. "Nothin' shall injure me."

At that, she flung away the yarrow stork and ran with all her strength towards the fading light at the centre of the monolith.

Printed in Great Britain
by Amazon